AMALTHEAN QUESTS
THREE

JERI DION

First published in 2019
This edition published in 2022 by
A.H. Stockwell Ltd.
West Wing Studios, Unit 166
The Mall, Luton
ahstockwell.co.uk

British Library Cataloguing-in-Publication Data: A catalogue record for this book is available from the British Library.
ISBN 9780722352304

I would like to say a big thank you to the following people that have supported me on the Amalthean Quests journey into publication:

My sister Linda, my friends of many years Jane and Bill, my niece Helen, and Richard and Rose for their patience and understanding.

And to others that have supported me along the way in the writing of this third book in the series.

Contents

Names and Abbreviations

DC	Discuss Centre
MLC	Medical Life Centre
SSWAT	Space Special Weapons and Tactics
Porto Compute	Pronounced Porto Compute
Auran	the team's name for the cruiser Auran Amalthea Three
CMD	Counter Medical Disc

Auran Amalthea Three Layout

FRONT AND REAR DECKS

LEVEL 1: Main Organisation Deck

Organisation Centre
DC (Discuss Centre)
Resources and Study Centre
Slazer Emergency Store and Charge Room 1A
Emergency Hatch for escaping Amalthea Three, which incorporates passage to Life Escape Pods (which are stored at the rear of the cruiser)
Automatic Total Shutdown Centre for the whole cruiser.

LEVEL 2: Life Deck

Medical Life Centre (MLC)
Emergency Treatment Room
Slazer Burns Centre (for the treatment of burns from weapon fire)
Dr Tysonne's Officette (incorporated in the MLC)
Medical Supplies Store
Body Scanner Room (for injuries)
Transpot Centre
Docking Bay with Boarding Tube
Leisure and Refreshments Centre
Male Sanitary Room
Female Sanitary Room
Pios Sanctuary Centre (cruisers chapel)

LEVEL 3: Quarters Deck

Main Crew Quarters (situated at the front of Auran Amalthea)
Tayce Traun, 1A
Marc Dayatso, 2A
Dairan Loring, 3A
Dr Donaldo and Medic/Nurse Tysonne, 4A

Second-Rank Officers' Quarters (halfway to rear of Auran Amalthea)
Kelly Travern, 1B
Lance Largon, 2B
Craig Bream, 3B
Nick Berenger, 4B
Sallen Vargon, 5B (until later during the voyage)
Aldonica Darstayne, 6B
Phean Leavy, 7B

Guest Quarters
Professor Maylen

Flight Hanger Bay Entrance

Flight Maintenance Unit

Quest Suiting-Up Room

LEVEL 4: Science And Botany Deck

Garden Dome (rear of the cruiser)
Plant Specimen Growing and Prep Room
Botany Study Centre
Astrono Centre
Dairan Loring's Officette
Sallen Vargon's Officette
Medical Experimental Lab B (larger facility than Lab A)
Botany Equipment and Seed Stores

LEVEL 5: Combat And Tech Level Deck

Combat Training and Practice Centre
Robot and Technical Service Section
Weaponry Design Centre (Aldonica's domain).
Gym and Sauna Rooms
Shower Rooms for Gym
Recreational Room (for sports)
Weaponry Testing Room
Engine Room
Electronics Centre (serving the whole cruiser)
Engine Access Shaft (for maintenance)
Access Room (for the main weaponry cannons for the cruiser)

LEVEL 5 (REAR): Freight Hold And Interrogation Deck

Interrogation Centre
Confinement Cells 1–9
Slazer Energy Force-Field Doors to Cells' Control Room
Cruiser Electronic Defence Operational Room
Invis Shield Control Room
Service Area (for Shuttles/fighters)

Team Members of Amalthea Three

Tayce Traun
Captain

Marc Dayatso
Commander

Dairan Loring
Lieutenant Commander / Astronomer

Lance Largon
Quests Specialist

Craig Bream
Computer Analysing Technical Officer

Kelly Travern
Navigationalist / Control Officer

Nick Berenger
Communications Chief

MEDICAL LEVEL

Donaldo Tysonne
Doctor / Laser Surgeon

Treketa Tysonne
Medic/Nurse
(née Stavard, Tom's sister from *Amalthea One*)

SCIENCE LEVEL

Sallen Vargon
Science Officer / Janitor Of The Lab Garden Dome

Professor Adrien Maylen
Creator Of The Reprogram-Of-Memory Technique
(Rescued During The Voyage)

Phean Leavy
Telepathic Guide To Tayce
(new member)

WEAPONRY LEVEL

Aldonica Darstayne
Weaponry Specialist/Creator

ON-BOARD COMPUTER TECHNOLOGY

Twedor
Escort And Romid To Tayce Traun
(Formally Midge, the guidance and operations computer on *Amalthea One*)

Amal
Female Guidance And Main Operations Computer
(Link-up to Twedor; Amal is short for *Amalthea*)

Personnel at Enlopedia Headquarters Base

Darius Traun
Admiral Of The Base
(Chief of Council; Tayce's father)

Lydia Traun
Deputy Councillor
(Tayce's mother)

Adam Carford
Admiral's Assistant
(also assistant to Lydia Traun)

Jamie Balthansar
Maintenance Chief

Jan Barnford
Chief Of Security Division

Empress Tricara
Teacher Of Gifted Ability Students
(friend and guide to Tayce; long-time friend of the Trauns)

Enemies and Criminals

Count Varon Vargon
Imposter/Councillor
(enemy of the Trauns)

Fatashia and the Cartarcan Pirates
All-Female Pirate Force

Dion
Ex-Leader Of The Boglayon Pirates

The Chillerans
Undercover Criminals Of Crocosmia 2 Base

The Green Tempest Keeper
Revengeful Being From Gruspan Space

Joshua Landor
Tom Stavard's Clone
(used by Count Vargon)

Retura Davin
Criminal Falsifying To Own Twedor

Aemiliyana
Witch Queen
(resurfacing from the Honitonian Empire)

Eltarin
Aemiliyanas Assistant
(emerges from the mysterious marble)

The Staners
Torturers And Kidnappers
(torturers of Dion and kidnappers of Andory Payturn)

AMALTHEAN QUESTS

THREE

Amalthean Quest Update

At the end of the second voyage Amalthea Two had been taken over by Chief Barnford by orders of the Enlopedian Council for Voyages, Missions and Assignments. Carlyle Cartarn in particular. But halfway to the headquarters base Chief Barnford had to leave the cruiser and head back to Enlopedia. An emergency had arisen which was far greater than the simple impounding of Amalthea Two. He was picked up by a passing Patrol Cruiser and flown on at high speed back to take charge of what he considered a tricky situation. His orders had come straight from Admiral Traun, telling him that he wanted him back as soon as possible. He left Amalthea under the leadership of Tayce to return to Enlopedia, even though it was very much against her principles to do so. She had to even though she didn't want to; otherwise she could have been thrown into the Enlopedian detention building for breaking rules.

As far as Dairan, Tayce and Marc were concerned, there seemed to be an influence a lot deeper than that of the normal council, over the cancellation of the Amalthean Quests voyage. But who and why? All the Amalthean team, after a meeting in the DC, decided they were going to get to the bottom of this suspicious deep undercover influence over the continuation of the Amalthean Quests. By unanimous vote the whole team decided they would be continuing on with the trip back to Enlopedia.

But what was about to unfold on the final stages of the journey? Would they make it?

1. Resurgence, Part One

In a stationary orbit it sat lifeless and scorched, obviously the victim of a 'fall-on' attack. The words to identify this vessel were half scorched away. All that remained were the letters to form the name '—THEA TWO'. On board this vessel, starting from what would have been the main Operations Centre and travelling through to the bow, was a scene of bloodied devastation. Members of the crew that normally undertook their every-dayon duties in the main operations centre of the vessel were now sprawled in different positions, over the surface of their consoles or on the deck floor, bleeding or dead. Some were lying where they had been struck down by whatever had boarded the vessel. Their injuries were the kind to signify they had each put up one hell of a struggle to try and stay alive. In the doorway leading to an obvious meeting room lay a young shapely woman of elegant beauty, her uniform scorched here and there, her face showing cuts and bruising. Was she unconscious or dead? It was guessed she had emerged from the meeting room to confront her on-board intruders, to be struck down in mid stride. Level by level – Medical, Science and Weaponry – the members of this crew were as the members were in the main operations centre, unconscious or dead. 'Thea Two' was not far short of an abandoned ghost ship, if it hadn't been for the crew. There was a faint beeping sound to signify a distress beacon was sending out a distress signal to any passing vessels, or hoped-for rescuers, who might be in the area. The signal would transmit all the way to the main headquarters base, to be alerted that an extreme emergency had occurred on board this vessel. But would whoever picked up the signal find this crew and save them before the inevitable occurred?

***

Three hourons later, out of the deepest darkness of the Universe they came. An Admiral's cruiser with medical facilities aboard – a hospital medical ship – and accompanying behind came a fleet of twenty service tow vessels. The Admiral of the leading rescue fleet that had travelled out from Enlopedia was none other than Darius Traun. He paced back and forth in thought in his command Officette, wondering what had happened and why in their destination of rescue. His features were etched with grave concern over what they would all find. Adam Carford, his assistant, shared his concerns in wondering whom they would find alive and who had done such an awful act of viciousness towards this crew in particular. Darius stopped pacing. He looked questioningly towards Adam, hoping for some slight piece of good news. Adam met his Admiral's look.

"Yes, Adam, anything to report?" asked Darius, ready to listen to anything new.

"Yes, the rescue team are in position to travel over to the cruiser. They report life support is slightly damaged but operational on board. They enquire whether as Admiral, and knowing your connections with the cruiser, you would like to accompany the rescue team?" informed Adam.

"Yes, definitely," replied Darius in a straightforward tone.

"Very well, Admiral, I'll let them know your decision," said Adam.

"When are they leaving?" asked Darius. "I want to be ready?"

"Chief Balthansar said he'll be ready in roughly ten cencrons," replied Adam, pausing and turning.

"Right, I'd better get changed."

With this Adam walked away with his Admiral's decision to go with the rescue team over to 'Thea Two' to inform Chief Balthansar. Darius glanced at the awesome sight of what was once the beautiful and graceful-looking exploration cruiser that was 'Thea Two', then walked off out of the pastel light of the Officette to get into a rescue suit, out of his Admiral's attire. His thoughts continued on the young leader of the crew. For she was none other than his daughter, Tayce Traun. As for the cruiser 'Thea Two, it was Amalthea Two, which was expected to return to base more than three dayons ago. Many of the rescue team who knew Tayce and the other members of the team felt bitter over the vicious and unprovoked attack. Darius was not alone in his feelings of suspicion. It was wondered whether Amalthea's attack was connected to the fact that 16 hourons or more previously on Enlopedia, after a weekon of suspicion, a temporary guest councillor named Cartarn had been arrested for serious dubious misconduct. Interrogated at great length by Darius and Chief Barnford, the prisoner, who had been heavily disguised, was revealed to be none other than the evillest man in the Universe, Varon Vargon. He had been sent to confinement pending a trial, but had escaped in the early hourons four dayons ago, picked up by a mystery vessel that was gone in the blink of an eye.

***

Half an houron elapsed. The rescue team and Darius Traun boarded the damaged Amalthea Two. The atmosphere was tepid, and in almost total darkness they arrived via Transpot in the corridor outside the Weaponry Design Centre on

Level 5. Chief Jamie Balthansar swore as his light pencil torch beam caught a still and bloodied form – one of the team. She was in a horrific state, scorched and bloodstained. This team member had been shot. Jamie held his breath, almost afraid to shine the torch any closer, but he knew he had to in order to identify who it was. He shone the light beam at the facial features, or what was left of them, to try and make out who it might be. He shook his head. She was once young and beautiful, her long blonde curly hair dishevelled and bloodstained. This was none other than Amalthea's weaponry specialist, Aldonica Darstayne. Jamie couldn't believe what he was seeing. He remembered her as such a fun bubbly girl. A young female medical officer came forth as Jamie confirmed who the young beaten female was. The medical officer requested Jamie keep the torch directed so she could begin to find out if Aldonica was alive.

She guided the medical Examscan around and about Aldonica, then looked up at Darius with intelligent green doll-like eyes and announced, much to everyone's relief, "She's alive. I don't know how, but she is. We have to get her back to the hospital ship immediately," said the medical officer, who then turned, summoning four members of her team.

"Give her the best medical treatment you can – top priority," ordered Darius.

"Yes, sir," replied the medical officer, heading away once Aldonica was ready to take back to the hospital ship.

Darius and Jamie exchanged glances of sheer disgust at the corridor's destruction all around them. Both plus a couple of Jamie's men, plus the medical officers and medics, continued on along the vandalised corridor in search of whomever they could find next. Jamie thought to himself as he went that the cruiser was going to take some repairing this time around, but he was certain Amalthea Two would return. The team moved on through what was left of the cruiser. On the Science Level the first death of the team was discovered. It was science, medical and botany officer Jaul Naven. He'd taken a severe beating, which had left his neck broken and massive exposed internal injuries, from which blood had oozed. One thing the rescue team and Darius Traun had found somewhat strange was that they had found Jaul Naven but no sign of Amalthea's science officer, Sallen Vargon. To make doubly sure they hadn't missed her, the search men checked all rooms and even the Lab Garden Dome. Not even her body was found. Darius was beginning to think his hunch was right: Varon Vargon was responsible and he'd escaped from Enlopedia after passing himself off as Carlyle Cartarn and abducted Sallen after the devastating attack on their present surroundings. If it could be proved Varon Vargon was responsible, he'd like to get his hands on the murderous bastard for what he'd succeeded in doing to Tayce and her team.

Jamie Balthansar could see Darius in blank concentrated angered thought. He put his hand on Darius's shoulder in a reassuring gesture, bringing Darius back to the present.

“Shall we go on, Admiral?” prompted Jamie in a friendly quiet tone. He could see what had happened to Tayce’s vessel was starting to get to his superior.

“Yes, let’s. I was just thinking of who could have done this,” replied Darius as they went on together.

Jamie hadn’t changed much in the last couple of yearons. Tall, broad-shouldered, the type of man who likes sport. His features still held that certain college-boy handsomeness. His hair, once totally brown, was now showing signs of grey through his never-ending workload and stress, which came with the duty of being a maintenance chief. The grey was mainly his sideburns and starting at the temples. However, he was as easy-going in nature as he always had been. Always willing to accommodate new ideas, new principles. He and Darius had become firm friends, and the dayon Darius took over Enlopedia was the day their friendship started, as they began to see things the same way in the various procedures aboard the base, needing his help, working together like some kind of small team. He and Darius walked on, Darius in thought, thinking if he was wrong about Varon Vargon causing the ambush on their present surroundings it was a good job that whoever struck the cruiser never did it monthons ago, when Nadinea Wiljan was aboard; otherwise it would have been further torture for Nadinea. Everyone continued on along Level 4 to the Level Steps, stepping over broken ceiling panels, avoiding dangling sparking cables in near-impossible visibility, having no lighting apart from their light pencils. Emergency power for lighting had drained. They went up the Level Steps, some carrying equipment that would be needed when more of the team were discovered, again stepping over various amounts of debris. Jamie was surveying the damage as he went, shaking his head as he made a note on his Porto Compute. Dr Carthean was the head medical officer. She followed her second team of medics and six of Jamie’s men, Darius and Jamie. They continued on to the top, pausing long enough on Level 2 to dispatch medics and some of Jamie’s men to check along Level 2. Darius gestured in the direction of the Medical Life Centre – or MLC, as it was known.

“Dr Donaldo Tysonne and Medic/Nurse Treketa Tysonne should be in the MLC along here. Give them the same top-priority treatment should you find them alive,” ordered Darius.

“Yes, certainly, Admiral,” replied Dr Carthean sincerely.

Dr Carthean was the head of the medical side of the rescue teams. She was a slim gentle-looking woman with mid-length blonde hair in a bob style and blue eyes. She ordered the deputy medical female officer and two of her medics to continue on along the current corridor whilst she continued on to Level 1 to Organisation in search of the others.

The Organisation Centre, Amalthea Two’s main operations point, was once the important centre of the whole cruiser. But now it was no better than a savaged pirate-raided area, with ripped-out interior.

***

Forty-five minons elapsed. Dr Carthean, Jamie Balthansar and Darius Traun all came through the open entrance, entering into what was left of Organisation. Dr Carthean raised her Wristlink at the unexpected sight of the various team members lying silently here and there in various positions, with horrific injuries, ordering more Hover Trolleys and medics to come to Organisation on Level 1 immediately. Jamie, whilst Dr Carthean put forth her orders, guided his light pencil torch around the various positioned team members, and Darius watched as he did so. Without warning the beam picked up Tayce. She was in a sprawled twisted position in the DC doorway.

"Oh my God, no!" said Darius without thought, in the tone of a concerned father.

Darius tore across what was left of the centre to get to his only daughter, fearing the worst. He was followed by Dr Carthean in hot pursuit, activating her medical Examscan as she did so, ready to guide it over Tayce. Darius knelt beside his daughter's lifeless body, fearing it was too late. Dr Carthean knelt on the other side and began guiding the Examscan over Tayce in her true way of a doctor taking charge of the situation before her. Darius scooped his daughter up in his strong arms, hoping the inevitable hadn't occurred. Darius looked towards Dr Carthean. Thoughts he didn't want to think – that he'd lost his daughter forever – were going through his mind and he was asking himself how Lydia would take the devastating news that their daughter would not be coming home again. He studied her features. To him she looked like the independent stubborn childling from Traun of old, especially in her injured and unconscious state.

"Well, Doctor, is my daughter alive? Is she going to be all right?" demanded Darius, almost afraid to ask.

"According to this, she's alive. It's going to be touch and go. She's very weak, but I have a strong heart reading, even though her other vital signs are faint. It would almost seem, from the readings I'm getting, it's as if she's in some kind of suspended sleep. I suggest we move her now to your on-board Medical Ability Centre. You four, come here with that Hover Trolley. I want this young woman moved to the Admiral's Medical Ability Centre and made top priority," ordered Dr Carthean in true command.

"Yes, ma'am," replied a female medic, coming forth in urgency.

The medic foursome quickly lifted Tayce on to a Hover Trolley and covered her with a heat sealant coverlet. Soon the Hover Trolley was being taken out of Organisation bound for Darius Traun's Medical Ability Centre. Darius watched as it went, hoping his daughter would be all right. More medic team members arrived from the hospital ship. It was a hive of activity and they began loading the rest of the Organisation team on to Hover Trolleys to take back to the ship. Darius requested Dairan Loring and Marc Dayatso be returned to his Medical Ability Centre also.

"Admiral, I don't know what caused this, but it seems to me this attack had a purpose and that was to wipe this team and cruiser off the face of the Universe. I've never seen such injuries," began Dr Carthean, coming towards Darius as the last of the medic teams moved out.

"Well, do you remember the escaped criminal Varon Vargon that left Enlopedia a couple of dayons ago?" replied Darius.

"Certainly do. I don't think anybody will forget that. I ended up treating the injuries of the two officers who were badly hurt when he departed. Do you think this is his handiwork? It certainly has a similar look to it."

"No offence, Doctor, but you don't know this barbarian like I do, if it's who we think caused this. He wiped out a whole world – my home world. He's killed a lot of innocent people – a lot more than this team. This is just a small act in his eyes. If Tayce gets to find out it's him, I wouldn't want to be in his boots. Revenge will be very strong in her mind. As she sees it, he owes a great debt to our people," expressed Darius.

"If you'll excuse me, Admiral, it looks like I'm needed," said Dr Carthean, beginning to move away.

"Yes, of course. The sooner this team is back to normal, the better," replied Darius, eager for the Doctor to continue.

Dr Carthean left Darius with an approaching Jamie Balthansar. Jamie had been surveying the damage around the cruiser so he would know what teams to place where when they reached Enlopedia, where the cruiser would reside for the next two to three monthons, whilst it was restored to full graceful glory. He came to a pause beside Darius.

"Good news: the hull is structurally sound. The damage caused is mainly internally to equipment, walls, doors and fittings – nothing that can't be put right. As for Twedor, who one of my men found on the lower levels nearly ripped apart, I'll have my Computer Design Team put him back the way he was before all this," assured Jamie, checking the inventory of what needed to be undertaken for the cruiser and Twedor to be restored to the way both should be.

"So how long do you think it will be before she's space-worthy again?" asked Darius, curious.

"Give or take, we're talking about two to three monthons," replied Jamie, checking his Porto Compute information.

"Good. You have my authority to commence work on this the moment we get back to Enlopedia. Anything else is shelved. I want every available man and woman you've got working on it. This takes top priority, by my orders. Well, she's all yours – I'll be on my vessel if you need me, to ask anything," said Darius, walking away.

"Very well, Admiral. OK, over here, men," said Jamie, ordering his men to come forth for their orders.

He began giving orders to his men to make sure Amalthea was secured, ready to be locked on via tractor beam from the service vessels, to be towed back to the Enlopedia Construction Port. Darius looked back as he reached the entrance, and Jamie acknowledged him with a farewell nod. Jamie's men, or some of them, followed Darius out to commence their work. Jamie could see his superior was putting on a good brave face over Tayce, and quite rightly so. He figured Tayce was a brave young woman in his eyes after what she'd just endured. Jamie sent orders out left, right and centre to different section heads, instructing them via his Wristcall on the current project that would commence the moment they arrived back. Time was not for wasting. He wanted the Amalthean Cruiser in the Construction Port like yesteron, when they docked. Amalthea was going home to Enlopedia, even if she was all the worse for an unprovoked destructive attack.

***

Outside in the Universe the twenty service tow vessels of Enlopedia, originally from Questa, activated their tractor beams at different sectional points around Amalthea Two. Green illuminative beams activated one behind the other, from each of the vessels, locked on to Amalthea. Once they were in place, Jamie Balthansar's voice to the head vessel pilot gave the word to commence the return journey. Slowly, at the lowest grade of speed, matched in unison by each tow vessel, Amalthea Two began forward on its slow damaged tedious journey under no power towards Enlopedia and the Construction Port, five hourons from the present universal bearing. She looked like she was limping home like an injured animal. No life, scorched here and there, on the outside hull the name '—THEA TWO' was clearly visible for all to see.

***

On Enlopedia, Five Hourons Later, Amalthea Two, worse for her attack, came into the area ready to be manoeuvred into the Construction Port where she would be docked for the next two to three monthons, whilst she was brought back to her former glory. People who knew of the Amalthean Quests team, couldn't believe what they were witnessing when the Admiral's medical team moved Tayce, Marc and Dairan in a strong security presence in the direction of the Medical Dome followed by Dr Carthean and her medical team with the rest of the Amalthean Quests team. There were various dark covered trolleys, signifying someone was deceased beneath. These were Jaul Naven and others of the team that hadn't made it through. The Amalthean team had come home from the voyage with orders to return, but not in the way they had been hoping to.

Darius Traun walked off his cruiser with Adam Carford. He glanced at his Wristcall time display. It was late. Any actions could be done at first light. He clapped Adam on the shoulder, informing him it had been one unexpectedly severe dayon when no one knew what the outcome would be. He could go off duty, and they'd meet up at first light next dayon in the foyer of the Medical Dome, unless something urgent came up. Adam nodded in agreement, heading off to his apart-house. As he walked across E City Square he glancing up to see Amalthea Two doing a final manoeuvre into the Construction Port through the glassene roof. He shook his head, not understanding why someone would want to carry out what they did on the Amalthean Quests team and cruiser.

***

Tayce, with her inner healing ability, during the night hourons in the Medical Dome slowly began to repair the damage done by the attack, on her cuts, bruises and internal tissue. Restoring her body back to normal health. Whilst this was happening, she lay in a private room, in deep sedation, being monitored. It was unseen – the ability to heal was undertaking what was hidden from the naked eye. A nurse walked into the room to check how Tayce was doing, then left none the wiser about what really was going on.

Night soon passed into dayon. Tayce was healed. She opened her eyes, looking around the white sterile room and catching sight of Dr Carthean when her vision cleared. She could see the Doctor studying the overhead monitor, and noticed her astonishment at what she was reading in the restored normal levels of health. Dr Carthean was aware Tayce was gifted, but found it baffling what had occurred to a very seriously injured young woman – namely, Tayce – who had been brought in so many hourons previous. She looked down at Tayce with the gentle look of a caring doctor.

"Welcome back. According to the readings I'm getting – though I don't know how – there is no reason why you can't leave the Medical Dome," informed the Doctor calmly.

With this and before Tayce could say anything further, Dr Carthean was briskly gone from the room after telling Tayce there was leisure attire in the closet for her to wear. Tayce found her attitude somewhat abrupt and didn't much appreciate it, but figured that for the first time in her medical career she was probably lost for words at Tayce's miraculous healing powers. Tayce slid from the bunk and headed over into the Cleanse Unit, discarding the medic-care gown on the way, before stepping into what she hoped was a really relaxing and soothing much needed shower.

***

Darius, Jan Barnford and Adam Carford entered into the treatment area. They were met by Dr Carthean, looking still somewhat surprised by Tayce's amazing recovery, when she'd been unconscious when she'd been discovered on Amalthea. Darius could see, as he approached the Doctor that her expression was slightly puzzled and, even though he knew he shouldn't, he found it amusing. Just as he was about to talk to her, she was summoned in the opposite direction by an alarm sounding from one of the Amalthean team members' computer monitors that had been studying their vital signs. Darius tried to follow, but the door closed and he was left outside with Jan and Adam, wondering what was going on within. To their amazement, the door nearest them opened and Tayce walked out in the leisure attire of top and casual trousers in beige and flat slip-on shoes. Darius, seeing her, crossed with overjoyed relief at seeing his only daughter back to normal. He took hold of her by the upper arms, studying her like the caring father he was.

"I guess you used your healing ability?" he asked, amused at her quick recovery.

"Yes, but at first I was beaten so badly I found it nearly impossible to summon the ability to do it. Then I had the powerful help of Emperor Honitonia. He softly spoke to me and guided me, and here I am. I want to know who attacked us, Father," she began.

Without warning, a team carrying medical equipment came running down the corridor. Jan quickly pulled Tayce back out of the way for her safety. The team hurried past into the medical treatment room where Dr Carthean had gone into previously. Tayce tried to see who it was in the room, worried it was one of her team, but the door shut after the team had entered. Darius turned and cautiously announced that from what he could gather all her team were spread along their current level in designated rooms. As for the person in the room, it could be any member of the team and he told her not to worry, they were in safe hands. A few moments elapsed, then Dr Carthean walked from the room. She looked somewhat disheartened, but tried not to show it. Some of the emergency team followed her on out, going back to their normal duty. Jan exchanged curious glances with Adam, wondering what had occurred. He had a feeling it had something to do with one of the team, considering what Darius had said about how injured everyone had been.

"Good to see you up and dressed, Tayce. It's good to see I have at least one less team member to worry about," said Dr Carthean light-heartedly.

"Who's in that room you've just been in?" asked Tayce, seriously interested.

"I'm afraid, Tayce, I am unable to divulge that information at the present time," she replied in true doctor's official tone.

"Don't give me your officialdom, Doctor. As team leader of the Amalthea Quests team, and captain, I have a right to know how my team are doing," demanded Tayce sharply, becoming upset. Her team meant a lot to her.

Dr Carthean refused to divulge the information just the same, and just looked at Tayce silently.

'She's back to normal,' thought Jan, lowering his head and smiling to himself.

Tayce though failed to see the amusement in the Doctor's refusing behaviour to divulge what she wanted. Darius suggested she come back later and that Adam take her to see Lydia. Tayce threw an unimpressed look at her father and sighed.

Jan decided to go with her as he wanted to talk to her gently about the ambush in space. Darius decided to find out who was in the emergency room and to tell Tayce later. He would have more clout than Tayce to get the information he wanted from Dr Carthean – she couldn't refuse not to tell him. Tayce walked on down the corridor, complaining that she hadn't been told who was in the room where the emergency was. She turned, throwing an unimpressed look back at Dr Carthean. She'd been treated once more no better than a childling back in the dayons of Traun.

"What's happened to Twedor and my cruiser – and spare me the cover-up stories to avoid hurting me?" asked Tayce suddenly as she walked along with Jan and Adam.

"As much as I'd like to tell you, it would be wise to ask your father. I have no idea – sorry," replied Adam, not prepared to disobey his Admiral's orders not to tell her.

They exited on the top floor, going down steps with a chrome rail that would take them back down into E City Square. Tayce wanted to get into some of her own clothes – she didn't much care for the attire the hospital had given her. It made her feel like a junior low-grade officer, not what she truly was – captain. All three hurried out of the Medical Dome into the square. People who knew Tayce were dumbfounded to see her as if nothing had happened, though less than forty-nine hourons ago she'd been brought into the base under heavy security on a Hover Trolley, unconscious. They smiled, welcoming her back. Some who walked past said it was good to see her safe and they would be thinking of the Quest team, hoping that they pulled through. Tayce was surprised at the overwhelming friendliness, concern and kindness shown by many people on her return. Without warning, Tayce caught sight of a tall blonde curly-haired young man. He was watching her every move in a silent, calm, interested way. For some strange reason, she found she was making mind contact with him. But she was feeling nothing but a blank strange softness. He was blocking her. Why was it that she felt she knew him, even though she hadn't seen him before in her entire life? He walked away and she continued wondering who he was as she entered the Vacuum Lift to take her, Adam and Jan up to Chief's Chambers, which were off her father's chambers. Tayce, as the lift began to ascend, toppled. Jan immediately steadied her, wondering if her apparently being back to normal was all a put-on and she really wasn't quite right at all.

"You all right?" he asked in a caring tone.

"I'm fine – just a bit tired, that's all," she replied casually, as if her topple was nothing.

The Vacuum Lift stopped on the destined Level and all three walked out and along into the Anteroom of her mother and father's chambers area. Adam let her go on in to see her mother first, as did Jan. They paused and stood talking over the Amalthean incident. Tayce entered in through the automatically opening doors of her mother's chambers. Lydia smiled a motherly smile, conveying that she was glad to see her only daughter back safe and sound. Crossing the room she held open her arms to Tayce. Tayce, upon reaching her, hugged her, glad to be back. Glad also to feel the motherly caring warmth Lydia was conveying as she held her. Tayce thought to herself that when the attack happened on Amalthea she had wondered if she'd ever see her mother and father again. Lydia, after a few minons, held Tayce so she could take a look at her daughter in a studying way.

"Something is wrong. What is it?" asked Lydia in a caring soft tone. She could see Tayce was troubled.

"Back at the Medical Dome the Doctor – I believe her name is Carthean – had an emergency in one of the team's rooms. A team hurried in with life-saving equipment, but when I asked her who it was she refused to tell me. I want to know – I have a right to know," said Tayce, growing stressed at the thought.

"Take it easy. Your father will find out all that needs to be known," assured Lydia, trying to calm Tayce like the true loving mother she was.

"Don't patronise me, Mother. I feel helpless, not knowing what's happened to Twedor, where my cruiser is or if all the team are alive or dead. This is hard for me and it's not fair," began Tayce, getting angrier by the moment.

"I understand, but there's nothing you can do. Come, sit down. You need to relax," ordered Lydia, guiding Tayce across the room to the mouldable soffette.

"No, Mother, I don't want to. I want to know what's happening. How do I know I'm not the only survivor in all this? Tell me I'm not – that Dairan and Marc aren't gone, Lance even," said Tayce, growing exasperated at the worrying thoughts that seemed to be bombarding her mind.

Lydia found it hard. She didn't know what to do to make things right for Tayce. She could see she was ripping herself to pieces emotionally with wanting to know about the others. She put her arms around her daughter, trying to make her understand all would be sorted. The double doors of the chambers drew apart and Jan entered, pausing discreetly, apologising for the intrusion. But he had some questions he needed answers to so he could put two and two together on what happened in the attack and hopefully begin coming up with the criminal who caused the attack on Amalthea. As much as Lydia really didn't want Tayce put under any more strain right then, she figured it might help to get the investigation under way. She looked towards Tayce, then agreed, then crossed the chambers to leave Jan and her daughter to talk. Before she left, she warned Jan not to exhaust Tayce too much. Jan nodded understandingly.

Tayce left the soffette and walked out on to the balcony to look down on E City. Jan sauntered out behind, wondering how he was going to ask the questions he had as gently as he could. Tayce looked up and caught sight of Amalthea Two, or what was left of her, up in the Construction Port.

"I can't get over the fact someone would want to just attack us in such a vicious way. You know we wouldn't investigate someone unless this base, Father or you requested it," began Tayce sadly.

"So it was totally unprovoked?" asked Jan, giving her a questioning look of seriousness.

"Definitely. You know we were on our way back here, much against my wishes," replied Tayce, not taking her sight from what was left of her once beautiful and graceful cruiser.

"It was out of my hands. I didn't want to do what I had to – believe me. I was a pawn in the council's hands, doing what they asked with little choice, just following orders," he said, sounding apologetic.

"Who do you think could be behind what happened?" asked Tayce, ignoring his apology.

"I didn't want to lay this on you right now, but there's a theory that it all comes down to a guest councillor. Something didn't fit in about him, so they called me back here quite out of the blue. Hence I left you for an emergency, as you know. As soon as I arrived back, I began growing suspicious about this guest councillor, and my suspicions were justified. Your father requested my immediate presence for a questioning session with him, regarding this councillor's conduct, and during the questioning we found him awkward and uncooperative. I realise we should have seen the signs that all was not what it should be, like it was with Layforn Barkin. By your father's orders he was sent to confinement pending further enquiries, only he didn't get there. He shot through and in the process injured quite a few of my men. It's a criminal your father needs to tell you about. I can't tell you who he is. It's better coming from him – sorry," said Jan. He felt he couldn't divulge at this point who the criminal was.

"Really! We never had any warning – no time to react. We were all busy at our every-dayon duties to return here. Then my team, one by one, Level by Level, section by section, were attacked. We heard the sounds of sudden muffled horrific screams. Whoever this attack force were, they rapidly swamped the whole cruiser in a matter of minons. I don't know what to say other than there's someone who could divulge what happened aboard – that's if her internal daily recording of our existence is still intact – and that's Amal!" announced Tayce, seeing in her mind's eye the scenes happening again as her team perished in Organisation. She fought back the tears.

"Really! Excuse me a moment – I need to make a call," he said, raising his Wristcall with a look of urgency on his features, responding to what Tayce had just said regarding Amal.

He contacted Jamie Balthansar and found him, appropriately, on board the damaged Amalthea Two. Jan immediately ordered him to hold on before removing anything to do with Amal. He said he was on his way up to see him. Jamie could be heard agreeing on the Wristcall. Jan ceased communication.

Before leaving, he turned, informing Tayce in case she didn't know that Jaul Naven and Deluca Marrack hadn't survived the ambush; also Sallen Vargon was missing from what was left of her team. Tayce was taken aback by the news, but realised at least she now partly knew what had happened to two of her team, even if Sallen was missing. Jaul Naven would be missed. He'd been a brilliant young member of the team. Jan, seeing her shock, reached out and put a friendly hand on her left shoulder, squeezing it in a reassuring way and assuring her they would get to the bottom of who attacked the cruiser and team. With this, he turned and left her standing in the middle of the balcony area and walked on back inside the chambers to head to the entrance.

Darius passed him on the way out. He crossed to walk out to join Tayce on the balcony. As he exited, he could see she had something on her mind.

"Why couldn't someone have told me before?" said Tayce, turning to face her father, far from pleased.

"Tell you what? What is it?" asked Darius, unsure of what she was asking.

"That Jaul Naven and Deluca Marrack didn't make it. Jan told me. He also said Sallen is missing."

"I'm sorry you had to hear it like that, but Dr Carthean felt it was too soon for you to be hit with this kind of news. Jan should have known better."

"Why! Because he had the guts to break it to me when you and everyone else didn't?" asked Tayce plainly.

Darius walked over and took hold of Tayce by the upper arms gently. He looked at her for a few minons. He could see she was bottling up all her anger and it was understandable.

"I hate this feeling, Father. Everything's out of my control – my reach even. I feel like I'm in the dark," she said, becoming upset, fighting back the tears.

"You've been through quite an ordeal. It's understandable, the concern you're feeling for Dairan and the others of your team. I bet there's a part of you right now that wants to go after who did this and has Sallen. Am I not right? But you can't – you just have to be patient," he said gently to her.

"Yes! Sorry, Father," she replied, walking into his now open arms, relaxing against his uniformed chest.

Darius hugged her, assuring her that they would get to the bottom of whoever attacked Amalthea in such a filthy merciless way. Darius kept from her his idea about who had done the dirty deed on the Quest team as he knew she would want to go after them and it was too soon. But she would be given first refusal to do just this once it could be proven who was responsible. He knew Jamie Balthansar at that moment had his whole team working around the clock to get Amalthea back to her former glory and space-worthy as soon as possible. Glancing back inside, he saw Adam standing waiting and suggested they head back inside. Once inside, Darius informed her she would be glad to know Dairan was not the one in the emergency room requiring the emergency treatment earlier. Sadly it was Aldonica Darstayne. She was going to need extensive medical treatment to reconstruct her facial features, but it was a treatment that had a very excellent success rate.

"Why don't you head over to the apart-house with Adam? He'll act as your go-between over the Amalthea situation as it stands and as it materialises. Would you mind, Adam?" asked Darius, looking at his assistant.

"No, of course not," replied Adam obligingly.

"All right," agreed Tayce – she was feeling tired anyway.

She began on across the Officette with Adam to the entrance. Pausing before leaving, she informed her father tiredly that tomorron she wanted to see the team and start sorting out getting back in space in search of Sallen. Darius nodded understandingly. Tayce continued on out with Adam. Darius watched her go, shaking his head. She never changed in her inner determination to get back to normal as soon as possible.

***

In the furthest north part of the Universe, far from Enlopedia, it was situated. The colour of jet, and looking menacing with it, it covered a diameter of two square milons and every point of it's lobster shape was heavily armed. It was in a stationary orbit, like it was just waiting for something to appear. On board it was lit with the kind of atmospheric lighting that conveyed that the crew and leader were under the order of evilness. Death and destruction were in residence. The leader, who was dressed in a close-fitting suit with a high collar in a dark slate colour, was stood looking every inch the evil villain and leader he was. He was in his late forties, tall but of no particular build, straight up, straight down. His hair was cut close to his head and in a platinum shade of grey. He spoke the words of commands as if he was too tired to talk. His words came from him like they were being dragged out of him under protest. He stood just behind one of his main operatives' chairs, watching the main screen before them. He was viewing with glee the Vidfilm of the attack on none other than Amalthea Two. Satisfaction could be clearly seen etched in his chiselled features, knowing he'd successfully accomplished what he'd set out to do: catching the Amalthean Quests team off guard, teaching the leader of the team a lesson she'd never forget and claiming what was rightfully his – his daughter.

***

Back on Enlopedia, Tayce entered the apart-house with Adam following on. She tried not to show it, but it felt strange not having Twedor with her, or Dairan. The place felt empty. Adam activated the lights and heating. Tayce crossed the room and stood looking out into the stars in thought. Adam, as the artificial fire display activated on the central wall, making the residence more cosy, could see she was in worried thought. He wished he could conjure up Twedor, but at least he would be able to keep her company at this uneasy time. Tayce turned, and Adam wondered if she had been reading his mind as she asked suddenly about Twedor.

"They say two more dayons and he'll be as good as new," assured Adam optimistically.

"Sorry, Adam, but it can't be soon enough for me. He knows when I need him to assist me," she replied.

"No, it's fine. He's been with you a long time. He's quite an extraordinary Romid," replied Adam, thinking how special Twedor was.

The front entrance chimed. Adam turned and walked to open it. He found a young blonde curly-headed male, standing at ease, waiting. He began nervously, saying that he was Phean Leavy and that Empress Tricara had sent him to see Captain Traun. He was from the Realm of Honitonia, but was living on Enlopedia as a guest of the Empress. Tayce, having listened to what was being said, immediately invited him in. Adam asked Phean for his Enlopedia security clearance pass disc/ID. Phean obliged, taking it out of the cream high-necked jacket and handing it to Adam. Adam studied the likeness, then nodded, suggesting Tayce call him on Wristlink should she need him. He would be with her father, sorting things for her for the next mornet. Adam could see the Empress had realised that at this moment in time Tayce needed someone to guide her and listen to her, after her ordeal. He was more used to being a duty man to her father, not a man tuned into the way she was feeling like Phean would be. He quickly excused himself and walked from the apart-house, leaving Tayce and Phean beginning to get to know each other.

***

In the Medical Dome, Dr Carthean was standing by the bunk of Dairan Loring. A nurse had alerted her to the fact he was showing signs of coming back to consciousness. The Doctor watched Dairan's features and the monitoring system. Both were showing signs of growing improvement. Dairan soon opened his eyes, trying for a few minons to focus through the blurriness. He found, when it cleared, he was staring up at Dr Carthean's gentle caring face. She smiled a reassuring half-smile.

"Welcome back, Mr Loring. You're quite safe. You're in a room in the Enlopedian Medical Dome," she assured him.

"Tayce! Where is she? Tell me she's all right. I have to find her. Ouch!" said Dairan, beginning to sit up and realising the pain was reminding him his ribs were badly injured and wouldn't let him.

"Relax, Mr Loring. She's been released from here and is back to normal health. I'll call her and let her know you're conscious," assured Dr Carthean.

"It's Lieutenant Commander, Dr Carthean," Dairan corrected her, in her address of him.

She didn't say another word, just ordered the medic/nurse to make sure Dairan never again got up from the bunk as fast as he had just done; otherwise he would undo what was healing nicely. He had sustained four broken ribs in his fight to protect Tayce. Dr Carthean walked from the room feeling a bit more at ease, pleased that at least two members of the ambushed Amalthean Quests team were well on the mend. Marc Dayatso was her biggest concern. If only she'd known what the enemy attack force had used in the weaponry that shot him, because so far whatever they had tried to counteract what was happening to his system clashed with his bloodstream. It wasn't looking good, but she wouldn't give up. She would pull him through this, she was sure, by trying different new antibiotics to rid him of the poison that was slowly destroying all his main bodily functions. She headed to contact the Admiral via Telelinkphone, to tell him Dairan was conscious.

It could be seen she was good in her field by the way in which she carried herself and held the presence of medical command. She was in her late forties, but didn't look a day over forty, because she looked after herself despite her gruelling hourons as head medical officer.

"Ten dayons, Admiral? You're asking the impossible," said Jamie Balthansar, taken aback by what Darius had asked, wondering if he'd heard right.

He was standing on board Amalthea Two with Darius Traun with men coming and going, ripping out badly damaged equipment around them. Jamie guided Darius into nearby quarters – the ones that had been occupied by none other than Jaul Naven, the unfortunate team member who had perished. Jamie pointed out he was stretched to the limit. He had pulled out all his men from what they were working on, on Enlopedia and other vessels in port, to prioritise the surrounding work. There was no one else he could pull in.

"I will do my best, but two weekons will be pushing it." Jamie didn't like letting Darius down, but he felt it was damned near impossible to do what his superior was asking.

"If you swing this, there will be bonuses for yourself and every man on the work expenditure accounts, upon completing a first-class job in half the normal time," suggested Darius.

Jamie knew his men would jump at the chance of more currency at the end of the completed job. He thought for a moment, then told Darius he would try – he couldn't promise, but he would certainly discuss it with his men.

Darius nodded in acknowledgement. "I leave it with you," he said, patting Jamie on the shoulder.

Darius walked away, leaving Jamie with the unenviable job of telling his men the cruiser was wanted earlier than was previously proposed. He knew he would pull it off as Jamie had never let him down before.

***

Two dayons elapsed. In the Robot and Technical Service Section, Twedor was stood on the bench, back together in his blue metlon casing with replacement parts. He was going through final tests of speech, movability and plasmatronic brain functions to make sure he was as he was before the ambush. A female tech officer attached micro pads to various functions, then stood back and keyed in the command for reading every function of Twedor, to tell that he was working as he should be. Tests were ongoing when a young blonde-haired male walked towards the female tech officer. He was one of Amalthea's team and someone that knew Twedor well. He still had slight bruising to his features and walked with a slight limp, but he was fit enough to be up and back on his feet, even if he had to check back to Dr Carthean in a dayon or so. This was Craig Bream.

"Hello! How's the little guy doing?" asked Craig casually, trying not to be nosey.

"Officer Bream, it's good to see you up and around. He's fine – fully functional, plus new add-ons. All that remains is for me to stand him down and activate him," she explained in an educated voice.

Right before Craig's eyes she did just as she said, pushing a small button on the small hand-held remote. Twedor lifted up off the workstation bench and was gently brought round and lowered to the ground before them. Craig gave a look conveying that he was glad to see his creation back in working order, instead of blown to smithereens like he had been back on Amalthea Two. The young female tech officer aimed a small round device at Twedor, like a wand, and pressed a button. Within minons Twedor began waking into a fully functional state.

"Where is this? Where is my mistress? Boy, you're a looker," announced Twedor, back to his usual old self, making the tech officer and Craig laugh.

"I guess he's back to normal," quipped Craig.

"Ha ha! He's ready to be handed back to your captain, that's for sure," agreed the young tech officer.

Craig waited until Twedor turned and was heading over to the entrance. Then he shook hands with the tech, thanking her for putting Twedor back together and making him better than he was before. Jenna, the female tech officer, blushed and informed him that it had been a challenge, but enjoyable. Twedor looked back for Craig. Craig walked away, heading back to the entrance, suggesting to Jenna that next time he was in port he'd buy her a drink as a thanks. Jenna smiled, watching them go, and called after Craig, agreeing and wishing him luck. He paused upon reaching the entrance and thanked her once again. Jenna sauntered across, saying she'd forgotten to tell him, Twedors new outer casing was now made in a tougher metlon and in two parts, so it was a lot less easy than before to dent or shatter. Craig nodded, amazed by her ability to discuss technology, as she couldn't have been any more than in her early twenties and fresh from tech academy. He said his farewells and walked on out, saying he'd see her next time he was in port. Jenna replied that she'd hold him to it. As he went, he figured he would tell Tayce all about Jenna. Craig continued on out of the building behind Twedor. Personnel that had taken a hand in putting the little Romid back together, with Jenna, looked on, pleased the little escort was back to what he should be. Craig thanked a few people for what they'd done, as he met them. At the end of the corridor, he exited back out into E City Square. He then began on the walk to Tayce's apart-house with Twedor walking at his side.

***

Darius Traun entered back into his Officette. Lydia was present and was about to give Tayce the news via Telelinkphone about Dairan. Darius paused until she was finished. She soon placed the Telelinkphone back on its base, giving a motherly look of concern. Darius noticed it immediately – he'd seen it many times before. As she looked at him, he gave her a questioning look, wondering why she'd done it.

"Is something wrong?" he asked, curiously interested, as her partner of long yearons.

"It's Tayce – I feel she's still very traumatised over this attack in space. It's as if she's hiding behind a tough shield. She's not coping too well, to my way of thinking. It concerns me she's bottling a lot up," confided Lydia, truly concerned, like the true caring mother she was.

"Relax – she'll be fine. It's been a really terrible ordeal for her, but she'll come out of it stronger. If she needs us, she knows where we are; but if you feel you want to have a heart-to-heart with her, then go ahead. But be prepared for her not to open up. She's trying to adjust to what's unfolded – it's hard, but she's coming to terms with it," replied Darius, trying to stop Lydia from worrying, as she had always been a bit soft when it came to their only daughter.

Lydia thought about what Darius said. She glanced at her Wristcall time display. It was the end of another duty stint, so there was no time like the present to do what Darius suggested – visit Tayce. She put a hand affectionately on Darius's arm. He reached for it, patting it gently in return.

"I'm going now. We'll eat in about an houron," she suggested softly.

"Why don't you bring Tayce? Considering the circumstances, it would be good to have a family meal. I'll arrange it while you're gone," he suggested.

"Don't see why not – it's a good idea," agreed Lydia in her usual soft tone, pleased.

"See you later. I'm going to check on the team's progress, I know Dairan and Craig are fine; I want to see how Lance is doing. Somehow I don't think Jonathan Largon would look upon it so good if I didn't look out for his son, considering the hospitality he and Adam showed Tayce when she arrived at Questa for the first time all those yearons ago," said Darius, knowing it to be so.

"See you later," announced Lydia, continuing on out, the doors opening before her as she approached them.

Darius watched her leave, smiling to himself. It didn't matter how independent Tayce was, or how old she was. Her mother would always treat her when in port like the naïve Traunian teenager she used to be, despite what she'd become. It made him recollect for a moment the times both mother and daughter, back in those past times, clashed over love and independence. Coming back to the present, he put the disk chips into the holding box then walked from his surroundings with thoughts of seeing how Lance was doing, hoping that everything would soon return to normality again.

2. Resurgence, Part Two

In the depths of space sat the most dark and menacing battleship imaginable. On board, the leader was standing before a grid-type force-field entrance of a cell in the Confinement Area. Inside was a rather official academic-looking man in his late fifties. He was of medium build, with close-cropped grey hair and mellowed features. The academic-looking man was none other than Professor Adrien Maylen, who at present was looking far from pleased at the leader before him. He'd been kidnapped from Enlopedia for who he was – the creator of the reprogram-of-memory technique. He was still in his duty uniform, after being taken from his Officette in late-duty time. What for, he had no idea, but he had a feeling it was something beyond the call of his normal duty.

The leader waved a black-gloved hand to gesture for the force-field entrance to be deactivated. Once it was gone, the leader walked forth, holding his look fixed on Adrien. On either side of him were his two officers, who quickly walked to either side of Adrien and stood ready to act on their leader's words. The leader slowly began in a tired tone, explaining the reason for Adrien being present. He said he had a problem, in the subject in which Adrien was qualified; so, if he cooperated, his life might be spared upon completion of the task he had in mind. Adrien refused to be intimidated by this leader before him and just listened. The leader continued to explain: Adrien would be taken to the on-board medical facility, where he was required to put together a machine that would be used for the reprogramming of memory and the replacement of memories the leader had on disk that he'd like Adrien to undertake. If he did not comply, then he could forget ever again seeing his life as he knew it on Enlopedia. With this, the Professor was led away, not communicating with the leader. It wasn't that he didn't want to – he was playing along with what was required of him until he could get the gist of what was happening. The tall evil leader watched Adrien leave with a sudden smug look crossing his ice-cold features, knowing he was going to achieve what he wanted. But Adrien wondered how he'd got hold of a disk containing past memories when all were destroyed upon 'mind wipe' before reprogramming took place.

Lydia Traun, back on Enlopedia, entered the apart-house of her daughter to find Phean, Craig, Tayce and a newly restored Twedor all talking seriously amongst themselves. Tayce's Telelinkphone sounded. She turned, reaching for it. As she placed it to her ear, Jan Barnford's voice came through.

"Do you have a moment? I've found something which I think you're definitely going to want to see. We recovered it from Amal's intruder memory cam," began Jan.

"Yes, of course. I'll be right there," replied Tayce, placing the handset back and rising to her feet.

"What's the problem?" enquired Lydia, interested.

"Chief Barnford wants to see me. Apparently he's uncovered something he thinks I'm going to want to see from Amal's intruder memory cam," replied Tayce as Phean and Lydia listened.

"I'm going with you," said Lydia with determination in her voice.

Phean also volunteered.

Craig decided to head back to his short-stay accommodation to get some rest. Tayce agreed. She could see he still wasn't right from the attack, considering he'd been discharged earlier that dayon from the Medical Dome. At the entrance they went their separate ways. Lydia, Tayce, Twedor and Phean all headed on down into E City Square to go to the Division Building to meet up with Chief Jan Barnford, whilst Craig walked with difficulty back to get some rest at his accommodation. Thoughts were going through Tayce's mind on just what it might be that Jan had found. Phean was reading her thoughts and assured her it would be OK. In a way Tayce was glad he'd helped her talk through the ambush and the fears of it happening again should she return to space.

Soon the foursome arrived at the Division Building. The desk clerk, who knew Tayce from previous visits, alerted his chief that Captain Traun had arrived. The double brown almost floor-to-ceiling doors opened to Jan's Officette and he strode out, gesturing for them to join him. With this, Tayce, Lydia, Phean and Twedor all followed Jan along a corridor of glassene partitions to a room at the end marked 'Viewing Room'. Jan opened the door, stepping aside to allow Tayce and the others to enter. Inside, the room was like a large cinema. There was a vast seating area and a central large ultra-slim screen on the main wall, with a disk-chip reader beneath. Everyone went to the front row of ten rows and sat down. Jan accepted a disk chip from an approaching slim female officer. He then began explaining as he crossed the floor and pushed the disk chip home in the reader.

"What you're about to watch is a scene caught by Amal on the intruder cam aboard Amalthea Two. I've tried to keep all the gory details out, Tayce. I've also highlighted just who really is to blame in this. Your father and I already have our theory who it is. I should warn you, you're going to be shocked," said Jan seriously in his usual gruff tone.

"Let's see it. Nothing shocks me in this Universe any more," replied Tayce, wanting to view what Jan had.

"All right, here goes," said Jan, turning and picking up the slim handset remote.

Crossing the floor, he aimed it at the reader and depressed a key. The screen came to life. The universal date and 'Amalthea Two' flashed across the middle in white lettering. The date felt like it was yesteron to Tayce. She was glad none of the others had to sit through the ordeal again. Scenes showing various parts of Amalthea in the near-darkness began showing on the vast-sized screen. Quickly the images showed the intruders and came in clear and sharp. Tayce gasped at the sight of the darkly clad leatherex-wearing invaders attacking her team. She had to look away at times, but when she looked back the familiar insignia on one of the intruders' uniforms said it all. Tayce couldn't believe it. She gave a look as much to ask was she really seeing what she was?

"Show it again – the insignia – and freeze it, if it's possible," demanded Tayce, rising to her feet alertly.

"Sure!" Jan replied, he could see Tayce had seen what her father and himself had seen.

Tayce recognised the familiar letters in the hexagonal shape in gold – 'CVVWA' – but wondered if she was seeing things. It sent a cold shiver up her spine at the mere thought of who was represented by some of the letters and what they stood for. She walked to the screen, then turned. The whole thing didn't seem right – no one had heard of the being behind the letters for yearons. She had been presumed dead.

"No, it can't be – she's dead. I heard she was killed by an inmate at the colony she was sent to to serve out the rest of her dayons after she pulled her last dirty act, but the initials don't quite add up. Hold on – it can't be. No, he's not been heard for yearons either," said Tayce, finding the whole thought perplexing, to say the least.

"Who?" demanded Jan, looking questioningly at her, wondering if Tayce's recognition matched her father's and his own suspicions and their connection to her attack.

"I recognise that symbol too, but I have to agree with Tayce: the woman behind those initials did die. She was apprehended during Tayce's last voyage. I can see where you're coming from, Tayce – it looks like her evil legal intimate joining partner, judging by those letters," spoke up Lydia.

"Excuse me, I would like to know if you think along the same lines as myself and your father," cut in Jan.

"And your theory along with my father's is?" asked Tayce plainly.

"The initials CVVWA are on the intergalactic criminal file as standing for Count Varon Vargon Warrior Army. Do you two agree?" asked Jan, glancing from Tayce to Lydia, with Phean and Twedor looking on.

"He's responsible for putting us out of action, nearly wiping out the whole of my Quests team. I'll make sure he pays for this," said Tayce under her breath. Upset beyond all recognition, she wanted to kill Vargon if she could get her hands on him.

"Take it easy, Tayce. Come on…" ordered Lydia, taking hold of her daughter, trying to calm her in her true motherly fashion. She understood her daughter's anger though.

"Jamie Balthansar had better complete the work on my cruiser in the time allocated. I want to get that evil bastard once and for all," she replied angrily, pushing her mother away, even though she didn't mean to.

Lydia thanked Jan for discovering just who it was who attacked Amalthea Two and the team. Jan nodded in acknowledgement and wondered what next move Tayce would make, considering her anger, which was justifiable. Phean guided Tayce on out of the viewing room, trying to get her to calm down, even though he was finding it very difficult as she was so wound up and so angry. Jan knew he had something to get on with. His and the Admiral's suspicions over the bogus councillor had been confirmed; it was the reason behind the team being brought home. Lydia hurried on out after Tayce, thanking Jan once again near the entrance. He nodded, exclaiming that he didn't think it was the end of it, judging by Tayce's fury – not by a long shot. He realised that in a way he would have acted the same as Tayce had if he had been in her shoes. First the Countess tried to finish her Amalthean Quests off, and now it looked like her evil partner in love and crime, the Count, was trying to do the same. But it also made Jan wonder where the Count had been hiding all the past yearons and why he had surfaced now. Was Sallen the key to the attack, so he could get her back on side? he wondered.

***

Four dayons later a ceremony of respect was held in honour of the Amalthean crew members who had perished in the attack. The surviving crew members that attended were now the whole team. Jaul Naven and Deluca Marrack were given a first-class space burial. Both Deluca's parents and Jaul's parents were present. The Navens had flown all the way from Canardan 5. It had been a simple but well-meaning affair. Tayce, being Jaul's captain, was to say a small speech to say how pleased she had been in her exchange officer. He had fitted into the Amalthean Quests team exceptionally well. Nothing was ever too much of a challenge for him. An official, also from Canardan 5, gave a small speech on how Jaul was a first-class student in his early dayons and how he would be missed. Tayce began at the podium, finding it sad to have to say the words to Jaul's parents, but she managed to sound professional.

"It's a sad dayon really. We're here to say goodbye, not only to family, but to two exceptionally participating team members I was proud to call part of my team. Jaul was a young man who came to us wanting to do more with his career, so he opted for a life on Amalthea and we were proud to have him. Deluca was somewhat reluctant to become part of my team. She was afraid she would leave behind all the people she knew, but after a while she said to me, 'Captain, I'm glad I joined your team. You gave me a purpose, other than being the daughter of Admiral Marrack.' She soon made friends on my team, so it's with equal sadness that todayon I hereby release Jaul and Deluca into eternity. May they find peace – we will miss you both," said Tayce in a soft sincere way.

Synthesised soft spiritual music began playing, fitting for Jaul's and Deluca's journey into eternity. Dairan slipped his hand discreetly into Tayce's, squeezing it affectionately. Each member of the Quests team stood in thought, each realising how lucky they had been. It could have been any one of them in the caskets before them, like Jaul and Deluca bound for internal peace before their time. Each gave a salute to Jaul's and Deluca's caskets as they began forth down the aisle to the exit. When Jaul had departed, Tayce handed the official disk chip containing the Javen cure. A drug Jaul had invented on Amalthea during his time on board – to Jaul's mother and father. They walked out and stood quietly talking with Tayce and Marc. They were a pleasant career-minded couple and did not hold Tayce responsible for their son's demise. After talking with the Navens, Tayce paused to talk with Deluca's parents, offering her sincere sympathy over Deluca. She explained that Deluca would want them to know she was well on the way to making them proud of what she was training to become on the Amalthean Quests team before what happened. Everyone on the team had taken Deluca under their wing to help her achieve what she wanted to do.

"Captain, there's no need for feeling so sad. As her father, it is I that should feel this. Thank you for your kind words over my daughter and thank you for giving her a beautiful send-off," said Admiral Marrack.

"Yes, Captain, you're not to blame. Marrack mourns Deluca too, and a ceremony is planned there in remembrance of her passing. If you are near Marrack and would like to attend, we would like you and your team to be there. It will be in a couple of monthons."

"Thank you. We will certainly try," replied Tayce calmly.

After the ceremony Tayce and the members of the team went for something to eat and drink in memory of both Jaul and Deluca with both sets of parents. Tayce knew she couldn't stay long – there were the preparations to get in order, to get the newly restored Amalthean cruiser back in space. She was more determined than ever to make Vargon pay for what he'd done.

Five dayons later, the whole Amalthean Quests team who had been released from the Medical Dome. In appreciation for Dr Carthean's round-the-clock care, whilst the team were all badly injured, they held a gathering of thanks in her honour. Aldonica Darstayne, who looked as if she hadn't even had the physiognomy-healing technique, looked as beautiful with her peach-clear complexion as she used to, before the ambush. The dinner had been a total surprise to Dr Carthean. She was overwhelmed by what had been arranged and modestly exclaimed that what she'd done was nothing more than her duty. She said it was nice to see such a fine crime-fighting team back where they should be, even if the leader of the team – namely, Tayce – chose to heal herself! Tayce glanced at Marc and laughed; he was doing the same, as he'd heard the same from Donaldo numerous times before. Donaldo was quick to agree with Dr Carthean, announcing that some people (mentioning no names present) like to make doctors obsolete. Everyone laughed, seeing Tayce was being made a joke of. Aldonica, turned handing a thank-you gift to Dr Carthean from the whole team for bringing almost everyone back together. Dr Carthean accepted the small gift of exquisite flowers. Music was laid on for the celebration evening to celebrate the almost regrouping of the near-deleted Amalthean Quests team.

Dairan turned as the entrance doors opened behind him. Phean Leavy entered. He glanced around for Admiral Traun and found him in discussion with Jamie Balthansar on the completion of restoring Amalthea the dayon after next. Darius stopped upon seeing Phean present.

"Can I ask for everyone's attention, please? I'd like to introduce you to the team's new telepathic guide and replacement for Jaul Naven – Phean Leavy," said Darius.

"Welcome to the team, Phean," said Dairan, stepping forward, hand outstretched for Phean to shake.

"Thank you," replied Phean, clasping Dairan's hand and shaking it.

Soon Phean was mingling with the team, talking and getting to know each member. Tayce watched discreetly, noticing, if appearances were anything to go on, that he was going to fit in in no time. But then she caught Marc eyeing Phean suspiciously at a distance. What was it he was seeing that she wasn't? She glanced back at Phean and, just for a split cencron, it was as if she was seeing an apparition of Tom, instead of Phean, in the midst of the gathering – his actions, the way he held his head and laughed. Tayce closed her eyes and told herself to stop it, it wasn't happening. She put the déjà vu down to nerves about beginning the new voyage. Anyway, whatever it was that Marc was concerned about, they would work through it and meet the problem, if there was one. '23:42' read Tayce's Wristlink time display as she lightly touched it and it illuminated. Dairan noticed and crossed to her, wondering what she was thinking.

"Do you want to leave?" he asked suddenly and discreetly, close to her right ear.

"Yes – good idea. It's been a busy dayon and tomorron is going to be just as crazy," she replied quietly.

Tayce crossed to Lydia, telling her she was going to leave. She was tired and tomorron was going to be a busy dayon, considering it was the final dayon before departure. Lydia agreed understandingly, saying she'd explain her sudden departure. With this, Dairan and Tayce crossed the room to the entrance, saying a goodnight to Marc and Lance. Tayce paused at the entrance.

"I'll see you all at some stage tomorron. If you have any problems or any worries about us heading back into space, my apart-house doors are open; if I'm not there Wristlink me and we'll meet up."

With this, she and Dairan walked from the centre of celebration in the newly renovated Assignments Building.

Darius stood in thought, watching both his daughter and Dairan leave. He was quickly brought back to the present time by Marc approaching. Marc noticed he seemed concerned about something, judging by his watchful expression.

"Excuse me here for being nosey – you look concerned?" asked Marc casually.

"No, you're not being nosey; and yes, I am. Before coming here tonight, I received word that the council are still demanding Tayce take an audience with them," replied Darius discreetly.

"She's not going to like it, considering what we've been through. Isn't there anything you can do? Lydia!" said Marc, acknowledging Lydia walking up.

"They say it's nothing more than a formality, though I have been requested not to attend," replied Darius, not too pleased by the fact.

"I hope they don't regret their actions – you know how angry she's going to be," said Marc, knowing the fact and considering that after all that they had come through the council were still demanding an audience.

"I was hoping that as I and Lydia here aren't allowed in, perhaps you'd escort her?" enquired Darius.

"What time does this all take place tomorron?" asked Marc, glancing around the room then back at Darius.

"0945 hourons. Think you can make it?" asked Darius.

"Leave it with me, though I don't hold out much hope on what kind of reaction you're going to get when she finds out she still has to face the council. She hates them – and considering what's happened!" exclaimed Marc in warning.

"We'll be prepared to hear her words of disgust," assured Lydia.

Marc, Darius and Lydia continued on, discussing Vargon's actions to throw out the Amalthean Quests voyage and how mysteriously it seemed it had led to the vicious attack on Amalthea Two for the sole purpose of reclaiming Sallen. Darius expressed how he didn't like the way in which Tayce seemed to be driving ahead in her determination to reclaim Sallen. He was concerned for her safety. Both Darius and Marc left Lydia talking with Jamie Balthansar and walked out on to the balcony in discussion of the voyage that in two dayons' time would be the third in the crime-fighting Quest concept. As Marc was once confidential aide to Darius, he always felt they had almost the kind of working understanding relationship a father and son might have; they could always discuss matters at great length and with mutual understanding. Marc had become a strong link with himself and Lydia where Tayce was concerned. Marc had lost all ties with his father a couple of yearons ago when his parents headed off on an Astro exploration and as yet hadn't returned. As far as he was concerned, Darius and Lydia were his family. The gathering continued on into the early hourons of the next dayon.

***

During duty time later that same dayon in the early mornet aboard the newly named Auran Amalthea Three Jamie Balthansar was instructing his men on the final tests and checks on different replaced equipment. Dairan boarded the cruiser with Craig Bream. Craig had been asked by Tayce to go in her place as Jamie had wanted to explain the new intrusion device that had been installed. Jamie walked to meet both Dairan and Craig with the understanding that they'd be returning to the scene of the ambush. Even though Amalthea had been refitted, it was going to be a bit unnerving for the two team members. Jamie was somewhat surprised not to see Tayce. Dairan caught the fact and explained her absence. With this, Jamie suggested they follow him up to Organisation. All three walked along the Level 2 corridor towards the Level Steps. Craig glanced at Dairan as they began up. He was finding the recurring flashbacks of what occurred the last time they were aboard hard to brush aside as they happened. Dairan clapped him on the shoulder in a reassuring way and informed him that it would get a lot easier – he'd see. They finally made it to Level 1 and entered into the newly restored Organisation Centre. Entering through the open doorway wasn't easy for either one of them. Jamie glanced around, allowing both Dairan and Craig to take a moment. There were three of Jamie's officers running checks. He could see Dairan's relief at seeing the Organisation Centre nearly back to its former glory as he looked back at the Amalthean pair.

"The intruder system operation is via two ways: via Amal, if she picks up the intruders, or via your navigational control console."

"How does Amal pick up the intruders once they're on board?" asked Dairan, curious.

"It's miraculous how we've done it in two weeks, but we've installed sensory detection all round the cruiser, integrating it into the main system. It doesn't matter how sophisticated the intruders' anti-detection device is, we have a system small enough to detect such devices. It scans and cuts through fields of anti-detection not normally detected with the equivalent of a naked eye. It's just been released from being a prototype."

"Yeah, but how can you scan something that's not there?" asked Dairan, not getting the idea. "Surely if it's not there, then it isn't."

"To you or me, no, but this kind of system has a kind of recognition pickup. When the corridor or wherever on aboard is more than your normal surroundings, you could say it sees the difference. In this case Amal will see there is something more than the normal layout of the cruiser and pinpoint that difference. Have you ever tried scanning your anti-intruder arm devices? They give off a minute signal in a high frequency that would under normal circumstances be hard to detect; but with this new system, the minon something isn't what it should be it's scanned, picked up and relayed straight back as 'intrusion on board'. Hence an immediate alarm sounding and a force field being activated around that being or whatever caused the intrusion in the first place," explained Jamie.

"Let's hope it works when we rendezvous with Count Vargon," said Dairan.

"Tayce knows, then. I knew she'd seriously want to take him on," said Jamie.

"Yes – very seriously. She's seething, you could say," replied Dairan.

"I'll leave you to wander around. Any questions, my men will be happy to discuss them with you and answer," said Jamie, heading away.

"Thanks!" replied Dairan.

Jamie left Dairan and Craig in Organisation studying the new operations on demonstration mode. Craig studied many of the new components he'd have to operate as part of his duty, on voyage, for tech overhauls and checks from time to time, to keep the cruiser ticking over. Dairan glanced at his Wristlink time display as he walked to the central star-chart podium. He leant on it, to take a look at the new display, but his mind was on Tayce, who'd be leaving soon for her audience with the Enlopedian Council for Voyages Missions and Assignments. He hoped she would manage to keep calm before them, considering how angry she was over the news of who was behind the attack. Men worked on around him in the centre, finalising tests and replacing panels for the last time before moving on somewhere else on board. Dairan glanced at the star chart, then around Organisation. Memories of the ambush suddenly flashed into his mind and were so violent it made him topple, but he managed to regain his footing, hoping no one noticed. Craig caught the act.

"You all right? If it's any consolation, I was fighting the same feeling when we came in here."

"Yeah, I'm fine," replied Dairan, feeling angry at himself for what had just occurred.

Both men decided to leave Organisation and head down and check out their newly refurbished quarters. Both were glad to leave Organisation for a while. A couple of Jamie's men talked amongst themselves, saying how it must be hard to return to the scene of an unprovoked attack and devastation so recent.

***

At the Enlopedian Council Building, Tayce, Marc and a newly restored Twedor entered the outer foyer. Tayce was finding it hard to keep her temper, considering what they'd just been through. She felt this audience with the narrow-minded bunch of no-good decision-makers was a total waste of time. She was not prepared to let her voyage go – not at any cost. A clerk stepped forth upon seeing her approaching quickly. Once he'd established it was Tayce, he proceeded to the designated audience chambers with her. The tall doors drew open. The young smartly dressed clerk entered, announcing Tayce. He stepped aside, letting Tayce go forth into the chamber with Marc and Twedor not far behind. She walked ahead of Marc in a determined way, into the centre of the white shiny-floored area before the council bench, and came to a pause. The five members of the council all looked down at her in their usual official stiff authoritative manner, silently waiting for her attention. Tayce didn't show any interest in being where she was. She just wanted to get what had to be said over and done with and leave.

"Good dayon, Captain Traun. The council members and I here present would like to firstly express how good it is to see and know that you and Commander Dayatso and your team have made a good recovery from your ordeal."

"Good dayon, gentlemen. My team are ready to leave tomorron, as are Twedor here and the newly named Auran Amalthea Three. Gentlemen, as much as I appreciate your concern for myself, Commander Dayatso and my team, I have a busy schedule before departure, so I trust this won't take long," expressed Tayce, to the point.

"We won't keep you any longer than is necessary. We believe your first Quest is to track down our bogus councillor, who resides under the criminal name of Count Varon Vargon. Would the aim of this Quest be classed as gain on your behalf, or would you class it as crime-orientated for us?" asked the sandy-haired councillor to the left of the head councillor on the bench.

"Both," replied Tayce, wondering why he'd asked, though she could see he was trying to trick her.

Marc, from behind her, was surprised the councillor asked what he did. What was he driving at? he wondered. Twedor stood silent, taking in the cold stiff authority of the scene. He knew Tayce hated anything to do with the council, considering what they'd done to her past voyages in an underhand way. Tayce stood silently for a moment in thought. The council before Tayce discussed amongst themselves for a few moments, then returned to her, stood before them in the white central circle. The head councillor requested she explain fully her answer.

"Count Vargon ambushed my cruiser for two reasons, one being that when my world was destroyed by him and his evil female partner they thought they'd rid the the Universe of me and my parents. They even went as far as to try and destroy my first Amalthean Quests voyage. He hates anything to do with Traun that's still in existence. The second reason was the apprehension of Sallen Vargon, once his evil daughter, who went through the memory-reprogram treatment and became my science officer. Our aim for part of this first Quest is to reclaim my valued team member and put a stop to Count Vargon once and for all. Does this answer your question, gentlemen? If you feel you want to offer this Quest to another team, which won't know Count Vargon like we do, then the decision is yours. The outcome might not be so successful," she said without further word.

"So this Quest would incorporate what we request of you in the apprehension of this Count Vargon?" asked the sandy-haired plumpish arrogant-looking member to the left of the head councillor, who was suspicious that Tayce would take on the first Quest of the new voyage just for her own gains in getting rid of Count Vargon once and for all – not that he blamed her.

"If you give me authority, I and my team will deal with him in our own way; or if you request, we will do our utmost to hand him over to Chief Barnford under strict guard. We work as a team," replied Tayce.

There was another few moments whilst the bench mumbled amongst themselves once more. Tayce glanced back over her shoulder and raised her eyes at Marc, as much as to say, "Here we go again!" She soon looked back to the front when she was asked further questions she felt were a waste of time.

"I take it you will take on numerous other Quests as part of your forthcoming voyage, along with this one?" asked a curly-haired councillor Tayce didn't recognise.

"Of course. Amalthean Quests is a voyage of Quests, criminal-based or rescue-orientated. We also hope that we can serve this base as we have done numerous times before successfully," replied Tayce.

"Captain, besides this Quest that we have asked you to undertake, our proposal on the decision regarding your third voyage is as follows: you will undertake a trial voyage for a yearon, and we will monitor your Quests during this time. If at the end of the yearon we feel your voyage is worth furthering for a further yearon, we will then consider it in depth, taking into account your achievements on this current voyage. Should we think you haven't done enough to justify a further yearon of the Amalthean Quests, your cruiser will be seized and impounded and your team disbanded and given other assignments," said the head councillor.

The look on Tayce's face said it all. She was furious beyond all recognition. She was fed up and tired of this no-good bunch of decision-makers, making decisions affecting her and the team's lives and careers.

"Then if you think the Amalthean Quests – a concept agreed by the late Jonathan Largon – is not worthy of that further yearon, I lose everything? No, Councillor Paytern, I flatly refuse your council's proposal here and now. There is too much risk. I feel you're asking too much. My team and I have done a lot for Enlopedia since the Amalthean Quests voyages first commenced in 2417. I know for a fact, if the late Jonathan Largon was alive todayon and could see the way you are handling his approved concept, he would make you answer for this decision over the future of my voyages," said Tayce in a slightly agitated tone.

"So your answer is one of non-cooperation – not taking up our offer?" asked Paytern plainly.

"Yes. Either you give me what I want or I will be taking my cruiser – which, I might add, is owned by me in spite of whatever upgrade she has – and Quests team either to work for another colony that appreciates our worth or to work for ourselves," said Tayce. She felt she was not prepared to accept the council's attitude any more.

"Captain, you believe very strongly about your Quests-orientated voyage, don't you?" asked another member of the council, a short stubby man with mellow features.

"Yes, I do, considering what we've accomplished in our two-yearon history, which includes rescuing people from the destruction of Questa, yes," replied Tayce plainly.

There was further discussion between the five middle-aged council delegates. Tayce glanced back over her shoulder at Marc, who winked at her, then nodded in agreement over what she'd just said. The council asked for her attention, bringing her back to face them. She turned back to them. They had decided there needed to be more to support her request for the continuation of her new voyage for another yearon. They needed to study more past voyage Quest material. They said they would give her their decision at first light in the mornet. After this time she could do what she considered right for her and her team. Tayce sighed, but reluctantly agreed.

She turned and began walking out, fuming that this bunch of no-good decision-makers were going to keep her in suspense for a further period of time; but she knew what the outcome would be should they refuse her. Marc and Twedor fell in on the walk out. Tayce did not look back. She'd decided she'd taken enough of this council and she wasn't going to put up with them any further than tomorron. Marc congratulated her on standing her ground. He knew her father would have been very proud of the way in which she had done so. Twedor patted her with his blue metlon hand, as much as to say, "Well done!"

"You sure did tell them. Couldn't have done it better myself," spoke up Twedor in his usual male childlike voice.

"Thanks, both of you, but we're not out of this yet. Tomorron we'll make a decision for us, that's for sure. Marc, will you tell the others? I want to find Dairan and tell Father what the outcome is," said Tayce.

"Sure! Before you go, are you going aboard tonight?" asked Marc, curious but not meaning to pry.

"Yes, I want to get the cruiser ready for tomorron, no matter what the council's decision may be."

"I'll meet you here tomorron then, for our final decision?" enquired Marc.

"0900 hourons – enjoy your last dayon here," said Tayce, teasing, walking away on across E City Square, calling Dairan via Wristlink as she went, telling him what had happened.

Tayce felt a bit more at ease and pleased with herself now she'd finally, after all the yearons of cruising, stood up to the decision-makers behind her voyages – namely, the council. Twedor noticed, in the way she was striding out in an elegant way, walking across the square, that his mistress was coming back to being the leader and captain she was, instead of being someone that had just been through a life-threatening ordeal. Dairan soon came into view in the area leading to the Construction Port. Tayce walked to meet up with him and tell him more fully what had occurred in the Council Chambers before they headed on to explain it to her father.

***

Nightfall came soon enough. Via Marc over Wristlink Tayce had requested everyone to be on board next dayon ready to commence duty. She and Dairan walked aboard Auran Amalthea Three, talking with Jamie Balthansar and accepting Jamie's assurance that everything was completed. They both headed down to their quarters. Both realised they were the only two people on the massive cruiser. It was a chance to relax in once more familiar surroundings before the commencement of the voyage next dayon, either with or without council's backing. No sooner had they dropped their holdalls off in their quarters than Dairan was heading away to the new Astrono Centre, to check all the information that would be needed to be at hand for departure next dayon, to be sent to the star-chart podium. Tayce headed up to Organisation with Twedor. She felt strange being back aboard, considering the last time she'd been on the cruiser had been during the ambush. As she neared Level 1 she tried to push the feelings of apprehension to the back of her mind, and as she continued on along towards Organisation she took deep breaths and told herself she was perfectly safe. Soon the feeling of being back in command came flooding back. She was very much relieved when she came to a pause just inside Organisation and looked all around at the many new consoles and the normal working environment minus the team. Amal picked up on her immediate presence.

"Welcome to Organisation, Tayce. What would you like me to attend to first?" asked Amal.

"Thanks, Amal. It's good to hear you again. Lock in departure time for tomorron – it's 10:56," commanded Tayce.

"Locking your request into my new memory backup system, for retrieval at the time specified," replied Amal in her female tone, politely and efficiently.

Tayce walked to where the new intruder-system controls on Kelly Travern's new console were. She sat down relaxingly in Kelly's high-backed new navy-and-chrome chair. Twedor stood at ease, on standby, watching his mistress run through pre-checks for the next dayon's departure. A while later Dairan entered Organisation to see Twedor and Tayce studying the VDU's slim display screen. He crossed the floor, glancing at his Wristlink time display. He came to a halt behind Tayce and leant on the back of the chair, arms folded, watching what she was studying. After a few minons Tayce looked up at him. Tiredness was etched on her beautiful features and showed in her sapphire-blue eyes. She smiled.

"Nearly finished. Kelly can run through the rest tomorron," promised Tayce softly.

"Do you have something in mind?" he asked softly behind her.

"It's 21:55 hourons and we're the only two on board. I figured we'd head for our quarters and celebrate getting this cruiser back, in some way," she said playfully.

She soon logged off Kelly's console and rose to her feet. She walked round the back of the chair, coming face-to-face with Dairan, who reached out, pulling her gently into his arms. Their lips soon met in a long lingering kiss. Tayce backed away slightly after a while and told him that, no matter what the decision was, in the mornet they were leaving port. Dairan nodded in total understanding agreement. He gestured for her to shush. Tayce wondered why, looking away then back. He slipped his arm around her waist, saying a goodnight to Twedor, and began guiding Tayce on out of Organisation, suggesting that whatever needed to be worried about should be forgotten from that moment until the next dayon. Twedor whistled in awe at the two, off to grab some time together before departure tomorron, then went back to communicating with Amal.

***

At first light next mornet Tayce was in the Cleanse Unit. She'd left Dairan sprawled in deep sleep in the bunk. She soon emerged, dressed, ready to head off for breakfast, then on to the rendezvous with the council in the Enlopedian Council Building to hear the final decision on the new proposed third voyage. She ordered Amal to wake Dairan in ten minons. Amal agreed. With this, Tayce walked on out of the Repose Centre and on through the Living Area, calling Twedor to follow on the way. The doors drew apart in front of her on approach and they headed off to get something to eat and drink.

***

Marc left the short-stay accommodation building dressed in his new Amalthean uniform, of black jacket and trousers with white trim and cream shirt. He looked, as usual, the handsome commander he was. Holdall in one hand, he walked through the corridor and out through the entrance to head across E City Square to meet up with Tayce in the Enlopedian Council Building. His thoughts as he went were on what the newly appointed delegates had decided to do over his and the team's future with Enlopedia. He wondered just what Jonathan Largon would have said in the light of the actions this bunch of decision-makers were undertaking. It never ceased to amaze him, the pathetic actions they took that weren't right sometimes. Empress Tricara was crossing the square with Auran Amalthea Three's newest recruit, Phean Leavy. He too was dressed in the new black-and-cream uniform with the 'QE' emblem on it in blue and green, the Q being blue and the E being green entwined, situated in the top left-hand side of the jacket. Tayce came from the Flight Arrival and Departure Dome down from the Construction Port. Marc glanced over to see her coming towards him. He had an idea she'd had a good night's rest aboard the cruiser, which he was glad to see. He wondered whether she would find it a little tough being back on board, considering the last time she was was when the ambush had occurred. He could see the strain of the ambush was gone, and in its place was the first-class look of a true leader, friend and captain.

"Mornet! Ready to find out if this council bunch have got their act together over our third voyage?" asked Marc, wondering.

"Of course. Even if they don't grant me my voyage under Enlopedia, I'm not changing my decision to leave port without their say-so," said Tayce in her true tone of determined leader.

"Mornet, Captain," said Phean politely.

"Ready to join Auran Amalthea Three?" asked Tayce, looking towards Phean.

"Yes, looking forward to it. The Empress here said it was your idea to have me on the Quests team – thank you," expressed Phean, pleased.

"It was partly my father, but he asked for my opinion and I found you handled yourself well through our crisis after the ambush in supporting me. Tricara, do you want to see me before we leave?" asked Tayce.

"No, it's fine. I've briefed Phean here on everything the Emperor feels you should know. I'll talk to you on the voyage. Just be careful when you come face-to-face with Vargon. Don't let him undermine you," warned Tricara kindly, as any good friend would warn another.

"Don't worry – I'm looking forward to coming face-to-face with that barbarian," replied Tayce, feeling the hatred once more rise within her at the thought of Count Vargon.

Tricara, noticing the way Tayce had spoken about Count Vargon, glanced at Marc in a concerned way. As Tayce glanced at her Wristlink time display, Marc informed the Empress discreetly that her concern was noted. Tayce suggested they get going – it was time. Marc casually ordered Phean to report to the Leisure Centre on Auran Amalthea Three. It was where the whole team were gathering. Phean nodded in acknowledgement. He thanked the Empress for her guidance and understanding to get him where he was. He then picked up his holdall and took Marc's and walked away in the direction of Auran Amalthea Three, which would be home for the foreseeable future.

"Shall we go? Twedor, catch Phean up – he may get lost aboard the cruiser," ordered Tayce.

"Yes, Tayce," replied Twedor, heading off to catch Phean up, calling as he went, until Phean paused.

Tayce and Marc continued on towards the Enlopedian Council Building to see the Voyages, Missions and Assignments bunch of decision-makers known as the council. In her mind, Tayce was having a feeling of what the outcome would be, and it would be no surprise if it turned out to be what she was thinking.

***

Up at the Construction Port the Amalthean Quests team members were all walking aboard in various groups to be aboard in time for departure. Lance was first to arrive, carrying his holdall and the box of personal belongings he wanted to take aboard. Nick and Kelly followed on. Kelly had visited Greymaren and had only just come back in the last ten minons. They followed Phean and Twedor on board with Craig Bream following on behind. Jamie Balthansar watched the team walk back aboard the new Auran Amalthea Three, feeling pleased he'd managed to bring the legendary team back together.

***

Tayce and Marc entered into the Enlopedian Council Building and were immediately shown into the chambers where she and Marc had been the previous dayon. As they both entered, it was like the delegates hadn't moved from their seats since the previous dayon. Tayce braced herself for their non-committal answer. Marc paused just a short way behind her, waiting also for the excuses the council were going to deliver. The head of the Enlopedian Council for Voyages, Missions and Assignments, Councillor Paytern began. He looked down at his Porto Compute, then amongst his delegates, then at Tayce.

Tayce said quietly, "Here it comes – wait for the excuses."

"After considering the evidence during the past hourons in studying your past voyage Vidfilm logs, we have come up with an offer that we consider slightly better than the first one. Of course, whether you decide to accept it is another thing. We are prepared to offer you a trial voyage of three monthons plus Quests. After this time, as stated, we will review your Quest reports."

"So it's a case of I can have my voyage, but for a trial of three monthons; instead of the yearon first offered and if you don't then feel that we have done well, even though we will have, you could revoke my Amalthean Quests, just like that – and this is your final offer," said Tayce, playing them along. She'd already made her decision on this latest offer.

"Yes, Captain, it is. Accept it or your voyage will be dismissed completely," announced Councillor Paytern, with the other delegates nodding in agreement.

"Well, gentlemen, your offer may be good for you, but it's not good enough for me. Get stuffed! Come along, Commander – we have a departure to undertake," said Tayce, turning and beginning back towards the entrance.

"Councillor Paytern, with your offer being the final one and my captain not accepting it, I just hope you don't live to regret it. Some day you might need our help," said Marc sternly. Then he turned and followed Tayce.

Chief Paytern announced to Tayce that she would never leave port – she would be stopped in her attempt to do so. Marc looked at Tayce, who had just paused and turned back with an expression of disgust. Councillor Paytern had just called an airless shot. It meant nothing to her. Auran Amalthea Three was hers.

"If you try and stop me I'm quite sure my father will dissolve this council," retorted Tayce.

With this, she continued on out through the chamber's opening doors with Marc in close pursuit. The Council for Voyages, Missions and Assignments made a comment on Tayce's file on Porto Compute, then shut down the file. They all discussed Tayce's behaviour as they left the seating area, surprised at the response that had come from an Admiral's daughter.

***

Out in E City Square, Dairan and Jan were talking with Admiral Traun about what was to be Tayce's first Quest of the new third voyage. None of them were aware Tayce was intending to do it without the backing of the Enlopedian Council for Voyages, Missions and Assignments. Dairan looked in the direction of the approaching Marc and Tayce. He could figure by the look of disgust on the normally breathtaking features of Tayce that things hadn't gone the way she'd hoped. He guessed they were on their own as far as representation of the base was concerned.

"Oh, by the look on your face it didn't go well. What was their decision?" asked Darius, seeing his daughter's cool disapproving face.

"We're going it alone. Goodbye, Father. Speak to you soon," promised Tayce, giving her father a hug then beginning away with Dairan and Marc.

"Hold on, young lady. What do you mean you're going it alone?" asked Darius, far from pleased.

"It's quite simple: the Voyages, Missions and Assignments council thought about my voyage overnight and offered me a three-monthon voyage, would you believe? At the end of that time, they say, they will review whether they will allow me to continue on with the Amalthean Quests concept. Well, I'm not prepared to kowtow to those decision-makers any more. As from this moment, I work for you and will still carry the QE emblem; but as for that bunch of decision-makers, they are no longer part of my voyage. I'd better go, Father – the team awaits."

"Tayce, hold up. If you need me and the SSWAT team, we'll be there – just give us a call," offered Jan.

"Right, thanks!" replied Tayce.

Darius ordered Dairan and Marc to take care of his only daughter where Vargon was concerned. Both agreed. Tayce, Dairan and Marc continued across to the walkway in the Flight Arrival and Departure Dome to head back to the Construction Port to leave. Jan quickly assured Darius that if Tayce wanted assistance he and his men would be there in no time. Darius nodded, glad of the fact. He watched Tayce and the others until they were out of sight, then walked with Jan on across the square in discussion about other things.

3. Vargon's Mendacities

Auran Amalthea Three was heading across the Universe well under way on the first Quest. One that no one on board was looking forward to, including Tayce. In Organisation Kelly had keyed in the new coordinates direct from a long-distance scan beacon that had been sent out in search of the destination port of the first Quest. Marc was leaning on the back of Lance's chair watching the universal information scroll onscreen during the download from the beacon's on-board tracking system. Without warning, it stopped mid download. Marc hit the chair back in anger. It meant Vargon had found out he was being rooted out and didn't much care for the fact that the Amalthean Quests team were on to him. Marc stood up.

"Work on what we could get. It will have to do. Maybe it will help us put a picture together of what we're up against," said Marc, far from pleased at the backlash from Vargon.

"Right, leave it with me," assured Lance.

Marc walked away from standing behind Lance's chair and sauntered on into the DC. As he entered Tayce was in heated debate over the Satlelink with her father at Enlopedia. She was refusing to do what he wanted her to do. He could hear Darius explaining that he would accompany Tayce – it was too dangerous to attempt alone. Tayce was furious and cut communications, refusing the offer of his help. She was not prepared to discuss it any further – they could handle what had to be done. There was a Quest to sort and plan. Marc glanced out through the sight port, trying not to listen to the conversation Darius and Tayce had been having. It wasn't the first heated debate he'd witnessed between father and daughter over the yearons. Tayce relaxed back against the high back of her chair with an exasperated sigh.

"How are the preparations going? Anything from our search-and-scan self-driven beacon yet?" asked Tayce, looking at him questioningly by the sight port gazing out into the stars.

"That's why I'm here, I think, and I'm almost certain Vargon's found us probing his whereabouts," began Marc, pacing.

"Really! Any feedback information, or did he destroy it in his usual careless style?" She looked at him, not surprised if Vargon had destroyed the beacon.

"I think we obtained enough info even if he did. Lance is piecing together what we managed to download. It should be enough to put together some kind of picture of what we're up against," expressed Marc.

"We got his attention, then. No doubt he'll be getting everything ready for another strike at us when we show up in his vicinity. Can't wait," replied Tayce.

"I agree," replied Marc, sharing her hatred for Count Vargon, even though he wasn't showing it.

They both continued discussing Vargon. Marc expressed his concern for her safety and put it in such a way that she wouldn't think he was telling her her duty. He understood her anguish and hatred for Count Vargon of the Vargon Empire. Marc was an inhabitant too of Traun and was present on that fateful night the Count had carried out his final bloody ambush on his home world before vanishing. Tayce got up out of her chair and walked round to the front of the desk where Marc stood. She paused before him, exclaiming she understood his concern. She said she herself had to admit she wasn't looking forward to the encounter with the man that took away their home world and friends. But Sallen was the main focus of the forthcoming Quest – besides taking on the Count, they had to get her back where she belonged.

"If you think for a moment, the whole team must be silently dreading this first Quest, not just us," said Tayce.

Marc nodded in total agreement. From out in Organisation, through the open doorway, Nick could be heard calling to Tayce to come out into the centre urgently. Tayce and Marc, upon hearing the urgency in Nick's voice, looked at each other questioningly, then hurried on across the DC to the entrance. They walked out into Organisation to find out what was wrong. Dairan turned to see her and pointed to the awesome sight on screen. Tayce's features took on a look of pure hatred at the being that was on the main Sight Screen. He stood looking as evil and as cold as the dayon Tayce remembered coming face-to-face with him on Traun all the past yearons ago. Behind him was a vast hi-tech interior. Tayce came to a pause beside Dairan. He glanced at her, noticing her cold angered look as she looked at the darkened evil features of a man she'd hoped to never see ever again – Count Vargon.

"I detected your attempt to gain the knowledge of my whereabouts, Traun – a foolish act," stated Vargon unemotionally through the screen.

"He's keeping the channel open. I can't cease communications from here," whispered Nick.

"You have something that belongs to Enlopedia and this cruiser. Where is she?" demanded Tayce coldly.

"Oh, you mean my daughter. Perhaps you should visit and find out," invited Vargon.

It was as if Dairan could sense something was about to happen. He reached out and grabbed Tayce. What followed could only be described as some kind of conjuring magic. A high-energy beam engulfed both Tayce and himself, abducting them from Organisation in a split cencron. Marc flew into a state of alert, ordering Amal in sheer panic to pinpoint the destination the force was retracting back to and bring Tayce and Dairan back aboard. Lance quickly joined Kelly in following the line of destination, so he could pinpoint the whereabouts of Vargon's orbital setting, so Auran Amalthea Three could enter the exact numerical reference and head off to rescue Tayce, Dairan and, hopefully Sallen. And perhaps someone else would be newly discovered to be on board also – one Professor Maylen. But it wasn't going to be easy. Vargon had left no trace of the retracting force. Marc, on finding this, cursed under his breath – something so unrepeatable that Kelly looked at him, surprised. Lance suddenly yelled out that he'd got a bearing. It had appeared quite unexpectedly. Marc crossed the floor, ordering him to have it transferred to the star-chart podium. Lance did as requested. Marc crossed to the central star-chart podium. It illuminated on his approach, bringing up the exact location of where Tayce and Dairan had been sent. Phean walked into Organisation at this moment, glancing around. Then he looked at Marc. Something was wrong – his senses hadn't been wrong after all. He sauntered over to Marc, who confirmed what he'd picked up earlier: Tayce had been abducted by an evil being known as Count Vargon.

Phean nodded understandingly. "Can I do anything to help in any way?" he enquired.

"Yes, take a look at this chart. Perhaps you can use your ability to stay in communication with Tayce?" asked Marc, hoping.

"Of course," replied Phean casually, eager to assist.

***

Tayce and Dairan both stood in the middle of a vast elaborate hi-tech Operations Deck. Dairan was holding Tayce protectively – not that she needed it. So where was Vargon hiding? In through the high square entrance on the other side of the vast space he walked in a slow precise way, his footfall making a sound on the shiny floor as he came forth. Tayce felt her skin crawl and a shiver run up her spine. Five yearons she had waited for this moment. So where had he been during all this time, whilst Carra and Sallen, in the first yearon of her voyage, wreaked havoc across the Universe? He snapped his bony fingers and in an abrupt tone ordered four officers to come forward, gesturing for Tayce and Dairan to be separated. As two officers grabbed Dairan, he struggled. His eyes darkened, showing his anger at what was happening.

"You see, Tayce Amanda, you're not the only one who has a cruiser that can take on numerous tasks. This battleship has capabilities beyond your wildest dreams. The task to bring you here was a mere simple act, and your commander no doubt found it frustrating when he attempted to block the source bringing you here and reclaim you," explained Vargon.

"You think you've got it all planned. Why have you rid me of my cruiser and team? What have you brought me here for? I have nothing to say to you, you barbaric murderer," retorted Tayce with cold hatred in her voice.

"At this precise moment I am aware that your cruiser is under some kind of invisible shield. What I brought you here for is to extract the code frequency. Then I can uncover your cruiser and finish what I set out to do two weekons ago," he said slowly and plainly.

"If that's all, you're wasting your time. You'd be the last one I would tell that to," retorted Tayce.

"This I anticipated. Men, if you please," gestured Vargon to his two remaining officers.

Before Tayce had a chance to react, the two officers grabbed Tayce's arms and secured them in a restraining hold behind her back. Vargon took a small square silver-toned device from his jacket pocket and held it so it faced Tayce. She struggled in the hold of the two officers and found her inner powers surfacing. One officer handed total restraint over to the taller, stronger officer and moved so he could take hold of Tayce's head and hold it facing forward. Vargon held the device right before Tayce's sight. It activated and pulsated white, blue and yellow lights in quick succession. Over Tayce's shoulder Dairan used all his strength to try and break free, but to no avail. He found it angering that he couldn't do anything.

"Give me the code and we can end all this," ordered Vargon in his slow, dragging tone.

"Never!" replied Tayce, using all her inner strength to refuse to cooperate.

"Soon this device will send you into a cooperative stupor, where I shall take the information I seek. It will leave you in a coma with its power, from which there is no known awakening. It would be wise for you to cooperate," said Vargon in a persuading tone, but Tayce refused to listen.

"No! You'll n-e-v-e-r g-e-t..." said Tayce, finally losing the strength to hold out as the device drained her powers and her will to fight the device's power.

"Tayce! What the hell have you done to her, Vargon? God help you when Amalthea shows up," shouted Dairan angrily, struggling in the hold of the other two burly officers.

"Silence him. Take him to join the Professor – now, men!" bellowed Vargon at his men.

Tayce looked like a drunken mess. Her focus was out, and she looked like she was drugged to the eyeballs. Vargon turned to an operative at the main console, ordering him to open communications to Enlopedia, Admiral Traun's chambers. The unemotional-looking being of medium height and build, dressed in a khaki-coloured body-hugging glove outfit, complied with his master's orders. Vargon waited. He was almost evilly ecstatic at the thought of showing Lydia and Darius Traun he had their precious daughter at his mercy. He reached out and took Tayce in a rough hold by the neck and brought her before him.

***

On Enlopedia in Darius's chambers, the wall Sight Screen came to life unexpectedly. Adam, Darius and Lydia stopped what they were doing and turned to see a sight on screen they thought they'd never ever see again. Lydia gasped as she saw Tayce in the strong grip of Varon Vargon. Darius's expression took on a darkened and enraged look. Lydia was speechless, thinking of Tayce in the barbaric hands of the man who had destroyed their home world. Darius ordered Adam to get Jan Barnford up to the chambers immediately. Adam didn't need telling twice – he briskly left the chambers.

"I thought you'd like to see my first on-board guest," said Vargon, holding a dazed, drugged Tayce, gleefully seeing Darius's fury.

"You harm her in any way further, man, and I'll personally hunt you down with a task force myself. There won't be a place you can hide, do you hear me?" said Darius, seething beyond all sense.

"That's if you can find my vessel. You were and still are no threat to me, Traun. How you became an Admiral is to me a complete mystery," said Vargon spitefully.

"I'm warning you, Vargon. God dammit, I should have had my forces on Traun destroy you when you declared war of possession over our world. I should have tried to stop you leaving this base," snapped Darius.

"What's stopping you now? But then again, you don't have the guts, do you, Traun? That's why you lost your home world."

On this communications ceased abruptly.

Darius turned to see tears streaming down Lydia's delicate cheeks. He pulled her into a comforting hug. In between sobs she confided her fears about what had happened to their only daughter. Darius assured her in a soothing way that there was no way he would allow Tayce to be another unfortunate victim of Vargon.

The doors to the chambers opened. Jan briskly entered, looking concerned.

"Admiral, I just received an urgent message from Adam – something about a communication from Count Vargon?" asked Jan, ready to take control of what needed to be done and glancing towards a distraught Lydia.

"You're damn right it's urgent! Sorry, Jan – that barbarian makes my blood boil," said Darius, calming. He hadn't meant to snap at Jan.

"Care to share what this is all about, sir?" asked Jan, somewhat unsure as to what had made his chief so mad.

"I've just received a threatening visual call on screen, from Vargon. He has Tayce. He seems to have drugged her in some way. We've got to get her out of there. I don't like the way this is looking. I don't want anything happening to Tayce. I told her she should have let me help," said Darius, pacing as he explained.

"Leave this with me. I'll have a team together and be under way in less than one houron," promised Jan sincerely.

"Good," said Darius with a nod and a sigh.

"I had a feeling it was going to come to this. The sooner I get out there the better," replied Jan impatiently, as he headed back to the entrance.

"Keep us informed out there," ordered Darius.

"Will do. Don't worry, Lydia – I'll get Tayce out of there in one piece," promised Jan. Then as the doors parted he nodded to Lydia and Darius.

Jan continued on out through the open chambers doors, on through the outer Anteroom in urgency, knowing what lay ahead and what he had to do. Lydia smiled, feeling a lot more at ease, knowing Jan was going out with a SSWAT team to save her only daughter. Adam entered the chambers. Darius explained that he wanted to hear any reports Chief Barnford sent back to base during the hoped-for rescue of Tayce. Adam nodded. Darius glanced at his Wristcall time display. He had to be somewhere for a meeting on the other side of Enlopedia and he was running late. He kissed Lydia on the cheek, exclaiming that he'd see her later at their residence. She agreed. With this, he briskly walked from the chambers with Adam.

***

An houron elapsed. Chief Jan Barnford and six of his top SSWAT officers were heading in a brisk manner across E City Square to the High-Ranked Arrival and Departure Area. They were dressed in their combat attire, looking like they had a mission of vital importance to undertake. Jan was talking to them as they went. It sounded like a briefing on what they could expect and what had to be done in order to rescue the Admiral's daughter.

Vargon had had enough of Tayce failing to give him the code. He let her fall to the operations-deck floor in an uncaring way. She looked like a discarded rag doll as she landed in a heap. She was bruised and cut. Vargon had had her tortured until he couldn't get anything more out of her. Angry at her refusal to give up the information he wanted, he ordered the same officers that had apprehended her earlier to drag her away and put her with the others – namely Dairan and Professor Adrien Maylen. Tayce was grabbed by the upper arms and hauled to her feet and dragged from the Operations Deck. Sallen walked in dressed in a lattice-design black-and-red body-hugging suit, in leatherex and Lycra. She looked every inch the evil daughter she used to be when she was back with Carra, her mother. Black eyeliner and immaculately applied make-up made her look the true evil part perfectly. Her hair was clasped up at the back of her head in a clasp. Gone were any traces of the Amalthean Quests science officer, who loved bringing on new seedlings and attending the Lab Garden Dome and cared about life and the people closest to her. Varon turned, studying her in a proud evil way. 'Perfect!' he thought. The Professor had done an excellent transformation.

"Was that Captain goody-goody Traun I saw, Father?" demanded Sallen, glancing back over her shoulder coldly towards the entrance Tayce had just been dragged through.

"Yes, she's resisted my attempts to get her to cooperate, so I have to think of some other way to extract the Invisi Shield code that hides the Amalthean cruiser. I want that code – I must destroy that cruiser. It interferes with our plans for this Universe," said Vargon in thought.

"I totally agree, Father. What about using the other member who came with her? I saw him being put in the holding cell?" put Sallen. Nothing would have pleased her more than to turn Dairan Loring against Tayce Traun.

"Yes! Dairan Loring! I could extract the code from his mind. He may not have such a strong mentality in refusing to cooperate as Traun," replied Vargon in continued thought.

"The Professor could be made to perform the task – that's if he values his life," added Sallen with malicious wickedness.

Now she was back in her old ways, though no one knew how.

"Your mother would be proud of you, my girl. She'd be pleased to see you have come back like this. Come – I think we'll try your idea," he replied, pleased.

He began on across the Operations Deck with the idea that if he could make Professor Maylen extract the information he needed – namely, the Invis Shield code to uncover Auran Amalthea Three – then he could destroy the so-called Amalthean Quests team finally this time. An evil smile crossed his chiselled features, almost reaching his icy-blue eyes. He paused halfway to the entrance. Turning, he ordered Sallen to help him – after all, two powerful thinking minds were better than one. This made Sallen smile, almost like an excited childling. She was only too eager to join her father in the proposed evil task ahead. Father and daughter continued on out of the Operations Deck, Sallen talking about her mother on the way.

***

Down in the holding cell, Dairan held an unconscious Tayce. Both he and Professor Maylen were really concerned that Vargon had gone too far and Tayce was going to need emergency medical treatment. Dairan though knew of Tayce's ability to heal and wondered whether it would materialise. Suddenly, as if by magic and to the Professor's astonishment, Tayce's injuries and bruising began to fade to healthy skin. Professor Maylen shook his head in awe.

"That's amazing. How does she do it?" asked the Professor, almost whispering.

"Tayce is gifted with an inner ability to heal herself," replied Dairan, looking down at her.

Tayce slowly opened her eyes. Focusing, she found herself looking up into Dairan's warm, caring brown eyes. She began sitting up and he helped her gently. Just like a blinding flash in her mind, Phean Leavy mind-communicated with her. She almost fell back against Dairan with the sudden onslaught of it. He quickly steadied her, introducing Professor Adrien Maylen to her.

"This is Professor Maylen, who was abducted by Vargon," introduced Dairan.

"Professor! Pleased to meet you. It's just a shame we have to meet under such evil circumstances," said Tayce, stretching out her hand to shake hands with Adrien, which he did.

"Did he get what he wanted?" asked Dairan, hoping not.

"No, I held out, as you could probably tell when they threw me in here. We've been brought here using what you could almost call mendacity," said Tayce angrily.

"Does it surprise you, where that bastard's concerned?," asked Dairan, disgusted.

"I have to agree. He brought me here under a convincing promise. I discovered too late that the reason he really brought me here was to get his daughter back to her evil self, though how he managed to find her old memories is beyond me. They were suppose to have been destroyed upon removal," added Adrien, thinking about it.

"Nothing surprises me about him. He's definitely got a plan – we need to be on our guard," said Tayce.

"To get his hands on Auran Amalthea Three, no doubt, finishing what he failed to accomplish two weekons ago," said Dairan, far from impressed.

"Could be, but I think it's something on a grander scale. Our cruiser is just what you would class as a fly in the ointment – something he could do without, something he'd like to get rid of. We have to stop him," explained Tayce.

Adrien and Dairan exchanged glances, as much as to say, "This is not going to be easy."

Tayce walked to the circular sight port. This first Quest was turning out to be not what she'd expected. Behind her the holding-cell force-field entrance opened. In walked Vargon's officers – the same four that had dragged Tayce and Dairan apart earlier on the Operations Deck. The first two officers grabbed Dairan. He struggled and both Adrien and Tayce joined in, trying to stop him being taken. Tayce was shoved with force across the cell out of the way. Adrien went to her aid. Next the Professor had a high-powered energy weapon shoved in his face and was ordered in one word to move. Both Dairan and the Professor were pushed ahead of the four officers, leaving Tayce alone in the cell. The protests could be heard from Dairan as he was hauled on down the corridor. Tayce's mind communicated with Phean, informing him what was currently happening. She closed her eyes and began hoping Phean was still in communication with her from earlier.

***

On board Auran Amalthea Three Phean suddenly turned, standing beside Marc, announcing that Tayce was in communication with him. Quite suddenly Marc and the whole Organisation team – even Twedor – were looking at Phean with great interest. They all wanted news on Tayce and Dairan. When Phean came back from the communications concentration, he began to explain that Vargon had taken Tayce and Dairan to get his hands on the Invis Shield code they were currently travelling under. Once he had the code, he would set about destroying their current surroundings. So far Tayce had been tortured by Vargon, but had not divulged the code and was getting back to normal with her ability to heal. At the present time Vargon had sent the same four officers who had thrown her into a cell to retrieve Professor Maylen and Dairan and taken them away under protest. Her guess was that they were about to take part in something further to gain the code. At the present time she couldn't say what. Marc was interrupted by Nick over his shoulder.

"Chief Barnford's Patrol Cruiser is coming alongside and he's requesting you meet him on docking," said Nick.

"Right!" said Marc, clapping Phean on the shoulder, ordering him to stay in contact with Tayce.

Phean nodded.

As Marc headed for the entrance, he ordered Phean to tell Tayce help was on its way and to keep him up to date with any further happenings. Phean agreed. Marc left Lance in charge, heading on out of Organisation in a brisk way to go and meet up with Jan Barnford.

Below on Level 2, the Patrol Cruiser docked home with Auran Amalthea Three, going through the procedures to enable Jan Barnford to come on board. The sound of docking home and locking in position could be heard in the inner docking-and-boarding area. A few minons later the Patrol Cruiser doors opened. Jan walked forth in his blue combat uniform, followed by six of his officers from the SSWAT team. The Docking-Bay doors opened just as Marc was coming down the Level 2 corridor to meet him. Twedor was by Marc's side. He wanted to hear all that was discussed between the two men for future retrieval.

"Let's hear what you've got so far?" demanded Jan in a no-nonsense tone.

"Sure. Twedor, escort Jan's officers here to guest quarters, then return to Organisation," ordered Marc. Much to Twedor's disappointment, he wasn't going to be allowed to hear what was discussed.

"All right. Come this way," said Twedor, sounding disappointed that he couldn't remain.

Twedor, feeling agitated, began off up the corridor followed by Jan's six officers, who were of strong build and of varying heights. Looking the true elite men they were, they followed on behind with their holdalls in their hands. Jan walked the other way with Marc, wanting to hear everything that had unfolded so far, so he could assess what they were up against in the abduction of the dirtiest kind. Both men walked up the Level Steps talking about Count Vargon, and Marc shared his concern for Tayce. Jan took a while to tell Marc how Vargon had suddenly appeared on screen before Lydia and Darius, with Tayce tortured in his grip. Marc, upon hearing this, shook his head, not the least bit surprised. They continued on along Level 1 at the top of the Level Steps, going on into the Organisation Centre. Lance turned at his position, explaining as they walked in how he had managed to get an image of the battleship, showing the vessel's size and how much weaponry the vessel carried. Both men listened, then Phean was introduced to Jan. Marc explained why Phean had become part of the team as a communications link with Tayce when normal communications weren't possible. It was proving very helpful. Jan nodded understandingly. Marc, as he and Jan headed towards the DC, ordered Lance to bring what information he had into the DC. Lance stood, gathering the information he had, and following on in urgency.

***

Back on board the Carra Lair battleship, Dairan Loring was secured to some kind of medical cream leatherex couch by energy restraints. He was secured at the ankles, waist, neck and wrists, unable to move. Vargon stood by Dairan's side, looking down at him, showing no emotion. Sallen, also showing no emotion, stood aiming a silver high-energy power rifle directly at Professor Maylen's head, looking at him coldly and intently, waiting for her father to give the order to act and let the Professor meet his end. Professor Maylen looked down at Dairan in an apologetic way. It was very much against his principles what Vargon was making him do. Adrien was a plumpish man, but by no means flabby. All his build was toned and well proportioned. He was around five feet eight inches in height. Anyone could tell he was a man of high standing and of an academic background. His features were weather-beaten yet mellow and showed kindness. His eyes were a warm shade of blue and held a friendly warmth about them. Adrien was furious with Count Vargon and he felt maddened at himself for allowing such a barbarian to fool him into working against his principles as a medical and scientific creator. He hoped as he looked down at Dairan that he wouldn't hold the act Vargon was forcing him to undertake against him.

"I think you know why you're here, Lieutenant Commander Loring. It's quite easy: I want the Invis Shield code that is used to protect your cruiser, which your captain failed to divulge to me. She is a pitiful true Traun."

"You're not getting anything from me either," said Dairan, adamant.

"Your stubbornness and foolish devotion to your captain will not help your present situation. If you give me what I want, I will release you and you can go free, back to your team and cruiser," said Vargon in a lying but convincing tone.

"So you can finish what you started two weekons ago? I wouldn't give you the satisfaction," retorted Dairan.

"You disappoint me and leave me with no choice. Professor, you've seen Loring's refusal to assist in the retrieval of the Invis Shield code. I would review your present situation – the position you're in – and think seriously. If you do not do as I require, my daughter never misses," said Vargon slowly.

Professor Maylen glanced at Sallen and her primed power rifle aimed at him. Her face, which once expressed gentleness, now conveyed cold, dark evilness. He could tell by her dark eyes that she wouldn't hesitate to kill him if Varon gave the word. Not wanting to dié, Adrien began to carry out what her father wanted, even though it was very much against everything he believed in as the upstanding man he was. Varon Vargon walked to him at the control panel.

"Show me Loring's mind. Show me the Invis Shield code and you may live," said Vargon in his usual slow plain tone.

"Why should I do this for a barbaric evil man like you?" said Adrien, turning and looking straight in Varon's face.

"Sallen here will make your current breath the last you take," replied Varon without further word.

"I'm sorry for this, Dairan," apologised Adrien, and he didn't care if Varon heard him.

Dairan was seething – not with Adrien, but with Vargon. But he knew he would get his just deserts. Silently inside him he apologised to Tayce and the teammates he'd spent so much time with for what he was about to divulge.

The laser crimson point on the overhead silver-toned arm manoeuvred up Dairan's uniformed body to his forehead, stopping just in the centre. It began to pulsate in a drawing movement, as if it was extracting something. It lowered to come into contact with the slightly tanned skin on Dairan's forehead. He began to sweat and his breathing became erratic. He could feel his heart beating in his chest and hear it in his ears. The thought of some machine surfing his every thought and memory was beginning to freak him out. There was a white flash, then a feeling of searing unforgettable pain in the middle of his forehead. The laser began its operation and pressed into his skin. It became like an intense burning, almost too much to bear as it progressed towards the thought region of his mind to extract what Varon Vargon wanted so evilly. Dairan's normally handsome features showed the fight he was putting up against the probing instrument. He almost wanted to cry out, but didn't.

***

On Auran Amalthea Three Marc had picked the Quest team: Lance, Craig, Aldonica, Phean, and Donaldo Tysonne just in case medical emergencies were to arise. Also Donaldo could handle a Slazer just as well as any other member of the team. Twedor was also going because he was now capable of taking part in Quests. Marc suggested urgently to the Quest team that had been picked that they should make sure their combat shooting skills were up to what they should be. If not, to get some practice in before the Quest. The ones that needed it knew it was good advice, as they knew what kind of evil merciless being Vargon was and what he was capable of. Jan Barnford backed Marc up in insisting everyone should be prepared. The picked members all sat around the DC listening to the briefing, but in each of their minds they were forming their own thoughts on what they might be up against, thoughts of the ambush creeping in from time to time. It was as if Jan could pick up on this as he announced that his officers were on the Quest to protect and assist; they had nothing to fear in the way of what happened previously in the ambush. Marc closed the meeting by announcing they would be in the orbit of the Carra Lair battleship in just on two hourons. Without warning, Phean grimaced in pain and almost passed out. He fought against the immense power that was smashing into his very existence. Donaldo jumped to his feet in the capacity of the cruiser's caring physician, going to Phean's side.

"Tell me what's the problem. Where's the pain?" asked Donaldo in true doctor's manner.

"No, no, it's not me. I'm getting a very violent feedback from Tayce. I fear it has something to do with Dairan. Tayce is telling me to change the Invis Shield code immediately," said Phean in between his perseverance to fight the onslaught of Dairan's torture and listen to Tayce's urgent words.

Abruptly it ceased and Phean slumped forward and passed out. Donaldo caught hold of him, pulling him gently up to rest back against the chair back, where he checked his vital signs with an Examscan, which he always carried in his pocket in case of emergencies. Both Marc and Jan looked on in wondering alarm and concern as to what could be unfolding on the Carra Lair.

"Amal, change Invis Shield to a random code now, please," ordered Marc.

"Changing code now, Commander," replied Amal.

Donaldo stayed with Phean until he regained consciousness, whilst everyone watched in concern for both Dairan and Tayce, knowing they themselves would not want to be where they were, at any cost. Marc hoped Auran Amalthea Three's last cruising steps towards the Carra Lair were quick. He didn't like the way things were looking. Phean finally regained consciousness. Donaldo made sure he was all right before returning to duty down on Level 2.

"What happened? Let's hear it," demanded Marc.

"Vargon is mind-surfing Dairan and for a split cencron there was a connection to Tayce. He was apologising to her at the same time she was communicating with me. He was doing his utmost in not divulging the Invis Shield code. The energy that flowed between Tayce and Dairan was strong and fed back to me. I got the full force. It was the equivalent of almost 5,000 volts. If it didn't kill Dairan I would be surprised," explained Phean, shaken.

"Poor Tayce – this isn't looking good," said Marc in concern.

Jan raised his eyes at the information and wondered how long Tayce was going to put up with her treatment at the hands of Vargon. He didn't like it one bit. This was turning out to be a messy situation and one that neither Tayce nor Dairan had anticipated. He couldn't wait to get the current situation sorted, even though they had to get to the destination port of Quest, to get aboard the Carra Lair and do what was needed to stop Vargon and get Tayce back where she belonged, either with or without Sallen.

***

On the Carra Lair, in the holding cell more than an houron later, Tayce was regaining her composure after the jolt that had hit her from what was happening to Dairan, though she hadn't been able to understand why she should have felt a sudden energy surge from him in the first place. It hadn't happened before and he wasn't gifted like herself or Phean. She had mind-linked with Dairan for the first time. Was it because they were thinking of each other and he was at a low ebb, or had the Empire of Honitonia stepped in for some strange reason? It puzzled her, to say the least. Tayce felt it was time to escape her unwanted surroundings. She had to rescue Dairan before Vargon went too far and killed him. She began looking around, and her eye caught something up high that looked ideal for escape. She climbed on to the stonex seat and went to the end and stepped up on to the arm, keeping her ears open for anyone coming. Balancing on tiptoes, she pulled hard at the white Platex panel. To her relief, it was what she thought it was. The panel gave, swinging open. Tayce dropped to the floor, unable to stand on tip-toes any longer. She swore on impact, then waited a few minons to get the feeling back in her feet. Then she climbed back up on to the arm and jumped, grabbing on to the ledge of the open hatchway. She heaved herself up and swung herself up into a tunnel, big enough to crawl through. Once inside, she pulled the hatch closed behind her. Crouching, she began to crawl along the hexagonal duct-type tunnel, which no doubt ran the width of the Carra Lair. She reached a junction and paused in thought, deciding which way to go next. She listened and could hear voices in the distance. She turned the corner and luckily went into what seemed to be an outside corridor duct. Going along with a crawling motion, she checked each grid she came to along the way. Finally she neared where the voices were coming from, looking through a small vent to see a corridor below. Tayce realised the voices were familiar, and they weren't Varon Vargon's or Sallen's. She pushed at the grid, giving it a hefty shove, but on doing so it gave way and she fell headlong out of the duct on to the corridor floor below, landing in an awkward heap. As Tayce righted herself, so a familiar hand came down to offer her a helping hand to help her to her feet. She looked up.

"Nice of you to drop in. At least we won't have to look for you," said Jan Barnford as she came to a standing position.

"How come you're here?" asked Tayce, straightening her uniform.

"Arrived just on ten minons ago. Marc put Auran Amalthea Three into hyper-thrust turbo," replied Jan.

"Let's go. Vargon is at this moment torturing Dairan and I don't want to waste any more time," said Tayce, beginning on up the corridor, very much back in command.

Jan reached for a high-energy rifle on the wall cabinet and ordered Tayce to take it. There was no telling what was going to happen. Tayce accepted it. He had a point, she thought. Sure enough, just as they were about to reach the end of the corridor, the evil Sallen stepped into view, accompanied by ten warriors all brandishing weapons, and they commenced firing. Action commenced. Firepower rang out on both sides. Sallen, suddenly seeing her warriors were at a disadvantage, backed up around the corner, allowing the men to carry on firing on the Amalthean Quests team and Jan Barnford and his SSWAT officers.

Tayce saw what Sallen was up to and called to Jan above the roar of noise: "I'm going after her."

It fell on deaf ears. Twedor slipped past Jan and followed in hot pursuit of his mistress – he was not going to let her go alone. Tayce rounded the corner to find Sallen gone from sight. With the gun fire dropping behind her, Tayce kept her gun primed, wondering where Sallen had vanished to. Twedor came to a pause beside her.

"Twedor, scan and find her," ordered Tayce commandingly.

"It appears she's heading to the medical facility," said Twedor.

"Really? No doubt to help Vargon finish what he set out to do. Not if I've got anything to do with it! Come on – stick close," ordered Tayce, going on.

"Right with you – let's get them," said Twedor, ready for action.

After wiping out the warriors in a powerful onslaught of weapon power, Marc asked Lance for a quick scan of where Tayce and Twedor were heading. Lance depressed a sequence of command keys and waited for the reading. It flashed up and showed two small purple circles heading up to the on-board medical facility. Marc turned.

"Start placing PolloAld bombs, Al, from here to the medical facility. Set them in places around the Carra Lair where the most damage can be caused.

"Yes, sure," said Aldonica heading away.

Jan ordered one of his officers to accompany Aldonica. Rob was his name and he was the tallest and broadest of all Jan's officers. He was along the lines of an American footballer in build. No one would dare argue with him if they found themselves in a confrontation with him. He went with Aldonica and they began discussing where it was best to place the twenty PolloAld bombs she had. They went off down the corridor, Slazers in hand. They had to move about the Carra Lair on full alert. Aldonica carried the silver-toned attaché case containing the twenty bombs ready to use.

"Father, Father, Tayce Traun has escaped from the holding cell and is heading here," said Sallen, running into the medical facility through the opening doors.

Vargon looked up, then hit the on-board alarm activation switch in front of him. The alarm sounded throughout the battleship. Professor Maylen looked at Vargon, then at an unconscious Dairan Loring, still lying on the couch from his mind surf. Vargon thought for a moment, then decided it was time to key in the Invis Shield code he'd managed to extract from Dairan to uncover the Auran Amalthea Three. He called Sallen, leaving the Professor without a care about what he was doing. They slipped out through the entrance and ran round the corner, but not before Twedor fired off a shot at Sallen. Both he and Tayce ran into the medical facility, which Vargon and Sallen had just left, to be greeted by Adrien and Dairan. Adrien was glad to see she was all right and ordered her to go on – he'd take care of Dairan and make sure he made it back to the cruiser OK. Just after Tayce and Twedor had retreated back out into the corridor to head on up to the Operations Deck, Donaldo and the others walked in.

"They've gone after Vargon – heading up to the Operations Deck, I expect," informed Adrien helpfully.

"Don, you take Dairan and Professor Maylen here back to the cruiser. We'll meet you there," suggested Marc in true command.

"Right!" replied Donaldo, crossing to Dairan and the Professor.

Marc and Jan and the rest of the Quest team and SSWAT officers hurried back out of the room and ran on the way to the Operations Deck, following the hand-held scanner in between dodging and returning Slazer fire to the advance second wave of fighting warriors. It wasn't easy.

***

Tayce reached the top of the steps that brought her up from the lower levels. Twedor was behind her. His mobility since being redesigned on Enlopedia had made sure he was as flexible as a small childling of around nine yearons old. Both paused, their guns ready. Twedor looked up at her, wondering what her next move was going to be.

She looked down at him, then announced in near whisper, "It's time to get back what belongs to me – a valuable member of the Amalthean Quests team."

Twedor nodded and began off on Tayce's given word. They walked cautiously, on alert, along the corridor and entered in through the wide-open doorway of the Operations Deck. On the far side Count Varon Vargon stood with his back to the entrance by the side of one of his main operatives. Sallen saw Tayce.

"It's Traun, Father. She's here," announced Sallen discreetly to her father, seeing Tayce over his shoulder.

"Just in time to see me use the code I so wanted. Just think you'll be able to watch your precious cruiser and team be destroyed once and for all," he said smugly.

"You actually think I'd be foolish enough to let you do what you're wishing for? Wrong move!" said Tayce, holding her gun primed to kill Vargon with a single precise shot.

"Oh, and why is that? Tell me, childling," he said, turning to face Tayce with an interest as to why she'd just said what she had.

"Why should I? You seem to have everything under control. Why let me stop you?" said Tayce, knowing the Invis Shield code had been changed as Phean had confirmed it with her earlier.

"You're awfully relaxed for someone that's about to lose everything. I demand you tell me," he replied without thought, as she had just made him very suspicious.

"No! You didn't really think I'd let you get your hands on my cruiser that easily, did you?

"If I want something, young Traun, then I find a way to obtain it, no matter what," he promised coldly.

Vargon turned back to the console. Tayce took aim. Even though she knew the Invis Shield had been changed it didn't stop her from wanting Vargon dead. She was about to shoot when Jan's hand touched hers on the firing button of the Slazer and he took hold of the gun to deter her going ahead with what she was proposing.

"Don't do it. I know how you feel, but don't," said Jan in a near whisper behind her.

Tayce gave him a disappointed look, frustrated that he'd stopped her from getting justice for her people. Vargon turned to see the gathered group, all ready to end his dayons, all with their weapons primed to open fire.

"What's the meaning of this? Intruders? Sound emergency alert in Operations," demanded Vargon, looking straight and hostile at Jan.

"I hereby impound this ship and place you under arrest by order of Enlopedia Headquarters Base for the many crimes you've committed, which are far too many to list. I would suggest you cooperate with my officers here. Let's go," ordered Jan, to the point.

His men had taken up positions and were aiming their Pollomoss handguns ready to shoot on their superior's command if Vargon failed to follow his orders.

"You might think, Chief Barnford, you have won in apprehending me for a possible trial, but not in this instance. Come, Sallen," said Vargon as if he was going to cooperate to a certain degree.

"No chance – she stays with us," spoke up Lance, stepping up and restraining Sallen with all his strength.

“Get off me, Largon. Father, please don’t leave me,” protested Sallen in Lance’s hold.

Without warning, halfway to the entrance and before Jan could give the command, Vargon disappeared in a cloud of green smoke, which made everyone cough and try and get their breath for a few minons. When it had cleared Jan cursed under his breath and ordered his men to stand down. Sallen cried out for her father to no avail.

“He’s gone from this sector. Wherever he’s gone I can’t sense his presence,” spoke up Phean.

Sallen, on these words, broke Lance’s grip and was about to strike at Phean, but a Slazer shot rang out and Sallen crumpled to the Operations Deck floor. Jan looked at Tayce, wondering if she’d done the inevitable and killed Sallen after all.

“It was set to stun, honest!” said Tayce, seeing his surprised questioning look.

Tayce felt angered by the fact he hadn’t let her do what she wanted to do – kill Vargon where he stood. He wouldn’t have had the chance to escape. Still, there was always next time – no doubt Vargon would surface somewhere during the present voyage. He was not the kind to sit back and let her continue with the Amalthean Quests if he could help it. He had one agenda only, and that was to finish the cruiser and her team off. Underfoot, quite suddenly, the first rumbles were felt from the obvious explosions of Aldonica’s placed PolloAld bombs going off at their set timing. Marc suggested they get going. Aldonica had just informed him via Wristlink that she’d just set the last PolloAld, and the others were due to detonate in the next half-houron. Lance hauled an unconscious Sallen up on to her feet. Jan glanced around to notice that where the operatives had been sitting the seats were vacant. They too had vanished.

Tayce wristlinked to Amal: “Get us out of here now, Amal,” she ordered urgently.

Marc contacted Aldonica, warning her to stand by as they were leaving. Aldonica could be heard agreeing. Everyone stood, ready to return to Auran Amalthea Three. The swirling energy aura of the Transpot took on around the group and removed them from the Carra Lair Operations Deck as it began to malfunction. Explosions erupted, small and large, as the PolloAld bombs did their work in wrecking the battleship.

***

Treketa awaited the safe arrival of the team. Donaldo had informed her Sallen was returning, but was unconscious. He had continued on to the MLC to get Dairan and the Professor sorted. The team arrived back in the swirling Transpot. Once fully present, Lance crossed, letting Sallen fall gently on to the ready Hover Trolley. Treketa raised her eyes at the familiar sight of the evil version of Sallen, but said nothing. Activating the trolley, she began forward, informing Tayce as the trolley rose on its cushion of energy that Donaldo wanted to see her when she was through making sure everyone was safely back aboard. Tayce nodded. Treketa walked away behind the Hover Trolley, heading to the MLC. Lance decided to walk along with her as far as the MLC in case Sallen regained consciousness and started any trouble. Tayce waited patiently as Aldonica and one of Jan's officers materialised back on board. The swirling motion brought Rob and Aldonica safely home. Jan sighed, relieved his best officer was OK. Marc hurried on out of the Transpot Centre, talking on his Wristlink, giving orders for Auran Amalthea Three to leave the orbit they were in. Jan stood at ease, his arms folded.

"In less than twenty minons the Carra Lair will be destroyed," said Aldonica

"Great job – well done, both of you." As Tayce said what she did, she felt it was a pity Varon Vargon wasn't going along with his battleship.

"It will take Vargon some time to get back into the spacial swing of things and come after his daughter. When he does, we'll be ready. Good work, Rob," said Jan.

"I'm glad we did what we did," said Aldonica, pleased.

"Not bad for a weaponry specialist. Nice work, miss," teased and praised Jan with a slight smirk on his face.

They began on out of the Transpot Centre. Aldonica headed away to the Weaponry Design Centre to offload her empty case that had held the PolloAld bombs. She said a friendly goodbye to Rob, who had helped her. He gave her a smile and informed her they would probably work again together sometime soon, so until next time. Jan and Tayce walked in the direction of Organisation. Further down the corridor, Rob and the rest of Jan's officers regrouped. Jan paused, ordering them to take a break, but be ready to leave to head back to base.

Tayce waited until the officers were out of the way, then began: "Why did you stop me?"

"From what?" he replied, wondering what she was referring to.

"From killing Vargon and doing the right thing for my people, also ridding this universe of a merciless being such as he is. One shot is all it would have taken – but no, you couldn't let me unleash on that bastard what he so rightfully deserved," she said, beginning to get angry.

"A trial is more adequate for the likes of him. Shooting him would have been too easy," he said back at her in a true chief's tone.

"Well, that's one thing he won't be turning up for, considering he did a disappearing act. Are you going to explain it to the council, because I'm certainly not?" she asked angrily.

"I'll handle it – drop the subject, please, Tayce," said Jan plainly.

"No, Jan. You might think you were protecting me, but when it comes to that bastard I didn't need it. I wanted rightful revenge for the brutally murdered people of my world – people who were my friends, colleagues, teachers and other people of my world, including childlings as young as mere infants. Think about it, Jan. Just how would you feel coming face-to-face with a man who had destroyed everything that made up your history and an ideal world, as you knew it?" retorted Tayce, now shouting at him in the middle of the corridor, just before the Level Steps.

"Next time I'll let you handle it," he said without further word as he could see she was furious.

Tayce said no more. She felt cross to think she hadn't been able to get rid of Count Vargon. She headed on up the Level Steps, not looking back at Jan, trying to calm herself on the way to Level 1.

"You've blown it, chief," said Twedor, seeing how angry his mistress was.

Jan sighed. Sometimes Tayce made his duty hard to do. He watched Twedor head on up to Level 1. He figured he'd get a cup of refreshing Coffeen, then head on up to Organisation and let Tayce calm down. He headed for the Refreshment Centre, thinking over what she'd blurted out at him about Vargon and her people.

***

Auran Amalthea Three left the current orbit. It left behind the vast wreck of the *Carra Lair*. Tayce had rescued Sallen, but had failed to end Count Vargon's days out in the Universe, and she was letting Jan take that information back to Enlopedia to the council. Oh, how she would love to see their faces when he told them! As for Sallen, she would get back her life and memories as a science officer with the help of Professor Adrien Maylen, who had backed up her memories during her reversion to being the evil daughter of Vargon. Adrien had saved the memories on a small chip and had placed it in his pocket when Vargon hadn't been looking. There would be a next time for herself and Varon Vargon, but next time Tayce had declared she wouldn't show him any mercy.

Dairan Loring had been the first victim in the first Quest of the new third voyage, but what had Vargon done to him besides having Adrien mind-surf for the Invis Shield code. Time would tell…

4. Converted Minds

Auran Amalthea Three was in after-duty hourons standby and cruise mode. Amal was in overall charge of the many functions that kept the cruiser travelling on through the night hourons. Sallen Vargon was in a sedated sleep until the next mornet, when, as it had been discussed, the medical computer system with help from Craig Bream and Professor Maylen would carry out the memory-reprogramme technique to put back the memories that were Sallen's (downloaded from Enlopedia) as a science officer. Chief Jan Barnford and his SSWAT officers had departed back to Enlopedia. He had to face the council with the report that he was responsible for Count Vargon's escape – something, he realised, he could have avoided if he'd let Tayce do the unthinkable and kill him.

***

Dairan woke in the double bunk he and Tayce were sharing. He slipped out of the grey silkene sheets, exposing blue silkene PJ bottoms. On standing, he looked like he was absolutely vacant in the eyes and in a daze. He stood for a few minons, then, as if being commanded by some unknown force, he headed over to the Living Area of the quarters to the entrance. Twedor suddenly activated from his standby mode, on Dairan passing. He silently watched Dairan go and watched him walk out through the entrance doors on reaching them. Tayce, after a few minons, rolled over in the bunk, thinking Dairan would be there. Suddenly she sensed something was wrong. She felt the space where he should be beside her, feeling only empty space where he had been lying. She opened her eyes, becoming fully awake in cencrons, with alarm, sitting up and looking about the dimmed surroundings only to find no Dairan. After listening to find out if he was in the Cleanse Unit, and finding he wasn't, she proceeded to get out of the bunk. Twedor came on full operational alert, seeing his mistress do so.

"He left the quarters about twenty-five minons ago. Something doesn't look right. He seemed strange," said Twedor.

"What do you mean, strange?" asked Tayce, frowning at what Twedor said.

"I did a quick scan of his vitals and it was like he was under some kind of influence," replied Twedor.

Tayce on this, reached for her long silkene 'D' gown and slipped it on over her long silkene chemise, doing up the tie belt as she went. Heading from the Repose Centre. Tayce ordered Twedor to follow her. They had to find out what was going on. Both hurried from the quarters through the opening doors into the Level 3 corridor, hurrying along towards the Level Steps. Listening as she went, all Tayce could hear was the sound of the cruiser's fusion quick-reaction engines. Once at the Level Steps, both went on up until Level 2. Tayce wristlinked Amal requesting Dairan's whereabouts.

"Amal, where's Dairan right now?" asked Tayce.

Twedor, looked up at her, wondering why she hadn't asked him as he was scanning Dairan as they walked up from Level 3.

"Dairan's here in Organisation. He's standing in the middle of the centre. His pulse rate is erratic," replied Amal.

"Watch him. I'm on my way up," ordered Tayce.

"Would you like me to notify Dr Tysonne that Dairan is unwell?" asked Amal.

"No not till I get there and see what's what," replied Tayce, thinking on what might be happening.

At the top of Level 1, both Tayce and Twedor walked along into Organisation. Dairan was standing with his back to her at Kelly Travern's navigational console. Tayce entered Organisation quietly, not sure what kind of reception she was going to get. If Dairan was under some kind of powerful hold, there was no telling how violent he could suddenly become when he knew she was there. She tried to see what he was attempting to do. Twedor looked up at her in a questioning way. Dairan turned, meeting Tayce's questioning look of suspicion as to what he was doing near a keypad console in Organisation, especially in the middle of sleep time. He walked towards her. Tayce glanced past him at Kelly's console to see if anything had changed on screen. Other than the home QE screen, nothing was showing. If there had been anything keyed in before her arrival she couldn't see it. Tayce's senses were giving her extreme uneasy feelings. She tried to quell the uneasiness as he came within touching distance of her.

"Is there a problem with our present course?" enquired Tayce, finding it difficult to sense any feelings in Dairan as he looked blankly at her.

He didn't answer.

Tayce decided to push past and check for herself. She began past and, without thought, he reached out grabbing her back – and not in his usual playful manner. It was brutal, and the pain seared into Tayce's upper arm. She'd never known such a tight hurting grip from him before. She looked up, shocked. His whole features had transformed completely into someone she didn't recognise. He now mysteriously had a moustache and beard and his eyes were motionless, dark and filled with evil. It was as if he would kill her, and it freaked her out. Who was this in Dairan's place? she wondered. Sure enough, it was Dairan in build right down to his hair, but that was where the resemblance ended. His behaviour was totally out of character, confirming something was inside possessing Dairan, controlling him, changing his features. He would never hurt her like this. She yanked her arm from his grip. He was not going to stop her from finding what whoever had control of him had done to the cruiser. Twedor didn't like the situation and was prepared to act to protect his mistress. He activated his Slazer finger, putting it on stun. It didn't look good between his mistress and Dairan, he thought. Tayce approached Kelly's console. Looking down, she began to key away to get information about what Dairan might have done. As it materialised, Tayce gave a wide-eyed look and her whole body filled with deathly dread. The destination was one no one with a right mind would ever think of keying, in, unless they wanted to end it all.

Tayce turned on Dairan, furious: "Phenomenon Space! Why, Dairan, why?" she demanded sharply of him.

He looked at her without any hint of remorse for what he'd done. There was nothing of the normal loving and friendly Dairan about him. Whatever was controlling him had drained him of any humanity he had. He came forth towards her in a frightening cold way. Tayce, still furious, found her power-ability senses rising to effect an angered defence against whatever he might do. As he went to grab hold of her in a vicious way, she used her power force against him – something she'd never had to do in the past and would never normally do. With the force she used, Dairan sailed back across Organisation, impacting on the star-chart podium, which knocked the wind out of him, dropping him to the floor. He hit the floor and looked up. The force which had taken him over suddenly diminished, as Tayce came forth angrily to knock him out, he put a hand out to stop her. His features ebbed back to the normal handsome Dairan.

"Tayce, no! It's me – stop!" shouted Dairan in defence, back to normal and feeling like he'd broke a rib.

Tayce slowly calmed herself. Following the use of her powers, she hated herself for what he'd made her do, but she'd had no choice in order to protect herself.

"I think I've busted a rib," said Dairan in pain, clutching his left side, where his ribs were.

"That's nothing compared to what you were going to do to this team. Amal, override the present set course immediately," said Tayce coldly, looking at Dairan with disgust and anger.

"Course corrected. We are back on the original course," confirmed Amal.

Twedor wasn't so sure things were back to normal with Dairan. He was still ready to stun him. In the Organisation doorway Phean appeared. He'd picked up that Tayce was in danger. He'd been in a deep peaceful sleep in his quarters, but Tayce's sense of sudden dread and danger had made him arrive in the present surroundings to help as her Telepathian guide. He stood silently watching. Tayce looked at him as Dairan staggered to his feet with no recollection of what had just occurred in the past twenty minons. Was this what Varon Vargon had done to Dairan? Why the sudden change in appearance? wondered Tayce. It didn't add up. Dairan looked at her, puzzled as to what had just taken place and found Tayce's plain look at him strange. He had no recollection of his actions and it concerned him what he'd done.

"I want you to return to your own quarters for the rest of this night. We'll talk at first light," said Tayce, leaving him with Phean and walking briskly on out, back to her quarters not looking back.

Dairan, unsure of what he'd done, went to follow after her. Phean stepped in his way, advising him not to. Dairan looked at him in a questioning way, feeling regretful and in pain, both at the same time.

"Let her calm down – go back to your own quarters," said Phean to the point.

"I think I've broken a rib," replied Dairan holding his left side in his ribs area.

Phean ordered him to remove his hand and placed his hand instead just a small distance from the area the pain had been emitting from. Within a few minons Dairan was healed. Phean suggested he head back to the Quarters Deck with him. Dairan didn't disagree. Phean wondered if Dairan had really returned to normal or whether this was a cover-up until later. It made him suspicious that Dairan was being so cooperative suddenly. He could quickly use his powers, which were higher in ability to Tayce's, to sort out anything that surfaced at a short notice en route to his quarters and report it to Tayce at first light. Both men walked along, heading back down to the Quarters Deck, Dairan expressing his concern about what had unfolded back in Organisation, though he still had no idea what happened.

Twedor remained in Organisation. He had to link up with Amal on a high frequency to help her further remove the remainder of any course entry to Phenomenon Space. To Twedor's surprise, he discovered their present surroundings had been set on a direct course to what could have been a journey of no return into a nightmare hell. Phenomenon Space was an area of the Universe that was worse than anyone's horrific nightmares. Upon entering the sector, whoever it was had their worst nightmare become reality to such a degree it would drive that person so insane that they wouldn't try to escape and would end up killing themselves with whatever was available to hand. If Auran Amalthea Three had continued on the unscheduled set course, the cruiser would be in the area within three hourons. Just in time for the team to encounter the full effect of each of their nightmare scenarios of no return before waking – hence sudden horrifying death. Twedor went about helping Amal make sure the cruiser did not divert back on to the course of no return. He had authority to change any course if it meant the safety of the whole team was at great risk, especially if it meant loss of life. He checked all traces of the course to Phenomenon Space were eradicated. Once it was cleared, Twedor checked they were back on the original cruise course, then broke his link with Amal, said a goodnight and walked from Organisation, heading on back down to Level 3 to check Tayce was all right.

***

Next mornet Tayce entered the Refreshment Centre. She needed her first cup of Coffeen of the dayon. It was like a pick-me-up and she needed it this mornet. Lance was present, eating his first meal of the dayon – some kind of wheat cereal. He looked up, noticing Tayce was quiet at the drinks and meal dispenser and was saying nothing as she selected her first meal from the meal selection system. He'd known her since childling dayons, when the Universe was a lot more peaceful than it presently was. There was something wrong. He could tell by the way she was standing silently that she was troubled over something. Lance said nothing for a few minons, just watched as she turned. He could tell she hadn't got much sleep in the last hourons. He could see she was making an excellent job of hiding the fact in his presence. He kept quiet. If there was one thing Lance had always found with Tayce, if there was something troubling her she'd tell him in her own time. She crossed and sat opposite him in continued silence. Tayce knew he use to meet Deluca every mornet for the first meal of the dayon and go through some new research. She thought he would probably prefer to eat his meal in silence in respect of the fact Deluca was no longer with them. Lance played along with her silence for a few minons, glancing out through the sight port into the starry spacial scape; then after a while he looked at Tayce, studying her in a gentle questioning way and waiting.

"Not much sleep, then? You look like something is bothering you?" he asked carefully. He wanted to know what.

"It's OK, thanks. I'm gradually working it out in my mind," she replied, saying no more.

"Mornet, you two. Is something wrong, Tayce?" asked Marc, crossing and grabbing a vitamin beverage from the drinks dispenser, also noticing she had something on her mind.

"What is it with this team? A person can't think things through on their own once in a while! Is this not possible any more? If one more of this team tries to be caring and understanding and asks me if there's a problem, I'm going to scream, so just leave me alone," said Tayce in a surprising outburst, leaving her meal and utensils and the table, hurrying from the Refreshment Centre near to tears.

She left Marc and Lance somewhat surprised at her outburst. They exchanged concerned looks at her rushing out. Marc's look was one of startled amazed curiousness. He knew Tayce was prone to put up with so much, then fire off at a moment's notice. But this was out of character. Something was troubling her deeply and it looked like it was close to home. He drank down his vitamin beverage – a nourishing mixture he drank every mornet before duty. It set him up for the dayon ahead and gave him the stamina boost he needed, being second in command. Lance rose to his feet, crossing to the waste panel. He prepared his disposable utensils to put them into incineration. Professor Maylen entered wearing an Amalthean Quests team uniform.

"Mornet, everyone. I think Tayce must have her mind on something important this mornet. She just ignored me in the corridor. That's not like her, is it?" asked Adrien, concerned.

"I've got to check this out. Something is very wrong," said Marc, alarmed.

He raised his Wristlink after disposing of his empty cup in the incinerator and requested from Amal where Tayce was heading at that moment.

"She is on the clear-vision walkway, Commander, and I'm reading her vital signs as distressed," announced Amal.

Lance heard Amal's reply and hung around until Marc had deactivated his Wristlink. He looked at him, wondering if he'd like him to help in any way. Marc suggested he head on to duty, but keep an eye on Dairan. Lance looked at Marc, surprised at his request, but agreed, heading on out. Twedor entered the Refreshment Centre. He wanted to inform Marc of what had happened during the night hourons before. Adrien pretended not to listen as Twedor began explaining to Marc the occurrence resulting in the sudden and deathly change of course and the act of Dairan stopping Tayce from reaching the navigational console to check what had happened, even though she eventually had. He found what had unfolded interesting. Twedor concluded by telling Marc how Dairan had changed totally in appearance and became extremely violent towards Tayce – so much so that Twedor was prepared to stun him with his Slazer finger. Marc gave an alarmed look, but nodded in total understanding of what Twedor was trying to express. He'd known Dairan right back from the beginning of the second voyage, and he'd never ever witnessed cruelty towards Tayce on Dairan's behalf. He found it totally strange and thought about it seriously for a moment. Adrien rose to his feet, apologising for intruding but saying he could tell by what Twedor was explaining thar their worst fears had been confirmed. Count Vargon had fed something in a liquid form into Dairan's mind whilst Sallen had him held at gunpoint during the probe.

"I couldn't do anything about it – I'm sorry, Marc," apologised Adrien sincerely.

"It's fine. I know what a bastard Vargon can be," assured Marc.

They both realised that, whatever Vargon had administered to Dairan in drug form, if they didn't do something soon he could turn more violent towards Tayce and even kill her when no one was around, or try to destroy the cruiser. Something Vargon would smile about. Marc realised he had to find Tayce. Adrien walked out of the Refreshment Centre with Marc in shared conversation, concerned for both Tayce and Dairan.

"What do you propose? This situation is obviously the result of what happened on the Carra Lair," confided Marc, worried and wanting to know what to do for the best.

"We get Dairan to take another scan/surf, only one a lot deeper. He would have to be sedated," replied Adrien.

"I'm quite sure whatever it takes to get him back to normal Tayce will agree with," assured Marc.

"I'll stun him," spoke up Twedor eagerly. He didn't like what Dairan had done to his mistress in the night hourons previously and it wasn't like he was breaking his Romid rules by stunning Dairan, though he was not permitted to kill someone unless absolutely life-threatening to his mistress.

"The offer is much appreciated, mate, but it has to be done medically. I have to treat Sallen in ten minons – Donaldo is putting her at the moment through pre-checks for the procedure. Find Tayce – tell her I will help and what I propose. As soon as I've returned Sallen to being your science officer and destroyed the 'evil daughter' information, I'll meet you and Tayce. When it's done, I'll contact you on Wristlink," explained Adrien.

"Right! I'll go and check on Tayce," said Marc.

Marc went on towards the clear-vision walkway. Twedor walked down at his side silently. Adrien headed on to the MLC. At the entrance his thoughts were on what he could do with Dairan, not knowing what Count Vargon had fed into the young man's mind. He entered the MLC, the doors closing behind him. Over on the far side of the centre Sallen lay under sedation on the cream medical bunk. Treketa stood by as Donaldo announced all final checks were complete. Adrien walked to the portable hand-held control and depressed the activation. The reprogram-of-memory machine sequence began booting up. The laser point on the long silver-toned arm manoeuvred into place at the central point of Sallen's forehead. It stopped, then began to pulsate. Sallen's evil thoughts, which her evil father had planted back in her mind, were slowly wiped away, transferring to a disk chip. Adrien, when it was completed, removed the disk chip, ordering Treketa to throw it into the medical incinerator. He then put the disk chip that contained the science-tech memories into the reader and proceeded to place the memories up until the point of the ambush back on Amalthea Two back into Sallen's mind, stopping short of the actual ambush by five hourons. Treketa took great pleasure in crossing to the medical waste incinerator and depositing the disk chip into it and pressing the activation key. The evil memories stolen from the Medical Memory Archives at Enlopedia were no more; the evil Sallen of Carra and Varon was gone, never to be found. The memories of gentle Sallen, science officer and lover of plants and the Lab Garden Dome, began entering Sallen's mind and giving her back her life as part of the Amalthean Quests team, bringing her back to the moment five hourons before she was abducted. Everyone present was waiting with eager anticipation, ready to explain innocently what Sallen was doing in the MLC. Sallen's features were clear, normal-looking now, with no traces of the evil black immaculate make-up that went to make up the evil daughter. Adrien checked the screen and keyed in the final sequence to complete the task. This closed Sallen's mind from receiving any more information disk-chip-wise, as all had been restored. This would return Sallen to a normal sleeping pattern. Adrien finished. His job was done. Now they had to wait for Sallen to wake in roughly one houron.

"We have another problem, Doctor," announced Adrien as the machine retracted back into its sleep state.

"Not with Sallen surely?" asked Donaldo, looking at Treketa then at Adrien questioningly.

"No – Dairan. You know we scanned him the moment we returned from the Quest?" asked Adrien.

"Yes – we didn't find anything out of the ordinary. What's happened?" asked Donaldo, wondering what was the problem?

"Yes, what is it?" added Treketa, exchanging concerned looks, interested, standing beside Donaldo.

"It would appear Vargon did do something quite alarming to Dairan: he gave him a drug that changed him. Around 0200 hourons last night hourons Tayce found him in Organisation with – would you believe? – changed features. It's not known how they materialised, other than it was due to something the Count did when Sallen had me at gunpoint. It would appear that when Tayce found him he'd keyed in a journey that would have taken us all into an area of space known as Phenomenon Space," expressed Adrien to both Treketa and Donaldo, who were totally surprised.

"That's certainly something the Dairan we know wouldn't do. He loves his life in the team and especially Tayce," said Treketa, shocked.

"You're right, Treketa. What do you want to do, Professor?" asked Donaldo, giving Adrien his full attention.

"Help get Dairan back to normal, but…" said Adrien, pausing in thought for a moment.

"Is there a problem? Surely it's just a matter of sedating him," said Donaldo in a questioning tone.

"At first that's what I thought, but it seems Vargon's much too clever. Whatever he'd done it allows Dairan to revert back to normal mode from time to time, without any recollection of what he's just done to Tayce or of nearly sending this team and cruiser to the equivalent of hell. He's unpredictable," replied Adrien.

"Tricky and dangerous," said Donaldo, now also in thought.

"How's Tayce? She's very close to him – he's her life off duty. Since Tom died, her husband, she and Dairan have grown real close," said Treketa, knowing so.

"Shocked, apparently, that he made her use her power ability against him," replied Adrien.

"That's terrible. Poor Tayce! She must be really feeling it," said Treketa, feeling sorry for Tayce.

"Marc's gone to find her and talk to her. I said we'd see how Sallen recovers, then I'll contact Marc and tell him what we can do, if that's all right with you?"

"Yes, fine," replied Donaldo with a nod, in thought.

All three turned to look at Sallen, then stood in discussion about what could be done to help safely catch Dairan and get him to the present surroundings for treatment. Behind them, on the overseer, Sallen's vital signs were returning to normal. She was coming home, so to speak, as science officer of the Amalthean Quests team and janitor of the Lab Garden Dome.

***

Phean, being Tayce's telepathic guide, had decided to step in and help Tayce. He had picked up that she'd felt bad about what she'd had to do to Dairan, sending him hurtling across Organisation earlier. He entered the clear-vision walkway in his soft gentle way. He walked towards Tayce, who had her back to him, just staring out into the passing stars in thought. He put a friendly hand on her shoulder, gently squeezing it.

"Tayce!" he said softly.

She turned, looking up, meeting his soft and caring Honitonian blue eyes. He smiled a reassuring smile, assuring her that everything would work itself out. Tayce knew she could confide in him. She had when they suffered the ambush back at the beginning of the voyage. Unbeknown to Tayce, Phean had another side to him too, but it was far from harmful. Both he and Tayce sauntered to the nearby seating in the ledge of the sight port and sat down. Phean used open communication – he'd done so since they'd first met.

"What's your greatest fear right now? Tell me," asked Phean, turning his head to face her, ready to listen.

"Losing Dairan. He's come to mean a lot to me, both on duty and off," replied Tayce, finding it easy to open up to Phean.

"If you would allow me, I'd like to help. After all, that's what I'm on board for; and, as you know, last night hourons I witnessed Dairan's out-of-character behaviour. I'd like to assist in any way I can to bring Dairan back to you. Let me give you some advice, just passed from the Emperor of Honitonia down to me: you have to put yourself above this, hold on to Dairan's true side. You'll be forced to feel you're doing wrong in the next couple of hourons, but all you have to do is believe Dairan will win through this, he'll come back. You must not falter," advised Phean carefully and gently.

"I understand. I guess I need to pull myself together, huh?" said Tayce.

"I wouldn't say that. You're very close to Dairan and you're frightened of losing him as you did Tom."

"How do you know about me and Tom Stavard?" asked Tayce, glancing at him, surprised.

"The Empire prepared me for life here. I had knowledge of your life with Tom, amongst other things. Please don't concern yourself – you've nothing to fear from me," said Phean in a soft tone of assurance.

At the entrance to the walkway, Marc paused with Twedor, watching the conversation between Tayce and Phean. Phean turned and rose to his feet, reminding Tayce of the message from the Empire of Honitonia. He then informed her that if she needed him she only had to mind-link and he would be there. With this, he walked from the clear-vision walkway, better known as the Think Tunnel, heading off down the corridor. Marc glanced after him in thought. Even though Phean was fitting into the team very well, there was still something strange about him. What, he couldn't quite put a finger on. Maybe it was the fact he was from Honitonia. Marc's Wristlink sounded in a sequence of small bleeps. He glanced at Tayce, then depressed the Comceive on his Wristlink. Professor Maylen's voice came through sounding urgent. He requested both himself and Tayce meet him in the MLC without delay. Tayce, upon hearing the urgency in the Professor's voice, rose to her feet as Marc informed him they were on their way. Marc deactivated his Wristlink and followed Tayce out of the Think Tunnel, heading back along Level 3.

***

Half an houron later in Organisation without any warning Dairan slipped back to Varon (pronounced Var-on). Vargon's orders of programmed mind control changed his appearance back to the bearded features once more to carry out the destruction of Auran Amalthea Three. He'd been discussing research information with Lance quite innocently, then his eyes took on a blank glazed look and his features began to change. Lance had given a taken-aback look and was slowly reaching for his Slazer in case he needed to stun Dairan. Dairan was totally changed to the point where his present surroundings no longer registered. Everyone in Organisation was shocked at the change in Dairan's features and what he'd become in cencrons. Lance got to his feet.

"Come on, mate – you don't want to do this," said Lance persuasively.

Dairan ignored Lance. He just looked at him with an evil cold glance. There was no emotion in his normally warm brown eyes.

"Nick, call Marc – tell him Dairan's working for Vargon again," said Lance.

Dairan pushed Lance with sudden force back against the console, so much so that it winded him. Kelly helped Lance to his seat. Behind them, Nick was alerting Marc to the fact of what was unfolding. Craig came into Organisation, wondering what was happening. Lance pointed to Dairan, who was now standing with his back to them, not moving.

"Let him go – don't stop him," shouted Lance.

Dairan continued on out of Organisation. Lance, getting his wind back, ordered Kelly to give him Track Vid Cam throughout Auran. Kelly did as requested. Lance tracked Dairan on the corridor Vid Cam. Nick soon joined Lance, watching Dairan head down the corridor. Kelly watched also.

***

In the MLC Marc's Wristlink sounded as he, Tayce, Professor Maylen and Donaldo stood discussing Dairan and how to go about helping to rid the revenge on Auran Amalthea Three from his mind. Marc answered the Wristlink. Tayce could hear Lance passing on the urgent information about just what was unfolding with Dairan. She began heading for the entrance, much to the others' surprise.

"Get everything prepared. Donaldo, you're with us. Bring your new Medical Crisis Kit. Come on, Marc – let's get this sorted," said Tayce, sounding the true captain, who had had enough.

They slipped out through the parting entrance doors and broke into a sprint down the Level 2 corridor to the Level Steps. Tayce, ahead of the others, paused long enough to grab a fully charge Pollomoss from the emergency wall store, setting it to stun as she continued. Marc caught up with her, Twedor not far behind, in hot pursuit with Donaldo, wondering what she was going to do. They all hit the steps, running down one behind the other. Lance kept Marc informed over Wristlink as to where Dairan was heading. The main electronics shut down for the whole cruiser. Tayce knew that under Vargon's fed orders Dairan would no doubt try and destroy Auran. If he gained access to the centre he would try to cause untold damage that could cripple the whole cruiser. She ran down the last flight of steps to get on to Level 5, followed by Marc, Twedor and Donaldo. Then she briskly walked towards the Electronics Centre. There, ahead, Tayce could see Dairan stood at the entrance, keying in his access authorisation code to gain entry. Tayce wasted no time – she took aim, put her feelings aside and spoke in a true tone of command.

"Step away from the entrance, Dairan. Now!" ordered Tayce in a no-nonsense tone.

Dairan turned his head in her direction and stared at her, then continued on with what he was doing.

"You leave me no choice, Dairan."

"Do what you have to do, Tayce Amanda," said Dairan in Vargon's tone, much to everyone's surprise.

He left the keying-in and proceeded towards her under ordered control. One thing was on his mind: if he couldn't get access to the Electronics Centre, then he would kill her instead. As he neared Tayce, she fired without thought. Dairan looked at her and all the strange influence of Vargon's mind control had vanished again. He was back in his normal control. He dropped to the floor with a startled look on his handsome features, wondering why she'd just shot him. Tayce lowered the gun, cursing Vargon. Donaldo came forth with the Hover

Trolley and Medical Crisis Kit. He set it down and activated the Hover Trolley. It manoeuvred into position to take Dairan on board. Marc slowly took the Pollomoss from Tayce's grasp, then hugged her. He deactivated the gun whilst Donaldo moved the Hover Trolley into position. He and Marc then placed an unconscious Dairan on board.

"How come Tayce got to shoot him? I could have saved all this as I did volunteer earlier," said Twedor.

"Are you going to be all right?" asked Donaldo, noticing Tayce in thought.

"Yes, I'm fine. It was just the thought of having to stun someone you care about," replied Tayce.

"Could have been avoided if you'd let me do it," said Twedor, his words falling on deaf ears.

"I understand, really. Would you like to come along and see what we find?" offered Donaldo.

"No one listens to the Romid," said Twedor, walking off, mumbling.

"I'll go on up to Organisation and take command. He'll be OK," assured Marc, squeezing Tayce on the shoulder.

"I know," said Tayce, feeling better, hoping she'd never again have to do what she'd just done.

Marc called out to Twedor, who mumbled something under his little Romid breath, but paused. Donaldo and Tayce walked to the Deck Travel, whilst Marc headed for Organisation. Strong electronic restraints were keeping Dairan on the Hover Trolley, just in case he came to and went back under Vargon's mind control and tried to escape and cause more havoc. They soon entered the Deck Travel and were on their way to Level 2. On Level 2 Professor Maylen was waiting as they came from the Deck Travel. In his hand, he held a deep mind-relaxant sedative in a Comprai Inject Pen. Donaldo took it, holding it against Dairan's upper arm. He pressed the release and the sedative hit home in Dairan's bloodstream. They all continued on along towards the MLC. Tayce explained as they went what she'd had to do. The doors opened to the MLC on their approach and they all entered. Sallen, who had gained consciousness and had been cleared by Adrien, stood just on the other side ready to head back to her quarters. Donaldo and Adrien continued on over to the medical bunk to prepare Dairan. Tayce paused in the doorway.

"Welcome back to the team, Sallen," said Tayce casually, sounding glad she was back, even though her mind was on Dairan's current trouble.

"I'm glad to be back. For a moment I thought I'd woken to an illusion, until I asked Treketa to pinch me. Now I know we weren't raided by that evil-looking vessel out in space," replied Sallen, thinking the ambush hadn't taken place at the end of the last voyage.

"Where are you going now? Shouldn't you be taking it easy?" asked Tayce in a concerned tone.

"My quarters. Professor Maylen advises me to take time to adjust from my illness. It was good of him to come on board and get me well. According to Treketa, it was serious. I'll also check on the Lab Garden Dome once I've cleansed and changed," said Sallen, having no real recollection of what truly unfolded or of being on the Carra Lair.

"We'll talk later if you want on what we can do next with the dome," assured Tayce.

"Yes, of course. I hope poor Dairan can be cured. Treketa told me he's been infected by a strange source," said Sallen, having no idea it was her father that had done the evil deed.

Tayce was pleased by the way in which Treketa had told a very convincing cover-up to Sallen, hiding what really happened other than the fact she had been through a mind change, back to the real Sallen. Tayce turned to see Sallen walk out of the MLC and the doors close behind her. At least one situation had been solved. She turned back to see Dairan stretched out, now under the laser arm of the memory-reprogramming machine. Treketa was attaching the Counter Medical Discs, to keep track of Dairan's heart rate, blood pressure and general vital signs during the memory deep-probe scan, to find what Varon Vargon had hidden deep, to surface later for his evil pleasure. Tayce paused, thinking that if only he hadn't leapt into the energy field from Vargon, on the last Quest, he wouldn't be going through this ordeal and she wouldn't have had to stun him. She guessed he'd done it because he wanted to protect her. The Professor key-pressed a sequence whilst watching the screen above Dairan's head. Dairan's memories flashed by on the screen, then, locked deep in the character area of his brain, it sat. Adrien sighed upon seeing what he feared. He turned, calling Tayce nearer. She was concerned as she approached.

"I'm far from pleased at this. Vargon has done a really evil job this time. There it is – the source that is causing all these life-changing occurrences. If it isn't removed extremely carefully, it will either kill him, or paralyse him for the rest of his life," said Adrien straight.

"My God, what can we do?" asked Tayce, almost speechless.

"It may mean travelling to Enlopedia," said Adrien quietly.

"That's a must if you decide it has to be done, but what happens if he reverts back into the problem in mid flight and goes berserk?" asked Donaldo, seriously concerned that any one of them on board could get hurt.

"There is a way to subdue this. We have to create a mind block. It would be something perhaps yourself or Phean could do, you both being gifted. This would enable him to reach Enlopedia safely," suggested Adrien.

"Tell me straight: can this be cured? Can you honestly promise it can be eradicated for good?" asked Tayce, greatly worried.

"I can't see any problem. The full procedure on Enlopedia will give me a better chance of removing the evil source without damage, with help from my team," he assured her with a reassuring kind smile.

"Then we'll do it. I need to contact my father, the Admiral, to make this a top priority. We'll need an emergency escort to your lab when we arrive," decided Tayce.

"I'll contact my team, have them prepare and standing by," offered Adrien.

Tayce headed back to the entrance to the MLC. As she reached the doors and they drew apart she glanced back at a lifeless Dairan before heading on out. Treketa crossed to Donaldo, telling him she was concerned for Tayce. He listened, taking on board what she was saying. Preparations began to find the ideal mind block for Dairan. Phean was requested to attend the MLC. Adrien and Donaldo discussed what needed to be taken into consideration, then Adrien used Donaldo's Officette to contact his team on Enlopedia to find out just what could be done and if his old team of extremely skilled experts could assist at the Complex for Mind Study, Health and Neurology.

***

Twenty minons later, Tayce entered Organisation. Marc looked up. She walked across the centre, ordering Nick to contact Admiral Traun on Enlopedia and have the communication transferred to the DC. Nick agreed, carrying out the urgent request. Marc ordered Lance to take over. He immediately did so. Marc noticed the worried look on Tayce's face as she passed. He walked on into the DC to see if there was anything he could do to help. When he stepped in, Tayce was on the Telelinkphone, talking with her father, explaining what had happened to Dairan and what she wanted, and asking if he could help. Marc leant on the door jamb, waiting to hear what was happening. Tayce soon finished her call, placed the ultra-slim handset back on its base and turned her attention to him.

"I've spoken with father. He said Dairan will be given top priority and first-class treatment. He'll make sure Professor Maylen has everything and everyone he needs to treat Dairan upon our arrival," said Tayce much relieved.

"I take it Donaldo and the Professor found something serious during the mind surf?" asked Marc calmly.

"Yes, Professor Maylen's found something deep locked away in the character part of Dairan's brain – the area that makes Dairan who he is. He's got to go to Enlopedia to the Professor's special Complex for Mind Study, Health and Neurology to get the treatment to erase the placed problem," explained Tayce.

"Do you want to go? I can take charge of the cruiser until you get back," he suggested.

"Actually, I was going to ask you to fly Dairan and the Professor there," put Tayce.

"Sure, I just thought owing to your close relationship with Dairan you'd want to follow what happens and be there, also to talk to your father regarding the proposal the council put to you and see if there's an update," suggested Marc.

"I would like to go, but what if…?" she began, but suddenly stopped.

"Vargon comes around? Tayce, I feel we won't be seeing him anytime soon, considering what Aldonica said she had done in the placing of the PolloAld bombs during our last encounter with him."

"You would call me if anything happens?" asked Tayce, studying him.

"Of course – I promise. Anyhow, you don't get to do much flying these dayons – you'll get rusty," he teased.

"Then that's settled – I'll fly to Enlopedia," she said, rising to her feet.

Tayce walked on across the DC, heading out into Organisation, telling everyone she'd see them in a couple of dayons, then leant close to Lance, informing him that if there was any trouble from Vargon she wanted calling and asking him to keep an eye on Marc in her absence. Lance agreed, wishing her all the best regarding Dairan. Twedor waited for Tayce by the entrance to Organisation. Both walked on out. Marc watched Tayce go, hoping Dairan could be cured for her sake.

***

One houron later in the Flight Hangar Bay Tayce was down in Quest 1, her shuttle/fighter, doing preliminary checks before departure. Twedor was by her side. Phean entered the bay and walked to Quest 1. Tayce looked to see him approaching then back to running the system checks with Amal. Phean soon boarded, pausing in the area just behind Tayce's pilot seat. She finished the final checks then turned to face him. Professor Maylen and Donaldo were approaching with a half-dazed Dairan.

Phean put a reassuring hand on Tayce's shoulder and smiled. "He'll be fine – you'll see. Do you want me to keep an eye on Marc whilst you're on Enlopedia?"

"Lance is; but yes, please keep me informed of what's happening back here," agreed Tayce.

"I'd better let you get under way. Safe trip. See you later," said Phean, heading on out of the interior of the shuttle/fighter.

Tayce looked at a now secured Dairan, in the passenger seat in a half-drugged state. She knew one thing: when she came face-to-face with Varon Vargon next time, she'd kill him. Even if Jan Barnford tried to stop her, she'd find a way. Professor Maylen sat opposite Dairan, securing himself for take-off. Tayce depressed a key that sealed the entrance doors. Marc came over the Aircom.

"Clear for departure when ready. Safe journey."

"Thanks, Marc. See you soon. Phean says he'll work closely with you while I'm absent," said Tayce.

"Right – I hope all goes well," replied Marc casually.

Tayce ceased communications and began powering up the powerful engines to full power, for heading on out of the Flight Hangar Bay. She manoeuvred Quest 1 up off the flight-bay floor. Ahead, the almost floor-to-ceiling hangar-bay doors drew apart. Tayce brought the Quest 1 into line ready to head off down the floor to the doors, pausing for a cencron, then headed on out of the bay through the open doors into space. Once clear of Auran Amalthea Three, she put the shuttle/fighter into top speed, shooting off into the Universe in the blink of an eye, destination Enlopedia. Professor Maylen, on board Quest 1, kept an eye on Dairan, making sure he was all right, carrying out constant checks with help from Donaldo and his Examscan.

"We'll be at Enlopedia in roughly an houron," said Tayce over her shoulder.

"You're doing your best, Tayce. Let's just hope we've done enough to hold what's happening to Dairan at bay for that long," said Adrien.

***

At Enlopedia Headquarters Base, Adam was in communication by Satlelink relay link with Marc, who was informing him Tayce was on her way. Once Adam placed the handset down on the desktop he headed on into the Admiral's Chambers to inform him as much. Upon entering the chambers he walked in on a conversation between Darius and Empress Tricara about important improvements at the schooling complex. They paused as Adam stood waiting for their attention. Darius looked questioningly at Adam, wondering what was wrong.

"Tayce is on her way here with Donaldo, Professor Maylen and Dairan," informed Adam.

"Contact the Complex for Mind Study, Health and Neurology. Tell them to stand by for their arrival," ordered Darius.

"Yes, sir" replied Adam, heading on back out to do as his chief requested.

"Did I hear him say Dairan?" asked Tricara in soft listening interest. "I heard a bit of the problem of what's happening – Phean has to report to me occasionally."

"Varon Vargon, in an attempt to gain Auran Amalthea Three's Invis Shield code, mind-surfed Dairan's mind. It's been somewhat of a tricky situation. He not only tried to kill Tayce, but he nearly sent the whole team and cruiser to the equivalent of hell – Phenomenon Space, would you believe?" explained Darius to Tricara's utter surprise.

"How awful! But why the need for the Mind Study, Health and Neurology visit?" asked Tricara.

"It would appear there's something left behind in Dairan's mind and it's changing him literally into a fighting machine at Vargon's bidding. What they have to do is extremely tricky and can only be done by the team here under Professor Adrien Maylen's guidance," explained Darius.

"Poor Tayce! Not only does she have to live in fear of that barbarian – who, I might add, should have been struck down yearons ago – she now has to deal with wondering if Dairan will return to the way he should be," replied Tricara.

"Believe me, after this I think if she comes face-to-face with Vargon again she won't take any orders not to do just that; she'll take matters into her own hands if I know Tayce," said Darius.

"Kill Varon once and for all, you mean?" asked Tricara casually.

"Yes! I think that man if you could call him that, had better watch his barbaric back," said Darius in thought.

"Are you seeing her when she arrives, only I'd love too as well?" asked Tricara.

"I'll tell her, but I fear her time will be filled with Dairan and returning to Auran Amalthea Three amongst other important issues."

"If she can't, I'll be out in space next weekon. I can drop by Auran Amalthea Three then. I'll leave the documents on the complex for your perusal and wait to hear what you think about my proposal," she announced casually, then headed on over to the entrance.

"It will get my reading attention, I promise. I will let you know soon," assured Darius.

Tricara walked elegantly from the Admirals Chambers, meeting with Lydia walking in. Both women met with a friendly exchange of greetings. They had been friends and business confidantes for many yearons when each had her own home world. Lydia entered the chambers and crossed to the Coffeen dispenser jug on the stand. She poured herself a refreshing cup and took the first sip, then sighed. It had been a busy couple of hourons in meetings. Darius looked up from the papers.

"I need this," she said, exasperated at what she'd had to endure in the meetings.

"Problem?" asked Darius, generally interested, as he always was in Lydia's business affairs.

"Nothing I can't handle. I have a group of off-base dignitaries who are hesitating in joining Enlopedia to exchange supplies and personnel, but I feel if I could just prove to them how Enlopedia has done in the last yearons, in contributing to the space economy since the demise of Questa, I could clinch a deal that would benefit us as well as them," explained Lydia, fed up.

"You'll win through – I know you. What about help from Waynard? He'd be ideal to do a talk. He has been with Questa and seen Enlopedia evolve. Maybe he's the ace you need," put Darius.

"Unfortunately he's on leave at the moment," replied Lydia, seeing that it would have been a good idea.

"Yes, but he'll back by first light. I can leave word you would like to see him tomorron, if you like," said Darius, sounding helpful.

"That would be great," replied Lydia.

Darius nodded and gave her a reassuring smile, then changed the subject, informing her Tayce had left Auran Amalthea Three just on a half an houron ago. Lydia glanced at her Wristcall time display. She wanted to meet Tayce when she arrived in port. Both she and Darius went through what had been happening that dayon aboard Enlopedia and what had come in from Adam in the way of things needing their immediate attention on the base – i.e. invitations, etc. They would do this every dayon of the weekon, and sometimes offer each other solutions to the many matters arising.

***

Out in space about two milons away and closing by the cencron, was Tayce's Quest 1 shuttle/fighter. Tayce, on board, glanced over her left shoulder in the pilot seat to see Dairan still in his calm glazed state. Looking back to see Enlopedia coming into view, communications began with the flight control for arrival and docking. An exchange of commands plus security checks was passed back and forth to enable permission to arrive and dock at the High-Ranked Private Port. Whilst this was going on, various vessels of all shapes and sizes, including Transpo Launches, departed, flying around Auran Amalthea Three's Quest 1 shuttle/fighter on their way out into space. Finally Tayce could head into the port designated area to complete docking.

Once accomplished, she soon switched off the small but powerful engines. Undoing her harness, she hit the entrance-hatch button. The entrance began slowly opening. Professor Maylen stood and crossed to step out into the outside. Tayce unharnessed Twedor from the co-pilot seat. He stood up. Tayce followed on out behind him. Professor Maylen's team introduced themselves to Tayce. There were both male and female members. The team soon were taking control and removing Dairan. Tayce stood to one side with Twedor in front of her. Dairan paused and looked at her, and for a split cencron it was as if he was somehow saying sorry for what had unfolded, that it was out of his control.

"We'll take it from here. I'll contact you on Wristlink the moment we're successful. Don't worry," Adrien said to Tayce.

"I'll wait to hear," said Tayce, concerned, wondering if everything would be all right.

The team, headed by Professor Maylen, headed away, with Adrien giving his orders as they went out of sight off towards the Complex for Mind Study, Health and Neurology. Tayce watched until they were all out of sight, with Donaldo following, then turned to slip the de-locking key in the locking port beside the entrance. Twedor waited patiently. Lydia came into view in her silkene trouser-suit-type uniform, in navy with a high stand-up collar. Tayce finished keying in the lock code to secure Quest 1, then turned to see her mother – something she was glad of. Lydia came to a soft pause, looking as beautiful and as graceful as ever.

"Welcome home. Are you all right? I've just seen Dairan heading with the Professor and his team to the complex for treatment," said Lydia, noticing her daughter's despondent look.

"I don't know what to think after what's happened," replied Tayce, downhearted.

"Come on – let's go home and have something to eat. We can talk more there," said Lydia in her true caring motherly manner, slipping her arm around her daughter's shoulders.

Lydia guided her daughter back to E City Square. Twedor walked along silently just in front of them, looking about, trying to avoid people as they walked out into the main walkway. As soon as Tayce emerged into the simulated natural light of Enlopedias E City Square, dayon-hourons personnel on patrol, or walking to their destination, welcomed Tayce back to base. As usual E City was growing busy with the changeover of duty personnel from dayon- to night-hourons shift, and after-hourons entertainment establishments were getting busy. Patrols changed over in the secure watchful locations, ever alert in case trouble broke out. Twedor slipped his blue metlon hand into Tayce's left slender hand, applying the right amount of gentle pressure to grasp. Mother, daughter and Twedor crossed the square, heading to the Traun residence, but as they went Tayce found her thoughts were on what Dairan was going through.

***

The Complex for Mind Study, Health and Neurology was a building overlooking Enlopedia Parklands, an area that had once seemed nothing more than a barren no-man's-land. But Darius Traun had put forth an order that there should be a peaceful and tranquil area at the back of the complex, so that anyone staying as a patient, receiving operative surgery or other treatment relating to the mind, could relax when recovering. The complex and grounds covered a vast area, roughly three-quarters of a milon in diameter. It was constructed around the same time Enlopedia became the new main base after the explosive demise of Questa. But to begin with the building was vacant and the grounds nothing more than rubble, until it was designated to Professor Adrien Maylen, who put forth his idea to build a complex related to the mind. Darius Traun gave the project his full backing and the complex was now joined with the Medical Dome. They worked together, both medically and professionally. On Level 2 Dairan Loring, under Adrien Maylen's orders, was booked in and guided by the medical staff ready to begin at first light the extraction and termination of what Count Varon Vargon had placed in the character part of his brain. A treatment that would hopefully restore him to his true being. A young female tech was close at hand behind the screen as he changed into the operative attire of plain cream leisure suit, vest and trousers in a casual design. Once Dairan was changed and ready, the young tech explained that the unit he was in would adequately take care of his needs for the duration of his stay. Dairan listened, nodding. The young tech handed him a Porto Compute for him to study and relax with, announcing that she would collect him in the mornet and he would soon feel sleepy as his sedative took affect. With this she walked from the room. Dairan stood and sauntered over to the sight pane. He looked out, down to the Parklands area, which was lit by decorative night lighting. The doors to the room opened behind him. Adrien entered carrying a Comprai Inject Pen. He crossed the floor as Dairan turned.

"More injections?" asked Dairan, hoping not.

"Sorry, Dairan – this is just to keep at bay what Vargon has placed in your brain. Tomorron we'll be removing what's there. It won't be long before you're back to normal," assured Adrien as he gave Dairan the injection.

"Did we come here alone – only I can't remember?" Dairan enquired.

"No, Tayce is here and Twedor. Tayce flew you here," explained Adrien, pressing the release on the Comprai Inject Pen.

"I see. Am I allowed to see her before we begin this lengthy procedure in the mornet?" asked Dairan softly.

"Unfortunately no. Right now she would rather you rest for this treatment tomorron."

"She doesn't want to see me. I understand, even though I can't remember what I did back on Auran. OK," said Dairan, disappointed.

"Get some rest. I'll see you at first light," said Adrien, patting Dairan reassuringly on the shoulder.

He then headed back to the entrance, walking from the white sterile room, the door automatically opening to let him through and closing behind him. Dairan turned back to look down on the Parklands below. His thoughts were on Tayce and what she might be doing right there and then. He felt isolated. He felt also he'd been wrenched from what his life had become and dumped in the middle of nowhere. 'Roll on tomorron,' he thought. After a while he walked back to the bunk as he was beginning to feel sleepy. He just had enough time to answer the medical procedure questions that had to be filled in on the Porto Compute. As soon as they were completed sleep took over and he was mornet-bound.

***

At first light once Tayce was up, cleansed and dressed she decided to head over to the Complex for Mind Study, Health and Neurology to see how things were progressing with Dairan. Twedor accompanied her, explaining how she had to meet up with her father later in his chambers. Daytime duty personnel were heading as usual to their duty. Tayce reached the middle of the square and saw Jamie Balthansar heading to the Construction Port. She decided to catch him. Glancing at her Wristlink time display, she knew she had time to talk with him to tell him there was a fault with the new intruder system.

"Jamie!" she called.

"Tayce, what are you doing here?" he asked warmly pleased to see her. "I didn't see Auran Amalthea Three dock."

"I've had to fly one of the team here. I just want to say the new intruder system you installed on Auran could do with a lot more work. It didn't stop myself or Dairan Loring being abducted by Vargon recently," explained Tayce in a point-blank way.

"Sorry to hear it. I'll send Craig Bream up-date modifications that have been done since we've installed it. Are you both all right now?" asked Jamie, concerned.

"I am, but Dairan suffered after-effects. He's the one I flew here with," replied Tayce.

"Is it serious?" asked Jamie, giving her his full listening attention, being her friend.

"No, but he should be fine once his treatment's through. I can't help but wonder if we had had a lot quicker pickup to detect Vargon's intruding device, to abduct us from the cruiser, we could have been prepared," said Tayce.

"Is Auran Amalthea Three here?" asked Jamie, looking where it generally docked.

"No, but Marc is in charge back in space. All you have to do is try the Auran frequency code. It should get you straight through," she suggested.

"Right – leave it with me. I hope Dairan's OK," said Jamie, heading away.

Both parted, going their separate ways. Twedor looked up at Tayce. He could see his mistress's mind was on Dairan by the thoughtful look on her face. The entrance to the Complex for Mind Study, Health and Neurology came into view. Tayce headed towards it in thought about what she might find when Dairan recovered. Upon approach, the clear-vision entrance doors automatically picked up her approaching presence and parted. Tayce walked through into what was like a large hospital foyer, with an almost wall-to-wall reception area on one side. Tayce approached, asking a pleasant-looking woman in her mid forties with short dark hair what clinic Professor Maylen was in. The female receptionist checked, then announced that the Professor was about to be in surgery, but if Tayce took the first-floor stairs to the next level his admin tech would be able to assist her. These words about Adrien being about to commence surgery meant one thing to Tayce: Dairan had hopefully begun the journey back. She left the desk with Twedor in tow, following the black-and-white signs to find Professor Maylen's clinic. Tayce soon found herself on the next floor. Medical tech personnel of different ranks and duties walked to and fro, going in and out of rooms carrying various objects and equipment. Some were guiding patients. Twedor was almost hugging Tayce's side as they headed across to the main clinic reception for that floor. He felt uneasy.

"Yes, Ma'am may I help you?" asked the slim female desk attendant.

"I'm Captain Traun of Auran Amalthea Three. Could I speak with someone connected to Professor Maylen?" enquired Tayce.

"Yes Captain, I'll call the Professor's admin tech," she replied.

"Thank you," replied Tayce, sauntering to join Twedor in the waiting area.

As soon as she entered the waiting area she crossed to the sight pane to look down on the Parklands. There could be heard behind her the sound of approaching footsteps on the shiny sterile floor. They came to a gentle stop. She was a slim almost petite girl, with strikingly beautiful alien features that resembled a china doll. Her complexion was bluey grey in colour, quite unique. Her eyes were ginger with a white pupil – again the shade was quite unique. Her hair was the same shade as her eyes – white and ginger in strands of each colour, which cascaded down around her shoulders.

"Captain Traun?" she asked, speaking softly.

"Yes, that's me," said Tayce, turning.

"I'm Amandina – Professor Maylen's personal admin tech. I understand you want to see Professor Maylen. I'm afraid he's in the middle of intricate mind-erasure theatre. Can I help with anything?" she expressed, clearly and politely.

"I just wanted to find out how Lieutenant Commander Loring is doing?" asked Tayce. "He's one of my team."

"I understand from the latest report that Dairan's doing well. He should be through the procedure in about one and a half hourons. I should call back later. Do you have a communications device I or Professor Maylen can contact you on, when he's through?" asked Amandina in a helpful tone.

"Yes! Tell him he can contact me on my Wristlink. He should still have his as he's on my team," pointed out Tayce in casual tone.

Both said their goodbyes and Tayce walked away back along the corridor to the steps down to the lower level, where she came up.

Twedor began: "Did you notice the way in which Amandina said Dairan's name? I picked up a slight elevation in her adrenaline levels, signifying interest."

Tayce laughed as she knew Dairan would never stray from her side, especially not being enticed by a low-level admin tech when he could have her, the captain of her own cruiser. Tayce felt she had nothing to fear and informed Twedor so. Twedor could tell Tayce didn't like the idea of some woman muscling in on Dairan in her absence, judging by the slight angry tone of her voice at the thought. Once down on the level where they had entered the building, both Tayce and Twedor headed back to E City Square with the happier notion that Dairan was doing well.

***

Dairan Loring lay in a large room surrounded by various pieces of equipment that were showing in 3D format the relevant area of Dairan's brain. Strangely enough, they showed a mass of dark greyish-green pulsating matter seated in an awkward position. Medical techs constantly watched and keyed in sequences of numbers to keep Dairan in a state of constant steady sedation and his body functioning normally. Professor Maylen was dressed in a navy surgical uniform and wore what resembled virtual-reality eye equipment. He slowly moved the long arm of the very slim laser using a slim hand-held keypad. The laser moved to Dairan's temple region and began pulsating an orange glow, slowly at first; then, as the laser rested on the skin of his temple, it began increasing speed. On the 3D screen image a thin pencil beam showed in grey heading to the pulsating mass. Vital signs were watched sharply every cencron for any sudden trouble.

"How are we doing? How are this young man's vital signs?" asked Adrien as he worked on.

"At present everything is holding level, sir," replied a medical tech beside Adrien, glancing at the screen readings.

"He must have a strong constitution to withstand what he's enduring," remarked Adrien's male system operator.

"Is that what's causing all the trouble, Professor?" asked a ginger-haired female tech with the name 'Judarn' on her uniform.

"Yes, it matches the being that placed it there. From what I can see he has increased the area of the brain that controls our dark thoughts and character, with the added bonus of a parasite life form that can make this young man change appearance too. It made him go from calm to angry in split cencrons; it also prompted the notion to act against everything he would normally believe is good," explained Adrien.

"What did he do, Professor?" asked a tall near-grey-haired male with 'Jarn' on his uniform.

"In Dairan's case he almost sent the Amalthean Cruiser into an area of space very widely known for all the wrong reasons named Phenomenon Space," replied Adrien seriously, his mind on the current procedure to erase, using the reprogram-of-memory probe, the whole alien intelligence that had been fed in by Vargon.

Silence filled the medical environment as progress was made in the following one and a half hourons. First there was the safe slow but tricky removal of the evil alien parasite Vargon had fed into Dairan's brain. Then the restoration of the area of Dairan's mind, making it seem like nothing had been there. Then the reducing of the swelling caused by the invasion of the alien intelligence and the constant watch for half an houron to see the return to normal brain activity. Finally Professor Maylen breathed a sigh of relief and removed his virtual-reality-like eye equipment, which had enabled him to do the tricky procedure. He glanced at the vital-signs wall monitor, demanding a final reading on brain function plus other vital signs. A ginger-haired female medical tech did as requested. But just as she turned away Dairan began going into mass convulsions. Adrien ordered the nearby Comprai Inject Pen. His nearest medical tech in the team of five handed it quickly over.

"What's happening, Professor?" enquired Jarn, concerned.

"It's nothing I didn't anticipate happening. It will be all right – it's just the removal of the alien mass has sent his brain impulses into override, causing massive spasms. It's temporary," replied Adrien administering the injection straight into Dairan's neck.

Everyone watched as the injection slowly stopped the convulsions and returned everything to normal. Adrien waited a few minons before nodding for Dairan to be moved back to the short stay room, where he would be kept under observation. The two did as requested. Dairan was moved back on to the Hover Trolley and taken back to the short-stay room to regain consciousness in his own time under watch. Adrien glanced at his Wristlink time display. He would check in on Dairan in an houron, when he should be fully awake. In the meantime he would contact Tayce. His admin tech, Amandina, was waiting for him. He crossed to her. She told him Tayce had called in in person to check and see how the procedure was coming along. Adrien raised his Wristlink and activated the Comceive button, which would connect him to Tayce.

***

Tayce and Darius were closing the end of the council meeting with the Council for Voyages, Missions and Assignments. They'd suggested, as she was on the base, they'd like to meet with her and her father. It had been a somewhat detailed argument and many points had been raised on both sides, but Tayce had achieved the ideal contract for her to represent Enlopedia. She'd stated that unexpected situations had arisen with the team and would continue to do so no doubt. She said the council should accept the fact they were an exploration team, upholding justice and travelling into strange territory where situations happened that were unavoidable. It was not like living full-time on Enlopedia, where security could be summoned in a moment. Darius, beside Tayce, stood silent yet proud of his daughter being firm with the council. It happened to be the same bunch of decision-makers she'd confronted at the beginning of her third voyage, just after the ambush. Things had changed since that dayon; now her father was present. He'd quashed the ban on family interference in council cases, making a new law as the Admiral of Enlopedia. Family would now be able to have a say in decision-making. The new conditions of the voyage contract were the same as Amalthea Two's. Auran Amalthea Three would carry the QE emblem on the outside of the hull and the team would take care of any Quests of importance that arose during the duration of the third voyage. The funding would be unconditional. Darius would hold the decision on expenditure, and the fact that mishaps with team members were bound to occur was acknowledged as acceptable. The Auran Amalthea Three voyage contract would be handed to Admiral Traun, to decide what to do with it, in the event of funding running out or the team wanting out. Tayce knew her father wouldn't stand in her way if she wanted to take her cruiser back on a single-handed basis again should the team decide they'd had enough. If and when the time arose, then she'd face what she would do. The council members stood. The head of the delegates addressed Tayce.

"I trust, Captain, that this latest proposal meets with your approval?" asked Councillor Paytern.

"Yes, Councillor, it does," replied Tayce, putting on a snobbish act.

Darius glanced at his daughter, somewhat amused by the fact the council hadn't forgotten the words Tayce had used in their last meeting before she stormed out. Councillor Paytern nodded to Darius and followed on out behind the other councillors. Twedor looked up at Tayce, asking did it mean they were back under the council's thumb?

Darius put his hand on Twedors metlon head and simply announced, "No, you're under mine, so you'd better watch your step."

Darius was joking, but Twedor didn't find it funny. Both Tayce and Darius laughed at Twedor's silence.

Tayce's Wristlink sounded on her right wrist. She raised her right hand and pressed Comceive. Professor Maylen's voice came through. He announced, as Darius guided Tayce with his hand behind her back on out of the chamber, that the removal of Dairan's brain alien had been a success. He suggested he give it an houron then go to the Parklands. Dairan would meet her there. With this, communications ceased. Tayce walked from the outer foyer of the council building with Twedor and her father. Both paused for a moment outside the building. Darius suggested that, as she had time before meeting Dairan, maybe it would be a good time to go and meet with Empress Tricara, who had wanted to see her. Tayce glanced at her Wristlink time display then agreed. Darius started away, but suggested that as soon as she'd been to the Parklands and found Dairan she should come up to his chambers before departure. Tayce nodded, continuing on across E City Square to the Schooling Complex for Gifted Students to see Tricara.

***

One houron passed. Dairan was fully conscious and had been checked over by Professor Maylen and was cleansed and changed ready to face Tayce. Adrien had brought in a personal Porto Compute to show Dairan what Vargon had made him do to Tayce. Dairan wondered if Tayce would ever trust him again, even though it wasn't him that had done the actions; it was the alien within him controlling him and making him do what he did. Would she still love him? he wondered. Adrien suggested maybe he should let Tayce find her confidence in him once again and to take things easy for a while – play it by ear, as they say. Dairan nodded in utter agreement. Adrien noticed Dairan was eager to leave. He was ready also to say his goodbyes to the team that had assisted him with Dairan. Together they began on out, back down to the entrance to the main complex.

Glancing at his Wristlink time, Adrien turned to Dairan en route. "We're to meet Tayce in the Parklands," he announced casually.

Dairan nodded, wondering how she would be with him.

***

Tayce finished her visit to Empress Tricara and briskly headed over to the Parklands, feeling a little uneasy about facing Dairan. Thoughts of what he'd done to her were still fresh in her mind, even though it wasn't Dairan at the heart of it. She soon entered the Parklands entrance with Twedor by her side. He glanced up at her as she came to a pause, seeing two male figures sitting on one of the stonex slab-type seats. One she could see was Professor Maylen, the other Dairan. Twedor picked up the uneasiness in his mistress's system. Dairan looked towards her, after a nudge from Professor Maylen told him Tayce had arrived. Tayce began down the path that would take her to him. Twedor fell behind. A sudden strong feeling of uneasiness gripped her. Twedor walked to be with Adrien, who had left Dairan to be alone with Tayce. Dairan stood and walked out to the centre of the path. He slowly walked towards Tayce, holding her look. The tension could be seen in Tayce's eyes. She glanced away, then back. Both came to a gentle pause and stood staring at each other for a few minons, each waiting almost for a rebuff from the other.

"Hello. Nice place to meet," said Dairan softly, almost apprehensively.

"Yes, we'll have to do this more often. The scenery is nice," replied Tayce casually.

Dairan gently reached out and pulled Tayce into a strong loving hold. She felt at first as if she wanted to push herself away, but as she reached the warmth of his body the feeling of wanting to do so ebbed away.

"I'm sorry I hurt you. I had no idea what was happening to me," he said softly against her ear as he held her.

"It's OK – it wasn't you," she replied with a sigh.

Dairan looked down at Tayce, then lowered his head, bringing his lips to meet hers in a strong, long kiss. Tayce could feel the sincerity of his feelings in his kiss. He meant what he said. Behind them Adrien smiled and Twedor gave a whistle. Both Tayce and Dairan broke apart and turned to begin the journey on back to the shuttle/fighter to begin the return to Auran Amalthea Three with the Professor. Tayce wristlinked her father en route to say farewell until they spoke and met again. He wished her luck.

5. The Cartarcan Pirates

The Quest 1 shuttle/fighter came in to land in the Auran Amalthea Three Flight Hangar Bay. No sooner had all engine power ceased than Marc's voice came over the Aircom requesting Tayce to go to Organisation immediately. It was urgent. But then it always was, thought Tayce as she left her pilot seat and proceeded outside into the hangar bay behind Donaldo, Professor Maylen and Dairan. Dairan turned, lifting Twedor down on to the bay floor. Adrien suggested he find his new duty place, the Medical Experimental Lab on Level 4. Tayce agreed, letting him and Donaldo head on out of the bay. She watched Adrien go, wondering how long he would be with the team – short term or indefinitely. Upon locking the Quest 1 with the usual procedure, she, Dairan and Twedor crossed to the entrance of the bay to head on up to Level 1 Organisation to find out from Marc just what was so urgent that needed her attention.

***

Lance Largon was receiving updated information direct from Enlopedia faster than he could sort it. Marc stood just behind him, watching as the information fed through on screen. 'Pirates!' he thought. Now, that was something that hadn't risen for some time. The race in this instance was the Cartarcan Pirates, an all-female group whose leader was more ruthless than Lord Dion. Marc and Lance continued studying and found some points in the incoming information similar to that of Greymaren's attack by the man himself. Tayce soon entered Organisation, walking to Marc's side. Dairan followed, interested to know what was so urgent. Marc ordered Lance to continue sifting the information; he'd be in the DC. Lance agreed. Marc ushered Tayce on into the DC, followed by Twedor and Dairan.

"Nick, transfer the waiting call from Admiral Traun to the DC," ordered Marc.

Nick began doing as requested. Tayce entered the DC and walked to her swivel chair. She dropped into it relaxingly, ready to listen. The wall Sight Screen activated and Darius appeared from Enlopedia. Dairan perched on the edge of the soffette arm, ready to listen. Marc paced. Twedor stood by Tayce's desk in the corner by her chair.

"I appreciate you've probably just stepped back aboard Auran Amalthea Three, but I need your and the team's help. In other words, I have your first official Quest under the new contract," began Darius.

"What's so urgent?" asked Tayce, giving her father her immediate attention.

"Less than four hourons ago, one of our new entente-cordiale colonies, A'Asia, was being manoeuvred into a new different orbit. This happens every two yearons, but this time it had to travel through an area of space known as Cartarcan Space, which is patrolled by a ruthless bunch of female pirates, namely the Cartarcan Pirates. They ambushed the two vessels towing the colony, destroying them, and the leader did her damnedest to make it clear that A'Asia was not welcome to travel through their sector," explained Darius.

"What's happened so far?" asked Tayce, trying to form a picture in her mind of what was happening.

"The Cartarcans rounded up the personnel of A'Asia and shipped them back to the pirate base. The General and his wife were amongst them, but their two young daughters, Kayleigh and Pia, were left behind on the colony. They ran away during the capture of their parents," informed Darius.

"What would you like us to do?" asked Marc.

"Find Kayleigh and Pia, then head to the Cartarcan Den and get those people back to where they belong on A'Asia," ordered Darius.

"Leave it with us, Father, though going into Cartarcan Space we may need backup," said Tayce, realising the possible danger of an onslaught battle at the base.

"Jan is aware of the situation and is standing by with his SSWAT team," promised Darius.

"I'll contact you just as soon as we have Kayleigh and Pia," replied Tayce.

"Lance is sifting through the finer points now, working out what we could face," spoke up Marc.

"Good. Use extreme caution and be on alert. They are cross-bred humans with a spacial background – that's all we know at the moment," informed Darius.

The Sight Screen deactivated. Tayce sat in thought. Dairan could tell by the look on her face that she was thinking of a plan of action and who to take. She began by naming the following members, Lance, Kelly, Phean and Donaldo, then glanced at Marc, requesting him to go also as he had a good knowledge of pirates. Dairan suggested he take command in her absence, if she wanted him to. Tayce nodded then rose to her feet, asking was the course set? Marc let the doors to the DC open, then explained that he wanted her to decide what she wanted to do – whether she went or not. They both continued on out into Organisation. Lance turned at his duty position, explaining that he had received course bearings from Enlopedia, and they would bring Auran Amalthea Three right into Cartarcan Space.

"Good! Kelly, key in a course to rendezvous us with A'Asia in Cartarcan Space, and put us under Invis Shield," ordered Tayce.

"Keying in request now. Going under Invis Shield," said Kelly over her shoulder as she did so.

"I've picked the Quest team. It's, Kelly, Phean, Donaldo, Lance and Marc, and I'm going too. Nick, contact Phean and Donaldo. Tell them the details of what's happening," ordered Tayce.

She glanced out through the main sight port into the presently clear, calm space, wondering what the all-female Cartarcan Pirates were like. Would they be as bad as Lord Dion and the Boglayons? She crossed to Lance, asking for everything he'd obtained on the Cartarcan Pirates to be transferred to her Porto Compute in her quarters. Lance nodded.

"Arrival time in Cartarcan Space is one houron forty-seven cencrons," announced Amal overhead.

Tayce, on this, knew this would give her time to cleanse and change and read up on the Quest information.

"Marc, you're in charge until the Quest. I need to cleanse and change before our next Quest. I'll be in my quarters," informed Tayce, walking towards the Organisation entrance.

"Right – I'll contact you the moment we arrive," replied Marc.

Twedor followed Tayce and stayed in high-frequency link with Amal so he could pick up finer points of information for the Quest. Dairan joined Tayce and they walked from the centre. Dairan noticed no one had mentioned what he'd done on Auran Amalthea Three a couple of dayons ago, nearly sending them all to their deaths. Perhaps they had put it down to a case of being out of mind and not being responsible for his actions, which, true enough, he wasn't; Varon Vargon was. Tayce noticed how silent he was as they began down the Level Steps to Level 3.

"No one blames you for what happened under Vargon's control, if that's what worrying you," said Tayce.

"I did wonder as no one's mentioned anything," replied Dairan.

"Well, don't – you don't need to. It happened, but it was just one of those unforeseen situations," said Tayce casually.

The three of them headed down to the Quarters Deck. Tayce's mind was on the forthcoming Quest.

***

Outside in the Universe Auran Amalthea Three cruised at warp 4 (470,000 milons a cencron). Her destination was Cartarcan Space, which the Cartarcan Pirates patrolled and called their zone. It was an area any traveller with any sense would steer well clear of and think twice before passing through. Their motto was 'We defy death', and anyone who strayed into their territory was used for instant target practice, or became embroiled in their malignant games to the death, which they considered fun. But Auran Amalthea Three was built to take on such female predators as mere competition. The leader of the Cartarcan Pirates, Fatashia, was going to meet someone who was her match – namely, Tayce! Auran Amalthea Three glided gracefully to the point of Quest.

***

A while later Tayce was cleansed and changed into a clean combat uniform and was sitting on the mouldable chair in the Living Area of her quarters, studying the information on Porto Compute relating to Fatashia, leader of the Cartarcan Pirates, and learning everything available about her. Dairan leant on the back of the chair looking at the curvaceous beauty on screen dressed in a tight-fitting leatherex bodysuit. He raised his eyes at her somewhat breathtaking attractiveness. She certainly had what any man would call sex appeal. Her big brown eyes showed a pupil like a fox's with a glint of enticement. Her hair started at her temples looking like reddish fox fur; then, as it reached the crown, it turned to ordinary human thick brown hair, which cascaded down around her shoulders in semi-curls.

"Wow – different! But she's one sexy female," expressed Dairan without thought.

"A lot of men have thought like you and have never been seen again. She's treacherous, make no mistake," said Tayce seriously as she studied the information before her.

Dairan walked round and sat on the mouldable chair arm, studying the information with Tayce. He figured that as he would be staying behind he had to know what the pirates were about, including their vessels and the sort of dirty trick tactics they would use. The description of the band of 130 or so female freebooters read like a combat and personal checklist.

- Origination: descendants of humans and foxes, created in a science lab by cross-breeding.
- Characteristics: fox-like cunning,very clever, ready to strike in a lightning-fast split cencron. The ages of the all-female force are from as young as sixteen to forty-five in human yearons. The leader, Fatashia, is the oldest. She has been in charge since an all-out territorial war of her elders in which her parents were killed along with all other grown-ups. Alone they continued and evolved to what they have become.
- Purpose: to capture any traveller passing through Cartarcan Space, raiding their vessels for anything worth the taking and selling for currency. Sometimes

they seduce their male victims then do away with them as they see fit. Many vessels are never seen or heard of again.

When the information study was through, Tayce rose to her feet and began pacing in thought, wondering how to handle this Fatashia and her sisters of piracy. 'I'll call a Quest meeting in five minons,' she thought, having come to a sudden conclusion of her thoughts and ideas. She raised her Wristlink, pressing Comceive and ordering Marc on the other end to have all members that were going on the Quest attend a meeting immediately. She was on her way. Marc agreed. No sooner had she ceased communications than she checked her appearance briefly in the imager to see she looked OK for duty, then headed on out with Dairan following. The doors to the quarters parted on approach and both she and Dairan passed through on the way to Level 1.

***

It was dark, with rusting sections here and there and armed to the limit with every kind of weapon for raiding and disintegration. It covered a diameter of nearly one milon and was stationary right in the middle of Cartarcan Space. Lights shone from within, signifying that Fatashia and her sisters were in residence. Aboard she was pacing with a certain prowess, like a fox summing up her prey before she strikes. Her eyes were dark and beautiful, but revealed a soul that was empty of all compassion. She rested her hands on her curvy hips and sighed, displeased. She'd received word from her spacial scouts that Auran Amalthea Three was about to become an unnecessary thorn in her side. Her near attendants, each varying in degrees of seductive beauty like her own, looked at Fatashia, waiting. Fatashia paused in her all-in-one leatherex body-hugging suit, in various shades of brown, khaki and grey. Her attendants, in the same attire as herself, would lay down their lives for their leader and mistress. She was considered their almost queen. Fatashia turned to her near immediate attendants, demanding overall information on Auran Amalthea Three.

"Its leader is a female captain by the name of Traun," informed Fatashia's assistant.

"Female? Interesting. Her crew?" replied Fatashia, pausing, interested.

"Fourteen members and one Romid. There are men in the crew," announced Tesha, Fatashia's near assistant, with a mischievous smile.

"Tesha, enough! What weaponry does this vessel have?" demanded Fatashia, barking at Tesha.

"Her weapon power is a match for us," said Tesha apprehensively. She knew Fatashia wouldn't want to hear what she had to divulge.

"What is it?" continued Fatashia, to the point, growing angry.

"Slazer swivel cannons on the front and rear, plus quick-reaction disintegration bombs. There could be more, but that's all the information we have."

"Outcome of these weapons if unleashed by this Auran Amalthea Three? How much damage?" persisted Fatashia, uneasy about what she was hearing.

"Immediate death and destruction of our race, leader."

"Do we commence attack on the vessel in question as soon as they enter our space?" asked another of Fatashia's shapely and beautiful sisters.

"Silence! I need to think – and remember who gives the orders around here," snapped Fatashia, suddenly feeling even more uneasy.

"You do, Vixen Leader," agreed Fatashia's sisters.

"Go, all of you, but keep me up to date on this Auran Amalthea Three as it's entering our territory of space," barked Fatashia in true leadership command.

"Yes, Vixen Leader," replied the all-female pirates at once.

The young pirates hurried from the command area of the Cartarcan Den – all except Tesha, who walked briskly but elegantly from her leader's sight. Fatashia looked at Tesha in a scrutinising way. Lately she knew the young woman was vying for her leadership position over the pack. She wondered how long she was going to tolerate Tesha. She was around her mid teens – a younger version of herself, with just as much guts and evilness rising within her. One dayon, if she wasn't killed, she would make a good leader.

***

On Auran Amalthea Three Tayce was explaining many of the pitfalls of the forthcoming dangerous mission – her first proper assignment, undertaken at her father's request. But the first priority was to rescue Kayleigh and Pia Starkern, two frightened but unpredictable childlings. These childlings had seen torture of the worst degree and saw their parents dragged away in a brutal fashion by the Cartarcans. Alertness was to be the word at all times.

"Any special weaponry required besides our Pollomoss?" asked Lance, leaning back in his chair.

"Not on the first port of this Quest. This is a two-tier Quest. First is the search and rescue of Pia and Kayleigh; second is going to involve entering the pirate den, and I have an idea on that when it arises," said Tayce, thinking.

"Because of the nature of the first part of the Quest, I take it that's the reason you want me along with my Medical Crisis Kit?" asked Donaldo, looking at Tayce questioningly.

"Yes, there's no telling how traumatically affected these two childlings could be. They may be just scared and not want to come out of hiding. Or they may rebel, thinking we're on the same side as Fatashia," replied Tayce.

"How can we make them see we're not the Cartarcan Pirates?" asked Lance.

"Because they'll see there are men in this team when we enter A'Asia," replied Tayce, seriously.

Amal, on the overhead revelation announcement system, informed Tayce that Cartarcan spacial outer rim was just being entered into. Tayce immediately finished the Quest meeting and headed out into Organisation to look at the main sight port. The doors opened before her. The team followed out behind. Dairan turned in the middle of Organisation, informing them that the A'Asia colony was ahead about half a milon. As Kelly reached her console, so Tayce looked past Dairan, asking if the Invis Shield was still in operation. Kelly confirmed as much, after a brief check. Tayce knew that, now they had entered Fatashia's territory, at any cencron she'd be sending a party to show a lack of welcome to her territory. But if Fatashias scanning equipment wasn't strong enough to penetrate Auran Amalthea Three's Invis Shield, they would be safe for a while at least – or so Tayce hoped. It would also make their rescue of Pia and Kayleigh a lot more easier. Tayce ordered the Quest team for the first part of the Quest to go and get changed and meet in ten to fifteen minons in the Transpot Centre. Everyone going took one last look at the stationary sight of A'Asia and headed away to get changed into combat attire. Marc excused himself and told Tayce he'd meet her in Transpot later. Tayce nodded. Dairan waited until Marc and the other Quest members had exited, then turned, asking was she sure she was ready to face the Cartarcan Pirates?

"We've a Quest to get started. If I need your help, I'll contact you," said Tayce without further word.

With this, she elegantly and briskly walked from Organisation leaving Dairan concerned. He felt her reply was a mere brush-off, hiding what she was really feeling. He focused on the nearing of Auran Amalthea Three to A'Asia. It wasn't what you call an attractive-looking colony. It covered an area of roughly three square milons, and steelex rails ran round the whole the lower half so that people or whoever could walk around the colony quite easily in its life-supporting field. The top half was a massive dome shape of steelex-and-glassene construction, showing square-shaped inner buildings. At present it looked what it currently was – vacant. The only two occupants were the childlings they had been asked to track down and rescue, Kayleigh and Pia. Dairan crossed to Lance's vacant research position and began to read the colony information from the layout currently on display.

***

Down in the Transpot Centre, the team were arriving for the first part of the Quest, walking in to wait for Tayce. Marc checked his Pollomoss just in case Fatashia and a couple of her female friends were waiting for them to Transpot into the colony and had somehow managed to break the Invis Shield whilst playing a sly trick to make them think she wasn't on to them. Lance and Kelly walked in discussing Greymaren. Phean followed in, dressed in his Quest combat uniform. Finally Tayce walked in with Donaldo. They walked to the Transpot group-marked area on the floor and stood along with the others, ready. Tayce gave the word to Amal through the overhead revelation system pickup (which Craig had fixed since returning to space) asking her to activate Transpot. In cencrons all the members of the Quest team were dematerialising in a swirling shaft from the Transpot, off to A'Asia, Twedor going also.

***

On A'Asia the atmosphere was one of coldness and deathly silence. All operations were in silent mode. All chairs at workplaces were pushed back as if personnel had gone for a break to return later. Computer screens were operational, showing the white wording 'A'ASIA SYSTEMS FAILURE' across the middle. No Securidroids were on patrol, which was standard security aboard a colony in this present century. It was a scene of total desertion. In the centre of what was termed the Task Centre the Quests team and Twedor arrived. Once fully materialised, everyone took a moment to look around the large square centre, at the rows of slim-screen computers, then at the spacial view outside the almost wall-to-wall sight port, which showed the glassene-and-steelex constructions that made up A'Asia. Tayce realised Craig should be with them, being the tech member of the team. She raised her Wristlink, pressing Comceive. Dairan soon answered at the other end.

"Send over Craig. Tell him to bring his Tech Kit. I've got something challenging for him," ordered Tayce.

"All right – he's on his way. What's it like over there?" enquired Dairan, interested.

"Deserted. There's a kind of eerie stillness and it looks like the main computers have been tampered with," replied Tayce in a whisper, glancing around her present surroundings.

"Standing by if you need me. There's no sign of Fatashia yet – our presence is still incognito," replied Dairan.

"Let's hope it stays that way. I'll take care of Fatashia later. Speak to you soon," said Tayce, ceasing Wristlink communications.

Tayce turned, ordering two teams to form – Marc, Twedor, Donaldo and Kelly in one and in the other herself, Phean and Lance. Marc nodded, calling to Kelly and Donaldo, suggesting they should start searching for Kayleigh and Pia on the lowest levels, leaving Tayce's team the two upper levels. Tayce agreed. She watched Marc and the others walk on across white shiny floor to the inner corridor entrance. Craig soon arrived and asked what was the problem as soon as he saw Tayce. Both walked to a computer workstation. Craig began keying in a simple sequence of commands to find a diagnostic reason why the main system wasn't working. He discovered someone in their present surroundings was logged into the system's command programme. Tayce glanced at him questioningly, coming to the conclusion it could be Kayleigh and Pia. He went back to keying in a sequence that would pinpoint exactly where they were. Suddenly Tayce's Wristlink sounded on her wrist. She answered whilst Craig continued.

"You've got company. A single fighter is heading to A'Asia and is closing in. It looks like it's searching – like it's suspicious someone's on board," warned Dairan.

"Thanks. Prepare to open fire if it gets near Auran Amalthea Three. Don't hesitate," ordered Tayce.

"You've got it," said Dairan fully understanding Tayce's command.

Dairan ceased communications. Craig waited after discovering the other user on the system at the same time as he was on it. Tayce prompted him to divulge what he'd discovered.

"They're on the next level – a study centre of some sort, though I can't tell who. That information is somehow withheld," apologised Craig.

"That's OK. We'll find out who. Is that the location that's flashing?" asked Tayce, checking the screen layout of the next Level.

"Yep!" replied Craig.

"See if you can get the defence system up on this colony. Fatashia's discovered we've arrived somehow. If you can't we'll have to try and rig some kind of barrier of our own to keep her at bay. Be careful – this isn't ours," warned Tayce as she walked on out, calling to the others to follow.

Craig watched them go, then continued trying to bring online the defence system and activate the barrier around their present surroundings. He noticed how cold and quiet it seemed – ghostly even – as he worked, but he'd been in situations like it before he'd joined the Amalthean Quests team.

***

On the lower levels, unknown to the team members that had just left the Task Centre. Kayleigh, the oldest of the two daughters belonging to General Starken, had constructed a force-field trap to protect her and Pia against intruders. Kayleigh was fifteen yearons old, but had the advancement in study and technology of someone twice her age. The trap was invisible to the eye and undetectable to any scanning equipment. It was a deadly trap in the waiting. The two girls lay in wait, hiding, and in the place Craig had discovered them – a study-type centre. Kayleigh watched, ready to activate her plan of action. Pia, the younger of the two girls, around four yearons old, was not so sure about her sister's grand plan. She just wanted her mother to come and get them. She was a pretty childling, almost doll-like and of thin build. Her long, straight brown hair was cut in a blunt way at the bottom of the length, in the middle of her back. In her arms she clung tightly to a soft toy that had seen better dayons, but it meant everything to her, in her world. She felt safe with it.

Kayleigh sprang on alert, seeing someone approaching her trap on the Vid Cam. Pia left their surroundings and ran out. Kayleigh called her back, but it fell on deaf ears.

***

Tayce walked on ahead of the others, Slazer in hand set to stun. She'd reached the corridor area where the trap was set. Pia suddenly appeared from nowhere, clutching her comforter. She stopped and stared childling like at Tayce in the middle of the white-floored corridor, not sure for a cencron what to do. The person she thought was her mother wasn't. Tayce looked at the childling as Pia realised Tayce wasn't her mother then watched her turn tail and run away. Tayce ran after her, but as she ran into the area where the high-density force-field trap was activated it was like a fly flying straight into a web. Tayce was caught in agony in the energy the trap gave off. Her Slazer imploded, the energy travelling up her arm and throughout her body. She cried out in agonising pain and lost all consciousness, hanging in mid-air. Phean and Lance took their Pollomoss guns out, taking aim to each side of the surrounding force-field trap and opened fire on full power. The shield fused out and Tayce dropped to the floor with a thud in sprawled unconsciousness. Both men ran to her side. Lance called Donaldo urgently on Wristlink.

"Don, get over here. It's Tayce – we've got an extreme emergency. She's not moving. Corridor one, Level 2, hurry!" said Lance, fearing Tayce had been killed.

"Let me try. Her body system has taken a extreme jolt. I'm not sure I can do anything though," said Phean.

As Phean was about to try and see if there was anything he could do, powers-wise, Donaldo and Marc came running up the corridor. Lance noticed Kelly wasn't with them.

"Where's Kelly?" asked Lance curious.

"She's still searching the lower levels for Kayleigh and Pia, with Twedor," replied Marc, watching Donaldo and Phean.

"I'll go – she shouldn't be alone, considering what just happened to Tayce," said Lance, beginning away.

Marc turned back to the emergency before him, in the form of an unconscious Tayce. Donaldo guided his medical Examscan all over Tayce, concerned it was too late. Pia slowly re-entered the corridor, totally afraid and came slowly towards them. Her small delicate face was tear-stained. All she wanted was her mother. She didn't understand what was happening, or who the people were surrounding the lady on the floor. Marc looked up.

"Is the lady hurt? It wasn't my fault – my sister did it. I said no," said Pia.

"Yes, she's very hurt," said Marc, trying to keep his cool, considering this young childling's probable age.

"Kayleigh shouldn't of done it," replied Pia, afraid.

Phean, sensing Pia was terrified, carefully walked up to her. She was one petrified little girl, he thought. He reached out his right hand and softly spoke to her, telling her who he was, that she was quite safe, that they were there to rescue her and her sister and that they were not the bad people that had come earlier. Slowly Pia walked up to Phean, took hold of his hand, then threw herself at him and hugged him tight. Phean was used to little childlings, having come from a large family in the Realm of Honitonia.

Tayce showed no sign of regaining consciousness. Her body had taken a severe electronic shock – enough to kill any normal human. Donaldo had managed to get a faint life-signs reading and wanted to head back to Auran Amalthea Three to treat Tayce as an emergency. Marc agreed, turning to Phean and suggesting he take Pia back with him whilst he went to find Kelly, Lance and Kayleigh Starkern. Pia, on hearing her sister's name, quickly spoke up, telling Marc where to find her. Marc, on this, set his Pollomoss to stun and headed off in the direction of the Study Centre, far from pleased. He had a feeling it wasn't going to be easy rescuing Kayleigh.

Kayleigh saw him coming on the corridor Vid Cam. Even though her sister had been captured, there was no way she was giving up without a fight. Suddenly the doors opened. She ran straight out, but wasn't prepared for Marc's quick reaction to apprehend her. He grabbed her by the upper arm, whilst putting his Slazer back in its holster. Once done, he secured her arms as she tried to struggle.

"Stop it. Pack it in, young lady. You're not going anywhere," ordered Marc abruptly down at her.

"Let go, you jerk. I won't cooperate. I hate you. What have you done with my parents, you pirate?" demanded Kayleigh, continuing to struggle against Marc's restraining persistence to not let her run off.

"If you'd quit struggling, I'll explain. Think about this: if I was a Cartarcan Pirate, why am I a man?" asked Marc. "They're all female, Kayleigh." Marc, shook her to stop her struggling, trying to make her see sense.

"Point taken. So who are you?" replied Kayleigh brashly. She wasn't afraid, unlike Pia.

"I'm Commander Dayatso. I'm with the Amalthean Quests team and your stupid trap, even though it might have seemed impressive to you, just nearly cost my captain her life," he pointed out angrily.

"How was I to know she wasn't a pirate? She's female," replied Kayleigh, throwing the fact back at him.

"You're coming back to the cruiser. We can reunite you and Pia with your parents and other people. Let's go."

Kayleigh turned, summing Marc up, wondering if she could trust him, considering how angry he was. At this moment Kelly Travern and Lance came up the corridor with Twedor. Kelly looked at Kayleigh, and she somehow recognised her. Kelly knew Kayleigh as their parents had met a couple of yearons ago when they both attended a conference. Kelly gave Kayleigh a kind smile of recognition and walked over to her, putting a reassuring arm around Kayleigh's shoulders and assuring her it would be all right, no one was going to harm her. Kayleigh glanced at Marc, still unsure of what her punishment would be, considering what she'd accidentally done to his captain. Marc raised his Wristlink and depressed

Comceive. He requested immediate Transpot. The small group disappeared in a swirling aura that went from foot to head, sending them back to Auran Amalthea Three. Marc walked away on the walk back to the Task Centre to meet with Craig.

***

Craig had had success and he was just adding the final commands via keypad to keep the erected defence barrier around A'Asia. There was a group of menacing-looking fighters hanging just a few milons off the bow. Craig could see them through the screen, which he had managed to make fully operational. Marc ran into the Task Centre, coming to a pause. He glanced to the sight on screen, then crossed to Craig, who was now placing the colony under computerised command, which he could temporarily control from Auran Amalthea Three.

"Ready to go. Everything under our control. They look like they mean business out there," he said, glancing out again before looking back to what Craig had done.

"Locking in final commands. I've routed operations to my console on Auran Amalthea Three, which can be done via high frequency," explained Craig, keying in the final command to seal the connection between colony and cruiser.

"Great job! Well done – good idea," praised Marc, somewhat amazed.

"Where's Tayce? Did she find Kayleigh and Pia?" enquired Craig, not taking his sight from the screen before him.

"Back on Auran. As for Kayleigh and Pia, we found them all right. They were in the Study Centre, where you said they would be," replied Marc, glancing at his Wristlink time display.

"That's good," replied Craig, giving one more glance over what he'd set up before leaving.

It was time to leave, to go back to the cruiser. He closed his Tech Kit and walked to be with Marc. They were soon transpotting off A'Asia back to Auran Amalthea Three, known most of the time, lately, by the team as just Auran, leaving behind a command for Auran to be in control of the colony. Craig knew he would have to run all the way to Organisation once he was back on board the cruiser, so he could check that computer operations were working as they should be after the link-up.

***

On Auran, Kayleigh, under Kelly's guidance, entered the MLC. She saw Pia sitting on a medical bunk looking clean and tidy, also a lot better than she'd been a couple of hourons previously. Donaldo was standing by an unconscious Tayce, who was lying on the examination bunk. Donaldo was watching Tayce's vital signs. She was slowly returning to normal, though he had had to give her a Select 2 injection, which would return her system through rest and boost to normal health. Kayleigh, a tall girl for her age, and leggy with it, almost froze when she saw Tayce. Her wide green eyes showed sudden great apprehension to go forward. Treketa walked over, suggesting Kayleigh might like to freshen up and saying she knew just the place. As Kayleigh passed Tayce, she did it in such a way that it was like a frightened mouse widely passing something fearful to avoid it at any cost. Treketa noticed how filthy Kayleigh's cropped hair was. Kayleigh looked like she was a proper tomboy – there was nothing feminine about her, not like her younger sister. Not what you would expect of the first daughter of a general. But Treketa figured it was Kayleigh's choice to be the way she was. In a way she guessed she must have been like Kayleigh when she was fifteen, when she was always Tom's shadow. But then, she wasn't a general's daughter. When she came to think about it, Tom was always dragging her out of scrapes. Kayleigh took Pia's hand and walked away with Treketa.

***

Two hourons later Tayce had been moved to her and Dairan's quarters, where she was being monitored by Amal. She still hadn't regained consciousness. Dairan was beside her, studying her, hoping she'd pull through. Tayce suddenly, to Dairan's surprise, sat up just as Auran Amalthea Three was attacked by Fatashia. Somehow she had managed to penetrate the Invis Shield. Tayce forgot about the slight fuzziness from the shock and became fully conscious, immediately beginning to get out of the double bunk to a standing position. Dairan waited to see what she was going to do, concerned she would topple. Donaldo suggested she take things easy as her system had taken a severe knock. Reaching for her boots, she requested an update. Dairan began filling her in on as much as he felt she could take: Kayleigh and Pia were safely aboard and Fatashia had manoeuvred her pirate fleet into position to attack. No more needed to be said. Tayce pulled on her boots and was heading on out of the Repose Centre, towards the entrance to their quarters. Twedor, who was doing a backup scanning of his mistress's life signs as she returned to normal health, followed on in hot pursuit. No sooner were they out in the corridor, and they were all heading for Level 1, than yet another weapon strike hit home on Auran's hull. Dairan reached out to stop Tayce falling sideways from the impact.

"Who the hell does she think she is, attacking this cruiser?" said Tayce, furious.

"Are you sure this is wise – you being back on your feet so soon? You suffered a hell of an electric shock, which would have been enough to put anyone else out of action for quite a few dayons, let alone a few hourons," he gently pointed out.

"And allow that pirate bitch to take this cruiser apart? Not if I've got anything to do with it," pointed out Tayce as she headed for the Deck Travel.

"What's your plan of action?" he asked, interested, walking to match her briskness.

"To rescue the A'Asian people and get their colony on through space to where it should be," replied Tayce with certainty in her voice.

"Marc said earlier that Jan is on his way out with his SSWAT officers," replied Dairan informatively.

"I hope his men have strong restraint. Fatashia likes nothing more than to seduce men who come into her spacial sector, and they never live to tell the tale," said Tayce, recalling what she'd studied earlier on her Porto Compute.

"I've a feeling this time she won't be so lucky with Jan's men. They are very duty-orientated and always on their guard for women such as she is and her no doubt womanly – or should I say foxy? – wiles. She and her sisters will be classed as 'strictly duty' and someone to be put a stop to. She'll be no different to any other persuasive female criminal," said Dairan.

"They're still men, and females of a pirate kind can be very persuasive, I feel I, Kelly, Treketa, Aldonica and Sallen should go in first, backed up by the male members of this team and Jan, if he wants to fall in with our plans," expressed Tayce, thinking.

"Women against women – now, that's different but interesting," replied Dairan, picturing it.

"That's a fight worth capturing," said Twedor.

They soon were whisked to Level 1 by Deck Travel. The doors drew open. Dairan let Tayce go first. She briskly walked out, heading into Organisation. Upon entering, she was greeted by the leader of the Cartarcan Pirates on the main Sight Screen, demanding to speak to the female captain of the vessel, the mere childling that thought she could just enter Cartarcan Space uninvited. Tayce came to a pause in a no-nonsense way, unimpressed by this Fatashia and her brash demand.

"You're talking to her. Hello, Fatashia," said Tayce, to the point. She resented being referred to as a mere childling.

"State the reason for your foolish arrival in our space," said Fatashia, finding Tayce more than she expected as a leader, comparing Tayce to herself.

"I'm Captain Traun, Fatashia. I wouldn't be in your space if it wasn't for the fact you attacked A'Asia en route to her new spacial sector." Tayce pointed out calmly, feeling she had just made Fatashia realise she was a match for her.

"You're trespassing. You are hereby ordered to leave this space at once. The prisoners from A'Asia are to remain here. If you persist in trying to rescue the citizens of A'Asia, you will be stopped by any means we choose to use," threatened Fatashia's coldly.

"Is that a challenge, Fatashia?" replied Tayce, waiting for Fatashia next move.

"If you feel it is, then so be it," replied Fatashia in a careless attitude, not bothered one bit.

The screen went to standby, turned blue then deactivated. Tayce turned, ordering Nick to tell Aldonica, Treketa and Sallen to meet her and Kelly in the

Transpot in fifteen cencrons. She then turned to Kelly, ordering her to go and get into combat attire – she was going along on the Quest too. Kelly nodded, leaving her seat. She briskly walked from Organisation. Marc turned, looking questioningly at Tayce, wondering if she was playing with fire. She looked at him, ignoring his look, then placed him in charge whilst she got the next phase of the Quest under way. He gave her a look of exasperation as she'd ignored his questioning look. He felt she was taking a risk. But it wasn't any different to any other times she had, even though this latest decision was downright irresponsible in his eyes. But that was his opinion, not hers. Dairan, Lance and Phean were picked for backup in team 2, and Jan's men would be further backup. Nick immediately announced that he would contact Chief Barnford and have him on standby. Tayce nodded in agreement, turning and heading towards the Organisation doorway. Lance, Phean and Dairan paused. Dairan assured Marc that Tayce would finish the current situation one way or another. Marc still thought Tayce was taking a very dangerous chance, heading into what he'd term the Foxes Den, and wild foxes at that. Amal had taken overall charge of navigation and research in Kelly's absence. Marc watched as the situation progressed.

***

On board the Patrol Cruiser Chief Jan Barnford was in the middle of team briefing, instilling the fact that the forthcoming particular band of human/fox-origin pirates were females that were not to be trusted, no matter how pitiful or coy they might seem. They would use any kind of persuasion tactics to get what they wanted, resulting in death. Under no circumstance were any of his officers to think of dropping their guard. These criminals were the enemy – they had attacked a colony of innocent people. These pirates might look appealing to the male eye, but if they got the slightest impression the women were trying to get them to drop their guard they had his permission to do what they saw fit and destroy them. Any slip-ups in letting this treacherous bunch make any officer drop his guard, he would be stripped of his rank and honour and his loved ones on Enlopedia would get to find out about his disloyalty.

"You have been warned. Is that understood?" asked Jan, walking back and forth before his men.

"Yes, sir!" came the loud response to their chief's stern words.

"Our duty is to assist Captain Traun and her team in rescuing the citizens of A'Asia, nothing more. Let's go," said Jan commandingly.

***

Fatashia, in the pirate high command area of her den, was yelling orders in every direction. Orders to prepare for battle. The 130-strong women/fox pirate army were putting into position every electronic elaborate trap they could, some were checking on their weapons. Some practising arm combat, all in preparation of the on onslaught of attack. Down in the holding area, the General, an Australton and head of A'Asia, suddenly could hear the immediate action unfolding somewhere ahead in the subdued light. Something was drastically up, he thought. His blue eyes glanced in a squinting way into the near-darkness, trying to make out any visible signs of just what was happening. His immediate personnel noticed the sudden growing activity too. The General, a man of stocky build, turned to his nearby assistant, a tall broad man in his mid thirties and of pleasant looks, discreetly informing him of the fact something was under way. It seemed like their captors were preparing for something serious. Suddenly the voice of a pirate could be heard stating they were about to be under attack. The General's assistant thought for a moment, then put it to the General that, as the pirates would be distracted, maybe if they could round up enough of the male Task Centre personnel, they could break out of their current detainment. General Starkern nodded. Turning, he gathered together some of the Task Centre members who hadn't been brutally injured by Fatashia and her gang. They were of various builds and ages and also from Australton. (The A'Asia colony originated from Australton and had been sent into space to study new sectors of the Universe every yearon – hence the shift in spacial reference and their need to travel through Cartarcan Space. About 1,600 men and women, plus the General's childlings, lived and served on A'Asia. Half though at present were injured.) General Starkern and twenty of his Task Centre members were in discussion about what they could do next, to thwart the female/vixen-cross pirates.

***

The Amalthean Quests women arrived at Fatashia's den. All were dressed in combat attire and each of them carried a Pollomoss poised for action. They crouched behind some storage containers to get their bearings in the near-darkness, so they could quietly assess the next step in their plan of action. Next Dairan, Lance, Phean and Twedor arrived and finally Jan's men behind that. Tayce gave the word. The women of the Amalthean Quests team ran to a nearby stonex cave area, just out of sight of the main entrance, on full alert. Dairan, Lance, Phean and Twedor ran to a nearby area of darkness in preparation as backup. In a typical defensive formation, Jan's men formed the final triangle for onslaught assistance, also primed to open fire. Slowly first Tayce and the female members of the Amalthean Quests team crept forth, followed by the men of the team, dressed in their combat attire, followed by Jan and his SSWAT officers. Pirate fighter craft were sat on a type of landing stonex area in preparation for warming up and launch. Lookout towers were quite visible to spot intruders. Slazer cannons were at the four corners of the bunker, assumed to be the Cartacan Pirates' Flight Area. Tayce checked all was clear, then suggested to the others they slip inside. But as soon as the Amalthean women stepped inside, pirates open fired. Tayce and Aldonica dived for cover one way, returning fire, whilst Kelly,

Treketa and Sallen, doing the same, ran into an alcove which was just enough to give them cover. Slazer shots went back and forth between the Amaltheans and pirates. Aldonica felt in her pocket and retrieved a Digit Bomb. She set the timer, then threw it on the silent count of three, over her shoulder. It rolled along the floor right into the female pirates' firing line. After a few cencrons there was a brilliant explosion.

"Yes!" said Aldonica triumphantly under her breath.

"Nice work, Al. Come on – let's go," commanded Tayce after checking that the first wave of greeting pirates had fallen.

Dairan, Lance and Phean fell in behind Tayce and the others as they headed further into the inner area of the pirate den. Jan had sent some of his officers to surround the whole den and take out any stray pirates; they also had been given the order to start rescuing the inhabitants of A'Asia if they reached them first. The remaining men of Jan's team followed up in the rear, behind the male members of the Amalthean Quests team, heading on into the entrance. Tayce glanced back over her shoulder to check backup was behind her. She then walked to a fork in the dimmest-lit tunnel.

'Which way?' she wondered, pausing.

Dairan came to a stop behind her, catching her up, as did Jan and his men.

"Problem?" asked Jan, noticing Tayce looking ahead from one direction to the other.

"Which way are the A'Asia inhabitants and which way is Fatashia?"

"Maybe we should split into two groups?" proposed Jan, knowing his men might find the inhabitants first.

"I'll take on Fatashia," cut in Tayce, determined.

"All right – you go that way, we'll go this. Be careful," suggested Jan, hoping his idea worked.

He hoped the inhabitants were the way he had chosen and Fatashia was the way Tayce was going, but above all else he hoped Tayce would be extremely careful in coming face-to-face with Fatashia.

"If anyone is interested, according to my built-in scanner Jan's directions are right," spoke up Twedor, behind Dairan and Jan suddenly.

"That settles it – let's go," Jan said, walking off.

He smiled to himself at the fact that Twedor had solved the problem of which way to head. He and his remaining men, plus Dairan, Lance and Phean, walked off up the left tunnel with its muddy-coloured floor and camouflage-patterned black-and-brown walls. Jan thought to himself that as with all pirate domains it was damn near impossible to see, and he could never understand why. Twedor had gone with the five female members of the Quest team in search of Fatashia, but halfway down the tunnel to their destination they were ambushed again. Suddenly there was an eruption of weapon fire on both sides. Even Twedor activated his Slazer finger and was returning fire.

“Pesky female pirates, take that,” said Twedor amongst the exchange of fire.

“Shall I?” asked Aldonica, holding another PolloAld Digit Bomb ready to throw.

“No, let’s force them back up the corridor. We must be near to where Fatashia is, judging by the way they seem to be trying to hold us away from that particular direction. Hold on to it – we may need to use it when we reach her,” replied Tayce.

“Right,” replied Aldonica, continuing to shoot back at the pirates.

The Amalthean Quests women continued firing in fierceness and drove the female pirates back up the corridor, slipping in and out of alcoves as they went to avoid being shot. Finally Fatashias second wave of female counterparts were forced back. Aldonica could see a tall entrance just at the end of their present tunnel. Tayce ordered her to stand by. Upon these words, Aldonica took the PolloAld and readied it as Treketa and Sallen shielded her. Tayce realised the female line of ambush ahead in the near-darkness had gone silent. She, Aldonica, Treketa, Sallen and Kelly cautiously peered up into the distance from the shelter of the last alcove they’d slipped into for protection from the weapon fire. They’d won! There were female fur-and-leatherex-clad pirates sprawled here and there on the floor, dead. Aldonica activated the PolloAld in her grasp and threw it. It rolled along the floor and came to rest at a tilt against the entrance to what was thought to be Fatashia’s command area. Aldonica glanced at her Wristlink time display, counting the minons to detonation. In the explosion, which everyone was surprised by, the entrance doors to the command area blew inwards. Tayce knew she was acting recklessly when she started forward, but she wanted this Quest over. Twedor went with her. Tayce, as the others wanted to follow on, turned.

“Act as backup. I want her to think I’m alone.”

The other women of the Quest team all looked at each other, alarmed, but did as Tayce ordered. Tayce and Twedor walked over to the sprawled bodies and on towards the entrance to the command area, where her senses were telling her Fatashia was situated.

Fatashia stood in the middle of the command area of her den brushing off her all-in-one body-hugging suit, angered by what had just occurred, but not aware of what was about to unfold. Tayce entered, using her powers before Fatashia had time to react. She held up her palm towards Fatashia and threw her with her powers across the cavernous command area. Fatashia landed with a thud, but was on her feet in no time, looking as wild as hell.

“Who the hell are you? Are you responsible for this attack on my command?” demanded Fatashia, her eyes wide with furious anger.

“What if I am? What are you proposing to do about it? It seems I have an advantage over you already,” replied Tayce, ready to strike again.

"We'll see about that. What's that thing at the side of you?" asked Fatashia, meaning Twedor, who stood with hands on hips, waiting.

"I'm Captain Traun, and this is Twedor. I came here firstly to give you some sound advice. Whether you take it is your decision, but the outcome for you should you choose to ignore my advice will not be good," replied Tayce.

"And that is – as if I'm interested to hear from a prissy captain like you?" replied Fatashia.

"Stay away from the continuing passage of A'Asia to its new bearings beyond this space you call home, or I will personally see to it the Intergalactic Criminal Punishment Life Colony is informed of your actions and you're out-of-spacial-sector activities towards the inhabitants of A'Asia. They would be very interested in your movements, I'm sure," warned Tayce.

"You bitch," said Fatashia, angered, and sprang at Tayce with claws that were almost talon-shaped and just as sharp, ready to tear Tayce to pieces.

Tayce winded Fatashia, much to Twedor's surprise, with a power strike to her midriff before she could reach her.

"You're wasting your anger on retaliation where I'm concerned, Fatashia," said Tayce, repeating the action she'd done when she entered the command area and sending Fatashia flying backwards again.

"Get out of here before I call reinforcements," retorted Fatashia, trying to recover from landing awkwardly from Tayce's strike.

"Go right ahead, though you'll probably find your sisters are no longer alive. You're on your, own Fatashia. You have been warned," replied Tayce calmly, not the least bit threatened by Fatashia's words.

"I don't believe you – they can't be, they just can't," retorted Fatashia, ready to explode, feeling the pain of her awkward landing and refusing to admit defeat even though her sisters were all gone.

"Come on, Twedor. We've delivered what we had to – let's go."

Twedor said nothing. He had been surprised by Tayce's actions.

Fatashia, as Tayce and Twedor walked from the dimly lit command area to meet up with the others, could be heard doing the equivalent of a fox cry, realising her sisters were no more. Twedor shook as the high-pitched sound hit his hearing sensors. Tayce had to steady him.

Once outside, the Amalthean Quests women and Twedor headed back to the rendezvous point to meet the others. Tayce acted like nothing had happened between Fatashia and herself.

***

Jan Barnford had successfully released the A'Asian prisoners and they were making their way back to the main rendezvous point. Some of the inhabitants were being supported by their crew mates. Jan was on his Wristcall to Tayce just as soon as they had reached the entrance. His concern was how were they going to get the 1,600 personnel swiftly off the pirate den back to A'Asia. Jan was interrupted by General Starkern suggesting maybe if someone could go to A'Asia and operate their body-transference system, they could go from their present surroundings back to their home in no time at all. Tayce, approaching, heard the General's words.

"General Starkern, I'm Captain Traun. I couldn't help but hear your suggestion. A member of my team, a tech officer, has been helping to keep your colony safely guarded in your absence. If you will allow it I can have him operate your body-transference system from our cruiser?" suggested Tayce.

"An excellent idea – yes, let's," agreed the General.

"I suggest you get the medical personnel and your first group of injured people together," suggested Tayce, walking away to contact Craig Bream on Auran Amalthea Three.

The General rounded up the first group and his medical personnel to travel to the colony, their home. Tayce soon walked back, announcing that Craig was ready and she had arranged for Dr Tysonne to help with the medical transfer. Dr Tysonne was heading to A'Asia as they spoke. General Starkern asked about his two young daughters. Kelly spoke up, announcing they were both safe and on Auran Amalthea Three. In no time at all the first group were ready and vaporising back to their colony. Jan ordered his men to spread out on standby in case there was any further torment from Fatashia, venting her revenge on behalf of her pirate sisters. All Jan's officers trained their Pollomoss mini cannons on the corridors leading to their present location. Within half an houron most of the inhabitants of A'Asia were back on their colony. Jan turned to Tayce suggesting she head back to Auran Amalthea Three as there was nothing she could do further in their current surroundings. He and his men would oversee things where they were. Tayce nodded agreeably, asking the General if he or his wife wanted to return to Auran Amalthea Three to collect Pia and Kayleigh.

Pallas was the General's wife. She was tall, slim and graceful-looking, in her early forties with a certain softness about her. She had short cropped hair, like Kayleigh's, but it looked neat and well styled. Her features were clear, soft and exceptionally beautiful. She had just the right amount of make-up to give her a natural look. Her eyes were the most startling emerald green imaginable. She wore a close-fitting uniform – a flight suit in a shade of mauve with white piping trim. Like Tayce, she wore cream boots.

Pallas looked at her husband, waiting for his decision, and it could be seen she wouldn't act without his say-so. He was the General, in overall charge of their colony, and she appreciated his upstanding command and his responsibility for all decisions.

"I don't see any reason you can't return to Auran Amalthea Three for our daughters," agreed the General.

"Then, Captain, I shall be honoured to accept your request. Thank you," said Pallas with a warm, kind smile.

"If you would like to come with me?" suggested Tayce.

The General watched his wife go with Tayce, seeing she would be well looked after. Then he went back to help organise the next team for leaving the surface of Cartarcus.

***

A while later Tayce, Pallas Starkern and the Quest team were back on board Auran Amalthea Three. Tayce, Dairan and Twedor escorted Pallas to the Medical Experimental Lab, where Kayleigh was with Professor Maylen listening to scientific stories. Adrien had offered to look after the girls when Donaldo had had to go over to A'Asia. Tayce and Pallas were the first to approach the clear-vision doors to the Medical Experimental Lab. The doors drew back. As soon as Pia saw her mother, she left the storytelling and ran across the lab, calling to her mother as she went. Pallas held open her arms to the little girl, scooping her up in them as she reached her.

"Has Kayleigh been behaving herself, Captain?"

"Kayleigh was bad, Mummy. She hurt the Captain," blurted out Pia without thought.

Kayleigh rose to her feet and walked towards Tayce, looking somewhat ashamed. She looked down then looked up, ashamed.

"Captain, I'm sorry. I realise my actions could have been serious – sorry!" said Kayleigh, almost whispering.

"Apology accepted; and if I had been in the position you were in protecting my little sister, I probably would have done the same as you. But some advice: I spent the biggest part of many yearons travelling this Universe alone, so be careful with your creations. The next person might not be so understanding as I am over what happened back on A'Asia," said Tayce.

"Thank you, Captain. I will. Perhaps we'll meet again one dayon. You've a wonderful vessel," said Kayleigh, relieved Tayce wasn't holding what she'd done earlier on A'Asia against her.

"Captain Traun, thank you for rescuing my daughters. I can't describe all the worried thoughts that were going through my mind about them, wondering what was happening," expressed Pallas.

"They were quite safe with us. Kayleigh, you keep up that imaginative mind of yours," said Adrien, standing and walking over.

"Yes, sir, and perhaps I can join the students at Enlopedia, like you said, one dayon," agreed Kayleigh.

"Well, girls, say goodbye – we're going home. Your father will be waiting," said Pallas softly.

Dairan stayed to talk to Adrien. Tayce turned to leave the lab and began to walk away with Pallas. The doors opened to the corridor. Twedor, Kayleigh and Pia walked out first. Tayce and Pallas walked on behind. Pia walked beside Twedor. She liked him and wished she could have a Romid too. Tayce and Pallas discussed the Cartarcan Pirates and the unfortunate mess that had materialised from just an innocent journey through Cartarcan Space. They all headed towards the Transpot Centre on Level 2.

***

An houron later it was decided that Auran Amalthea Three and it's Quest shuttle/fighters would assist at certain points on the colony, plus the Patrol Cruiser, all using high-energy tractor beams to tow the colony the rest of its way to its destined new orbital bearing. It took just on three hourons, as it was a slow process moving in exact unity with each Quest shuttle/fighter and Patrol Cruiser, with Auran Amalthea Three as backup, so as not to damage any of the vessels. Finally, after the manoeuvring of the colony to its new orbit the Quest shuttles/fighters deactivated their tractor beams and flew under the controls of Dairan and Tayce with Lance, Phean and Aldonica back to the Flight Hangar Bay on Auran. The Patrol Cruiser also deactivated its tractor beam and, after an exchange of farewells between A'Asia and Auran, shot off back to Enlopedia. Once Tayce was back on board the cruiser, she wished the A'Asia General luck and success in the new orbit, then Auran Amalthea Three went to warp 5 and headed on across the Universe to the next Quest.

6. Truans In Distress

Pellasun was the destination of a security high-ranked Transpo Launch. Aboard were two security officers escorting Admiral Darius Traun for his progress and design meeting for the new surface base. Pellasun was fast becoming Pellasun Traun 2, through the base being constructed on its surface. Darius had sent Jan Barnford to check out security two weeks prior to his visit, to make sure all procedures were still being followed. Jan had done it once before, at the end of the second Amalthean Quests voyage. Carlyle Cartarn had thrown everything into turmoil at that time, in holding everything up because of his bogus actions. But it was all in the past, thought Darius as he studied his forthcoming questions and the changes needing to be dealt with on his arrival.

Without warning the Transpo Launch was struck by an invisible force, like a kind of energy wave. Darius lurched in his safety harness and his Porto Compute dropped to the floor.

"Apologies, Admiral" came the voice of one of the security officers, who was piloting the Launch.

Darius slipped away his Porto Compute into his silver-toned attaché case, locking it securely with his code of authorisation. Within cencrons whatever had attacked the small Transpo Launch was boarding in the form of an unwanted party. Quickly the two black leatherex-clad rough-looking aliens cold-bloodedly shot the two security officers in their seats, then turned, aiming their guns at Darius. Darius gave a horrified stare, then the Slazer of one of the boarding enemy aliens went off and everything went dark.

***

Tayce and Dairan were out in space, practice-flying just a short way away from Auran Amalthea Three. It was something they liked to do, just to keep their edge when they needed to use skilled flying techniques. It was during a sharp turn in a computerised flight-path manoeuvre that Tayce suddenly felt the impact of what had occurred to her father during his transit to Pellasun. The incident hit

Tayce like a lightning flash in her mind. She completely lost control of her Quest at high speed. It spiralled out of control, diving towards a planet in the vicinity of Auran Amalthea Three. It was a planet shrouded in mist. Dairan ordered her abruptly to pull up and pull out. The Quest, as much as Tayce fought to bring it under control, wasn't responding. It was diving too fast and was too out of control to bring back under her operation. Tayce continued with every ounce of strength to try and do what Dairan was ordering her to, but without much luck. The computer system had locked in a spiralling downward motion. She was heading straight into the mist of the brown-and-yellow planet and straight for the surface. Dairan's brown eyes were alert with concern and he was angered to think there was nothing he could do to stop the inevitable from happening right before him. He contacted Auran Amalthea Three in urgency.

"Marc, it's Tayce – she's in trouble. She can't pull up. The system's locked her out and she's gone into a nosedive. She's heading for the surface of the planet about a milon from here," said Dairan over Aircom in urgency.

"Go after her," replied Marc abruptly, greatly worried it would be the end of Tayce.

"It's dense down there. Not even my on-board scanning system can break through the thickness of the mist for a Quest search. She could crash anywhere," continued Dairan, not liking what he was thinking.

"Head in so far as you can. See if you can get any readings at all. We'll try from here," replied Marc.

"Going in now. Contact you soon, hopefully," promised Dairan, cutting communications.

Dairan manoeuvred his Quest shuttle/fighter into the dense yellowish misty atmosphere, and one that he considered might not be breathable. He began thinking the worst, that if the crash didn't kill Tayce the atmosphere might. He knew she was an experienced pilot, but the conditions she was flying under and through would test her skills. The dense atmosphere engulfed his Quest in no time as he dived downwards. He immediately tried scanning and heading to different areas, but without success.

***

On the surface a dark cloaked and masked being paused in mid stride crossing rocky terrain on a hill. He was tall and muscular, but the cloak made him seem bigger than he was and showed his broad shoulders. He looked skyward to see the out-of-control Quest hurtle out of the dense atmosphere and head straight towards the surface a short way away from him. He took a pair of viewing glasses out of the pouch he carried and activated them, placing them to his dark-brown eyes, wondering who the hell was crazy enough to fly like they were. He watched with interest, trying to pinpoint the name on the craft, but it was difficult considering the immense speed at which it was travelling. He continued to watch until impact, then realised that if there was anything or anyone that could be salvaged, or injured, it needed checking out. He dialled a number on a device he held in his black-gloved hand and in a few cencrons he'd vanished, reappearing just a few minons from the crash site. The Quest was silent, but smoke was bellowing out around it. He walked over to where the entrance hatch was and was astonished to see the name on the side, 'Quest 1', then in small black lettering underneath it read, 'Auran Amalthea Three fleet'. He ran a scan over the craft, waiting for a reading. One life sign; all power failed. Nothing he wasn't expecting. He aimed his Slazer, firing at the de-locking mechanism. The beige entrance hatch slid back enough to get his broad hand into the gap and push it further back. Once the gap was wide enough, he cautiously entered, going into the forward pilot section. Tayce was slumped over the controls. He reached out with his hands, taking hold of Tayce, moving her back into her pilot seat. He shook his head upon seeing her beautiful breathtaking features and knowing who she was. He couldn't believe in all the Universe, and of all the planets she had to crash on, she had fallen into his backyard.

"Fairness!" he said in disbelief, raising his eyebrows and pulling back the hood of his cloak to expose dark curly hair.

There was only one being that ever called Tayce by this term and that was none other than Lord Dion, who had led the Boglayons in her last voyage to abduct Nadinea Wiljan, and before that had raided Greymaren with a liking for Kelly Travern. He removed his black leatherex glove and felt for Tayce's pulse on her delicate neck. 'She's weak,' he thought. He quickly raised the dialling device that had brought him to his present surroundings. He placed a half-moon-shaped flat disc on Tayce, then looked around for the on-board Medical Crisis Kit and food provisions. After putting another disc on these items, when found, he scooped Tayce out of the pilot seat in his strong arms, pausing for a split cencron thinking he'd heard something fly past. Then when it seemed like nothing, and whoever it might have been didn't return, he proceeded. Depressing the dialling device, he vanished with Tayce and the provisions, leaving Quest 1 abandoned where it had crashed.

***

Without any success finding Tayce or Quest 1, Dairan flew back to Auran disheartened by the fact that Tayce was back on the surface injured or dead, but his on-board surface scanner wasn't strong enough to detect her. He brought the Quest shuttle/fighter in to land in the Flight Hangar Bay and brought it in to a gentle landing on the bay floor, next to the vacant space Tayce's normally occupied. He wanted to be back out searching for her, but Marc had ordered him to return and the fuel cell on the Quest needed charging before he did. A lot could happen in that time, he thought as he began climbing out of the Quest. Twedor came to meet him as he did so. He waited as Dairan connected the fuel-cell charge hose to the intake on the shuttle/fighter, then together they began on out of the bay, off towards Organisation, hoping Marc would be able to throw some light on Tayce's whereabouts. Secondly, Dairan wanted a word with Phean. He knew that if Tayce was alive on the surface Phean would be able to pick up the fact. He also wanted to know what had made such an experienced pilot such as Tayce suddenly lose control in the practice flight. Twedor glanced up at Dairan as they walked up the Level Steps. He could see he would rather be back out in the Universe searching for Tayce than heading to the Organisation Centre.

They soon entered Organisation. Lance looked up whilst continuing the atmospheric-penetration scan of the planet Tayce had crashed into – something he was finding extremely difficult because of the denseness of the vapour the planet was shrouded in. Marc was stood watching as the pointer on screen slowly moved to the next planetary area of scan. He then walked away, leaving Lance to continue and to let him know the moment he found Tayce's Quest 1. Lance nodded. Dairan followed Marc across the Organisation Centre to the DC. They both walked in, followed by Twedor. Marc continued over to Tayce's desk and around to sit in her chair. Dairan perched on the edge of the soffette arm.

"We think we know why Tayce lost control of Quest 1," began Marc.

"Really? Why?" asked Dairan, fully interested.

"I received a communication from Adam on Enlopedia about twenty minons ago. Darius was en route to Pellasun Traun 2 about two to three hourons ago via Transpo Launch, with two security officers. It was attacked, the two officers were killed and Darius abducted," explained Marc seriously.

"God! Any idea as to who?" asked Dairan, almost stunned by the news.

"No, all the rescue people found was the Transpo Launch adrift and the burnt remains of the two security officers, whoever they were. They weren't after the information on Pellasun Traun 2 – Darius's attaché case and Porto Compute were still aboard," explained Marc.

"How's Lydia taking it?" asked Dairan. "She must be really worried."

"She is, but Adam is giving her all the support and assistance she needs to track the abductors," replied Marc.

"Wish we were in a position to assist. If only we could find Tayce through that dense atmosphere, we could help," Dairan replied, thinking as much.

"My thoughts on what made Tayce lose control: whoever abducted Darius, used some kind of drug that temporarily made both father and daughter communicate in a thought-transference way. Hence she lost control and is somewhere down on that planet's surface," said Marc, turning to look at the planet where Tayce was through the full-length sight port.

"But it would have to be a pretty unusual drug," replied Dairan, thinking.

"Maybe so, but with the kind of villains we've come up against lately anything is possible, and there is also a slight telepathic link between Darius and Tayce anyway. I remember it from yearons ago," replied Marc.

Out in Organisation there came a shout from Lance to summon Marc. Both he and Dairan stood and hurried out into the DC, across to Lance's position. Lance pointed to an odd shape on screen that nearly resembled the outline of Tayce's Quest 1, with some blurred italics along the side.

"Put extreme magnification on. See if we can bring it up any clearer," ordered Marc.

Lance keyed in a sequence on his console to bring the image up to full clarity, but what appeared was not what they had expected. It was another vessel, which had been on the surface for yearons and covered an area roughly half a milon in diameter. Dark in colour and looking like it had seen better dayons, it rested in the thick greenery. Marc looked at Dairan. They couldn't fathom what this of all vessels was doing in its present surroundings, for this was a vessel belonging to a humanoid male they thought had perished after their last encounter with him: Dion, the leader of the Boglayons tribe of pirates. Marc's mind began to work overtime, wondering whether Dion was alone or if this vessel was a resting place for new pirates with Dion as leader once again. He ordered Lance to scan at maximum depth for life signs. Dairan was growing anxious, eager to go back to the surface and search with his Quest. Marc had a feeling, glancing at Dairan's face, that he was probably coming to the same conclusions as he was – that Tayce was pirate bait once more, in the hands of a man who called her 'Fairness' with ulterior motives. Dairan wanted to get going. He'd seen enough and thought the worst for long enough. Lance came back after a more in-depth scan, but with news that didn't confirm anything solid.

"I pushed scan to its highest degree of penetration and filtration, but something is stopping the reading. If there is life down there, there's no way I can find it," announced Lance, feeling disappointed.

"Damn! That's just like him – if he's down there he'd be undetectable," expressed Marc, beginning to pace Organisation, far from pleased.

"Perhaps if I can modify a Quest, you could head back down and get close enough for a clearer reading," offered Craig from his tech position.

Marc knew it was his place to make sure the team were safe in Tayce's absence under his command and the last thing he wanted was to get anyone killed in sending someone – i.e. Dairan – back to the surface if Dion wasn't alone. Tayce would, firstly, never let him forget his neglectful actions and, secondly, never forgive him for getting the man she loved killed through stupidity. He paused mid pace, turning to Craig and asking could a Quest defence shield be modified enough to protect the craft during the atmosphere scan whilst travelling to the surface, and to stop any interference to electronics? Craig nodded suggesting Aldonica assist him on the shield. Marc agreed. Craig left his seat and hurried from Organisation, taking his Tech Kit with him. Marc then turned, advising Dairan to grab a chance for refreshment and saying he'd call him the moment everything was ready to go. Dairan nodded, then walked from Organisation with Twedor looking out at the planet.

***

Back on the planet surface, inside the vessel that had been identified as Dion's, Tayce woke. Focusing up into the bright light above her, she lay still, almost too petrified to move. She realised she wasn't on Auran Amalthea Three or in the interior of her Quest. The tall dark-haired cloaked being from earlier stepped into view above her. The familiarity of who it was hit her, but she wondered if her mind was playing tricks – maybe she had hit her head on crashing. Was it Dion? But there was no smell of Vardox. He just stood studying her in the dimmed light. She recalled the first time she'd encountered him like it was yesteron, the way he had made her want him intimately. God, she thought, had he abducted her from her Quest and was she his captive? No chance – this wasn't happening, she thought. He pulled back the hood of his cloak to show the handsome smouldering pirate features, the beard and dark curly hair that she knew too well. He leant over her more closely. Tayce stared into his dark-brown eyes and quickly found out he hadn't lost the strong, powerful yet playful enticement of seduction. She looked away. He smiled, knowing he'd captured her again in his powerful hold, then reached out his broad hand and gently took hold of her chin, turning her to face him. Tayce looked plainly at him, almost with hatred. She wanted to lash out.

"Relax, Fairness. I'm removing a dressing – you were hurt during the crash," he firmly ordered her.

"Get off me, you bastard! I thought I'd seen the last of you," she said, pushing against his strong arm to no avail.

"Nice to see you too, Fairness. Now keep still," he ordered in the voice of an authoritative former leader.

"What am I doing here? If you kidnapped me, you won't live to tell the tale when I'm rescued," she protested.

"You crash-landed on the planet surface. I saw you coming into land – if that's what you call it. Hell of a flight! God knows why, but I rescued you from the present weather conditions," replied Dion.

"Oh, I suppose you think I should thank you. Forget it," she said, starting to sit up.

As Tayce did so, all the drowsy effect of her impact against the control panel of the Quest came rushing back. She swayed. Dion reached out, taking hold of her supportingly by the upper arm. She pushed him away and proceeded to stand on her feet. Dion stood back and watched, somewhat amused by the fact that, even after all the time since he'd last seen her, she would rather escape into the night hourons' poisonous atmosphere than remain in his company one more cencron. He watched her stagger to the doors, showing the edge of determination mixed with drowsiness. It was one hell of a comical sight, he thought, smiling to himself. He walked slowly over as he could see that in the next ten cencrons she'd drop like a stone. He tried not to burst out laughing at her actions. Tayce paused and looked at him half drugged. It happened, but Dion used his extreme force, keeping her in mid fall until he could scoop her up in his arms and carry her back to the bunk unconscious.

He left her, knowing she'd wake later much stronger. He realised that if she was on his current surroundings then the Amalthean Cruiser had to be in a near orbit too. Maybe this was a way at last to leave the far from perfect environment that had been his home for the past four monthons or thereabouts. He crossed to prepare refreshments – something he once thought he would never see himself doing as all their meals on Boglayia were prepared by female attendants. It was evident to see, though not quite understood why, that Dion had become a changed person. There was no sign of his leadership of pirates. All that was evident was his powerful force and commanding voice and what he called Tayce: Fairness. But was he hiding them truth for some reason?

***

Adam Carford was in communication with Marc over the Satlelink relay link. Both were discussing Darius and Tayce. Marc was explaining what had been discovered so far regarding Tayce and the crash site. Aldonica and Craig entered the DC and paused. Their job was done – the modifications to the Quest were complete. Marc quickly informed Adam that he'd update him as soon as there was any news on Tayce. Adam agreed, then closed communications. Marc sat ready to hear what had been done to the Quest. Aldonica began explaining, then finished by saying that she and Craig had both run checks. Marc rose to his feet, ordering Aldonica to go to the surface of Olarintz and commence the search for Tayce with Dairan. She agreed. They all walked out into Organisation just as Dairan was walking through the main entrance to the centre.

"Dairan, everything is ready. Aldonica is going with you to keep an eye on the modifications," said Marc.

"Fine – let's go," replied Dairan, already beginning to move away.

Marc watched both Amalthean members leave, hoping they would both be safe on the surface. There was no indication of what was on the surface of Olarintz awaiting the pair. Marc crossed over to Lance, ordering Nick to stay in communication with Dairan for as long as possible. Nick agreed, slipping on over his ear the Microceive, ready. Lance began announcing there was still no change in his scan of the surface, but he might get a better reading when Dairan managed to penetrate the dense atmosphere later. Twedor felt at a loss as he stood by Lance's console. He realised he should have ignored his mistress's words not to accompany her when she went out on her practice flight. When would he ever stop listening to her, in order to protect her! Maybe she wouldn't be lost if he'd gone. Lance looked at him, noticing him silently watching what he was doing in research and patted him on her head. He could tell he was lost without Tayce.

"She'll be OK – you'll see, mate," assured Lance.

"As I'm not required I'm going on walkabout," said Twedor, heading off to find Professor Maylen and to see if there was any assistance he wanted.

***

Out in space the modified Quest shuttle/fighter headed to the muddy brown-and-yellow planet, known as Olarintz, in search of Tayce alive or dead. On board, Aldonica ran constant checks using her Porto Compute, keeping an eye on the level of readings relating to the modifications as Dairan flew the Quest expertly into the dense yellowish atmosphere. Suddenly electronic magnetic strikes of lightning danced off the Quest, but, owing to the changes both Aldonica and Craig had made, the Quest held solid against all that was being thrown at it.

***

Tayce was woken once again by the announcement from Dion that it was time to eat and that she should at least try – it would help to get her strength back. Tayce sat up. This time there was no dizziness; she felt more her normal self. She kept her eyes fixed on Dion. She didn't trust him and thought of all the beings to get stuck with on a strange world it had to be him! She swung her legs round and dropped to a standing position. The air was cold – not the least bit warm like the atmosphere on Auran, she thought. Why hadn't someone tried to rescue her by now? she wondered. Dion picked up his thick warm cloak and crossed, draping it about her shoulders.

"I don't want you to freeze to death, Fairness. If your team arrive they'd probably pin that on me too as well as what you just accused me of – kidnapping. Now sit and eat while it's hot," he ordered in his commanding leader's deep voice.

"What is it?" asked Tayce, disgusted by its creamy uninteresting appearance.

"Food! It's probably not what you're used to, but it's nourishing," he replied.

Tayce nervously dipped the spoon-shaped utensil into the triangular brown dish, scooping out a spoonful of the thick cream-broth kind of mix. She looked at Dion, wondering if it was all right. It looked disgusting, but he was tucking in and enjoying it. But then, he was a pirate and a Boglayon – anything would be appealing to him, she thought. Something had changed with Dion, or was this a clone sitting opposite her? He hadn't mentioned his men or his old lifestyle; he seemed to be alone. But as she studied him she could pick up that this was the real thing. What, she wanted to know, was going on? He seemed to be considerate, out of character. He was normally full of himself and trying to seduce her with his powers of immense seductiveness. She went back to the creamy uninteresting food on the spoon. Even though she knew she was going to hate the taste, she put it in her mouth, bracing herself.

After the first taste, which didn't seem too bad, she began: "I want to know what's going on. Did you force me out of the sky? Where are your men? Do you have them ready to take over Auran when she appears in orbit? How gullible do you think I am? In spite of all this kind action towards me, I'm not fooled, Dion, for one minon," she firmly informed him, leaving the meal and rising to her feet.

"You have me so wrong, Fairness. There is no one else but me here. I've been alone on this planet since you finished off my men on our last encounter with you, over that Wiljan girl," replied Dion, his eyes like the old leader she once knew, dark and alert with sudden fierceness.

"Why a sudden change in attitude, rescuing me and the whole hospitality scenario?" Tayce continued, suspicious.

"Would you rather I left you to die, like the old me would have done?" he replied, trying to keep cool.

"You're avoiding the question," replied Tayce, looking at him suspiciously.

"All right, I figured the moment you came hurtling out of orbit, if I rescue you, your team will come looking for you and I can get off this far-from-perfect environment and start a new life," he replied.

"So you do have an ulterior motive. Thought so," said Tayce, not surprised.

"No, those dayons are truly over. Trust me, Fairness, I've changed," he replied, trying to convince her.

"Trust you? You might sound convincing, but you've got to prove it," replied Tayce, trying to sense if he was telling her the truth with her powers.

"All right, if you get me off this planet I will help you with one Quest and not put a foot wrong, then you can drop me off at a base somewhere and you'll never have to see me again," he put to Tayce, rising to his feet.

As he stood studying her, she felt the Dion of old trying to entice her with his muscular dark charm and powerfulness that tugged at her emotions, playing with them playfully, just like he'd done the first time, back at the Boglayon hideout. She turned away in thought for a moment. He smiled, knowing he'd played with her feelings again. Tayce felt that if she returned with him there would be a strained atmosphere on Auran. But maybe there was to be a Quest – the reason her father had flashed into her thoughts earlier could mean a possible Quest. He was in danger. Maybe if she could trust Dion for this purpose, letting him help her find her father, then maybe he would prove that he had changed. He was looking at her as she turned. He was waiting for her to believe him, just for once. Fair enough, he had rescued her from her Quest and made sure she recovered from her ordeal. But their encounters of old kept crawling back into her mind, and she wondered whether she could trust him or not.

Suddenly overhead there was the sound of a vessel and it seemed to pause. Tayce looked up. Dion reached for his handgun as he looked out. He announced to Tayce that bandits had visited the planet before. He then reached out using his powerful force and brought Tayce towards him, just like he had done in the first encounter, but for protection this time. He held her in a tight protective grip. Tayce felt his warm closeness, trying to ignore the fact he'd gripped her tightly and reminding herself that it was for her own protection. She looked out through the same circular sight port, but all that could be seen was the dense atmosphere.

Behind them, the main entrance to their current surroundings suddenly opened. Dion aimed his gun towards the entrance whilst holding Tayce. Slowly what or whoever was coming in did. Dairan and Aldonica entered wearing portable breathing equipment. The scene of Dion holding Tayce in a tight grip didn't look harmless in Dairan's eyes. He raised his Pollomoss handgun and took aim. The entrance behind them closed. Aldonica's hand went for her gun to back Dairan up. Dairan was looking mistrustfully and angrily at Dion. It was a stand-off. Dion slowly and gently released Tayce. He didn't push her across what he'd made a Living Area, which must have once been the command deck; he let her stand before him and lowered his gun slowly.

"Dairan, lower your weapon – that's an order. There's no trouble here," assured Tayce.

Dairan looked from Tayce to Dion, not quite understanding why Tayce was ordering him to put his Pollomoss away. 'What is going on here?' he wondered. Dion was a criminal of the worst kind. Had something happened during the crash-landing on the surface to make Tayce want to trust him?

"I gave you an order, Dairan. Dion's coming back to Auran with us," said Tayce seriously.

"What! You've got to be kidding," protested Dairan, wide-eyed with surprise.

Dairan and Aldonica took off their masks and looked at each other, somewhat amazed. Something had to be drastically wrong, they thought. But Dairan knew he couldn't force Tayce to reconsider her decision – she was his superior and the head of Auran.

Dion stood silently behind Tayce. He could see it wasn't going to be a friendly welcome or atmosphere on Auran judging by the current atmosphere. He began to explain that if he hadn't rescued Tayce the team would be without their captain. He said it was Tayce's idea – she'd assist in getting him off Olarintz and in return he would help with a Quest as a kind of thank you.

Tayce thought to herself, 'That's news to me,' but didn't say anything.

Aldonica couldn't believe what she was hearing. Dion, pirate leader, a man with a lot of power and clout and one who had also hurt Nadinea Wiljan, was being nice. She wished someone would pinch her.

"Right, let's get going. I don't want to be on this planet any longer than need be," said Tayce.

Dion grabbed his cloak, which Tayce had discarded, then handed portable breathing equipment to Tayce and slipped one on himself. All four headed back to the entrance of the imperfect vessel. Dairan wondered what Marc would have to say about Dion's arrival. He had a feeling there would be a showdown between Marc and Tayce because of her decision. It would be like the old earth saying, many centuries ago, *'Light the touchpaper and stand well back.'* All four headed back to the awaiting Quest.

***

On Auran Amalthea Three Lance had picked up four life signs from a scan of the Quest returning to the cruiser. Nick suddenly gave a look of shock and amazement at what Dairan was telling him over his Microceive. He unintentionally let an expletive go, which made Marc turn, taken back. He'd never known Nick to swear before in everyone's presence.

"I can't believe what I've just heard and you're not going to like it," said Nick, shocked, still not sure he'd heard right.

"Do you want to tell me?" asked Marc, noticing Nick's outburst.

"Forgive me for saying this – you need to brace yourself," advised Nick, trying to return to normal.

"Go on – what?" prompted Marc. Nothing surprised him where Tayce was concerned any more.

"Tayce is bringing the pirate leader Dion back aboard. It appears Dion rescued her from the Quest when it crashed – that's what Dairan's just told me," explained Nick, seeing Marc's look of increasing anger at the mention of Lord Dion.

"What the hell is she up to? Is she crazy? Tell Donaldo I want him ready to Examscan Tayce on arrival," said Marc, far from pleased, wondering if Dion had somehow brainwashed her into bringing him aboard.

"You've got it," replied Nick, turning back to his console and carrying out Marc's orders.

"What are you thinking?" asked Lance, looking questioningly at Marc.

"Dion's a criminal. He must have tampered with Tayce's mind with his immense power force or she wouldn't do what she's doing to get him on board. There's no telling what's in that evil mind of his," said Marc, far from pleased.

"Information states the vessel he's no doubt been using has been on the Olarintz surface for more than four monthons and is in no fit state to fly, just exist on. It looks like this time he's simply rescued her and held her sheltered after the rescue," said Lance.

"I don't know – he's tricky. So what do you think?" asked Marc, interested to hear Lance's thoughts on whether they should give Dion a chance to explain his coming on board.

"If it was me, I'd keep an open mind on his arrival, hear him out. If he tries anything, have him sucked out through the airlock. You know Tayce – she's not going to like it if you don't hear his reason for coming aboard, even if you don't like the situation," replied Lance.

"Much appreciated, thanks. I'm going down to meet the Quest. As soon as they're back aboard, Kelly, get this cruiser out of our current orbit – just as soon as they land, just in case Dion has invited company to show up when he's on board," ordered Marc.

"You've got it," replied Kelly obligingly.

Marc walked from Organisation, ordering Twedor over his Wristlink to meet him by the Level Steps on Level 2. He then broke into a sprint, going down the Level Steps to Level 2, where Donaldo was coming along the corridor. Both men continued on down towards Level 3. Marc explained what had happened. Donaldo found the information surprising and agreed Tayce should be examined on arrival. Twedor was silent at Marc's side, but knew his mistress wouldn't bring Dion back aboard without a good reason. Marc checked his Pollomoss was fully charged in his side holster, just in case. Donaldo wondered if Marc was slightly overreacting, but then again the pirate leader was unpredictable – there was no telling what he'd try. They walked down on to Level 3 to head to the entrance of the Flight Hangar Bay.

***

Dairan flew the adapted Quest shuttle/fighter out of the planet's dense atmosphere and back into space. The atmosphere on board was strained and silent because of Dion's presence. Tayce was far from pleased. Fair enough, she herself knew what Dion had been; but if he was the old Dion, why didn't he leave her to die on the surface of Olarintz after the crash? Her mind ability was telling her to look deep into his true motives. She silently did so, and as she did he looked at her, but didn't fight her. He opened to what she wanted to read. Tayce found nothing other than what had happened in his past, and some of it was far from readable or endurable. Dion sighed, studying her with dark eyes, then, as she broke contact, he looked to the front for the rest of the journey. Aldonica glanced from one to the other discreetly, but said nothing.

***

Dairan flew the Quest back in through the open hangar-bay doors then slowly manoeuvred the controls to bring the shuttle/fighter in down on to the bay landing space. Marc, Twedor and Donaldo could be seen standing waiting. The Quest engines soon ceased. Dairan released the entrance hatch via the controls, from the front. Tayce released her safety harness and was first out of the Quest, followed by Dion, Aldonica and Dairan. As soon as Tayce set foot on the bay floor, Donaldo requested that she accompany him to the MLC. Much to his relief, she agreed without seeming suspicious. Tayce turned, ordering Aldonica to escort Dion to guest quarters. Aldonica nodded, but was on her guard as she suggested he follow her. The air could have been sliced with a Slazer knife, it was so silent. Marc stared at Dion mistrustfully as he walked past in the company of Aldonica. Tayce caught the mistrustful look, but she could understand his reasons, considering Dion's past. She walked away with Donaldo and Twedor, off to the MLC, leaving Marc and Dairan in silence until she'd gone.

***

An houron later Tayce was in a clean uniform and in the DC, having been given the all-clear by Donaldo. She was on the Satlelink relay link with her mother, discussing her father's disappearance and who she thought could be responsible for his abduction en route to Pellasun and why. Marc entered the DC and stood in silence. Lydia knew about the on-board guest. Even though she mistrusted the barbarian as much as the team did, if he was determined to put right his past and help in the safe rescue of her husband then so be it. She would put a good word in for him if he arrived at Enlopedia for a trial of his past misdemeanours. She would also compile a report describing how he helped in the rescue of the Admiral of the base.

"Well, life on this base must go on. I have a meeting to attend to in your father's absence. Must go," said Lydia, downhearted.

"Don't worry, Mother, we'll find him," assured Tayce.

She looked at Marc. She could tell he wanted to tell her she was an idiot for bringing the likes of Lord Dion on board and get his grievance out in the open. She ceased communication, waiting for him to start.

"Have we left Olarintz's orbit yet?" she asked, rising to her feet.

"Yes, heading on to another as we speak," snapped Marc abruptly.

"Marc, if you've got something to say, say it!" commanded Tayce. She didn't like his attitude – he'd looked like thunder ready to erupt ever since she'd arrived back on board.

"All right: what prompted you to bring that evil son of a bitch on board? You know what he's capable of," barked Marc, getting it off his chest.

"It's my decision, not yours. He's changed," replied Tayce to the point, almost shouting.

"Ha! You're the only one to think so. Criminals like him don't change; they make you think they have. How do you know right now down in those guest quarters he's not scheming some takeover of this cruiser, and that somewhere out there his men aren't just waiting around for his orders?" continued Marc, his eyes like fire and a face of pure anger to match.

"I don't have to justify my decision to bring Dion on board to you, Marc. Dion has agreed to help find Father, and that's all he's here for," retorted Tayce.

"As you say, it's your decision. I just hope you don't live to regret it," he said in an angry whisper.

"Dion has been trapped on Olarintz for more than four monthons with no means of communication. How is he supposed to contact his men, if they exist?" demanded Tayce, growing tired of Marc's attitude. It was time to clear the air.

"I still don't trust him, so don't ask me to work with him," replied Marc, calming down.

"Dion rescued me from my wrecked Quest. He didn't have to. I would have died in the thick gaseous atmosphere if he hadn't. He offered that if I got him off Olarintz he would help with a Quest. I began thinking about Father and told him what had happened and he agreed to help," explained Tayce, trying to remain calm.

"Are you mad! How do you know he wasn't the one to arrange such an act?" said Marc.

"That's enough. I won't tolerate this nasty vendetta you have against Dion any longer. So he's done things he's not proud of, but he saved my life and right now he has useful knowledge of many if not thousands of criminal groups, any of which might have abducted Father. You might not like the fact he's on board, but he's all we can hope for in digging deep to find Father safely. He's right at this moment with Twedor going through the kind of groups that would be interested in carrying out such an act, to trace their activity, hoping a match can be found for the flight path Father's Transpo Launch was taking," said Tayce plainly.

"OK, point taken, but it still doesn't stop me from wondering if he'll turn back to the evil side any time soon. I'll be keeping a close eye on him," said Marc.

"As you feel like this, for this particular Quest in finding Father I am hereby ordering you to your quarters off duty until we find him," said Tayce calmly.

Marc gave a surprised look. He could see she was serious and he knew she would also tell her father when he was found how he wouldn't cooperate. He had to think quickly on this. He respected Darius, and Darius had always treated him like the son he never had. The last thing he wanted was to have Darius look down on him because of his intolerance towards Dion. Tayce looked at him, waiting for him to say something. Her patience had run out. He decided to cooperate, exclaiming that he would help, but if Dion stepped out of line and reverted back to pirate leader he would not be held responsible for his actions against him. On this, Tayce agreed. He walked from the DC. Tayce sighed and headed out to join the others in the centre. Sometimes, she thought, Marc was hard to work with.

Dion walked in with Twedor. He looked at Tayce and together they returned to the DC. Everyone looked at him in uneasy wonderment as he passed through. Tayce crossed back to her desk and he followed with a printout on the group suspected of being responsible for Darius Traun's abduction. He set it down in front of her and stood back. Dairan sauntered in discreetly, making sure Tayce was all right after Marc's outburst. Dion wasn't fazed by the fact he was the most hated man on board right then. He was used to it. But he was there to help Tayce get Darius back, and that was all there was to it.

"This group only abduct high-ranked dignitaries," explained Dion, perching on one of the soffette arms.

"Why? Why my father? That's what I'd like to know. What's their purpose? I can see they could kill him, judging by this," replied Tayce, seriously studying the information.

"They extract any information that's important to anyone who wants to know and they sell it on the unauthorised market. The Chillerans lie in wait, attack in the blink of an eye – in and out and get what they want. That's their motto. They do it under an invisible shield. They've probably had someone acting undercover on Enlopedia, and when they heard information that your father was leaving for the new proposed second planetary base they followed and all hell broke loose."

"What's the worst they could do to him?" asked Dairan, at ease, listening.

"Extraction of the mind. In some people or beings it's been known to leave permanent mind absence. They no longer know who they are or what they are. They lose any recollection of life as that person or being once knew it. Some – sorry Fairness – are known to have been killed," explained Dion as gently as he could.

Tayce, on this, rose to her feet. Pushing passed Twedor, she ordered Dion to follow. He turned, walking behind her as she went across to Kelly. Kelly turned. She despised Dion for what happened in the past between them, but tried to do her best to lock it away in the back of her mind, putting on a brave face and adopting a calm approach to what Tayce wanted. But Dion looked at Kelly, reading her mind with his powers to see what she was keeping from him. Upon finding how she felt, for the first time in his galactic life he found himself understanding her hatred. Tayce quickly broke the look between the two and ordered Dion in a commanding tone to give Kelly the orbital bearings of the group's hideout, Crocosmia 2 – the quickest route. Dion glanced at Tayce. She was giving Dion a warning look, that if he stepped out of line he'd regret it.

"Careful, Fairness. Distrust can be a dangerous thing," he said close to her ear in a teasing whisper.

Dairan watched the exchange. He wondered if Marc's suspicions had some truth in them. Tayce left Marc in command. She wanted to talk with Professor Maylen regarding what could happen to her father and find out if there was anything he could do to help. Before leaving Organisation she discreetly warned Marc that if there was any trouble she'd get to find out, make no mistake. She asked him to try, if not for his position on Auran, then for her father, to refrain from any confrontation with Dion. With this she continued out of Organisation. Marc continued on with what he was doing at that moment.

***

Two hourons elapsed under the immense strain of having Dion, once pirate leader of the Boglayons, on board. Auran Amalthea Three was closing in on Crocosmia 2, home of the Chillerans, who had Tayce's father. Tayce had spoken with Adrien Maylen, who was willing to help in any way he could should her father have been the victim of a mind wipe when the Quest team found him. Tayce had picked the Quest team and, as it was more than an houron to the Quest, she decided to head to her quarters to relax. It had been a hell of an experience so far, and having Dion on board was no joke where the team, and particularly Marc, were concerned. She had had Nick Berenger put a screen communication through from her quarters via Satlelink relay link to Enlopedia. She began thinking as she went about what Dion had told her about simply having passage off Olarintz and being dropped off at the first available port after the Quest to find her father was achieved. But had he really changed in wanting to flip over to the good side? His approach to Kelly in Organisation earlier made her wonder if he had left his old ways behind him. Was Marc right – was it just a concealment of what really lay beneath to fool her of his true intentions? Later she was busy discussing with Jan Barnford about any chance that there might have been any reports of a new pirate group being formed under Dion's lead. She had to know, to put her mind at ease regarding whether he was in fact alone and genuine. Jan was speechless when he heard what had happened to her in the past twenty-five hourons or more, but warned her for her own sake regarding Dion to be extremely careful. He said he would look into her request in the meantime and get back to her as soon as he could. Tayce nodded, then ceased communications.

Quite suddenly she felt a presence in the Living Area behind her. She smiled as a soft warm breath blew on her neck, figuring it was Dairan off duty early and he was playing the silent teasing game. She relaxed, beginning to enjoy the sudden alluring closeness. His hands came around her middle from behind and he pulled her back against him. Totally thinking it was Dairan, she relaxed, giving in to the sensual warm pleasure of totally succumbing to the persuasiveness of the allure she was beginning to experience. Then he spoke, and much to her horror it wasn't Dairan, but Dion. Somehow he'd entered her quarters and was about to make her the object of warm powerful desire she couldn't escape from. Just like the first time they had met. She struggled in his warm strong grip. She didn't want this.

"Relax, Fairness. Stop struggling. You know you're enjoying this feeling – go with it," he whispered close to her ear, using his powerful powers of wanting and seduction, but in a gentle way.

"Get off me. Let me alone," she protested, pushing against his strong hold, but to no avail.

"You owe me. It's just been a matter of time before we would end up like this, and you know it," he continued in his old seductive whispering tones.

"I knew you couldn't change. You got what you wanted – your passage off Olarintz. I'm now beginning to wonder if I should have abandoned you there," she protested in an angry whisper, still fighting the strong unwanted feelings he was making her feel.

He quickly turned her to face him, and she spun roun, looking straight into his dark-brown pirate eyes. She had to admit what he was doing to her was pretty damn awkward to resist all over again, like their first encounter. But she had to at any cost. She broke his stare and looked away. She wanted none of what he was doing in using her mind, driving her on.

"Look at me, Fairness. No one need ever know of this moment," he continued, now looking deep into her telepathic sapphire-blue eyes as she looked back at him.

"I won't play your games. Let go of me," she persisted, pushing hard against him with both hands.

"Drop your defences. You know I'm more powerful than you could ever imagine," he replied in a voice that would crumble any woman's objections.

"You've tricked me into getting you here – you haven't changed at all."

She continued to push and hold him at bay.

"Give in to the powers of my mind and stop this. Don't spoil what could be beautiful between us. I hold the key to your father's safe return," he insisted whisperingly, not letting his grip loosen one bit.

Tayce wanted to cry out for help, but Dion sensed she wanted to and he couldn't allow it. He put a stop to it. Tayce felt her telepathic ability to fight him rise within. She tried to communicate with Phean. Again Dion blocked her. Why had she been so stupid as to trust him? she wondered. There was no way out of the situation. Without warning the entrance intercom/sounded. Dion quickly covered his tracks, erasing what had gone on between his and Tayce's minds, knowing one dayon they would continue this encounter uninterrupted. He erased what had just happened between them, just like it had never happened at all, replacing it with the thought that he'd simply visited her quarters to suggest he accompany the Quest team to Crocosmia 2 as he now had the layout of where the Chillerans could be keeping her father. Tayce wondered why she was so close to him and stepped away quickly. She ordered whoever it was to enter. The doors drew back. Dairan entered, asking why the doors had been locked, then looked at Dion with questioning wonderment, asking himself what he was doing present. Tayce looked at Dion, agreeing to his request and telling him that it was a good idea he go along. Dion, before pretending politely to leave, planted in Tayce's mind the thought that they would rekindle what they started sometime in the near future. When Dion was gone Tayce found herself baffled regarding what had just happened and what he'd said telepathically. But Dion had locked their close rendezvous in her mind, to trigger, like he'd said, sometime in the future. Dairan wondered why a smile of great amusement had crossed Dion's malicious features as he walked on out, like he'd done something no one would ever find out, that only he knew.

"We'll be arriving on Crocosmia 2 in roughly twenty minons," said Dairan.

"Fine! The sooner we can get this over, the sooner Dion can be off this cruiser," said Tayce, checking her Pollomoss handgun on the soffette.

Something Dairan found strange was that she'd always kept her gun close to her. Just what had really taken place between Tayce and Dion in their quarters? he wondered.

Tayce headed for the entrance. Pausing, she asked what was he waiting for. He shrugged his shoulders. He guessed he'd never find out and continued on out behind her.

Crocosmia 2 was like a silver-toned ball with spikes going out in all directions, covering a diameter of a milon in any one direction. Lights shone from the small square sight ports. It looked no particular threat to anyone in appearance, just like an ordinary space colony in a permanent orbit, there to serve passing travellers. It didn't look the least bit like it represented the abduction of Darius Traun. It had been discovered that there was a ring which ran round the inner centre. This was the weaponry ring, from which lasers of purple energy could be released simultaneously by on-board command against any enemy closing in. What Crocosmia 2 didn't know was that it was about to receive uninvited visitors: the Quest team.

***

In the Transpot Centre, Dion walked in, checking one of Auran Amalthea Three's Pollomoss hand Slazers. It wasn't what he was used to. He was used to something more sophisticated with a lot more clout. This was more in the toy class, but he guessed he'd have to get used to it. Tayce, Lance and Dairan entered the centre. Finally Aldonica, with her usual shoulder pouch of weaponry gadgets, walked in. Donaldo and Professor Maylen entered the centre and stood ready to help Darius Traun when he arrived back on board. The Quest members walked into the area for departure via Transpot. Twedor ran in and stopped just in front of Tayce. He was going this time, whether she liked it or not. Transpot activated. The Quest team and Dion were gone in cencrons to Crocosmia 2, and Donaldo and the Professor exchanged glances, as if to say, "OK, all we can do is wait."

***

Crocosmia 2 had a typical sterile environment – something the team were expecting on arrival. It was a businesslike atmosphere, mixed with utmost secrecy. The team and Dion began alertly searching for the Holding Area. Dairan walked unfortunately right through an invisible intruder beam, starting the alarms sounding – an ear-splitting whine. Before the team could move, they were surrounded by bald-headed beings, human in statue and appearance with purple eyes that had small black pupils, wearing military white all-in-one suits, brandishing flat disc-shaped weapons. Tayce looked around. Dion was gone.

There were ten beings surrounding the team, all aiming their weapons with intent on Tayce and the others.

"I'm Captain Traun and I'm here to take one of your prisoners. I want to see who is in charge here," demanded Tayce commandingly.

There came a reply, but it was incomprehensible gibberish, like a lot of childlings all talking at the same fast speed. Everyone looked at each other, wondering what had been said.

"What did he say – I'm assuming it's a he?" asked Dairan discreetly.

"Twedor, repeat what I've just asked and try and find a match for their language, please," ordered Tayce.

Twedor repeated Tayce's request once more and the same gibberish emitted from the beings. He recognised the language and answered, much to Tayce's and everyone else's surprise. The beings then lowered their guns and gestured for Tayce to accompany them, beginning to move away and splitting into two teams, some falling back around the Quest team as if protecting them. Tayce wondered just what Twedor had said. Whatever it was it seemed to be getting results. She and the others were being led along sterile cream corridors, through sections and up steps to other levels quite obligingly. Twedor was in discussion, but Tayce noticed he seemed to be putting on an astute attitude. She wondered if this was how these beings usually behaved. She knew she'd like to know what was being discussed. Finally Twedor turned, informing her that he'd informed the Chilleran guards that they were from the Intergalactic Criminal Court Colony Policing Division and if they did not cooperate they would investigate Crocosmia 2 for their conduct and the operation would be shut down. Tayce gave him a surprised look and silently hoped the real McCoy never got to find out they'd been impersonated. Sometimes Twedor surprised her.

They came to an area that was open-plan with floor-to-ceiling white heavy doors at the far end of the room. Tayce was suddenly suspicious. Dion, where was he? If that barbarian had run off he'd feel the wrath of her power to make him pay and she'd hand him over to the Enlopedian authorities. They walked on as the doors ahead opened back into the wall on either side. They entered a large official chamber. Inside, Dion and Tayce's father were waiting. But there seemed to be a glazed strange look in her father's eyes, as if he was in some kind of mind suspension. She'd seen it before. Twedor came to the side of her.

"What would you like me to ask?" asked Twedor.

"That we be allowed to take the Admiral and leave in peace," replied Tayce.

Twedor began addressing a very official-looking female in a slim white robe standing before them, making the request Tayce had asked him to make. Tayce was looking at Dion. He was somewhat amused about something, but what she couldn't read and she looked at the female Twedor was addressing. Lance, Aldonica and Dairan all stood with their hands resting on their Pollomoss guns in their holsters, in case they needed to act at a cencron's notice. Tayce felt slightly agitated about dealing with these Chillerans. She felt second-rate behind Twedor. Why couldn't they have had some kind of translator present? But it was a good job Tweedor was present and could put her questions across. It concerned her though just what he was saying to get her thoughts across.

The exquisite looking female with the same eyes as her guards (purple with a small central black pupil) looked at Tayce and beckoned her forward from the group. Dairan watched with alertness just in case this female tried any tricks to hurt Tayce. Considering Dion seemed to be on her side, he didn't like it. There was no telling what kind of deal might have been sneakily discussed behind closed doors, especially as Dion was talking discreetly with other Chillerans in their unusual dialect. 'What is unfolding here?' wondered Dairan. He was ready if action was needed.

The female leader before Tayce snapped her slender fingers at the nearest bald-headed aide. He walked towards her dressed like the rest of the race in a white suit. He handed her a small flat disc shape. She placed it against the side of her neck, then as it changed from red to blue, then to yellow and blended in with her olive skin, she began to speak in normal English even thought it was a bit disjointed.

"Your father's information will be most useful to us, Captain. Our people collect information throughout the galaxy and it is kept until needed," she began.

"The information you've gained is no doubt totally top secret. Why did you abduct him and kill two security officers belonging to our headquarters base?" demanded Tayce, trying her hardest not to sound angry.

"It is a result of taking high-ranking dignitaries. It is unfortunate it had to happen, but must be done in order that we can study information that is stored within the abducted being's mind, Your father's knowledge will be kept for future reference – if not for our race, for others in our master system for future retrieval, to be used to learn about the past of your home world," she announced politely.

"He doesn't look right. I've heard you take someone's mind and destroy it with your readings," said Tayce.

"I must apologise. Some of our subjects that we study put up a resistance against allowing us to do our study, and even though we mean no harm quite a lot of our past subjects have sadly died. Your father has a very strong constitution. He will return to normal health in approximately three hourons. You will need a medical being to watch him during this time," explained the leader.

"You might like doing this study, taking from people such as my Father, taking subjects at random as you so choose. Take some advice: not everyone comes willingly. What's more, if my father doesn't make a full recovery then our headquarters base will be sending out a task force to see to it that this scheme you're running will cease. Do I make myself clear?" asked Tayce in a no-nonsense way.

"I have noted your comments and advice, Captain. You are free to leave. Take this being called Dion with you, and if he visits this world again I will be forced to take action against him," replied the leader, looking at Dion with disgust.

Tayce could only deduce by the leader's angered look in Dion's direction that he'd tried his mind tricks on her, but to little avail. Nothing would have surprised her. Dairan and Lance walked on either side of Darius, guiding him carefully on out. Tayce grabbed Dion by the arm and ordered him to move with one hand on her handgun. He looked at the Chilleran female leader and gave an amused look that said it all, then walked on out of the chambers. Twedor walked with Tayce, glad this Quest had asked for his ability with languages. The doors closed behind the Quest team, Dion and Darius. Quite suddenly weapon fire erupted from the Chilleran guards. 'Damn that woman,' thought Dairan. She'd given the order to more or less not let them escape off Crocosmia 2 alive after Tayce's threat. He also wondered if this onslaught had something to do with Dion and the way he'd smirked upon leaving the chambers.

"Lance, call Kelly on Wristlink. Tell her to get us out of here now," ordered Tayce.

"You've got it," replied Lance, raising his Wristlink and doing as requested.

As the weapon firepower sailed back and forth, the Quest members, Dion and Twedor returned firepower to protect Darius Traun. In the moments that followed the Transpot engulfed the Quest team, Darius and Dion and they vanished in a swirling motion of energy out of the dangerous situation they'd suddenly found themselves in. The Chillerans' rapid fire soon ceased and the ones that weren't dead or injured went back to their duty, whilst the others were carried away to be treated or ejected into space.

***

On Auran Amalthea Three Donaldo Tysonne came forth as the Quest team, Darius and Dion materialised back aboard. Without warning, Darius passed out, collapsing, but Dion and Lance, who had hold of him, steadied him enough to get him to a Hover Trolley, which was in position for Darius to lie on. Donaldo pushed a button which brought the Hover Trolley back to a position to begin off out of the Transpot Centre. Professor Maylen went with Donaldo, secretly keying away on a scanner that would tell him what kind of brain activity Darius had after his mind treatment by the Chillerans. Tayce could see her father was in safe hands. Aldonica and Lance followed on out, going back to their duty. Dairan excused himself, leaving Tayce and Dion looking out of the Transpot Centre sight port at Crocosmia 2 getting further and further away. Tayce turned.

"Just what did you think you were playing at on Crocosmia 2? Isn't there any woman's mind you won't try and play your games on?" demanded Tayce, angrily looking at him.

"Why, Fairness, I sense you're jealous. She was rather fun, though. I have to keep a healthy mind above all else," he said with a cheeky grin.

"You disgust me, but apart from that what did you find on Crocosmia 2 apart from trying your tricks on the leader's mind?" asked Tayce. She figured as he wanted to turn over to the good side he'd tell her.

"That it's a base this Universe could do without," he offered sensibly, but he wasn't prepared to divulge any more.

But Tayce could read between the lines that what was going on on Crocosmia 2 was far from lawful and at present they were getting away with it. It was time to bring the base and its occupants to justice before someone else became their next unwilling target, the victim of the equivalent of a mind purge, for study.

"I feel they're disobeying the space law and committing two offences: abduction and unwilling mind purge. There's no telling how many other laws over the following yearons they'll break. It's time to bring them to a halt," decided Tayce.

"What are you going to do – destroy it?" asked Dion, seeing the thoughtful look on her face and realising that she was in two minds whether to or not.

"Do you have a better solution?" she asked to the point, much to Dion's surprise.

"Let me finish it for you. I know the exact location of strike that will assist your weaponry specialist's Digit Bombs. In ten cencrons they will wipe the Universe of any further Chilleran activity," he volunteered.

Tayce raised her Wristlink, activating it. Amal came on air. Tayce then ordered her to take one following command from Dion. She then held the Wristlink so Dion could give the command to match Aldonica's discreetly placed Digit Bombs placed earlier on the Crocrosmia 2 base. He took hold of her hand, glancing at her teasingly in his tantalising manner. She looked away as he continued on, voicing his command to unleash a succession of three Slazer cannon shots in the centre of the weaponry ring around Crocosmia 2 base. Tayce then pulled her hand free, deactivating her Wristlink. Firepower was unleashed as requested towards the Crocosmian base. As impact occurred a shock wave travelled back to Auran Amalthea Three. Tayce was thrown forward and not where she wanted to head. In order to stop her hurting herself, Dion took advantage, embracing her, using his full power of possession with little mindful effort. His powerful actions caught her off guard. She fell towards him, giving into his want for her for the first time.

With a snap of his fingers they were in Tayce's quarters. He made her look into his dark eyes and in a split cencron he'd put her under the full powerful influence of his sensual pleasurable force for the first time since the first voyage. In the moments that followed he drove her to the end of the Universe in the sensual powerful orgasmic forces he possessed, taking her almost to oblivion. He had at last won her against her objection not to succumb to his powerful mind. She was one sensual and telepathically charged woman in his eyes. He knew he could play and enjoy to achieve his ends as he had wanted to with her for some time. But she would always be special to him.

***

Dairan an houron later had been searching for Tayce. Her father had regained consciousness and was asking for her. Twedor did a scan of the cruiser and found her, much to the little Romid's horror, but he didn't say anything to give away what had happened before he'd found her. In no time Treketa was running down the Level 2 corridor, Medical Crisis Kit in hand, to meet Dairan on the Level 3 steps. They rendezvoused with each other and Twedor. As they approached, the quarters doors drew apart. As they did so, Tayce was found on the floor.

Treketa set down her Medical Crisis Kit. Opening it, she took out the medical Examscan, crossing as Dairan lifted Tayce up into a sitting position and held her in his arms.

"Twedor, who else has been here in the last hourons?" demanded Dairan.

"Dion has been the only one," replied Twedor, scanning for traces of who had been present.

"I don't know what went on here, but she's very weak. He must have used immense power force, according to these readings. Don't worry, she'll fight back and I'm going to give her an injection to help her," explained Treketa.

"God, why did she trust him?" said Dairan, shaking his head.

He was disgusted to think that Dion had taken them for fools and no doubt jumped cruiser. But then, perhaps it had been his plan all along. Marc had been right not to trust him. Dion had used them just to get back in space. Slowly, before him, Tayce began to regain consciousness, slowly coming back to normal as soon as Treketa had administered the injection to help her.

"Scan the cruiser. Find out if Dion's still on board. If so, I want a word with him," Dairan ordered Twedor.

After a few cencrons of scanning the whole cruiser, Twedor came back to say that Dion was nowhere to be found. He'd vanished, but where to? He'd surface again, and next time he was Dairan's to answer to. Next time too Dairan had a feeling Tayce was not going to tolerate him in her presence. Dion had lost any trust she had had for him.

***

So Darius Traun had been rescued; and as for the Chillerans and Crocosmia 2, they weren't going to cause anymore trouble. As for Dion, well, he had set out to do what was asked of him, but he had also got what he wanted from Tayce by making her surrender to his powerful force. If he returned to Enlopedia he knew what his fate would be and the outcome would be a termination of his life.

7. Forces and Reflections

Darius Traun felt his unscheduled visit to Auran Amalthea Three had been a somewhat short one. But there were urgent matters to attend to back on Enlopedia. The rescheduling of the meeting on Pellasun Traun 2 was one of his many important matters needing his constant attention. It had been four dayons since he'd been given emergency mind and medical treatment for what the Chillerans had done. Darius's mind had been locked in total suspension, which only tricky treatment by Professor Maylen and Donaldo working as a small team could cure. Tayce during this time had, as always, put her father's welfare before her own deep problem over her encounter with Dion. Sure enough, she'd recovered from his extreme sensual mind invasion, rendering her unconscious. But she was still left with restless night occurrences during her dream sequences, living the ordeal over again, plus he'd planted recurring pleasure sequences to appear when she least expected it to happen during sleep. With the greatest determination to hold them off, she'd fought hard not to succumb to those totally mind-blowing, strong sexual feelings, so much so, every night Dairan would have to wake her, greatly concerned. Darius, being her father, could see something was bothering her as they walked along the corridor to the awaiting SSWAT Transpo Launch, which had arrived from Enlopedia to take him back to base. He slipped his fatherly arm around her slim shoulders and gently prompted her to tell him what was hurting her so much, as she seemed silently preoccupied at times. He also told her Dairan was greatly concerned – enough to confide in Darius that he was worried about her.

"Come on, young lady, I've seen that look numerous times in the last couple of dayons, like your mind is somewhere else other than here. Tell me," prompted Darius gently.

"I can handle it. You've got urgent business waiting for you on Enlopedia," replied Tayce, almost snapping.

"Oh, you can? Then why is it Dairan is so worried about you? He said you've been moody and snapping at Twedor here and the rest of the team lately, as if something is greatly bothering you. And he also told me you've been having uneasy nights, to say the least. Also Marc backed up Dairan in being worried about you. Out with it," ordered Darius in a true fatherly tone to encourage Tayce to open up.

"All right, Father, if you must know, it's Dion," replied Tayce, reluctant to say anything.

"What's he done? He seemed a changed man on the Quest to rescue me, for which I'm grateful," said Darius, listening, surprised.

"No, it's OK. I'll work through the problem. You'll miss your Transpo Launch flight back to Enlopedia – the courier is waiting," said Tayce, wondering if she was doing right in telling her father what Dion had done.

"That can wait. I want to hear what this is all about before I leave, and I want to know now, young lady, so start talking," he said, getting stern with her.

He came to a pause and took hold of her gently by the shoulders, making her face him. Tayce looked down. Looking up, she found her father looking questioningly at her, waiting to hear what Dion had done. Tayce began as Twedor who had walked down with them paused and stood listening, hearing from his mistress why she had been like the leader from hell, rather than the calm pleasant and authoritative captain she generally was.

Tayce slowly began explaining what Dion had done, from the moment he'd rescued her, right through to his extreme sensual mind invasion and the recurring nightmare. How had she thought she could trust him and that he'd reverted back to his old ways? He'd fooled her, in other words.

Darius, upon hearing what Dion had done, shook his head. We all make mistakes, he thought, though he had told her time and time again not to trust the likes of the former Boglayon leader. Now she'd learnt her lesson the hard way. He reached out and brought her into a fatherly understanding hug, knowing in this instance it was something she was going to have to take care of in her own way. After a few minons Darius let Tayce go, informing her that if Dion showed up on Enlopedia he would be arrested on sight, pending trial. What he'd done had broken yet another law. Extreme sensual mind invasion was a severe crime and death was the penalty. They continued along the corridor towards the Docking-Bay doors. A female Enlopedian bodyguard/courier was standing on Auran Amalthea Three, waiting just inside the Docking-Bay doors to escort her Admiral aboard. She smiled pleasantly in greeting.

"Greetings, Admiral. Ready to return to Enlopedia?" asked the tall, pretty female brunette bodyguard/courier.

"Yes, let's get under way," replied Darius in his usual pleasant Admiral's tone.

Darius turned and, before leaving, pulled Tayce into his arms for a farewell hug. Then he held her slightly away, suggesting she never trust the likes of Lord Dion again, and advising her to tell Professor Maylen what Dion had left her with. He might be able to help. Tayce gave her father a look he'd seen numerous times before, conveying that she'd think about it. As her father, the Admiral of Enlopedia and the person in overall charge of her team, he quite firmly suggested she sort out her problem soon, before it took her over. Nothing would make the likes of Lord Dion so happy as if she messed up, he told her. She agreed with his stern words. Sometimes as old as she was, and despite who she was, when her father gave her an order she still felt she should see sense, but right up until that moment she hadn't. Tayce glanced at Twedor, then back at her father, meeting his concerned features. After a few minons he smiled, assuring her that everything would be back to normal soon, she'd see. he glanced at his Wristcall time display.

"Good luck, Father. I hope everything gets sorted out regarding Pellasun Traun 2."

"You take care too. You know I'm just a call away," he assured her.

"I will," replied Tayce.

She watched her father walk over to the Docking-Bay doors and pause. He turned as he reached them.

"By the way, I hope to see you at Enlopedia this coming Saturday," he announced.

"We'll be there, don't worry – and this cruiser," promised Tayce in a sincere way.

"I look forward to it. We like to see this cruiser in port, you know. It's not often we get her there. Everybody expects to see the marvellous graceful sight she is when she pulls into port. Twedor, you look after Tayce here," ordered Darius.

"I will, sir," replied Twedor obligingly.

Darius walked off on to the Transpo Launch. The young female bodyguard/courier walked on behind. The Docking-Bay doors soon drew closed, with the sound of compressed air, sealing father and daughter apart once more.

Tayce began on the walk along the second level corridor when without warning she vanished in the blink of an eye in a brilliant light. Twedor was startled for a few moments, as the brilliance of the flash knocked out his sight sensors. When they cleared, Tayce was nowhere to be found. Twedor immediately sounded the alarm and headed to Organisation as fast as his metlon legs would carry him. His mistress had been stolen and he had to find out who had done it.

***

Tayce arrived at her unexpected destination to find Phean Leavy also present. They were surrounded by a white fog, as far as the eye could see. It was like dry ice on a film set. They were somewhere in the Empire of Honitonia, she thought. But why had they been removed from Auran. Out of the vapour Emperor Honitonia walked towards them in his Telepathian-Realm uniform. What did he want? wondered Tayce. Didn't he like visiting her cruiser any more? Poor Twedor, he must have thought she'd been kidnapped again. But then, he would know what to do in the situation that had suddenly unfolded. Phean looked at Tayce. He was just as startled as she was to find himself in the Realm of Honitonia. The Emperor came to a pause before the pair of them quite calmly. Tayce braced herself for what was about to occur, or for what he had brought them to the Empire for. It was making her feel uneasy. He looked into her mind. The power was stronger than anything she'd ever encountered, Phean had to steady her. The Emperor examined every inch of thought and memory, knocking down the barriers Tayce tried to put up to stop him. She felt this was mind intrusion and she didn't like it. She fought until, like with Dion, she passed out. Phean caught her quickly, gently supporting her as the Emperor found what he was searching for: the nightmare scenario Dion had placed where he wanted it to be repeated. The Emperor raised his hand, holding it just above Tayce's delicate and beautiful face. A small purple energy ball appeared and he formed a claw-like grip with his hand around it. The ball grew and began to spin. He held it near to Tayce's forehead. With the smallest amount of effort, the purple glow entered Tayce until gone. Then within cencrons it reappeared, turning to a darker shade of energy. The Emperor guided it safely away from Tayce and crushed it to nothing. The nightmare scenario was over, involving Dion, or so he thought. He couldn't see anything else, but it was difficult to tell as Tayce had fought hard against what he was doing, unwilling to let him walk through her mind for the eradication of the dream sequences.

"Phean, you've been with Tayce as part of her team since the team's ambush. Has she used her higher mind defence power ability much at all?" asked the Emperor, surprised he'd found she hadn't.

"Only when fighting a being known as Lord Dion, but she doesn't have the idea she can make full use of her gift to sort the smallest of problems out, with little effort, sir," replied Phean.

The Emperor put his hand on his chiselled chin in thought. It seemed to him Tayce had suddenly lost all faith in using the pure potential of her ability. The Empire Higher Minds had been right: she needed to go in for a weekon of one-houron training to hone her skills.

"I'm hereby ordering you to do this training. Phean, no matter how much she protests, this must be achieved – do I make myself clear? She must be tested and made to realise she needs to use her ability more," ordered the Emperor.

"Yes, sir, absolutely," said Phean in a polite obeying tone.

The Emperor continued to explain that the one-weekon training to hone Tayce's gift had been set by the Higher Minds to see she was worthy of keeping her gift. The one-houron daily training would be mixed with her Amalthean Quest duties, starting from the present time for a test on the following Saturdayon, and he was not to let Tayce refuse it on any account. Phean's duty, even though he was a member of the Amalthea Quests team, was to the Empire as a whole. Phean agreed, but had a strong feeling this was not going to be easy. He knew Tayce could be adamant, but duty must take first priority. She began regaining consciousness. The Emperor had one bad point to make regarding Tayce's training and testing and it wasn't something he wanted to do. The Empire Higher Minds had decided if Tayce wasn't worthy and failed to reach the desired grade in a weekon, then she would be stripped of her gift, her mind would become like a normal thinking human's, Phean would be removed from her life and any connection with the Empire of Honitonia would be severed forever.

Tayce regained full consciousness. Phean helped her to her feet. The Emperor, when he could see she was fully awake, began explaining what was required of her, without letting her interrupt. He then warned Phean further: he had one weekon from the present point in time before the test and he was not to let anyone down. He looked at Tayce, pointing out that this meant her too. She would not only be letting herself down in failing what was set before her, but if Phean failed to help keep her powers he would be removed from Auran Amalthea Three forever, taken away from the career he had come to love and always wanted. Tayce could see both points. The Emperor was right – she didn't want to lose Phean. She thanked him for removing the nightmare scenario implanted by Lord Dion. He nodded with a smile, as much to say she was welcome. Then he placed both herself and Phean back on Auran Amalthea Three using the equivalent of the Transpot, only Honitonian-style, with extreme powerful force.

***

Marc turned in Organisation, pulling Dairan quickly out of the way as Tayce materialised back on board. They both looked at her in a somewhat surprised and questioning way, wondering where she'd been in the last houron since seeing her father leave the cruiser. Tayce, once fully materialised, noticed Phean wasn't back with her.

"Amal, scan the cruiser and find where Phean Leavy is please," ordered Tayce.

"Phean is in the Lab Garden Dome," announced Amal.

"I want a word in the DC," said Tayce to Marc and Dairan, heading on across Organisation to the DC.

Both agreed. Marc clapped Lance on the shoulder before walking away from his high-backed swivel chair at research, asking him to continue on with the Quest that was just materialising. Lance continued on, sifting information coming in in his usual way. Marc briskly headed across the centre to the DC's open doorway, following Dairan on in.

Professor Maylen entered Organisation. He paused on approach to Lance, who looked up questioningly, wondering if he could help.

"I want a brief word with Tayce, if she's in, only Admiral Traun contacted me on Satlelink and wondered if I could help with a small problem that had materialised," said Adrien.

"She's in, but having a discussion with Marc and Dairan about something. Go on in – there shouldn't be a problem," replied Lance.

"I'll wait if you don't mind?" put the Professor – he didn't want to appear intrusive.

Lance decided to explain what he was working on to help pass the time while Adrien waited.

***

In the DC Dairan was perched on the edge of the desk whilst Marc perched on the soffette arm ready to listen. Tayce began, saying that Emperor Honitonia had taken her to the Empire via the usual way and was sorry for making everyone worried when she'd suddenly vanished.

Twedor, who had followed Marc into the DC, suddenly spoke up: "She did a disappearing act on me," said Twedor.

Tayce patted him on the head in a gentle sorry gesture, saying how sorry she was but it couldn't be avoided. However, she began to explain what the Emperor wanted, and both Marc and Dairan listened. Tayce paced as she went through what she would have to endure for the next weekon on board, arranged around her duty, and telling them she needed their total cooperation to provide cover at times.

"You'll get it. Just tell us when you're going for the houron's training and either one of us will take command – right, Dairan?" asked Marc, glancing at Dairan questioningly, waiting.

"Sure, we want you to keep your abilities. We both know you'd be lost without them," replied Marc.

"Thanks, you two. It means a lot to have you say that. As you both know, my gift is my life. Without the many energy techniques that are going to honed, my life just wouldn't feel the same again. If I fail I shall find it very difficult to revert to being just an ordinary ex-inhabitant of Traun," expressed Tayce.

"Being an ordinary Traunian isn't so bad, you know," said Marc, knowing so, as he was one.

"It certainly comes in handy having the many abilities, though I think Donaldo gets a bit peeved when you get someone well without his medical intervention," said Dairan, amused.

"He's right," agreed Marc, smiling amused.

Tayce turned her attention to her father being told she had a problem, and she informed them that the problem had now been sorted and everything was back to normal, like it never happened. Dairan kept quiet and discreetly glanced at Marc. They knew what Tayce was on about – namely, the encounter with Dion. Marc began telling Tayce a Quest was materialising at present, to change the subject, and added that Lance was getting more and more incoming information as they spoke. Tayce advised him to make it official, should it look like it would be. She wanted all the information when it had finely been sifted, if it became official. Marc nodded, rising to his feet; then, before leaving, he checked to see if there was anything else. Tayce shook her head. The DC doors opened and Marc returned to duty. Dairan let them close behind him and rose to his feet. Crossing, he pulled Tayce into his arms gently.

"I was really worried about you when Twedor here said you'd vanished, when he ran into Organisation," he said softly, close to her ear.

"I never thought I'd end up where I did, in the Empire of Honitonia. It was weird," she replied lightly, feeling the secure warmth as he held her, which felt good.

"To be honest, I was beginning to think that maybe Dion or Vargon had made a galactic U-turn and come back for you," said Dairan, then he kissed her on the forehead.

"No, thank goodness! Now we've duty to take care of and a possible Quest. We'll continue later," promised Tayce, breaking away from him gently.

"Not so fast, Captain Traun. I might not be able to see you in the coming dayons with your extra training," he said, pulling her back to him.

"Dairan! We've got duty," protested Tayce, laughing as she tried to break free.

"I know," he replied, not letting it happen.

She gave into his wants and he began kissing her in a soft way, which made her respond. Quite suddenly the DC doors opened behind them and Professor Maylen entered. Upon realising he'd interrupted an intimate moment between them, he smiled and then looked out through the sight port, realising they hadn't obviously heard him enter the DC. He coughed. Tayce immediately broke away, apologising to Adrien. Dairan winked at her, then turned, heading on back out into Organisation. Adrien smiled, finding the whole moment quite amusing as on the way out Dairan looked back guiltily, having been caught.

"Sorry to spoil your little interlude," said Adrien light-heartedly.

"No, it's fine. How can I help?" asked Tayce, returning to her chair.

"I've received a call from your Father. He said he wondered if I could help. You seem to be having problems with a nightmare situation. I'm here if I can help – you only have to ask," he politely offered, like the true friend he'd become.

"Thank you, but the problem's been sorted now," assured Tayce kindly, thinking it had.

"That's good. There is one more thing I'd like to say: I'm enjoying being a part of this team," expressed Adrien, pleased he was one of Tayce's crew.

"It's an honour to have you with us. Stay as long as you like," replied Tayce, glad to hear he was happy being on her team.

"I see you and Dairan are as good as new after his mind-takeover problem?" he asked, pleased.

"Yes! It was a little shaky at first, but we're OK now," assured Tayce with a smile.

"Do you mind if I stick around for this Quest? It looks interesting, judging by what Lance is saying."

"Of course not. Who knows, we may need your help?" agreed Tayce.

Adrien smiled, then turned, going back out through the opening DC doors.

Tayce turned her seat to look out into the passing Universe in thought. One thought occupying her mind was what the test would be like in a weekon's time. She hoped it wasn't like the last one. She also realised it was her bornday in a weekon too. She hoped the two didn't collide. She'd hate to endure a test on her bornday. She guessed this was why her father said he wanted her on Enlopedia in a weekon – to share the special dayon with her. She thought over what kind of enduring tasks Phean would set before her. At least one thing was good regarding the test week: Dairan and Marc understood her predicament. Also the team would be accommodating to her plight. They were a good team, she thought.

***

Roughly an houron later, all information was in on the Quest that had been materialising by the minon. What had started out during the previous hourons as a small blip on the research scanner was now a small exploration craft with no engine power and low-level life support. Operations were on minimal too. The vital signs of one humanoid male on board were discovered to be weak – it seemed too far-fetched to think they might apply to a normal person. That was impossible to believe. Marc in Organisation ordered Lance to put up the vital-signs readings of the humanoid aboard the craft and transfer them through to Donaldo for him to run a medical vital-signs comparison check with a former member of the team, comparing the incoming data with the computer memory-bank profile for that person. Discretion was the word. Professor Maylen, who was present and interested to see what was going on, couldn't understand why all the hype and secrecy was necessary over one being. It puzzled him why the information when found should be kept under wraps. Marc turned, seeing him curious about what was unfolding regarding the craft's occupant. He discreetly left Lance's side and guided Adrien to one side and proceeded to explain what was what regarding the situation.

After a few minons the feedback came back from Donaldo in the MLC via computer link. It was a confirmed match with a former team member that both Lance and Marc knew well. Marc knew he had to find a way to gently break the news to Tayce – there was no telling how she was going to react to it. He was expecting the worst. One other piece of information intrigued Lance about the craft's occupant. There didn't seem to be any memory pattern from the brainwave activity report, and Lance drew Marc's immediate attention to the fact.

Marc ordered Kelly to increase speed to bring Auran within docking-procedure distance of the craft. Kelly nodded, carrying out the request in urgency. Marc turned to look out through the main sight port, wondering just how he was going to handle the rescue Quest. He had to protect Tayce at all costs from discovering the true identity of the craft's inhabitant. Then it came to him:

he could get Phean to request his first lesson with Tayce, honing her powers, at the same moment they brought the craft's inhabitant on board, and get him into the treatment area without Tayce being suspicious. He walked out into the Level 1 corridor, checking he was out of earshot of the rest of the team. He raised his Wristlink, contacting Phean with his proposal.

"Phean, it's Marc. When I give the word, schedule your first lesson for Tayce, to hone her powers. I know this is short notice, but I need you to keep her mind off what's going to unfold in the next houron," said Marc.

"Sure, of course. Problem?" asked Phean, but ready to do as Marc had requested.

"We have a situation regarding her past and we need to get things sorted before she faces what's happened," confided Marc in near-whisper.

"All right, I'll be standing by. I'll be in the Armed Combat Centre," agreed Phean, understanding what was happening. He could sense it was a situation that needed to be handed delicately.

"Great – speak to you soon," replied Marc, signing off.

Marc depressed the Wristlink Comceive and lowered his wrist before going back into Organisation. Adrien glanced at him questioningly as he walked in. He explained what he'd managed to do. Adrien listened, though he had a feeling it was a bit underhanded not to tell Tayce or they should at least break it to her gently. She'd be furious should she rumble what was unfolding, and there could be trouble for him, but he guessed Marc knew what he was doing, having known Tayce a lot of yearons and being her commander.

***

The mysterious craft was diamond-shaped. She covered a diameter of roughly half a milon. She was nothing too elaborate or to make a fuss over. In fact she looked like she had been dragged out of a galactic auction sale, purchased at the lowest bid. Mainly grey-and-white in colour, a decorative crimson stripe ran around the central part, like it was joining the upper diamond shape to the lower section. She drifted on no particular path, slowly turning this way and that. Auran Amalthea Three as she neared the craft's orbit looked overpowering, yet graceful beside the little craft. A name began to materialise in black lettering: **'ALENEA 2'**. Alenea 2 had no weapons aboard, which signified she was purely for exploration. But whoever this stranger was, he certainly had to have a death wish considering there were pirates and the likes roaming the Universe, always on the search for new targets to ambush for possible spoils, to fetch a good sum of currency. Auran manoeuvred into docking position.

***

Marc in Organisation gave the word to Phean via Wristlink discreetly. He waited a few cencrons to hear Tayce's Wristlink bleep in the DC, then he heard her say loudly, "What now?" Then he discreetly ordered Nick to have Donaldo meet him at the Docking-Bay doors in twenty minons. Nick nodded.

Tayce soon walked from the DC looking far from pleased. Marc turned, trying to look completely innocent, even though he knew what was going on. Tayce exclaimed that she had to go on her first test, she didn't know how long it would last and that it was a shame she couldn't be part of the materialising Quest. Phean had requested her presence in the Armed Combat Centre, and under the rules of Honitonia if she didn't attend these sessions it wouldn't look good when she came to the end test. With this, she walked from Organisation. Marc waited until she'd gone. Twedor followed her down the corridor – he was instructed to help keep her away from what was going to materialise.

Marc went into action. He turned, ordering Kelly to dock Auran Amalthea Three with the craft before them and make it as smooth as possible. Dairan crossed, awaiting his orders. Marc turned, suggesting he stay in command and if Tayce asked anything about the Quest, when she came back from the first training session, to tell her anything other than the obvious. Dairan totally understood, thinking about what he'd said. Marc ordered Craig to accompany him and to bring his Tech Kit. He then turned to Lance, calling him also as he'd done all the research on the craft and her mysterious inhabitant. Dairan turned his attention to the main sight port and watched the approaching craft as Auran neared to dock at a slow speed.

***

Tayce stepped down on to Level 5, wondering to herself what the first training session would entail and thinking that next time she'd like more notice when she needed to attend. After all, she could have been in the middle of an important planetary visit. She headed along in thoughtful silence. Twedor, beside her, was in his own way trying to understand his mistress's apprehension about what lay ahead during the honing session. He could pick up in her vital signs that she was apprehensive, to say the least. He couldn't understand it, considering she was undertaking the honing to keep something that was special to her. She turned the corridor corner and was soon entering through parting doors, leading into the Armed Combat Centre. She walked up the narrow shiny-floored corridor with Twedor following silently just behind. They reached the entrance to the Armed Combat Centre. Tayce took a deep breath and readied herself for what might be expected of her within. Twedor was looking up as she looked down, readying herself.

"You'll do this, Tayce," offered Twedor encouragingly.

The doors drew apart. Phean stood waiting. He was looking out of the sight port and turned to face her with a gentle caring smile of reassurance. He picked up her feelings of fear of the unknown. She had a lot to achieve in the coming weekon if she was to hold on to her abilities. He walked towards her, and as he did so he explained that, just because he was to be her trainer during this weekon, he was by no means going to lecture her; it was not his style. He was her friend and guide as normal. His duty was to make her use her powers to the best of her ability and find out what was holding her back and nurture them. Without warning he entered her mind, shielding his own Honitonian secret that could not be divulged at any cost. It was forbidden. He began searching for past occurrences and situations where she'd wanted to use her powers and been afraid of the consequences if she did. He found the wrongful encounter with Dion, where she'd been left unconscious in her quarters. This was something Phean found strange, as he had thought it had been removed by the Emperor on their last encounter. Tayce shut him out quickly, surprised he'd found it, breaking contact.

"No, not that memory," she snapped, surprised it was still present as, like Phean, she'd thought the Emperor had taken it away in their last meeting.

"Trust me – I'm not here to harm you. I need to find out why it didn't leave you, so I can help. I won't let anything happen. If I feel it's becoming too painful I will break the contact at the point where you're not happy to continue," he said softly to her in a reassuring manner.

"I can't relive that memory – sorry – at any cost," replied Tayce, turning away from him in the centre, realising all the Emperor must have done was lock the last encounter with Dion away in the deepest part of her mind.

"Tayce, I have to cover all ground to find the root of your apprehension to go further with your powers. You can do this – please trust me," said Phean, trying his utmost to persuade her.

"All right, but you promise you won't make me live that memory again?" she replied, scared to endure the situation all over again.

"I promise," he said in a sincere way. He could see his task wasn't going to be easy.

Twedor watched on. He could see his mistress was going through the equivalent of hell, having to endure situations she'd rather forget and had hoped had gone forever. But he could see Phean's point: he couldn't help her if she didn't help him. Phean entered her mind once more, gently. Soon the memory of the full-on unwilling powerful encounter with Dion flooded back into Tayce's immediate thoughts. How he'd made her feel. Phean appeared beside her in the sequence as if in a flash, so he could see what needed to be done to help her push her powers to their fullest potential. He was able to read why she wasn't fighting back the onslaught of extreme sensuality Dion was making her feel. How the powerful lord had brought down her defences one by one.

"Rid your mind of all unnecessary outside thoughts and influences. Focus on this situation that's before you now. Concentrate and keep thinking this is just a memory, it's not real. Now take the situation in hand. Let your powers grow to make his presence decrease and push the memory away for good. Don't stray. Stay with the point of dispersing this memory – keep going until it's gone," ordered Phean in a guiding way.

Tayce listened to Phean's gentle prompts and commands and found her confidence growing. The pupils of her eyes lit up with the Telepathian bright blue force as she took control and expanded with her powers. She felt pleased with what she was achieving – something she had been afraid to attempt before, but was now finding increasingly easy. Phean calmed her, teaching her the highest degree of control over the memory situation. He studied her in a caring way as she calmed back to normality and her eyes returned to their normal sapphire blue. She'd done well, he thought, for a first session. She'd accomplished the power of dispersal of unwanted memories.

"You've just taken the first step forward in fighting and controlling a situation – previously something you were afraid to accomplish. Well done. I saw what your problem was. Tricara taught you some things, but not how to take the situation in hand powerfully and turn it to your advantage, for termination," explained Phean.

"I've always been afraid to do what I've just done around the team, in case they found it strange and lost faith in me being captain. I shrank from attempting such a situation. I guess it made me feel the way I did," confided Tayce.

"I understand, but don't Marc and Dairan know you possess this gift? All you have to do is forget everything around you, like you just have, and focus on what is right before you. In time the team won't notice what you're doing is strange. I'm going to, over the next couple of dayons, teach you new things you'll be able to do with your ability – things you never thought possible," said Phean.

Then he saw the look of apprehension creep back into Tayce's face.

"Sorry – some of this is new to me. We need to take it slowly," said Tayce, sounding apprehensive.

"No problem," replied Phean in an understanding tone.

Tayce realised Phean was going to give her the confidence she lacked. Maybe this weekon wasn't going to be bad after all. They both crossed and sat down on the training bench and began talking about her Telepathian abilities and how she'd discovered she was gifted, plus why the memory of Dion hadn't entirely vanished for good. Phean then told her what they would be trying in the dayons ahead. After a while he suggested they try some more training, and they crossed back to the training protection mats in the middle of the vast centre.

***

Marc and Donaldo paused at the Docking-Bay doors on Level 2. Alenea 2 had docked with Auran Amalthea Three successfully. The doors, on Amal's clearance, slid open, revealing the entrance hatch of Alenea 2. Craig waited for Marc's orders to get the craft open. Marc gestured for him to go ahead. Donaldo stood, new Medical Crisis Kit in hand, Hover Trolley nearby set in a position ready to take the occupant back to the MLC for possible treatment. Craig attached a small, slim, square device to the main mechanism panel and activated it. A sequence of flashing multicoloured lights began in a sequence one behind the other, then the sequence all turned green to signify the hatch was unlocked. After a few cencrons the entrance began opening, parting top from bottom and retracted up and down into the Alenea 2 hull. A tepid atmosphere wafted out to meet them. Marc waited until Lance had checked that his readings on his hand-held scanner were all clear to proceed, then they went forth cautiously. Marc, having known this original team member, felt strange, knowing the vital signs they'd detected on board were ones that matched those of someone he once classed as a friend. Marc realised it would be like coming face-to-face with the clone of his old friend. He braced himself as they ventured into the pilot area in the untidy interior of Alenea 2. Rounding the corner, Marc's heart almost skipped a beat as he came face-to-face with a sight he thought he'd never see again, reminding him of his Amalthean Quests One past. 'God,' he thought, 'this is damn weird and eerie!' Every inch and build of the humanoid seated before him, right down to the trademark moustache, was plain to see.

"This can't be happening – he's dead," said Marc, in shock, without thought.

"Let's get him to the MLC," said Donaldo, remembering also whom this humanoid resembled, but putting the fact aside and taking the situation in hand. The humanoid needed medical attention urgently.

Lance, also having known the original team member this humanoid resembled, looked at Marc, finding it hard to believe the resemblance too. Donaldo confirmed that this particular male was showing signs of being a clone of the original. He didn't know how at the present time, but the Examscan had confirmed as much. It was hard to believe this human male was an exact replica in every particular of the original team member that had perished back in the first voyage. Marc just couldn't stop staring in disbelief as Lance and Donaldo carefully lifted the unconscious male on to the Hover Trolley then placed the heat-sealant blanket over him. He continued to watch on in amazement as Lance handed the ID wallet to him. He flicked it open. The identification stated the name 'JOSHUA LANDORZ'. It was hard to believe this was the name of the unconscious being before them. Donaldo hurried away up the corridor to the MLC. Lance shook his head in total disbelief, wondering what Tayce would say when she discovered the truth of what was happening. Marc suggested he find out, from the Alenea 2 computer, the reason for the present course Joshua Landorz was on.

"Study every inch of the travel journal and see what information can be gained – what makes this Joshua tick."

Lance nodded in total understanding.

Marc left Craig and Lance to it, heading on after Donaldo.

***

An houron passed. Tayce and Phean walked from the Armed Combat Centre with Twedor. Tayce was feeling pleased her first training session with Phean had been a success. In a way she had regained her confidence in using her mind to fight the likes of Dion, should he decide to return. Plus she'd now learnt to make Twedor become invisible in an aura and could communicate with him via her mind. Twedor was silent beside her. He was still feeling the effects of being used as her training tool. They all began on up the Level 5 corridor, discussing what had been achieved further. Through the sight port as they turned the corridor corner Tayce caught sight of the Quest-orientated craft Alenea 2. Phean acted as if it was the first time he knew anything about it and joined her in crossing to the sight port. Tayce could see the craft was docked with them and gave a taken aback look, wondering why she hadn't been informed. Phean glanced at her, wondering how he was going to take her mind off the fact they had seen the very thing Marc had wanted her to be shielded against. Tayce walked away from the sight port, wanting to know what was happening. Why hadn't she been informed they had a Quest rescue under way? Phean sensed her growing anger and followed her with Twedor. There was no stopping Tayce when she was determined to find out what was going on. They soon reached the Level Steps, which Tayce ran up in urgency. Phean followed, reading Tayce's thoughts about Marc. Phean had a feeling the cover-up of the identity of the on-board guest was not going to work. They reached Level 1. Tayce ran along and into Organisation, wanting answers.

Dairan turned, surprised to see her, and pretended quickly nothing out of the ordinary was going on except that they'd just rescued an injured pilot.

"Why didn't someone inform me of what's going on, considering the craft is docked with this cruiser? What's happening so far? Is the pilot alive?" asked Tayce abruptly, far from pleased at being kept in the dark.

"Marc is in the MLC. He says he'll let us have the report on the pilot's condition as soon as Donaldo has thoroughly examined him."

"Alien or human?" demanded Tayce plainly.

"Humanoid – that's all I know at the moment," replied Dairan, pretending he didn't know any more.

Phean glanced at Dairan. He considered he was doing a good cover-up, but he could see Tayce was not the kind of woman to be fooled easily. With every question she asked about the Quest, Dairan did his best to steer well clear of the fact that their on-board guest was a clone of the late Tom Stavard, Tayce's legal intimate partner. Dairan found it hard to lie to Tayce, but it couldn't be helped. He had a feeling there would be a backlash from the fact, when she found out. Lance – of all the moments! – walked into Organisation carrying the disk chips from Alenea 2 and went straight to his research console, followed by Craig carrying his Tech Kit across to his console, not saying anything although Tayce was looking at them both questioningly. She felt a nagging feeling something wasn't right and she was being shut out of what was happening for a reason.

'What is going on here?' she wondered.

She crossed to Lance, trying to see what he was doing – loading some kind of information nervously and discreetly so she didn't see it.

Dairan quickly thought of a way to get rid of Tayce out of the centre until the time was right and Marc could explain what was what. 'Sallen!' he thought. He quickly walked away cautiously into the DC, raising his Wristlink and calling Sallen in the Lab Garden Dome. He knew that earlier she'd said she wanted to see Tayce. Sallen soon answered and agreed upon listening to why Dairan needed her help. Dairan exited the DC when the call was through. He was glad to see Tayce hadn't even noticed he'd left the centre for a minon.

"Sallen said she wanted to see you down in the Lab Garden Dome," spoke up Dairan on approach to her.

"Now? Why, is there a problem?" asked Tayce in surprise. She thought everything was going fine.

"Haven't a clue, only she wants to see you," replied Dairan.

"All right, but I want to find out about this Quest just as soon as Marc returns. At the present I feel as if you and the rest here are keeping something from me. I'm not stupid, Dairan," she said, discreetly giving him a look that conveyed as much as she passed on the way to the entrance.

She walked from Organisation, not looking back. She felt slightly angered to think the team were hiding something from her. If they didn't start telling her soon, she would take matters into her own hands and start doing her own investigation into who the craft's occupant was.

"Prevaricator," said Twedor, looking up at Dairan, then he hurried on out after his mistress, far from impressed.

"What did he just say? What did he just call me?" asked Dairan, not catching what Twedor had called him.

"It means someone who gives false or evasive information, and you're doing well at that," said Kelly over her shoulder.

"Great! Now he's got it in for me. You know the situation – it's difficult," expressed Dairan, feeling slightly angered.

"Marc should have come clean – she's going to find out eventually anyway," said Kelly.

"I know she will, but we're trying to break it to Tayce gently," said Dairan, knowing as much.

Kelly was right, thought Dairan. Marc had put him in an awkward situation he didn't want to be dragged into in the first place. He didn't like it. He turned to watch the information Lance was studying on screen. He felt a little less uptight since Tayce had left the centre.

***

He was laid out on the medical bunk. Donaldo was puzzled by the readings he was receiving from Joshua Landorz on the overseer and Examscan. He had brain activity, but it was like the lights were on and no one was home in memories that would have been the original team member's memories. The doors behind Donaldo opened and Adrien walked in, looking at him questioningly, asking what could he do to help? Donaldo showed him the readings proving there was brain activity, but that was all. He was hoping he could use his expertise to discover whether this was the real thing somehow, or a clone of the original recognised member of Amalthea One reproduced in some strange way. Adrien, on this, crossed to the newly installed Memory Probe Portable Computer. He took hold of the pads and crossed back. He placed them on Joshua's forehead, where the memories and everything about him could be read and played back as images on the screen, to confirm whether it was the original team member, long since thought dead, or a clone. Adrien picked up the hand-held slim panel and activated the sequence with a keyed-in command which would gain them all the knowledge they wanted. Both stood watching the screen where they hoped past memories would appear. But nothing. Joshua Landorz had had what was the equivalent of a total mind wipe. Everything his ID had stated, including that he was in his mid forties, was all they had. Where memories of a normal existence should have been there was nothing but blankness, causing the screen to be blank and the message to flash up **'MEMORY VOID'**. Adrien checked for any trace of whether memories had been present and removed, then came back. There was a trace; but when they were wiped wasn't long ago and it hadn't been carried out in an easy way, judging by what he could see. It could be seen that they were removed during some kind of force wipe. Marc listened and shook his head in utter disbelief – what some criminals would do to get their galactic kicks! But that was 2422 and crime seemed to be on the increase. Every minon in the last six monthons new criminal bands were rising up out of nowhere.

Behind them the MLC doors opened. Marc turned to see what he hoped he wouldn't see: Tayce walking in. Donaldo quickly covered Joshua's features with the heat-sealant blanket. Marc walked towards Tayce. Upon reaching her, he quickly grabbed her by the arm and suggested a quiet word out in the corridor, guiding her back out through the MLC's open entrance doors. Tayce didn't like the rough way in which he'd grabbed her, and once outside she pulled her arm free with a displeased look on her face to match.

"What the hell's going on, Marc? What is it you don't want me to see in there? As Captain of this cruiser I have a right to know," said Tayce angrily.

"Take it easy. Sorry if I hurt you – it's just I'd rather break this to you before you see what's in there," he began trying to calm her.

Tayce folded her arms and gave a look of 'Let's hear it – I'm listening'.

He began explaining as calmly as he could with gentleness that the occupant of Alenea 2 would come as somewhat of a shock to her if she saw him without being prepared first. Tayce listened, gradually losing her sulky look. Then came the words that shocked her to the core.

"The occupant of Alenea 2 is a clone of Tom, in every striking resemblance."

Without thought of what she was doing, and in shock, she slapped Marc across the face hard. Marc for a few minons winced at her uncontrollable strike, but put it down to stunned and hurt shock. Tayce looked at him, not knowing quite what to say she was so stunned at his words. He suggested she let him accompany her in to see this clone of Tom.

The doors drew apart and Marc led the way, apologising for keeping her in the dark, and explaining that nobody was quite sure how she was going to take it. Now, he said, she would understand why he had sworn Dairan to secrecy – he'd done it to protect her. Joshua, to everyone's surprise, was awake and sitting up. He looked across the MLC with a motionless look in his eyes. Both Donaldo and Adrien looked at Marc, wondering if he was doing the right thing in letting Tayce see Joshua. Marc silently voiced that it was OK, he'd told Tayce. Marc left Tayce to walk on alone. She continued, finding it near impossible to forget all the past memories of the man she first loved and lost. They flashed into her mind once more. Adrien stood in discreet discussion with Marc, whilst Donaldo watched Joshua with Tayce.

"I'm Captain Tayce Traun. You're on the Auran Amalthea Three. You're quite safe. Welcome aboard. I can't ask you where you're from for obvious reasons. We rescued you. My doctor here will take good care of you. You've nothing to fear. We are going to do everything we can to help you where we can," said Tayce softly, finding it difficult to talk to a man that in appearance resembled the man she once loved and thought gone forever.

"I wish I knew who I was Captain," replied Joshua as if Tom himself was talking to her.

The sound of Joshua's voice was like being hit by a force from the blue. He sounded like the real thing. Tayce felt a feeling rushing through her that was making it hard to stand on her feet, she was so near to fainting. She turned and walked back across to Donaldo, finding it strange beyond belief what she was enduring.

Adrien was coming up with an idea. Every space traveller carried an ID wallet, and the disk chip held within contained entire memories up until the moment the named person left port for the first time and the information was recorded via the vessel's medical computer. If this Joshua Landorz had his disk chip in his wallet, or on board Alenea 2, then it would be a simple case of putting back what had been removed to a certain degree. Upon listening, Tayce suggested Adrien go ahead and do what he had to. Twedor, who had been with Tayce all the way through, was standing staring at this Joshua Landorz, trying to sift through his

Plasmatronic brain to discover why Tom Stavard didn't speak to him. As in the first voyage he had been the main operations and guidance computer, it didn't occur to Twedor that Joshua hadn't any memories or that this could be a clone of the real Tom. Tayce walked towards him, guiding him on out by his small Romid shoulders. The doors opened and they passed through out into the corridor in silence. As the doors drew shut behind them, and they walked off to find Treketa, Twedor looked up, seeing the near-to-tears look on Tayce's face.

"It must be hard for you – he looks just like Tom," confided Twedor understandingly.

"Yes, very. It was like looking at a mindless version of him. It gave me the creeps, to be honest," confided Tayce as they went. She'd always been able to be open with Twedor, right back since the first dayon they met.

"If you don't mind me asking this, did you think Tom had returned from the dead?" put Twedor.

"No, because I know Tom was killed on the first voyage," said Tayce sorrowfully.

"This has to be the weirdest situation I have ever witnessed," said Twedor, shaking his metlon head.

"That isn't Tom back there. I would know him if he'd come back by some means," replied Tayce.

"You'd think they would have given him some memories. He looks weird," said Twedor.

"Twedor, that's enough. Mr Landorz can't help the way he appears," replied Tayce, hearing enough.

They both stepped down on to Level 3. Tayce was wondering how Treketa was going to take the news she had to deliver. They walked along to Treketa and Donaldo's quarters. Tayce paused upon arrival at the entrance doors, knowing what she had to say wasn't going to be easy. She pressed the intercom system. A few minons passed and the doors drew apart. Treketa stood wondering why Tayce was suddenly visiting.

"Can I come in? I've something I need to tell you – it's important," began Tayce.

"Sure! What is it?" asked Treketa, concerned that Tayce was so pale. "You look terrible."

"Did you find it strange Donaldo put you off going on duty suddenly?" asked Tayce, entering the quarters.

"Yes, I did. The way he suddenly suggested I take time out didn't seem right. Why?" replied Treketa.

"I think you'll need to sit down for what I'm about to tell you," said Tayce slowly as Twedor listened.

Treketa did as asked, wondering what Tayce was going to say. It looked serious. Was it something to do with her duty? No sooner had she seated herself on the nearest mouldable chair than Tayce began.

"I've come to tell you some news that less than half ąn houron ago Marc was slapped for, and I figured you would probably want to do the same to Donaldo when you found out, so I thought it would be better coming from me."

"You hit Marc? Tayce!" said Treketa, trying not to laugh.

"I did, but it was shock, believe me. Anyway, the craft that's currently docked with us had a humanoid male clone on board. We have him currently in the MLC. And before you think about rushing to help Donaldo I wanted to be the one to tell you what you should be prepared for," began Tayce, wondering if the shock revelation would be too much to take, as she herself was still coming to terms with what had unfolded. She readied herself.

"What? Tell me – what is it?" asked Treketa, noticing Tayce finding what she had to say awkward.

"His name is Joshua Landorz, but he's identical in every way to… Tom… our Tom."

"Are you serious? A clone! How did they do it? This takes some getting used to. How?" asked Treketa, almost speechless, feeling the full force of the shock.

"I don't know, but somehow, somewhere someone managed to get hold of Tom's DNA," replied Tayce.

"I want to see him," said Treketa, wanting to see for herself what Tayce was saying about the resemblance to her once much loved brother.

"I'll contact Donaldo, let him know you're coming. There is something you need to know though," expressed Tayce.

"What?" asked Treketa, still shocked.

"He's under medical and mind treatment, supervised by Donaldo and Adrien. He has no memories of his past at present."

"Why?" she asked curiously, interested.

"They seem to have been wiped by force, probably by the lot that attacked his craft. Whoever did it erased everything," said Tayce carefully. She could see Treketa trying to come to terms with what was being said.

"In a way it must be terrible for him, walking around resembling a dead person and not knowing who he is," said Treketa, forgetting the fact that Joshua was a clone of her brother and feeling sorry for him.

"Are you sure you want to do this?" asked Tayce, reading Treketa's thoughts and finding they were on Tom.

"Yes! I'm going to see him eventually."

Tayce, on this, raised her Wristlink, contacting Donaldo. Upon him answering, she explained that Treketa had been told and wanted to visit the MLC. After a few minons silence, Donaldo agreed apprehensively, wondering if Treketa was doing right. He ceased communications. Tayce checked with Treketa again. She felt all right to meet Tom's clone, Joshua. Upon her nodding, Tayce decided to leave her to go on alone. The doors to the quarters opened as Tayce approached them. She turned as Treketa assured her she would be fine. With this, Tayce continued on out, slightly concerned Treketa was wanting to see Joshua/Tom so soon after receiving the shocking news. Marc met her as she reached Level 2. Both looked at each other, wondering what to say, considering she'd given him a hefty slap earlier.

"I guess I owe you an apology. I didn't mean to hit you quite so hard – it was shock," said Tayce.

"Forget it. It was purely reaction, but next time a little lighter, please. It still smarts," said Marc teasingly.

Both laughed, enjoying the moment. Marc then reminded her of the reason he'd done what he had, hiding the information on the Quest. He knew how much deep down Tom had meant to her and he didn't want it to make her feel like her whole world had just fallen down around her again, as it might have if he'd just come straight out with it hurtfully.

"Thank you and sorry again," said Tayce softly, appreciating the fact.

They hugged each other in a friendly way, then both walked on to Level 1, Marc asking how her first training session with Phean had gone.

***

In the next four dayons Tayce, amongst her ordinary duties, made regular visits to learn more from the training sessions under Phean's guidance, going through past situations ready for the test which unfortunately would take place on her thirtieth bornday. Borndays weren't like past-century birthdays, where thirteenth, eighteenth, twenty-first and fortieth birthdays were particularly well celebrated; if a bornday had a zero in it, then it was celebrated more than others. Tayce wasn't relishing the fact that the unexpected might befall her on this special bornday, especially as she could lose her powers and Phean on the same dayon if she failed. But, despite it all, she was learning new skills she could use during the present voyage if she still had them after the confrontation test, with Emperor Honitonia and the Higher Minds of the Empire watching on. Joshua Landorz was scheduled to go straight into the Complex for Mind Study, Health and Neurology on Enlopedia for treatment to put back his memories from the disk chip. It was strange to think someone so like Tom Stavard, Tayce's dead husband and Treketa's much loved brother, was on board Auran Amalthea Three. There was a certain mysterious air about Joshua, that Tom once possessed. Treketa had guided him for strolls around the cruiser – not that any of it registered, but, like Treketa had said, it gave Joshua the exercise he needed to keep him mobile. Tayce was glad in a way that the likeness to her brother had been quickly adjusted to by Treketa. As he came towards both herself and Marc it was like looking at a vacant version of Tom. There was no recognition, only blankness. Tayce found she couldn't bring herself to hold a conversation with him and let him pass in the company of Treketa in silence. It was horrible, she thought.

Auran Amalthea Three on Saturdayon began the last houron's journey to Enlopedia. It was 08:35 in the mornet.

Tayce woke slowly to the words from Dairan; "Happy bornday," he said in a whisper.

She opened her eyes, looking up into his warm brown ones looking down at her. She didn't know why, but at that moment she began thinking that if Tom hadn't been killed at the end of the first voyage she would have been waking up beside him with the same soft bornday words. Dairan smiled, wondering what she was thinking. Tayce was glad he was there. He loved her just as much, if not more, than Tom had. Tom loved her in his own special way when he was alive, but somehow this love was a lot different, more strong, between her and Dairan than it had been between her and Tom. He leant over and softly kissed her on the lips. Her Wristlink sounded on the bunk-side top, breaking herself and Dairan apart.

"Here!" said Dairan, reaching over for her Wristlink and handing it to her.

"Thanks!" she replied, taking it from him.

She pressed Comceive. Nick came on the air. He exclaimed that they had an urgent problem and asked could she go to the Refreshment Centre immediately? Tayce slid out of the bunk, exclaiming that she'd be there soon. She said she needed to cleanse and change first and that Marc would have to take charge of the situation until she arrived. Nick agreed. Tayce crossed to the Cleanse Unit in her full-length grey silkene chemise, wondering what was so urgent. Dairan smiled to himself at the appealing slim shape of Tayce as she walked away, then thought to himself that he was glad this Joshua Landorz hadn't affected her enough to put a halt on their relationship.

In the Refreshment Centre the whole of the Quests team were gathered in honour of Tayce's special dayon. Presents to Tayce were piled on the table. Nick kept watch so they could surprise Tayce when she arrived. It had all been a cover-up. There was a problem in the present surroundings: Amal was left in overall charge of Auran Amalthea Three as she headed to Enlopedia. Everyone present felt at a loss, waiting for Tayce's arrival. Time passed and she could be heard walking up the corridor with Twedor. Dairan had slipped back to his own quarters to cleanse, change and pick up his gift and was already present. Tayce rounded the corner, wondering what she was about to find.

Everyone yelled quite unexpectedly, "Surprise! Happy bornday!"

There was a lot of laughing as Tayce was truly shocked and surprised at what they had done for her special dayon. She felt overwhelmed by the moment and the generosity of her team around her. Dairan picked up a glassene of a mixture of citrus juice and Stavern. Crossing, he suggested everyone raise a toast.

"Tayce, this bornday is a special one and you're special to all of us in some way. Happy bornday. May your cruising in the stars go on forever," said Dairan.

Tayce smiled and was hugged gently in turn by each of the team. Dairan, after sipping his drink, presented Tayce with his special gift, which the whole team were in on. It was a small velveteen box. Tayce looked at him. He prompted her to open it. Glancing around at her team, she could see something was being played out before her as they stood around smiling. Marc also nodded for her to continue – he too was in on what was about to unfold. She slowly opened the lid and gasped at the beautiful sparkling ring within.

"Tayce… let's begin to make our arrangement legal," said Dairan, referring to their being together.

"Is this a proposal, Dairan Loring?" she asked, amused, with a smile on her beautiful face.

"That's exactly what it is," he replied with a smile, studying her lovingly.

"I don't know… should I? All right, I accept," she said, laughing at the fact the team around her were all holding their breath in case she said she wouldn't.

Everyone cheered in the room as Dairan placed the beautiful sparkling diamond-and-sapphire ring on Tayce's finger. It sparkled as the overhead lighting shone on it. Both hugged. Tayce then went on to open her presents from the team. Phean Leavy handed her his gift, which turned out to be a red crystal. He informed her, as she looked at it, that it would serve her in moments of loneliness and doubt; she could use it with one of the teachings of the past weekon to make her happy. The celebration continued. Lance and Sallen gave her new in-bloom plants for her quarters. Marc gave her a replica of the Jewel of Traun – a diamond star on a gold-coloured chain. It was certainly turning out to be one special dayon.

***

On Enlopedia in the Celebrational Hall personnel were hanging colour banners and matching celebratory fabric drapes under the supervision of Lydia Traun. This was where Tayce was going to celebrate her special milestone bornday. Both Darius and Lydia had decided, because on Tayce's last bornday she was busy trying to survive alone in the Universe after Traun's destruction, this thirtieth bornday should be celebrated in style with all the people that had come to know her over the yearons. Lydia was busy talking to the catering techs, explaining what times she wanted drinks served and so on. Chief Jan Barnford sauntered in, glancing up at the personnel getting the banners and drapes right, occasionally arguing to get them where they were supposed to go.

"Looks good, Chief," praised Jan, walking over to Lydia.

"Do you think she'll like it? I hope I'm doing the right thing," confided Lydia.

"She'll love it. I'm here to inform you that security will be tight for tonight so you've no need to worry about any unwanted guests. In actual fact, as well as myself being present, I've some of my SSWAT officers out of uniform in their best attire, under strict instructions to watch for any kind of trouble – not that we're expecting any," explained Jan.

"Did you receive your orders from Darius to escort her here?" asked Lydia, hoping he had.

"Don't worry, I've got a good plan. I'll see you later," he promised, turning and beginning away.

"Good luck – she doesn't fool easily," pointed out Lydia, laughing.

"Tell me about it, Chief," said Jan over his shoulder, smiling at the thought that Tayce wasn't easily fooled.

Jan approached the entrance to the vast hall, passing personnel checking what was needed on the long table where food would be laid for a buffet, heading on back to his Officette in the Division Building. It crossed Jan's mind that numerous times before celebrations had been gatecrashed by criminals of the worst kind. This celebration had to be tightly watched, considering Tayce was the Admiral's daughter. Especially with the likes of Varon Vargon and Lord Dion in the Universe at large.

***

An houron later, Auran Amalthea Three was just completing docking procedures. Joshua Landorz was prepared for transfer to a team that would be waiting in port to take him to the Complex for Mind Study, Health and Neurology for his treatment. The team were on leave until Auran Amalthea Three was going to leave port. Tayce couldn't understand why the team seemed in a hurry to be off to Enlopedia without her. She thought they would head for a drink on Enlopedia to celebrate her special bornday. She guessed the dayon was over and felt sad, but tried not to show it. Jan Barnford walked into Organisation unexpectedly. He looked calm and serious, so as not to raise suspicion about what he had to do. He was playing along with the Admiral's plan to get Tayce to her party. Tayce turned, meeting his serious look, wondering what was wrong. He began in a pretending way, saying he needed her urgent help on a matter on Enlopedia. It was very important and couldn't wait. Tayce agreed, leaving Marc and Dairan to meet her later. They too were in on the surprise plan. Both Jan and Tayce began off towards Enlopedia. Both Dairan and Marc broke into silent laughter at Tayce's seriousness and Jan keeping his straight appearance, making his unofficial duty look official. They secured the cruiser, turning over control to Amal. Dairan headed on out to go and get changed whilst Marc checked with Donaldo on Wristlink that their on-board guest, Joshua, had been successfully transferred over to the team; then he too walked from Organisation.

***

At 19:45 hourons on Enlopedia guests were arriving in the High-Ranked Arrival and Departure Port for the thirtieth-bornday celebrations of the Admiral's daughter – namely, Tayce. She, however, elsewhere was finding it strange that she'd had to go and change into a celebrational evening gown to help a dignitary out of a very serious and sticky problem. But she'd gone back to Auran Amalthea Three, using her mind ability to travel from one spot to another, known as a 'jaunt', to arrive in her quarters, where she quickly changed her attire. Jan had explained that he would meet her at the Docking-Bay doors as he had to change also. He was discreetly keeping Darius Traun in the picture via Wristcall as the situation was unfolding and also called Adam Carford when he was en route to meet up with Tayce.

After a while Tayce emerged from Auran Amalthea Three, thinking to herself that this so-called dignitary had to be someone high up, because she would normally take on such a duty in her uniform. She glanced at Jan, thinking how handsome he looked. As they headed back to E City Square, Jan began telling her there was something she had to know.

"You look quite breathtaking in that gown. Dairan's a lucky man," said Jan in a raised-eyebrows complimentary way with a cheeky off-duty smile.

"Thank you – anything to keep up the official representation of my father's base," replied Tayce, not knowing what was about to unfold.

"This is quite a tricky but serious situation. We figured you are right for the job, as it requires the utmost deference," announced Jan seriously, but knowing otherwise what was about to happen.

Tayce looked at him, giving him a taken-aback look, wondering why her father hadn't called her on the cruiser to inform her of this problem. They crossed, heading towards the Celebrational Hall entrance. Everything was quiet within. Tayce began getting a little unnerved, especially because of where they were heading.

"What's really going on here, Jan? Tell me," began Tayce, finding her feelings were being alerted to uneasiness suddenly.

"All will be revealed just inside," promised Jan.

The doors opened and a triumphant cheer of "Happy bornday, Tayce!" erupted as she walked into the warm air that rushed out to meet her, and everyone soon in turn came forth to wish her a happy bornday one by one. She was overwhelmed beyond belief by all the guests that had gathered. Many had known her since her first dayon as leader of the Amalthean Quests, in her first voyage. She looked at Jan and mischievously gave him a look that said she would get him back for what he'd pulled off. He smiled a mischievous smile. Dairan soon reached her and took hold of her hand, squeezing it reassuringly. He was dressed in celebrational attire. He gave her a warm smile. To Tayce's surprise as she looked around the vast hall, among the crew members from as far back as her first voyage were Mac Danford and Duncan Leyres. Among other guests she recognised were Governor Cinva, Prince Tieman, and this was to name but a few of the many people she'd helped along the way.

Halfway through the celebration Empress Tricara and Phean Leavy walked towards Tayce. Lydia crossed also. Tayce, upon seeing them, realised it was time for her test. She glanced at Dairan. He met her worried look and immediately knew something was wrong. Tayce silently told him it was time for her test of powers in the Realm of Honitonia. Dairan knew this forthcoming feat wasn't going to be easy for her and he understood her apprehension as she looked at him. She realised at least she'd managed to have a good celebration for her landmark bornday, also she had cut the most beautiful cake with a Slazer knife. Her father had given her the best gift she could have – the key to the first luxurious dwelling of the latest architectural design on Pellasun Traun 2, when completed. When she wanted to head off home during breaks from the cruising life she could head there and relax.

"Here goes! See you soon, one way or another," said Tayce, frightened by the fact she could lose her gift this time around.

"I'll be waiting for you. Good luck," said Dairan, then kissed her on the cheek.

Within moments a blinding white-and-blue aura surrounded Tayce and Phean, making guests gasp at the sudden spectacular vanishing act. Darius quickly assured everyone it was nothing to be concerned about, and many that knew of Tayce's gift understood just what had happened. Tricara assured Dairan that Tayce would be fine, he'd see. Darius could see Dairan was at a loss, so he sauntered over to talk about Pellasun Traun 2. Marc grabbed a drink from a passing hostess and crossed to give it to Dairan, suggesting he enjoy the rest of the celebration – it would be what Tayce wanted. Marc guided him over to meet some people from other Amalthean Quests voyages he hadn't met before to share memories and to take his mind off worrying about Tayce.

***

The bornday celebration continued well on into what could only be termed the early mornet hourons of the next dayon. Dairan stayed until last with Marc to take Tayce's many gifts back to the cruiser. He didn't fancy heading back to empty quarters, knowing Tayce wouldn't be there with him. There had been almost 200 guests, including plain-clothed security. Many had been disappointed at Tayce's sudden departure, but understood why they couldn't say farewell to her. Dairan, Lydia and Marc expressed that they would pass on to Tayce that they had had a great time. Everything was quiet. The remains of the bornday – streamers, etc. – were strewn about the hall floor. Dairan, with an armful of presents, followed on behind Marc, pausing for a minon at the entrance and glancing back, recalling the excitement of the celebration. It made him smile. He then continued on out, allowing the cleaning techs to move in and cleanse the littered hall, to restore it ready for the next occasion. As for Joshua Landorz, he was safely on Enlopedia in the hands of people who could restore his true identity.

8. The Green Tempest Keeper

Dairan was in his and Tayce's quarters relaxing, listening to music in the off-duty hourons – the artist was one of Tayce's favourites. As he relaxed into the mouldable chair, so his mind wandered to Tayce. It had been three dayons since she and Phean had disappeared in a white-and-blue aura from the thirtieth-bornday celebrations. No word had emerged from Honitonia as to when both would be coming back to where they belonged. He stretched and sighed, wishing it would soon be over and Tayce would be back. He then glanced at his Wristlink time display, rose to his feet and walked over to the Living Area sight port.

Pausing before it, he looked out and silently said to himself. "Tayce, where are you? What's taking so long?"

It was as if the Empire of Honitonia had heard him, as behind him Tayce materialised in a blinding white flash. Dairan turned in time to see her moan and collapse against the nearest wall. He acted in a split cencron, going to her aid and catching her in mid fall. Scooping her up in his arms, he carried her to the soffette and set her down gently. Raising his Wristlink he called Donaldo in urgency.

"You'd better get down here and bring your Medical Crisis Kit. Tayce is back. She just collapsed."

"On my way. Stay with her," said Donaldo on the other end of the Wristlink.

Dairan ceased communications and crossed to the Repose Centre to fetch a coverlet from the emergency store. Hurrying back, he shook it out fully upon approach, then laid it over Tayce up to her shoulders to keep her warm. She began to regain consciousness. Opening her eyes, she looked up and found him looking back at her in worried concern. Without warning, once her vision had cleared she sat up and hugged him tightly, glad to be back. He was surprised by her sudden actions. He then put his arms around her, hugging her tightly in return. He took it that she'd finished her test and was back on the cruiser for good. He could feel, even though she was holding him like he was the last thing in the Universe, that her grip wasn't as strong as it generally was. She was like someone weak summoning every ounce of strength, glad to be held. Behind him the quarters doors opened and Marc and Donaldo entered. Donaldo had his Medical Crisis Kit in hand. Tayce, seeing them over Dairan's shoulder, let him go, dropping back on to the soffette cushion.

"Dairan, can I take a look?" asked Donaldo, wanting Dairan to move to one side so he could examine Tayce with the Examscan to see what state she'd returned in.

"Oh, sure – sorry! Go ahead," replied Dairan, moving up by Tayce's head, to the end of the soffette, and standing up.

Donaldo activated the medical Examscan, guiding it slowly all about Tayce, letting it pick up readings for her whole body. He then waited for the LCD reading of diagnosis information for possible treatment to appear. He rose to his feet.

"I'm assigning Tayce here at least five hourons of sleep and rest. Her body is exhausted. I'm going to give you, Tayce, a Select 2 injection. This will knock you out for a couple of hourons. It will also aid your strength to return," said Donaldo seriously.

He reached into his Medical Crisis Kit and retrieved his Comprai Inject Pen, loading it with a cartridge with the right amount of Select 2. He returned to Tayce, pressing the Comprai Inject Pen against her upper arm and pressing the release button. As the Select 2 hit her system, Tayce looked up at Donaldo, tired. If she had been stronger she would have refused the treatment. Donaldo smiled at her in a reassuring medical and friendly way. He then turned to Marc and Dairan, standing and explaining that Tayce would be under sedation in a matter of cencrons, then she'd be unconscious for four to five hourons. All they had to do was make sure she remained in her present surroundings for the duration, to enable her to recover from the exhausting ordeal.

Marc thought about what Donaldo was saying.

"Twedor's here. He can watch over her and make sure she doesn't go and walk about in a drugged state. But with the doors locked there's a downside to this: what if she should have to escape in an emergency?" asked Marc.

"Relax – I still have my powers," said Tayce weakly behind them, hearing what was said.

"OK then, you just relax where you are," said Donaldo, looking down at her.

"Can I suggest something? Why not put a temporary force field outside in the corridor, just for the required time, and one I can unlock should an emergency arise," spoke up Twedor.

"Good idea – that's what we'll do," said Marc, patting Twedor on the head for making a good suggestion.

Marc raised his Wristlink, putting in place what was to be done, authorising with Amal for Twedor to shut down the force field in an emergency at a moment's notice. Dairan glanced at Tayce, seeing she was now in peaceful sleep. He decided to leave Twedor with her and return to duty.

Donaldo closed his Medical Crisis Kit and picked it up, following Marc on out. Pausing, he glanced back when he reached the entrance at a peaceful sleeping Tayce, thinking she'd be all right. The doors to the quarters opened and they walked back out into the Level 3 corridor. Dairan glanced back over his shoulder at Tayce too, then continued on out into the corridor. Twedor meantime walked over to Tayce, scanning her to make sure she was all right and she was just sleeping as prescribed. In his memory he ran through the many times he'd been there for her and realised it was too many to remember. 'Poor Tayce!' he thought. 'She must have gone through some gruelling testing at the Realm of Honitonia to be knocked out as severely as she had.' But he would be her little escort and security guard again whilst she slept, like many times before, until she awoke.

***

Sallen left the Lab Garden Dome in Phean's hands. He'd arrived back on board just after Tayce, but unlike Tayce he'd been able to recover from the test quicker than she had, being someone who came from the Empire Realm. Sallen, now knowing Phean was safely back, could visit Marc for she'd come to her decision on what they had discussed earlier. She headed to the Deck Travel on Level 5, thinking over in her mind what she was going to say. Upon reaching the doors to the Deck Travel, she pressed the request key and soon the doors were opening before her to walk aboard and she was on the way to Level 1.

***

Marc and Dairan parted from Donaldo on Level 2. 'Four more hourons and duty will be finished for another dayon,' thought Dairan. Marc could see Dairan looked better for his ordering him off duty earlier, to take some rest, as he'd been on duty for a straight twenty-five hourons and had found out through Amal as much. Marc knew what long duty stints were like. He'd done many during his lifetime. It could cause accidents and more, not being fully focused in one's duty. But he'd understood Dairan's actions. He didn't want to think Tayce wasn't in the quarters when he went there. But Marc didn't want Tayce blaming him for Dairan ending up in the MLC through long unnoticed duty hourons.

They soon were entering Organisation. Lance looked up from his duty position. Marc announced that Tayce was back safe and sound, but exhausted, and was resting in her quarters so he was in charge until she returned to duty. He then walked on into the DC, leaving a much happier team, as they too had been wondering how Tayce was getting on in the Realm of Honitonia. Dairan crossed to Nick for any reports from Enlopedia. Nick handed him the small collection of printouts, on which he turned and went on into the DC with them. Sallen entered Organisation, continuing on through to the DC and pausing in the doorway.

"Is it all right to see you now?" she asked.

"Sure! Come on in," said Marc in a casual tone, beginning to give her his full listening attention.

"Phean's back. He's fine. He's in the Lab Garden Dome. How's Tayce? Did she make it?" enquired Sallen in a caring way.

"Exhausted. Donaldo had to give her a Select 2 to aid her recovery," replied Dairan.

"Really! Maybe I should postpone this meeting until everything is back to normal and Tayce is here," suggested Sallen.

"No, I'm in command. I can handle any problems you or any others of the team have – maybe not like Tayce, but I'm here and listening," said Marc casually.

"I've come to a decision about something I've been thinking about for some time, and it involves a chat we had some time ago. You suggested I think things over – well, I have. I'm leaving the cruiser and the team. I know this has probably surprised you, but it's the thought of that barbarian Vargon, who thinks he's related to me and could return any time. I'm not happy about that. I don't want this team to endure any more of his actions because of what he thinks he has over me, I'm sorry, Marc," said Sallen, meeting Dairan and Marc's disappointing looks at her decision not to remain on board because of her true identity, which was unbeknown to her.

"Sallen, Tayce would tell you as much as I will, you can't give up your life here and all your friends because of a man like Vargon. You're a good member of this team and we will protect you if he surfaces again," said Marc, standing and walking forth from behind Tayce's desk, saddened to think she was giving up all her hard work on board just because of fear.

"Sorry, Marc, but my mind's made up I'm heading back to Enlopedia. It's time for me to try out something new. It's not that I haven't enjoyed my time here – I have, but it's time to move on," she replied casually, but feeling the sad disappointment of both Marc and Dairan as a result of what she was doing.

"If you're sure that's what you want, I'll arrange for a Transpo Launch to pick you up," said Dairan, understanding her decision, but he felt sorry to see her leave. She'd been an excellent member of team, despite what she once was in her old past.

"Will you thank Tayce for me, for all that she's done?" put Sallen softly.

"Of course. She'll be saddened you've decided to go, but she'll understand," assured Marc.

Dairan walked out into Organisation, wishing her luck. He crossed to Nick, requesting he arrange for a Transpo Launch with security to collect her and take her to Enlopedia. Nick, upon hearing Dairan's request, gave a surprised look. Then he looked at Sallen, not knowing what to say regarding her sudden decision, but he, like Marc and Dairan, fully understood that her life hadn't been easy with Count Vargon around or her mother. Sallen had to go and pack so she'd be ready by her pickup time. Kelly turned, saddened to see her friend leave and stood giving her a hug, wishing her luck in her new venture and telling her she would be missed by the whole team. Everyone else did the same – they hugged Sallen goodbye and wished her well. Sallen explained her reason for leaving and further added that the decision hadn't been taken lightly. The whole Organisation team present understood.

"The Transpo Launch will collect you at the Docking-Bay doors in an houron. Good luck," said Nick with a kind smile, wishing she wasn't leaving. They'd become good friends.

"Thank you, all of you. I'll probably see you on Enlopedia or Pellasun Traun 2. Come and look me up – don't be strangers," said Sallen hopefully.

With this, she turned and walked towards the entrance, pausing and turning back for the last time, thanking everyone once again for making her part of the team. Then she continued on out of the centre, off to pack in her quarters. Dairan watched her go, thinking to himself that he hoped everything would turn out the way she hoped in her new venture. She deserved to succeed. Marc stood in the DC doorway watching her also saddened that Vargon had forced this young reformed woman to do what she felt she had to do in order to avoid his evil attempts to get her back as his daughter, even though this time the memories had been destroyed.

***

Tayce was in Phean's thoughts as he sat at the work console in the Lab Garden Dome's side Officette. He was concerned about her, even though the Emperor had ordered him to leave Tayce for a period to adjust to the new abilities she'd gained and the dispersing of ones no longer considered worthy of her. Phean closed his eyes and concentrated, trying to reach her. But, strangely, he found she couldn't be reached, which he found somewhat concerning. He could feel her presence aboard the cruiser using his powers, and see where she was in her quarters, sedated. He decided he'd leave her a while longer. Maybe his concern was nothing. He just wanted to know, as her friend and guide, that she was all right. He continued on with the new duty of being in charge of the Lab Garden Dome.

***

It was two hourons later. Auran Amalthea Three had just departed from the Transpo Launch collecting Sallen and had travelled on into a new unknown area of the Universe. It was an area that somehow didn't feel or look like normal space. For some strange and eerie reason, on board twice the power had flickered and computers had gone off line to standby, but no one could explain what was materialising. Not even Lance at his research console, keying away, trying to find out something to enlighten everyone about where they were. There wasn't anything out of the ordinary surfacing other than that they were travelling into new territory. There were a few important changes, but nothing to cause immediate alarm even though the atmosphere said otherwise aboard the cruiser. Everything was eerily calm. All that could be heard was the sound of the operational cruiser in transit. Then it hit hard. The cruiser jolted sharply, rocking from side to side. Power throughout the entire cruiser drained fast and everything went into off line standby mode again, making the low-grade operations systems cut in, until they were draining as well. The Organisation team had been thrown into a state of chaos, unsure what to do next as everything was failing around them.

***

Down in Tayce's quarters, she'd been flung from the mouldable soffette on to the quarters floor. She was now wide awake and wondering why she had Twedor prodding her in the ribs with his metlon hand. She slid away so he could move freely, as he was stuck on his back. She realised she must have been thrown off the soffette, and knocked him to the floor.

"I know some women throw themselves at me, but you, Tayce!" said Twedor light-heartedly.

"Sorry, Twedor. What's happening? All the power's down and backup is on line."

She sat up carefully, glancing at her Wristlink time display. At least she'd had some rest, she thought. Getting to her feet, she helped Twedor up on to his just as another powerful strike hit the cruiser's hull. Twedor shook then gained an upright position again, with Tayce's help. She knew she had to find out what was happening. Concentrating for a few minons, using one of her new powers, her whole attire changed and she looked fresh as if she'd just cleansed and changed. Even her hair was clasped up in a ponytail. She relaxed, getting her thoughts together on what to do first, even though her head was throbbing from the Select 2 injection. Twedor whistled in disbelief at how she'd gone from one appearance to another in a matter of cencrons. Even his sensors couldn't believe what they'd picked up, she'd changed so fast.

"Nice change," said Twedor, impressed.

"Something isn't right on board. Come on, Twedor," said Tayce, walking to the Living Area entrance doors.

"But, Tayce, you can't leave – the doors are locked. You'll have to wait for me to bypass the security put in place plus the force field. It will only take a couple of moments," announced Twedor as they neared the entrance.

"I don't think you'll need to. Main power is down, but you'd better check in case backup has reinstated it to a certain degree. We don't want to get a shock or worse if we touch to check," said Tayce.

"Just checking with Amal and scanning for force field. No force field so far, but the doors are locked. You'll have to do a manual override," said Twedor.

Twedor watched as Tayce placed her right hand on the mechanism panel by the entrance and concentrated. A glow materialised and travelled all around her hands, then shot out to find the mechanism built within the wall. Tayce quickly pressed an inset panel and the panel gave, sliding back, revealing the controls to pull, turn and press for the doors to be operated manually and to be pushed apart. Tayce manipulated the controls and then pushed the doors apart using her inner-strength ability, stepping out into the near darkness of Level 3. Calming down, she reached for her new light pencil torch with a wider and stronger beam and activated it. Twedor walked out through the doors behind her. Tayce turned, taking hold of his metlon hand to help him.

Once clear, Twedor did a scan of the whole cruiser. Tayce waited. He soon announced that Craig Bream was in the Automatic Total Shutdown Centre for the whole cruiser, on Level 1. He was locked in. Tayce knew they had to head there first to rescue Craig. Both walked in the direction of the Level Steps, with the torch beam showing the way ahead. It was eerie dark and the temperature was slowly dropping, owing to losing half their power. They began up the Level Steps, shining the torch all the way ahead as they went from Level 3 to 1. As they reached Level 1, there could be heard the sound of someone hammering to get out. Twedor ran another scan and soon pointed to the Automatic Total Shutdown Centre doors. He headed straight for them, identifying where the hammering sound was coming from. Tayce followed and was soon pressing the inset cover to expose the internal opening mechanism by the entrance. Like before, to manually open the doors she pressed it home.

The doors opened and Craig fell out, righting himself to stop himself falling to the floor. He was much relieved to be free.

"Thanks! Nice to see you back," said Craig, getting his breath back as the air was running thin in the centre.

"You're going to have to increase the life-support setting in there – it's set too short. What hit us?" asked Tayce, wondering if he knew.

"Just after the first strike knocked everything out, I checked with Lance. There was no vessel and nothing else out of the ordinary being detected. It's strange why we should keep losing power," replied Craig, thinking about it.

"How come you were in there?" asked Tayce, glancing behind him.

"Some of the system operations blew on the first strike. I went in to see if I could correct it. As soon as I stepped in, the second strike hit. Sparks flew from various panels and the doors closed, locking me in."

"Do you think you could get life support, heating and all the doors operational in the next ten minons?" she requested, hoping so.

"I'll give it a try," replied Craig, thinking how best to go about doing so so quickly.

"Great – I'm leaving you to it. I'm heading on to Organisation," Tayce replied.

“Give me a call if you need any help getting in there,” he said, walking back into the open Automatic Total Shutdown Centre to begin work.

“OK – will do,” said Tayce, continuing on with Twedor.

As she reached the Organisation Centre, closed doors greeted her. Twedor tried to do a penetration scan so he could detect who was inside, but for some strange reason he was finding it near impossible.

Turning, he began: “There’s some kind of high energy just the other side of these doors. I can’t read who’s inside. It would appear the second strike to our outside hull is the cause of the block in my scan,” he explained.

Upon this, Tayce knew she had to gain entry. This was her cruiser and if there was an uninvited guest inside she wanted to oust it, even if it had a damn good explanation for the attack! Like earlier, she did the same with the inset cover to the mechanism by the entrance doors, and pressed the lever after ordering Twedor to activate his Slazer finger and stand by in case whatever was inside decided to fire off a round of weapon fire and take a walkabout throughout the rest of the Levels. They had to bring whatever was inside down before it happened.

The doors gave, opening. Nothing emerged from within. Twedor looked at Tayce. She raised her eyes, wondering why nothing had rushed out. She slowly ventured towards the opening gap as the doors retracted back into the wall on either side with a helping shove. Tayce shone the light pencil torch inside into the near darkness. Nothing– no sign of any intrusion. Tayce’s torch picked up the first of the team. It was Dairan. But it was as if he was frozen in time, in mid walk across the centre. Tayce moved on to the others. Kelly, Lance, Nick and Marc were all in the same frozen state, in mid movement, working or whatever action they were currently undertaking when the mysterious force hit the cruiser. In a way it would have been funny if it wasn’t serious. Something had invaded the cruiser to cause what had happened. Scrutinising the various amusing looks and poses the team had paused in, Tayce wondered why the present situation should have presented itself. Then she saw the strange green aura around Marc, like a kind of energy shield. Was this the uninvited guest, or was it a side effect of the injection Donaldo had given her earlier? Twedor picked up on her look of concern, studying what had presented itself before them.

“What’s up? What is it?” asked Twedor, seeing her look at Marc.

“I’m not sure, but for some strange reason there’s a green aura surrounding Marc,” said Tayce, wondering why.

“I can’t see it,”said Twedor.

Tayce braced herself for what lay ahead inside, wondering if what attacked the cruiser had control over their current surroundings, waiting for her within. She slowly sauntered into Organisation, Twedor not far behind with his Slazer finger set to stun. As she came face-to-face with Marc, so she could see his handsome eyes were glazed and fixed and looking straight at her, motionless. Tayce found her breathing beginning to get tighter as she reached out cautiously to touch him. In the meantime Craig had walked into Organisation, saying he needed to get to Amal's console. But he quickly paused, amazed at what he was seeing – his teammates frozen in time. He crossed to Tayce, looking at her still studying Marc, trying to make something out of what had happened. As Tayce touched Marc's face, so his hand suddenly came up and grabbed her wrist quickly. Tayce wanted to panic, as his eyes had turned to a luminous green like some kind of light had been turned on. Tayce struggled in the tight grip, about to use her powers to break free. Twedor fired his Slazer finger at Marc. Marc's grip loosened around Tayce's wrist and she fell back rubbing it, wondering what the hell was going on. Craig gently grabbed her out of harm's way. He studied Marc, who had felt the impact of Twedor's shot, falling to the Organisation Centre floor. It freaked him out.

"You all right?" asked Craig, concerned.

"I'm fine. What's going on? What's causing this?" replied Tayce.

Both stood looking at Marc crumpled on the floor, out cold, with the green aura still around him. They were wondering what was going to happen next.

***

Down on Level 4, Professor Adrien Maylen had, strangely enough, not been affected by what had hit the cruiser and had managed to slip out through the open Medical Experimental Lab doors. A light shone in his direction and the slim shape of Aldonica Darstayne followed on behind it. She too was unaffected. Upon reaching him, she was glad to see he too hadn't been affected by the force that had hit the cruiser. They both decided to walk up to Organisation in the hope that they could find out what was happening. Both, to take their mind off the eerie-darkness type of ghost ship feeling, discussed Sallen's untimely departure. They reached Level 2 and could hear the sound of someone trying to break out of a locked room. Both paused, looking at each other questioningly, wondering if they should go and check it out. They felt it might be whatever had a hold over the cruiser, waiting to get them. Adrien thought for a moment, then had an idea: it could be Donaldo and Treketa trapped in the MLC. Aldonica agreed. Taking out her Pollomoss handgun, she suggested they find out. Both headed along Level 2 towards the MLC. Aldonica was ready to open fire should something leap out and attack them when the doors opened. Upon approaching the doors, Aldonica called out, asking who was inside.

"Is that you, Donaldo?" asked Aldonica, poised for whatever might come through the doors.

"It's us – we're trapped, but we're OK," called out Treketa.

Aldonica quickly put her Slazer away and looked for the panel beside the doors to manually open them, the same way Tayce had done for Craig earlier. Some entrance doors had mechanism panels on the outside, some on the inside, like Adrien had found in the Medical Experimental Lab. Aldonica soon had Treketa and Donaldo free.

Adrien turned to Donaldo. "You'd better bring your Medical Crisis Kit. There's no telling what we're going to find."

"Right – I totally agree," replied Donaldo, stepping back into the MLC to grab his kit.

Once everyone was ready, they continued on along Level 2 to the Level Steps, heading to Level 1, thinking about what might lie ahead, waiting on the next level in the near darkness.

***

Twedor ran a scan over Marc, who was still lying silently on the floor, where he'd dropped. Tayce looked out through the main sight port. To her utter surprise, they were surrounded by a lime-green luminous cloud, which hadn't been there when she looked earlier. Craig looked up and saw it too, before going back under Amal's console to restore main operations to normal. He was ready to activate all on-board systems. On the count of three, he keyed in the reset sequence and pressed the activation key. Amal flashed back into life, but was silent for a few minons as she began coming online, activating everything aboard, which signified she was undertaking a cruiser-wide scan at the same time. Life support, lighting, etc. came on one by one until everything was fully operational, as it should be.

Donaldo and Adrien were first into Organisation. Donaldo set down his Medical Crisis Kit upon reaching Marc. He looked out through the main sight port, then took the Examscan out of the Medical Crisis Kit and did a quick scan of Marc's lifeless body. Treketa looked around at the others slightly unnerved by their stationary frozen state. Donaldo found the LCD reading somewhat amazing.

"I don't know what to make of this. Marc is showing large amounts of high-voltage energy – enough to kill him – but he's still alive somehow," said Donaldo, baffled.

As the lights illuminated Organisation, it was hard to think the person on the floor before them was Marc, everyone's friend and team commander. Greenish patches were appearing on Marc's face, neck, body and hands. On this, Donaldo said he wanted Marc in the MLC for observation and treatment. Tayce nodded. Treketa crossed to Tayce.

"Are you OK? How much sleep did you manage to get earlier?" enquired Treketa like a true medic.

"Enough to tide me over. I'll be fine. You'd better take my Pollomoss in case he wakes up," said Tayce, handing Treketa her Pollomoss handgun as a precaution. It was fully charged.

"What about Dairan? He looks like he's still under whatever this is. He looks weird, stood looking in mid conversation with Marc, frozen," said Treketa, finding it creepy that Dairan was now looking forward into nothing.

"Don't worry – I've an idea that might just work to bring him back to normal."

"Be careful. You know what happened the last time he was possessed," reminded Treketa, remembering the time Dairan was under the influence of Vargon's mind control.

"It will be different this time," assured Tayce, knowing she now had more power ability.

"Don't overtax yourself if you're looking to use your powers. We don't want you joining Marc in the MLC," replied Treketa.

"I'll be fine – honest. Just take care of Marc," replied Tayce.

Treketa picked up Donaldo's Medical Crisis Kit whilst Donaldo and Adrien began getting Marc to the MLC. Tayce turned, looking at Dairan, wondering how was she going to bring him out of his current suspended state without trouble? She remembered her empire test and placed her hands on Dairan's chest, concentrating on removing the hold this green phenomenon had over him. It was hard to fight with the strong immense energy hold. But she increased her ability to match it, to withdraw it from him whilst protecting his heart. At last it dissolved and the green light in his normally handsome brown eyes began to fade and his eyes returned to normal once more. He stood for a few minons shaking his head in disbelief, unable to comprehend what he'd been under the influence of, but he was now back to normal. He looked at Tayce, relieved to see she was OK. Both hugged for a minon.

Amal announced behind them suddenly, "Life support fully operational. All on-board operations are back online. Heating and lighting is restored."

"Thanks, Amal," said Tayce, glad at least the cruiser was back to normal.

'Pity the immediate team weren't,' thought Tayce as she looked at Lance, Kelly and Nick.

There was only one thing the four of them – Aldonica, Craig, Dairan and herself – would have to do, and that was to find out what they were up against in this green phenomenon that had engulfed the cruiser and certain team members. Tayce and Dairan pulled Lance's chair out from his research console and Tayce began to key in a request for computer scan information on the green phenomenon currently surrounding the whole cruiser and affecting the frozen-in-time members of her team. Aldonica took Nicks Microceive off. Dairan pulled Kelly gently out of her chair and guided her into the DC, where he set her down on the nearest soffette. Quickly returning to Kelly's duty position, he sat down at her console in her high-backed chair, beginning to key in a request for their current situation. Twedor watched on.

"According to this, we're in the grip of what's known as Gruspan Space, home of the Green Tempest Keeper, who's the powerful keeper of this section of space in the form of a pure, powerful white-hot energy being," said Tayce, studying the information before her on screen.

"Someone not to be messed with by the sound of it," said Dairan, listening, glancing at her.

"Poor Marc! How can we stop this keeper? There must be something we can do," said Aldonica.

"We could keep him as reserved power – we could go well into the next century," said Dairan, joking.

"Dairan, it's not funny – it's serious. We're talking about Marc here. Just think for a moment what he must be suffering under the control of this so-called Green Tempest Keeper," said Tayce, not impressed.

Twedor wasn't impressed either with Dairan's comment and was giving him a Romid look of disgust.

Without warning the intruder alarm sounded. Aldonica turned at Nick's console, announcing that Marc – or should she say the Green Tempest Keeper? – had escaped from the MLC. Tayce looked at Dairan in alarm, then decided to find out just what this so-called powerful keeper wanted with her or the cruiser. She stood, beginning across the centre when Marc appeared suddenly in the doorway, possessed by the keeper.

"I want answers. What are you doing on board this cruiser? Why take control of my commander?" demanded Tayce.

"Human, female," it stated through Marc, slowly, like it was difficult to talk.

"I'm waiting for an answer. Have we strayed into your territory without your permission? Then we'll leave if you'll leave this cruiser," continued Tayce, standing her ground, ready to use her new powers if she had to.

"I seek revenge. Beings like you trespass in this sector too many times. Retaliation for the lost inhabitants of my sectoral world because of your kind. Possession of your commander is a small payment for past deaths and destruction of my race. A small price you will pay for my kind in his death once I gain what I want," the being said through Marc as he glowed before her, looking at her in a threatening way.

"We'll change our course if you release my commander at once. There's no need for killing others because of what's happened to your people," continued Tayce, continuing to stand her ground.

"Releasing your crew member is not an option. You come," replied the keeper through Marc.

He raised his hand palm, facing outwards, and suddenly a beam of white light omitted from it, hitting Dairan in the chest lifting him up off the floor. Dairan silently screamed in agony as the force burnt and sent him sailing back across the centre out of the way. He impacted with the side of the main sight port with a thud, which winded him and almost rendered him unconscious. Craig turned to check he was all right. But by the time he checked and looked back to where Marc in the keeper's hold had been, he'd left the centre, taking Tayce with him.

***

Phean Leavy walked from the Lab Garden Dome, brushing the authentic brown soil off his uniform. For some strange reason he was picking that up Tayce needed assistance urgently. Then, abruptly, just as it had started, it ceased. He raised his Wristlink, contacting Organisation just to check everything was all right. To his surprise, Aldonica answered. She informed him of what had occurred. Phean, listening, knew Tayce would use the ability he'd taught her and she had been tested for, if need be. But he also knew he had to try and help. Aldonica added that Marc could be killed if Phean was thinking of trying anything daft to save Tayce. Phean, on this, assured her that there were other ways to save Marc and Tayce – she'd see. With this, he ceased communications, deactivating his Wristlink. He opened his mind, using it like a cruiser-wide scanner. He searched for Tayce, then the powerful Green Tempest Keeper / Marc. He then begrudgingly began off, heading to Level 3, where Tayce was in the company of the Keeper/Marc.

***

Tayce couldn't understand why he was taking her along Level 3. What did he have in mind? she wondered. If he was seeking revenge, then surely he would have headed for the nuclear quick-reaction engines. Marc, in the hold of the Keeper, paused outside Marc's quarters. Why here? she wondered. The doors opened and Tayce was pushed inside carelessly. She glanced back, giving Marc an angry stare. It was hard to keep her mind on the fact that the Keeper was inside her friend, a person she'd come to treat almost like the brother she didn't have. She could see the Keeper was controlling everything in Marc, against his will. Every time the Keeper moved Marc's head to look at her, it was disturbing to say the least. A shudder ran down her spine the feeling was so unnatural. She picked up on the fact that the Keeper was making Marc convey that he was interested in her for all the wrong reasons.

'This is certainly not going to happen,' she thought. 'What would be gained by such an act?'

"What do you hope to achieve here? These are just quarters belonging to my commander," said Tayce ignoring the unwanted wanting looks and not liking what she was reading about the Keeper's intentions.

"I want to gain knowledge of humanoid close intimate contact. You will show me," the Keeper said through Marc.

"You only have to study information in our library database to gain this knowledge. You don't need to find out in other ways. Or you could read my commander's memories," pointed out Tayce.

"I want experience of this occurrence. You will give me this or your commander will die," said the Keeper, beginning to drain the life out of Marc.

"Killing my commander won't gain you the knowledge you seek," said Tayce, refusing to play along with what the Keeper wanted. It was against her and Marc's way towards each other.

"You're forgetting, I'm within your crew member. I can kill every cell and everything that goes to make up his existence with very little effort. I would think carefully, female, about what you decide in the next moments. For the man whose body I occupy, these could be the last moments he exists," the Keeper warned, displeased that he wasn't obtaining what he sought.

"Never. I value the person you control with the highest respect and I won't let him do something that's so against his character just because you want it to happen, so you can gain knowledge of learning intimate contact. It's not happening," replied Tayce, ready to use her highest degree of power force to rescue Marc and destroy the Green Tempest Keeper once and for all.

The Keeper fell silent within Marc for a few moments. Had she called his bluff and was he searching Marc's memories instead of using her for what he wanted to gain? He was doing just this – searching Marc's mind for the most recent situation with a female in intimate contact. Then, without warning, he made Marc do what he wanted. Without his own control, or thought, Marc reached out, pulling Tayce against her will into his arms roughly. Tayce, on this, commenced her powers and together power hit power. But the Keeper showed an edge over Tayce. Though she fought hard, he made Marc kiss her in a strong passionate wanting way. Tayce tried not to respond. She and Marc didn't feel the least bit towards each other like the Keeper wanted. They were friends, not lovers, and never would be anything more.

Behind Tayce, in the quarters entrance, Phean appeared, catching the full-on unwanted embracing scene. Sensing Tayce needed his help, he commenced his own higher-energy force to assist, telling her they'd do it together. The Keeper saw Phean through Marc's eyes. He turned Marc's head to face him with an unimpressed and angry look. His eyes were lit with the powerful burning force. Phean raised his hand, palm facing towards the Keeper and the Honitonian higher energy power was emitted, heading straight into Marc. Together Phean and Tayce joined energy forces strong enough to break down the Keeper's energy hold over Marc. Tayce further protected him against being killed, keeping him alive in the immense bombardment. In the power struggle between the Keeper and Phean and herself, it was going to be a long fight, thought Tayce.

***

The cruiser's on-board power fell and rose a couple of times during the fight between Tayce, Phean and the Keeper. In Organisation the team members that had been frozen in suspended time came back to their normal selves. Aldonica smiled, seeing Nick looking normal once more. She removed his Microceive, handing it back, stepping away from his duty position when he'd gained his full comprehension of the present.

"That was totally weird. Have I been somewhere?" asked Nick, not sure of what happened.

"In a manner of speaking, yes, and it's not over yet," replied Aldonica as he sat at his console.

"Kelly, stand by to get this cruiser out of here," ordered Dairan, worried about Tayce as Auran began to rock in the turmoil created by the Green Tempest Keeper in his attempt to get what he wanted.

"Ready on your word," replied Kelly, fighting the rocking motion to get back to her seat.

Auran Amalthea Three took a real pounding from the forces created by Gruspan Space as the Keeper fought to hold on to the cruiser and Marc. But through the rough turmoil the whole Organisation team rode it out. Kelly glanced out through the main sight port. The bright-green field that had been all around the cruiser was slowly receding. She brought Dairan's attention to the fact. Dairan's mind began wondering what was going on on the lower levels between Tayce, Marc and the powerful Keeper.

***

Finally the Keeper withdrew out of Marc in the same powerful way he'd taken control, moving towards the outer quarters wall of the cruiser in all his powerful brilliance. Marc dropped to his knees in the Living Area of the quarters, exhausted. He fell silent, out cold on the floor. Phean continued to drive the Green Tempest Keeper from the cruiser with Tayce. He slowly ebbed out through the wall back into space. Tayce calmed. It had been quite a feat, but it was over. She raised her Wristlink, ordering Dairan to get the cruiser out of their current sector immediately, go to hyper-thrust turbo and put some distance between them and Gruspan Space. Dairan agreed. Before ceasing communications she requested Donaldo to go to Marc's quarters. It was an emergency. Upon Donaldo agreeing, she ceased communications, lowering her Wristlink and turning to see Phean now sitting on the edge of the soffette arm, looking slightly drained from assisting her. She crossed, concerned.

"Thanks for your help. I couldn't have done it without you. You OK?" she asked in a caring way.

"That has to be the toughest energy fight I've had so far. Glad I could help though. Are you all right?" asked Phean in his usual gentle way, realising she'd used her new powerful force full on for the first time.

"Fine! Like you, I'm a little shattered. He wasn't prepared to give up without a fight, was he?"

"No, but we won. When Aldonica told me what had happened I knew I couldn't let you take this on so soon after the ordeal of your test," he said casually.

"What you saw between me and Marc – it didn't happen. It stays inside these quarters. It was merely the force of the Green Tempest Keeper, nothing else," said Tayce seriously.

"Sure – no problem," he replied, understanding.

Behind them, the doors to the quarters opened and Donaldo rushed in, Treketa not far behind with a Hover Trolley. Donaldo set his Medical Crisis Kit down once more and took out the Examscan. He looked at Tayce, meeting her concerned look, noticing what Treketa had said was true. She still looked like she'd only got a small amount of rest before the present situation had kicked off. He turned his immediate attention to Marc, seeing the patches of green still present from when the Keeper had first invaded his body. Slowly they began to fade before his eyes. Phean and himself moved Marc on to the Hover Trolley, then he checked the LCD reading and suggested they should get Marc to the MLC quickly. Tayce moved out of the way to one side, watching, worried, as Donaldo led the way for him and Treketa to return to the MLC to get Marc's treatment under way. Tayce followed on behind towards the entrance. She felt tired, and justifiably so considering she'd gone three dayons without much sleep, plus she was still feeling the sleepy after-effects of the Select 2 injection she'd had only just on two hourons previously. She wanted to see that Organisation was back to normal, so headed there before anything else.

Halfway up the corridor she paused to look out through the sight port, staring out into the now calm Universe once again, glad they were out of the Keeper's area of space. She stood in thought for a moment, thinking about the forced encounter and the one-off kiss between her and Marc, hoping it wouldn't happen again. She wondered too if the Keeper would have killed her when he'd gotten what he wanted. It was best forgotten, she thought. She carried on to the Level Steps.

***

Dairan noticed as he glanced around that Organisation was getting back to normal. Lance was back keying in a sequence to scan the immediate area of space, to give an update on whether or not they were clear of the phenomenon known as Gruspan Space. Kelly was back running operations checks and Craig was continuing repairs on the damage that had been done. Twedor was assisting him. It was good to see things were getting back to the way they should be, the cruiser running smoothly. Lance turned, looking up and seeing Tayce walk in.

"Welcome back. How do you feel?" he asked pleasantly.

"I feel shattered, between you and me. But everything is back to normal, I see, thank goodness," replied Tayce discreetly.

Dairan waited by the DC doorway as she walked over. Noticing she looked all in, he fetched her a refreshing cup of Coffeen, figuring she could do with a pick-me-up. He headed on back across Organisation once he'd retrieved the Coffeen and entered the DC to give it to her. He looked across and saw her resting back against the chair, having drifted off into a deep sleep. He smiled, understanding that she was exhausted. He set down the Coffeen on the desktop and walked around to her. Gently, even though he didn't want to, he woke her with a gentle kiss on the cheek, speaking her name.

"Tayce! Come on – I think you'd better go and get some rest. I can take care of anything here," he said softly, looking down at her as she woke and looked up at him exhausted.

"No, I'm fine. Is that a Coffeen I see? I could really do with that," she said, looking over at the cup.

"You can take it with you. You need to continue your rest and this chair is not the proper place to get it," he said persuasively.

"But I'm fine – honest. Just give me that cup of Coffeen and it will pick me up," continued Tayce, determined not to go off duty.

"You're not fit for duty. Take this Coffeen and head back to our quarters – that's an order from me," he replied gently, but determined to get her to rest.

Tayce looked at him, amused. Dairan assured her that the cruiser would be in safe hands for a couple of hourons until she'd recharged her batteries. He told her he would contact her if anything unusual came up needing her immediate attention. Tayce reluctantly agreed and further announced that the moment Marc showed signs of improvement she wanted to know. Dairan nodded. Tayce stifled a yawn. He was right: she'd only had a couple of hourons sleep under the Select 2. Maybe some people could survive, and she generally could cope, on that; but after having a double dose of draining her strength and mind, she guessed he was right this time. She headed on across the DC in the company of Twedor, who informed Dairan he'd watch Tayce. Dairan watched her go, then followed on out to check what was going on in Organisation.

***

Marc Dayatso in the MLC was lying in an unconscious state on a medical bunk. Treketa handed Donaldo the Comprai Inject Pen and treatment cartridges he needed to aid Marc's full recovery. The overhead scanner was giving Marc's immediate body system and function readings. As the cruiser's main medical man, it concerned him that any moment Marc's body could go into a total shutdown because of what he'd gone through. He frantically loaded the necessary cartridges into the Comprai Inject Pen and administered them one by one whilst keeping his eyes on the overseer screen above Marc. Treketa looked at Donaldo, noticing the anxious concern on his face. Slowly, bit by bit, Marc's body began to respond to treatment and to come back to normality.

"Come on, Marc – fight. Don't give up," said Donaldo as he watched the overhead screen with Treketa.

Treketa watched on as Donaldo quickly and expertly treated Marc with more injections, hoping it wasn't too late to bring him back on the road to full recovery. Suddenly Marc's whole body arched and fell back on the bunk and his vital signs rapidly began to climb. Treketa sighed, as did Donaldo. They exchanged looks of great relief. Marc was on the return to normal health.

"We'll need to keep him monitored for the next couple of hourons, but I am confident he'll be OK."

"Right, I'll place a CMD on his wrist. It will help alert us to any sudden changes. I'm hoping, though, we don't get any," said Treketa, looking back at Marc, now comfortable.

She pulled up the coverlet to Marc's shoulders, glad Donaldo had managed to bring him back. He was a good friend and the team and Tayce would be lost without him. She stood watching the still-increasing readings on the overhead screen above him. Donaldo crossed to the Officette to let Organisation know the progress report on Marc and that he was coming back to them.

***

Auran Amalthea Three, known as just Auran by the team, had resumed cruise warp 5. All functioning power was restored to normality. It had been a strange Quest of sorts. Tayce had returned to the cruiser after her test at the Empire of Honitonia and kept her old powers, gaining new ones, and then they had entered Gruspan Space, home of the Green Tempest Keeper, who had powerfully tried to claim Marc as his next victim to gain intimate human knowledge – though why, no one knew. The Keeper almost killed him, and would have done so if it hadn't been for Tayce and Phean joining forces with their powerful abilities and the expert medical knowledge of Donaldo Tysonne. Sallen Vargon had decided to return to Enlopedia. She couldn't face any more hostility from Count Vargon, considering she didn't know him. To her, he was a threat she could do without. Their experience in Gruspan Space would make an interesting report back to Admiral Traun on Enlopedia and it would warn others never to venture into that area of space again for fear of being used in the Keeper's search for knowledge with the threat of death if they fell into his hands.

9. Unlawful Connection

Several dayons later Dairan was on duty in charge of Organisation. Both he and Lance were watching what could only be described as erratic flying on the near-vicinity scanner. Then Nick announced he was receiving a distress call from the vessel showing signs of erratic flying. Tayce heard what was happening through the open doorway of the DC and immediately came out to see what was unfolding. She walked from the DC, having finished her report to her father on Enlopedia about Gruspan Space and sending it via her Porto Compute. She walked to where Lance and Dairan were. Nick let her hear the distress call. Dairan recognised that the voice making the distress call was suddenly becoming more alarmed. Tayce turned, giving him a questioning look, as if to ask why? Marc at this point entered Organisation, having returned to duty after recovery from the ordeal at the hands of the Green Tempest Keeper. While Marc was under sedation in the MLC Professor Maylen had wiped the memory of the shared kiss which had taken place during his controlled seduction, by orders of Tayce to avoid any awkwardness between them on duty and as friends. As far as she was concerned it never happened between them. Now their friendship was just as it had always been – casual.

"The voice on that message is my little brother, Matt," began Dairan seriously.

"Really? How old is this little brother of yours exactly?" demanded Tayce, wondering if he had a pilot's licence. Considering the erratic flying, it seemed that it was rather like a youngster out for a joyride.

"Sixteen," replied Dairan, unimpressed by his little brother's antics, finding them downright irresponsible.

"Lance, run a scan over the vessel. See if Matt is travelling alone, or if the vessel's been taken over by someone else ordering him to call for help under forced pretences," requested Tayce.

Lance nodded, immediately doing as requested. He could see neither Dairan nor Tayce were pleased. Dairan was growing both angry and concerned beyond belief. His little brother could be in some kind of danger – there didn't seem to be any reason for the stupid manoeuvres he was pulling. After all the lectures he'd given him in the past about fooling around in space! It was stupid and dangerous.

"I've an urgent call coming in from Admiral Traun," said Nick suddenly.

"I can take it if you want to check this out," offered Marc.

"Yes, please. Nick, transfer the call to the DC," ordered Tayce.

She then went back to continuing with the matter in hand. Matt Loring seemed to be in trouble, as his erratic flying wasn't changing in heading towards them. She recalled how dangerous it had been when she was first flying out in space in her early dayons. Matt Loring was matching her, as she was back then, in his apparent inexperience as a pilot.

Lance's scan revealed one occupant, male, in the vessel before them, but there was also another very faint life sign aboard. He couldn't quite identify what or who it was no matter how hard he tried. Dairan frowned, worried. He looked at Tayce, not liking the situation at all. Tayce, on this, turned to Kelly.

"Put tractor beam in place. Bring the vessel aboard through decontamination into the Flight Hangar Bay. Have Donaldo stand by for an emergency," said Tayce as Dairan watched on.

Marc soon emerged from the DC, giving Tayce the information on her father's urgent call. It was regarding the sudden disappearance of a young female singing sensation, the daughter of Councillor Paytern. Her name was Andory and apparently she had been kidnapped en route to Pellasun Traun 2. She had been due to arrive at Pellasun Traun 2 in three dayons, but instead the Councillor, her father, received a panicked muffled message of help from the young woman, then a ransom call backed by a threat. Nothing more.

"I know you don't much care for Councillor Paytern, but your father has asked you take this Quest. Do we agree?" he asked discreetly.

"As it's come from Father, yes, I'm giving it to you to get started," she announced.

"No problem," replied Marc without further word

"I'm going to find out just what this vessel Matt is flying has aboard," she replied, wondering.

"Sure! I'll see what I can find out out by the time you get back," replied Marc.

"Come on, Dairan, you too, Twedor – we may need you," said Tayce, heading for the entrance.

Twedor crossed Organisation to follow Tayce and Dairan on out.

Marc began thinking about all the unusual aliens and people they'd either rescued or encountered so far. This Andory was high on the list of glitzy people. A new list, he thought! He smiled to himself, thinking how Councillor Paytern had gone through Darius Traun to ask Tayce for her assistance. He continued on with tracing the final steps of this Miss Paytern with Lance, so they could start action in finding her. If they pulled it off, the Councillor would owe Tayce.

***

Outside Auran Amalthea Three was latching on by tractor beam to the small grey vessel and taking steps to bring it through decontamination into the Flight Hangar Bay. No one on board the cruiser was aware of the fact there was an unseen second person on the vessel and one Tayce wouldn't be pleased to see any time soon. On board the small vessel, in through the front sight port, Matt Loring could be seen sitting with a look of frightened apprehension, thinking of just what lay ahead for him and his uninvited unconscious guest, who had suddenly materialised on board groaning in pain during transit. What reception was he going to get when Tayce discovered whom he had aboard? Matt was like Dairan in appearance, but younger, with the same short dark-brown hair and brown eyes. Matt knew his brother was part of the Amalthean team and he no doubt was going to crucify Matt for flying so stupidly when many times he'd told him not to and stressed how dangerous it was.

***

Back on Auran Amalthea Three, Dairan walked beside Tayce, turning over in his mind how he was going to handle the stupid flying actions of his little brother and wondering what Matt was doing so far from home. Tayce glanced at him, seeing the thoughtful angered look on his normally warm handsome features, realising it was a good thing she couldn't read those angered thoughts at that moment. 'God knows what they would be!' she thought, as he looked fit to burst.

Dairan was still in silent angered thought as they rounded the corner, entering into the Flight Hangar Bay. He'd not said a word since they'd stepped down on to Level 3. Tayce looked across to see the small round grey vessel beginning final decontamination procedures. Suddenly she was filled with a sudden feeling of déjà vu of the unwanted intimate kind and a name: Dion. It happened just for a few cencrons then faded away. She brushed it aside, concentrating on the small vessel coming in to a landing position after decontamination. Both Dairan and Tayce waited until the landing procedure was complete, then walked towards the entrance. It slowly opened on approach.

After a few cencrons Matt Loring stepped out cautiously. He quickly asked if there was a medical doctor on board as he had an injured unwanted guest. As if by coincidence, Donaldo and Treketa ran into the Flight Hangar Bay. Donaldo glanced around, looking for the emergency. Matt called him over to the entrance and showed him inside, where he could see who it was. Tayce stood waiting, none the wiser about who was on board, but her feelings were giving her strange familiar unwanted vibes once more. After a few minons Donaldo stepped back outside, wondering how to tell her who it was. He glanced at Dairan, then Matt, who were watching what was unfolding before them, concerned they'd walked into an elaborate pirate trap of some sort and Matt was somehow connected.

Dairan walked over to the vessel's entrance, looking inside to see who the injured unwanted guest was. His eyes turned a dark shade of angered brown. He grabbed his younger brother by the breast of his uniform and threw him hard up against the outer hull in anger fit to burst.

"What's wrong? Tell me now! What is it? Who's inside?" demanded Tayce, trying to prise Dairan off his younger brother, worried he was going to do something he would later regret.

"He knows, don't you, Matt? What's he doing with you? Tell her," snapped Dairan, holding Matt hard against the outer hull, not calming down.

"I had pirates chasing me, but they weren't after me. They were after whoever has materialised into my control area using some kind of energy transfer. He was near to unconscious when he arrived. They worked him over good. He didn't tell me who he is before he passed out," explained Matt.

"Right, who is it – though I probably have a perfect idea with the feelings I've been getting for the last half an houron?" asked Tayce, growing furious to think that Dion might be back in her life again.

"Treketa, let's have that Hover Trolley, please," said Donaldo. He decided he'd rather let Tayce see who it was for herself.

The Hover Trolley was activated inside the vessel and the injured being was placed aboard. Soon Donaldo came out with Treketa, letting the Hover Trolley come forth before them. The bloodied and beaten bearded features were the first thing Tayce saw of none other than Dion. She'd been right, she thought. She couldn't believe what she was seeing. She looked at Dairan, then Matt. Whoever had beaten Dion had given him a lesson he wouldn't forget any time soon if he survived. They had worked him over hard.

"I want the full story later. In the meantime, you can show Matt to the guest quarters – and please refrain from killing your brother en route," said Tayce discreetly close to Dairan.

With this, Tayce walked away across the Flight Hangar Bay behind Donaldo and Treketa, now leaving with an unconscious, badly tortured and near-to-death Lord Dion on a Hover Trolley. Were they too late to save him? wondered Tayce as she looked at the battered and bleeding bearded features of the man who had left her on her quarters floor the last time they'd met. His attire was burnt in places and ripped. It looked as if he'd been tortured. But it didn't make sense. Dion was once the leader of a pirate tribe. Why should his own kind attack him? After all, that's why he'd escaped after what he'd done – to continue on with his old ways. He obviously couldn't change what had been bred into him for many yearons. A part of her wanted to feel sorry for him – it wasn't his fault he couldn't change. It was in his blood. As they say, once a space pirate, always a space pirate.

"Tayce, I'll call you if he regains consciousness," said Donaldo.

"Keep him in force-field restraints. I know he's badly injured, but I'd feel a lot happier," ordered Tayce casually, calling after Donaldo.

"All right – as you wish," replied Donaldo, but he felt she was overreacting. Considering the condition Dion was currently in, it would take a miracle for him to start his old tricks on Tayce or cause trouble.

Tayce let Donaldo go on to the Deck Travel to take Dion back to the MLC. Twedor looked up at his mistress as they began in the other direction towards the Level Steps. He could see she was in deep thought over the situation that had arisen in the last moments regarding a man she never wanted to set eyes on again.

"Anything you want to talk about? It might help," offered Twedor.

"I can't understand why Dion's own kind would torture him like this. He's supposed to be extremely powerful and he generally can handle himself in combat very well. It's puzzling as to why he should come here," said Tayce, thinking as they went.

"Maybe whoever did this withdrew his powers from him before they tortured him," offered Twedor.

"There's more to this, I'm certain. Just as long as he hasn't brought trouble to this cruiser!" said Tayce.

"We'll be prepared if we get a follow-up attack of sorts," replied Twedor.

Tayce began on up the Level Steps, still in thought over Dion's somewhat unusual and unexpected arrival. Twedor walked beside her. He knew what reaction Marc would give when he found out Lord Dion was back on board. It wouldn't matter whether he was injured or not. Marc despised Dion and everything he stood for – particularly after what he'd done to Tayce before he'd dematerialised off the cruiser the last time. Twedor glanced at Tayce as they walked up the last flight of steps on to Level 1. He figured there was going to be an outburst when she told Marc.

***

Half an houron elapsed. Dairan had shown Matt to the guest quarters after giving him the third degree as to why he'd flown solo and in an irresponsible fashion across the perilous Universe. Dairan ordered him to be up in Organisation on Level 1 in forty minons. He would be required to explain his connection with the passenger he'd been carrying. With this, Dairan left Matt sitting on the mouldable soffette and walked from the quarters with darkened angered eyes and a far-from-pleased expression on his face. He wasn't prepared to forgive Matt so easily, considering whom he'd just brought back on board, even though not intentionally. He briskly headed to the Level Steps, wondering what Tayce was going to say, considering his little brother had brought Lord Dion back into her life again.

***

Marc a while later, was standing in the centre of Organisation, giving Tayce a look that said he wondered if he'd heard right. But then, so were the surrounding team. Dion was back on board, unconscious in the MLC. Tayce looked at Marc, then around the centre at the various far-from-pleased questioning looks from her team. The tension was so tight and silent that it could have been sliced with a Slazer knife. Tayce turned and walked into the DC. Marc was silent, still trying to get his head around what she'd just announced. Then he ordered everyone back to taking care of the present Quest, to find Andory Paytern. The team around him slowly went back to their current tasks, but Lord Dion was on their thoughts. They were wondering how he'd come to be back on board when a monthon ago he'd left the cruiser, going back to his old lifestyle. Marc walked across the centre, entering the DC. Tayce was stood looking out of the sight port in thought. Marc entered, pausing just inside the DC. Tayce turned, picking up his presence.

"That was uncomfortable out there. They're concerned about Dion's sudden arrival. I wonder why he's back here, particularly after what he did last time," said Tayce in a near whisper and deep in thought.

"They're as shocked as we are, we all feel disgusted by the fact he nearly left you for dead on his departure. How else do you expect anyone to feel, considering we nearly lost you?" replied Marc directly.

"I don't like him being here any more than you do. I couldn't just chuck him out in space with the kind of injuries he has, even if you could," said Tayce spitefully, looking directly at him, knowing he would.

Marc threw his hands up as a sign of surrender. He knew it wasn't like her to do it either. He'd gone too far. He knew she wouldn't have just left Dion to die in space, despite what he'd done. She'd changed a little since her test – Before she probably would have ejected him out of the airlock without a thought. But he could see, despite what Dion had done the last time, that now he was aboard she wanted to find out what had happened and how young Matt Loring was connected in the way he had brought him to the cruiser.

"Maybe we ought to question this Matt Loring?" suggested Marc softly.

"Don't worry, I've already done that," said Dairan, walking into the DC.

Both Marc and Tayce looked to him questioningly, waiting to hear what he had to say. The Telelinkphone sounded on Tayce's desktop. She turned, picking up the slim cordless handset. Donaldo was on the other end. He requested her urgently in the MLC. Tayce agreed. Placing the handset back, she began across the DC to the entrance, ordering Dairan to tell Marc what he knew from talking to Matt. She said she'd be back as soon as she found out what Donaldo wanted. Twedor wasn't letting her go alone – he followed on. Marc knew there was only one thing Donaldo could possibly want Tayce for, and that was Dion. Secretly he hoped he was dying, considering the bad unlawful things he'd done to date. He smiled, wondering if this time around Dion was faking his injuries just to get back on board. He was in for a hell of a shock if he had as Tayce was now stronger in her powerful ability to fight him if she had to, despite his near-to-death condition. He would fail miserably. He and Dairan began discussing Matt Loring and his involvement with the sudden arrival of Dion.

***

Tayce briskly hurried down the Level Steps on to Level 2, followed by Twedor trying to keep up with her urgency to reach the MLC. She could suddenly feel Dion's presence as she headed on along Level 2 to the MLC doors, but it was weak. It still slightly unnerved her, after what Marc said about him leaving her for dead and jumping cruiser the last time she'd seen him. She paused before the doors, glancing down at Twedor, then stepped into the pickup sensor area for the doors to automatically open. As they drew apart, the waft of warm sterile air came out to meet her.

She and Twedor walked in to be greeted by the form of Dion, now in a medical patient attire, lying on a side medical bunk. Donaldo looked up and crossed to her.

"He's barely conscious, but wants to see you. His injuries are too much for you and me to do anything about. He's not expected to survive much longer," said Donaldo quietly.

Tayce looked to where Dion was lying, then nodded. Donaldo let her walk forth and stood discreetly to one side, observing as Tayce drew near to where Dion could see her. He was ready to act should he need to save her.

"You're a sight for sore eyes, Fairness," said Dion with great difficulty, turning his head to face her.

"Who did this to you?" asked Tayce, to the point, looking down at him, ready to listen, but finding his injuries were awful to look at – not that he no doubt deserved them for all the wrong he'd done.

"Would you believe my own kind?" he replied groggily, looking back at her with bruised eyes.

"Donaldo said you had something you wanted to say to me?" asked Tayce, to the point.

"I can do you no more harm, Fairness, believe me. Fairness, in my jacket pocket is a disk chip. I believe you're looking for a young woman named Paytern. Am I not right? This disk chip gives the exact whereabouts of this female. You have to act fast and get her out of where she is. If you want to save her for her daddy, you must do this within forty-nine hourons. She's in great danger. They know she's the daughter of a councillor as it is. I saw what they had in mind for her. They stole my powers and beat me to what I am before you. Does this tell you what they could do to her?" put Dion, making the greatest of efforts to speak.

"How can I believe this? You've lied before," replied Tayce, wondering whether he was leading her into an elaborate pirate trap of some sort and they'd be raided. He'd let her down before.

"I apologise for what I did to you the last time we met. It was wrong, but even pirates have feelings and deep down I think a lot of you, Fairness. You're different from other females I've encountered. When I left here, I knew what I had done to you could have killed you and I would be killed for it if I was found, so I laid low for a while and decided to become a spy. Hence I found your young woman's whereabouts. She is with the worst form of pirates you could ever imagine," he replied, looking up at Tayce in true agony.

"Worse than you? That's hard to believe. I didn't think there were any. We thought you'd gone to forge a new tribe," replied Tayce softly, looking down at him, seeing suddenly that he could do her no more harm as he was so near to death.

"They tortured me and stole my powers – for being nosey, you could say, and letting them think I was on their side, pretending to be one of them just so I could gain and pass on information," he continued.

"My father was willing to have all charges dropped against you when you said you wanted to be good. I can't believe I'm saying this, but is there anything I can do for you?" said Tayce, feeling for the first time a bit of sympathy for a man that had always done her wrong, who had used her mind for the wrong reasons.

Donaldo and Treketa stood exchanging surprised discrete glances, amazed at what Tayce had asked him. But he was in no shape to spring any surprises. The torture he'd received from his captors had drained him of all the great powerfulness that had made him the character he was. There was nothing left. His normally strong muscular body had been shattered so badly that time was not on his side. Dion reached out his hand, taking Tayce's delicate and slender hand just as Treketa was about to go for her Slazer and Twedor activated his. Tayce was somewhat surprised at first and wanted to pull free, but felt the soft warmth of his grip.

"Bring me back to who I was," he said jokingly, making light of the moment even though he knew it was impossible.

"You know we can't. If I could, I'd have to turn you over to the authorities," replied Tayce softly.

"Fairness, I want you to know you were extra specially precious to me. I saw something in you – a strong spirit – when we first met, and even though at times you were afraid of me and showed me that fighting spirit, determined not to trust me, you had nothing to fear. Like I said, you were different from other women, and I respected that. In answer to your question about doing something for me, besides bringing me back, would you honour me in burying me here in space?" he asked, his life fading.

"Yes! You saved my life on Olarintz – it's the least I can do," replied Tayce, forgetting the worst aspects of their past.

"We'll meet again somewhere in time, somehow. Thank... you," he said, fading out.

Without warning the medical monitor alarm sounded and Dion's vital signs dropped to nothing. Death was confirmed by Donaldo quietly. All life signs were reading deceased. The pirate leader, once of the Boglayons and a man to be feared, was gone from the Universe to eternity. Tayce turned away for a few minons. She couldn't understand why she felt so near to tears. It was ridiculous. Maybe it had been his confession before he died that had hit her. Treketa crossed and handed her the disk chip, saying nothing.

"Prepare him for ceremonial burial in his attire," ordered Tayce.

"Tayce, he did all those bad things. Are you sure?" put Treketa, surprised.

"Yes! This request is in honour of the fact that back on Olarintz he could have left me to die after I crashed, but he didn't. It's a kind of payback, that's all, for saving my life," replied Tayce as she glanced back at Dion's still form.

"As you wish," replied Donaldo, stepping in, also somewhat surprised that she was doing what Dion had asked.

Tayce glanced at the now deceased Dion once more, eyes closed, gone forever. Then she began towards the MLC entrance, not glancing back, thinking to herself she'd once had thoughts of killing Dion, but now he was gone. She began remembering their first encounter, when he was leader of the Boglayons and had almost crushed her hand. It was strange to think his own people had stolen his powerfulness, turned on him and tortured him so much he died. It was weird also that he should have crawled to her. Now she was giving him a space burial.

Just as she was about to walk through the parting doors, Donaldo announced he'd get Amal to notify her when the burial was ready to commence. Tayce agreed, continuing on out and taking the disk chip back to Organisation. Dion had risked his life and torture to obtain it. Twedor deactivated his Slazer finger, walking alongside Tayce.

"Are you all right, Tayce? I think maybe he got to you – am I not right?" put Twedor gently.

"Let's just put it this way: maybe he wasn't such a bad man, but was led into the wrong kind of life," replied Tayce quietly, looking down at Twedor, thinking about the fact.

***

Marc was watching over Lance's shoulder in Organisation, as the Destination Scan Probe was searching the vicinity of the supposed whereabouts of Andory Paytern. But this was not the first attempt. It was the third. So far each time the scan probe either blew up or malfunctioned for an unknown reason. Marc was growing impatient. Dairan was watching also, interested to find out if the latest probe, which had been modified to withstand stronger interference, would go all the way to its destination and send back what they needed.

Matt was sitting in the DC, waiting to see Tayce under Marc's and Dairan's orders. He wondered what she was going to ask him. He couldn't tell her any more about what had happened where Dion was concerned. Tayce soon entered Organisation. Crossing, she handed the disk chip to Lance.

"Here – a present from Dion. It'll help in finding Andory Paytern, and we have less than forty-nine hourons to rescue her before it's too late," said Tayce.

"A gift from Dion, you say? What's he promised this time in order to give it to you?" asked Marc, waiting for the latest surprising promise the Pirate Lord had no chance of fulfilling.

"There isn't one… he's dead!" replied Tayce, snapping back at him.

"Come again? Did I hear you say dead? You mean the Universe is finally rid of the leader of the—"

"That's enough! That's an order. And if you must know, he didn't return to his old lifestyle; he became a spy, hence Andory's whereabouts are on that disk. He was tortured by his own kind, who were trying to get it. Pleased?" snapped Tayce, continuing on into the DC without further word.

Marc raised his eyebrows. He was left speechless as to what to say next. He figured he'd hit a raw nerve, but why, he had no idea.

Lance dropped the disk chip into the reader and soon the small screen in front of him began showing information about vital points and passageways to rescue the Councillor's daughter. Lance didn't need telling his next orders. He transferred the destination coordinates straight into Kelly's console, and she immediately locked in the quickest available journey. Auran Amalthea Three went to hyper-thrust turbo speed and headed off across the Universe to get to its destination in time to save Andory Paytern.

Dairan shook his head at Marc's attitude. He could have shown more respect, allowing for the fact Tayce was feeling a little sensitive over what she'd been hit with regarding Dion. He continued across Organisation, going on into the DC. He wanted to put to Tayce what Marc had in mind for Matt, considering he'd left Earthonex, their home, not wanting to go back. Tayce was standing looking at Matt, listening to what he had to say about his untimely meeting with Dion. She wanted to hear Matt's side of the story, and it matched what Dion had told her. For the first time in his life, he hadn't lied. She walked around the back of her desk. Matt wondered what she was going to say to him next. Dairan suddenly began explaining that life on their home world had become difficult. Matt, being the only brother left at home, couldn't take any more. Everything that went wrong he was blamed for, for no reason at all. Their father came down on him, saying he ought to make a life for himself instead of just spending his time fooling around. He'd grown fed up and decided to take off in search of Auran's present course, hoping he could join the team somehow. Tayce listened to what Dairan said. She glanced at Matt, considering where he could be best placed on board – somewhere that would accommodate his age and no doubt low experience. He really was too young at sixteen to be on the cruiser, but she decided she was prepared to give him a monthon's trial, to see how he worked out.

“Would you wait outside, Matt? I want to talk to Dairan here,” said Tayce casually.

“Yes, ma’am,” he pleasantly replied, walking out the DC.

Both Dairan and Tayce stood waiting until Matt had left, then stood in discussion about the pros and cons of having such a young member on board.

“He should really be going back home. He’s really too young to be out here in space, let alone here on Auran. However, I think we could do something for him. I can’t put him on duty in Organisation, though I could find him something below Levels. Leave it with me a moment.”

“I’ll wait,” said Dairan, glad she was giving Matt a chance.

Tayce, as Dairan paced the DC, contacted Aldonica on the Telelinkphone. Aldonica soon answered, though busy. Tayce explained about Matt – who he was and what she had in mind. There were a few cencrons of silence, then Aldonica agreed. Tayce suggested she come to Organisation and the DC to discuss the finer points. Aldonica agreed, saying she was on her way.

Tayce replaced the handset, relaxing back in her chair. She could see they were travelling at hyper-thrust turbo as she glanced out through the sight port at the stars speeding past. This made Tayce realise that the coordinates for the destined port of Quest had been officially logged in and they were on their way to rescue Andory Paytern.

Soon the DC doors opened and Aldonica entered, out of breath. She gained her breath and relaxed, ready to listen. Tayce suggested she sit down for a moment, then explained what she had in mind. Aldonica didn’t see any problem with the idea. Dairan, on Tayce’s request, called Matt back into the DC. Matt entered, feeling apprehensive.

“Matt, this is Weaponry Specialist Darstayne. She’s agreed to take you on as her assistant for the period of one monthon. If you work hard and prove yourself to be a valuable member of this team, then at the end of this time we will look at you remaining on the team. If you don’t work out, you will be flown home by Dairan here. Is that understood?” asked Tayce whilst Aldonica listened.

“Yes, Captain, and thank you,” replied Matt, grateful for his chance.

“One thing: when we are on board we call each other by our Christian names, but when we visit somewhere important you address visitors and us by rank, unless otherwise stated. You will also behave at all times on board and when we visit planets or go on Quests. Finally, if you are asked to help on this cruiser in an emergency – it happens – you do it. We all work as a team,” explained Tayce. “Understood?”

“Yes, ma’am,” said Matt, feeling a little daunted.

Aldonica soon took Matt under her wing and headed towards the entrance of the DC. Dairan waited until both had gone from earshot, then thanked Tayce.

“Don’t thank me yet. He has a monthon to prove himself,” pointed out Tayce.

Tayce was keeping an open mind on Matt joining the team. First of all he was to young to be on a vast cruiser such as Auran Amalthea Three, and he would be especially at risk in the line of danger because of his age and inexperience. A crime-orientated cruiser was really no place for any lad of sixteen without first-degree knowledge or experience of a sudden crisis or emergency. But what had made her give him a chance wasn't the fact that Dairan was Matt's older brother or the fact he wanted to escape his home world. It was because he wanted to do something worthwhile, become something. Dairan knew in his heart Tayce was right: Matt had to prove himself as a team player. And he understood that her decision was the only decision over his little brother's future. She was Dairan's superior, despite what they were off duty.

Both walked out into Organisation to see how the Quest to rescue Andory Paytern was coming along. Upon exiting the DC, Tayce was greeted by a very unusual corkscrew-shaped vessel in the colours of green, brown and purple. It was hardly a friendly looking vessel – quite the reverse, with armament points here and there, protruding from the shape. Lance looked up at Tayce as she neared.

"Hardly inviting, is it?" he said, glancing at the sight that almost filled the entire centre of the sight port.

"Can you detect if Andory is on board?" asked Tayce.

"Unfortunately they have an impenetrable shield. It's impossible to get any kind of readings," replied Lance.

"Scan for a weak point. It's generally at the point emitting the shield," ordered Tayce.

"Tried that. Their shield has no weak points. If we open fire, we'll get the feedback. I've done some serious research, I can tell you," explained Lance.

"Nick, get Phean up here. I've an idea," ordered Tayce, thinking of something that might just work.

"You're not thinking of doing what I think you're going to do?" asked Marc, giving her a 'come on, think about this' look. He had a hunch she was going over to the vessel before them, which he thought would be unwise.

"Going aboard – breaking through their shield, in a manner of speaking – yes!" replied Tayce.

"You're crazy. Look, I don't much like Dion and all he stood for, but look what they did to him," pointed out Marc, alarmed that whoever was aboard the vessel could do the same to her.

"This will be different, you'll see," replied Tayce, not letting on what she had in mind.

Sometimes he wished she wouldn't act so irresponsibly. Did she have a death wish? Because it sure looked like it from where he was standing. This looked like a no-win situation and he didn't like it.

Tayce turned her attention to the vessel for a few moments, then turned back, ordering Lance to show her the layout of the vessel if there was one among Dion's information. Lance replied that Dion did have a rough layout. The scan probe with the modifications had managed earlier to scan a more in-depth layout before the vessel picked up the probe and blocked their intrusion. It almost destroyed any real layout when the shield was activated to keep the scan out. Lance keyed in a command, bringing the sketchy information up plus what information Dion had gained. Both studied it for a moment, much to Marc's concern. He figured it to be to downright dangerous to go aboard. He had no idea what Tayce was going to try. Phean ran into Organisation.

"You wanted my help?" he said, coming to a pause.

Tayce gestured towards the sight port, then explained about the non-penetrable shield surrounding the vessel with the name Stangrim along the side. Phean listened as Tayce put forth her idea. He thought about it for a moment, then agreed. Together, under the watchful looks of the team, they both concentrated. After a few minons, using their minds and powerful abilities, while physically remaining in Organisation they crossed space towards the Stangrim and invisibly walked through the defence shield around the one-and-a-half-milon-in-diameter vessel. Once they reached the other side, they boarded, searching (still using their minds) for the shutdown controls for the defence shield. Phean took hold of Tayce's hands to steady her in Organisation. He communicated with her via his mind as they continued the search, checking she was all right. This had been her first time to try to penetrate a force field using linked minds. The last time they'd shared powers was when they'd driven the Green Tempest Keeper from Marc and the cruiser. Tayce replied that she was OK, suggesting they look for Andory as they went. Phean agreed.

Phean soon found Andory. She had, as usual, been tortured. Her young beautiful pop-star features and slim shapely figure had taken a severe beating. Phean felt her pain and upset. Tayce found the deactivation main point for the vessel's defence shield, sending a powerful energy surge so strong through the system it burnt out within minons. Tayce suggested they retreat back to Auran. On this, both brought their powers back to Auran across space and back aboard, slipping through the Invis Shield, back into their present position, standing facing each other in Organisation. Both slowly opened their eyes, glancing around at the surprised faces of the team, including Marc. Who were impressed.

"Andory's on board. They've tortured her. I saw her lying on the floor of a cell," explained Phean.

"Their shields are down," called Kelly, checking.

"Let's get Andory out of there," said Tayce in urgency.

"Who are you taking aboard?" asked Marc, curious.

"Phean, you, Marc, and tell Aldonica to join us and bring her PolloAld bombs," said Tayce.

"Do you want me along?" asked Craig.

"Yes, just in case we can't easily get Andory out of the surroundings they've placed her in. Also check your handguns are fully charged – we don't want any failures over there," replied Tayce seriously.

Marc turned, telling Dairan and Kelly to stand by and have Donaldo ready to receive Andory for medical treatment. Dairan nodded. Marc, Tayce and Craig, who'd just finished telling Aldonica it was Quest time and to bring her PolloAld bombs, she was needed, followed on behind with Twedor. Dairan turned his attention back to the sight port. It suddenly crossed his mind that the Stangrim could leave the orbit she was presently in, if she so wanted, taking the Quest team with them. He crossed to Lance, putting this to him. Lance agreed.

"Amal, is it possible to stop that vessel in our orbit from leaving if we wanted to?" asked Dairan, standing half facing her and the main sight port.

"I can cast a temporary freeze on all its operations, Dairan," suggested Amal.

"Then do it, please, Amal," ordered Dairan seriously in a commanding tone.

"Temporarily freezing all operations to manoeuvres of the Stangrim leaving orbit. Now activated," she replied precisely, to the point.

Dairan stood in thought, wondering just what kind of race lay ahead on board the Stangrim for Tayce and the team in the rescue of Andory. Donaldo and Treketa entered Organisation to find out what was happening. Donaldo announced that Dion was ready for space burial. Dairan nodded understandingly. He began explaining about the Quest and how Phean had seen Andory in what appeared to be a holding cell. She would need medical attention upon arriving on board.

Treketa began describing Andory, saying she was quite a female idol in her music career. She generally used quite a lot of special effects as part of her act and most of her appearances were sold out within a short time. Many of her disk-chip compilations had been hits. It wasn't music that was mainstream; it was something young and trendy.

Dairan wasn't surprised. He'd heard some of Andory's music and the one's he'd heard were fair with a rhythmic beat, fit for youngsters in their teens. But there had also been ones she'd recorded that were romantic, which he'd liked.

Nick behind them announced that Tayce was ready to transpot and Matt was on his way to Organisation, as she wanted him to be kept an eye on in her absence. Dairan nodded, knowing his little brother was likely to start mischief when bored. Both Donaldo and Treketa jokingly teased that Dairan wished his little brother had remained at home, now he was his babysitter.

***

On the Stangrim the head of the obvious crew of brutal murderers and pirates stood. He was furious, demanding to know why they couldn't leave orbit. He was a big-built man with cruel, uninteresting features, which at the present time were in full scowl. The group surrounding him were a true bloodthirsty, mean-looking lot. Their uniforms were a loose baggy top and trousers in a dirty purple colour. The marauders were of various heights, builds and ages, ranging from around seventeen to fifty-four and there wasn't a good-looking one amongst them. There was a mark of their brotherhood right in the centre of each of the men's foreheads, in the shape of a small black triangle with a jewel inset. But was it more than just a jewel, or was it some kind of weapon or scanning reading device?

"What's taking time? Get this vessel under way. I want that female at auction before first light. She'll fetch us a nice tidy sum, being a councillor's daughter. You sort this, otherwise I will be forced to do to you what I did to that no-good idiot of an ex-pirate, Dion," said the leader, putting his hand on the shoulder of the nearest team member, giving him an evil look that meant what he said.

"I'm trying, honest I am. According to these instruments there's no reason why we're stationary," replied the group member as if afraid of his leader.

"Find a way to get us out of here, I'm warning you, you useless fool," barked the leader.

"Yes, master, leader," replied the group member, fumbling over the controls at hand.

"Sir, our shields are depleted," announced another adjoining member.

"Something or someone has done this. Scan the Stangrim and the immediate area of the Universe, now!" bellowed the leader in fury.

He had his suspicions – not that they would do him any good. Auran Amalthea Three was undetectable as usual, despite being within a five-milon orbit of the Stangrim. It wasn't clear what the Stangrim and its crew's purpose was. Dion hadn't exactly said, only he'd pretended to gain their trust in order to convince them he wanted to join his own kind. They were just known as another strain of murderous pirates out to make a fast amount of currency, and they didn't care how they got it or who they got it from.

***

The Amalthean Quest team materialised aboard the Stangrim. Their intruder anti-detection was activated, making them undetectable to any device that could otherwise pick them up. Craig carried a small pouch which contained his Tech Kit with the right devices to gain entry to Andory's cell. The vessel wasn't badly lit – it was natural lighting. Marc checked the hand-held scanner, which was protected by the anti-detection field. Phean informed him there was no need as he could pinpoint Andory's whereabouts using his sensing technique. Tayce gestured for him to continue. Once the destination was discovered they all set off with their Pollomoss handguns poised, ready to use them if something suddenly appeared, but they hoped nothing would. Otherwise it would raise awareness of them being present, even though they were under anti-detection. Tayce watched ahead as they alertly proceeded. Phean paused, explaining that Andory had a visitor in her cell.

"Who?" asked Tayce in a whisper.

"He's certainly not a fan, let's put it that way. She's up ahead to the left," replied Phean, breaking into a sprint, forgetting the fact that he was supposed to be under Tayce's orders, and she'd told him not to leave the group.

"Aldonica, start setting those PolloAld bombs. I want this band finished," ordered Tayce.

"You've got it," replied Aldonica in a whisper.

Twedor stayed with Aldonica whilst she twisted the setting and clamped the PolloAld bombs on the corridor wall beside the inset pillars, where they would do the most damage when they exploded. Tayce ran on with Marc to rescue Andory. All paused outside the circular entrance doors of the cell. Tayce looked at Phean and read his mind. Andory was being tortured once more for further information about her father. Tayce gave the word – on the count of three. Then she and Marc stood ready, Pollomosses primed on the entrance.

Phean held his hand with palm facing outwards and concentrated. A white beam of light blew the doors wide open. Then he used his gift to brutally throw the grubby-looking lecherous Stangrim crew member off his feet and hard against the far cell wall. The torturer dropped to the ground and remained silent, out cold. Tayce went into the cell and over to a cowering Andory.

"Andory, it's all right – you're safe. I'm Captain Traun of the Amalthean Quests. We're here to get you out," said Tayce, appalled at Andory's injuries, trying to comfort her as she sobbed uncontrollably.

"Thank you. Can we get out of here? I can't take any more," said Andory, shaking and tearful.

"Yes, easy," said Marc, steadying her as she almost toppled on rising to her feet.

The team all got together. Aldonica ran into the cell with Twedor, exclaiming that if they didn't get out of their present surroundings soon they would be in danger. They'd been spotted. Company was on its way and they would be pinned down with no escape. Tayce nodded and heard boot steps approaching to confirm what Aldonica had said. But how had they been spotted unless…? And then Tayce looked down at her Anti-detection device. It wasn't lit. It had suddenly failed.

"Time to leave, I think, unless we want a full-on fight to our deaths," said Tayce.

Marc raised his Wristlink with the other arm supporting Andory. He contacted Kelly back at Auran, but all he could get was static. Craig checked his scanner. The cell they were standing in was constructed to block out any communication devices.

'Brilliant!' thought Tayce.

The advancing boot steps were growing nearer by the cencron. Phean used his powers.

"I can hold them back long enough so we can go on to a section of corridor further up, where we can get a clearer signal to leave," volunteered Phean.

"OK, let's go. Marc, look after Andory," ordered Tayce as they headed out of the cell, guns poised, heading on up the corridor to a point from which to contact Auran Amalthea Three.

Marc shielded Andory as they progressed up the corridor. Phean followed on behind, using his powers to hold the advancing Stangrim Marauders at bay, but he could only do it for so long. Weapon fire erupted. It was firepower on both sides as Tayce and the others fired back in retaliation and tried to get themselves into an area where they could Transpot off the vessel alive. As soon as the signal was clear enough to send word to Kelly to Transpot them back to the cruiser, it was done and immediate Transpot took on, sending the whole team and Andory away from the onslaught of weapon fire from the Stangrim Marauders back to Auran Amalthea Three.

***

On arriving on board Auran Amalthea Three, Andory suddenly passed out. She'd collapsed from all the torture she'd suffered. Marc caught her gently mid fall. He scooped her up and placed her on the awaiting Hover Trolley. Tayce watched on. Donaldo informed her, as he prepared to move Andory to the MLC, that Dion was ready in the Pious Sanctuary Centre for his space burial. Marc suggested she go on; he'd head back to Organisation and inform Councillor Paytern that Andory was safe and get them under way for Pellasun Traun 2. Tayce agreed, guiding Twedor on out of the Transpot Centre.

"I'll take care of Andory – get her treated and cleaned up. Speak to you soon," said Donaldo heading away.

Donaldo took the Hover Trolley off out of the Transpot Centre with Treketa, heading on back to the MLC. Craig and Aldonica walked on out back to the Weaponry Design Centre. Phean waited for Marc and together they began off to Level 1 in discussion about the Stangrim Marauders. But as they walked, Marc realised Tayce was facing the space burial of Dion alone. He knew she did feel something for him, though he couldn't understand why considering his original lifestyle of old, which for some strange reason she'd forgotten. He raised his Wristlink, contacting Dairan, informing him that he was on his way back to Organisation and that Tayce had gone with Twedor to give Dion his requested space burial. Marc pointed out that maybe he should discreetly check out how Tayce was doing. Dairan saw his point and agreed, ceasing communications.

***

Tayce and Twedor reached the entrance to the Pious Sanctuary Centre Chapel. Tayce braced herself, then entered as the glassene-and-steelex frosted doors drew apart in front of her. Ahead was the standard burial navy-coloured casket. It was hard to imagine it belonged to Dion. All he was and stood for was gone.

"Soft music, please, Amal, befitting for a passing to eternity," ordered Tayce without taking her eyes off the casket, suspended on an energy beam.

"Commencing requested music," replied Amal.

Over the sound system light orchestral music was played, befitting the occasion. Twedor paused, allowing his mistress to go on alone, to proceed with Dion's request to be given a space burial. Tayce walked up the aisle until she came to the head of Dion's casket, where she came to a gentle stop. Silently she said to herself that even though Dion was once a pirate leader, a wrongdoer against many races, he was a great man of his time and a man of power. His last act was a far cry from the man who had done numerous wrongs. This act was one of two that he had done after he'd converted to the right side of the spacial law. He'd save Andory's life. The other was saving hers on Olarintz. Tayce realised that, unless by some marvel, Dion wouldn't return again. She knew she would no longer feel that overpowering presence. She would never again hear him use the name he called her: Fairness. She began to commit his body to space, feeling somewhat sorrowful despite what he'd done.

"I, Tayce Traun, hereby commit Lord Dion, once leader of the Boglayon Pirates, to a journey through space and time, to eternity, erasing all wrongdoings he has done on this plane, allowing his body to travel to where he may find peace," she announced.

Tayce pushed a small silver button on the flat console at the side of her. Dion's casket began moving forward towards the exit doors to be jettisoned into space.

The entrance doors to the Pious Sanctuary Centre opened suddenly behind her. Tayce flinched. She was so engrossed in watching Dion leave Auran Amalthea Three for the last time she never heard anyone walk in. Dairan casually and slowly walked towards the moving casket, then to Tayce. He too was thinking it was the last time they'd see Lord Dion. Slowly he made his way towards her with Twedor watching on.

"Marc said you were doing this. It's an end of an era for him, isn't it?" asked Dairan, softly coming to a pause at her side, watching the final moments of Dion's final departure.

"Yes, but at least he did one good act before he died, he apologised to me for all he'd done when he left me in the condition he had in my quarters on his last visit," replied Tayce, watching the casket's final moments.

"You saw something that none of us saw in him, didn't you?" asked Dairan, curious.

"It's strange really – even though he did what he did to me, I feel he wanted to revert to the good side of the spacial law. He was afraid he would be targeted for attempting it, which he was on the *Stangrim*, he was in a no-win situation, because they tortured him for trying," replied Tayce.

"Your father said he would have made sure he would be cleared when you were rescued on Olarintz. I can't understand it – maybe he couldn't leave behind what he was in the days of his leadership," replied Dairan.

"Yes, also he could have realised that if he appeared on Enlopedia he would have been arrested on sight, and he couldn't take that chance," said Tayce.

"Well, I know I never thought I'd say this, but I hope he finds some kind of peace where he ends up," said Dairan sincerely.

"That's good of you to say," said Tayce, pleased.

"Tell me one thing if you can: why are there so many pirate races in the Universe?" asked Dairan, looking to her.

"I've no idea, but someone from my home world, Traun, had a theory," replied Tayce.

"Really? What?" prompted Dairan.

"He used to say they must have run out of places of evil and wrongdoing on Earth 1, in which to conduct their criminal acts, so they continued to gather their spoils in the wider Universe," replied Tayce casually.

"He could have a point," replied Dairan, thinking about it seriously.

Tayce turned now that Dion's body had been jettisoned into the Universe and headed for the exit. Dairan reached out, grabbing her back to him gently. She sailed back in front of him, protesting that they had to see about heading to Pellasun Traun 2. She pulled loose of his gentle hold. He walked after her as he wanted to officially ask her in their current surroundings to become Captain Traun Loring. It seemed befitting and he told her so. Tayce felt she didn't want to listen at that particular moment – they had a Quest to complete. She stopped and turned.

"No, Dairan, this is not the right time. Later!" said Tayce, continuing on to the exit with Twedor following on.

"So when is the right time officially?" he asked after her, wondering why not when they were in a chapel?

"Not right now – duty comes first. Ask me again officially at the end of the current voyage," said Tayce back over her shoulder, nearing the Pious Sanctuary Centre exit.

Dairan was left standing in thought, watching her leave and Twedor follow on, wondering if she'd got cold feet and changed her mind about becoming Captain Traun Loring. He slowly followed on, considering the promise she'd made about giving her final answer at the end of the current voyage, tossing it over in his mind. Would she hold to it? Had she changed her mind and didn't want to say anything. He knew he shouldn't be thinking it, but wondered if her refusal to let him ask her in the present surroundings was due to the fact she might have felt something for Marc and not said anything when the unplanned kiss between them happened when the Green Tempest Keeper was aboard. He quickly brought his thoughts back to the present as he exited the Pious Sanctuary Centre and the doors closed behind him.

***

Auran Amalthea Three headed for Pellasun Traun 2. It was only one more dayon before the grand opening ceremony, when every delegate and planetary high-ranking being who wanted to be part of a space spectacle would descend on the new sister colony to Enlopedia from planets, ports and stations throughout the Universe.

***

Andory Paytern was safe and her wounds were found not to be too serious. She was assigned guest quarters where she could rest until they arrived. Tayce gave Andory free access throughout the cruiser until that time. Andory was taken by the team's easy-going friendliness. She could see her father, Councillor Paytern, had been wrong to join his colleagues in feeling undecided about the continuation of the Amalthean Quests at the beginning of the voyage and she would tell her father so when they next met. She thought he was wrong in his decided actions. This she told Tayce. This pleased her, considering the run-in she'd had with Andory's father at the beginning of the third and current voyage. Also now that she'd rescued Andory, it would prove to Councillor Paytern that he had been wrong in his actions and in future he wouldn't think twice about allowing the Quest-orientated-type voyages to continue.

***

Matt Loring had arrived during this latest Quest. Tayce had been a bit apprehensive about letting such a young man be on board as part of the team. But she was giving him a chance and time would tell whether he would be staying permanently. Matt had been assigned Deluca Marrack's old quarters. Tayce felt it had been a mixed Quest. Dion had shown up near to death, and before dying in the MLC had apologised for his past treatment of her. He was a man that would be greatly missed in a way. Andory Paytern had been rescued, which would put Tayce in Councillor Paytern's good books, she hoped. They had encountered and rid the Universe of another criminal race, the Stangrim Marauders. It certainly had been a Quest with unlawful connections.

10. Another Strike for Vargon

A daylight planetary world with exquisite plants, bushes and flowers, with areas of green outstanding natural beauty. There were also landscaped lawns and architecturally designed fountains. A parkland with waterfalls. Buildings of all shapes and designs. This world had been turned into a true living, breathing paradise and working environment, which included many exotic varieties of small and large birds and animals, both friendly and wild. Dwelling on the ground and in the trees roaming and flying. What was once known as just Pellasun was now known as Pellasun Traun 2.

***

Chief Jan Barnford's second phase of patrol officers were arriving by Patrol Cruiser to join the 100 already drafted in and present on the surface. This latest batch were his elite officers, the SSWAT. They would mingle with others for the official opening of the newly constructed colony complex of cream architectural design, known as Main Complex. In through the main glassene-and-chromex doors of the two storeys, Pella Square could be seen – an area with a mottled grey stonex floor and a central fountain, one of three on the overall colony. This one was in chrome with the initials 'PT' entwined. Cascading through was light-blue water and below it was a seating area around the whole fountain for people and aliens to sit for a while, for various reasons. Elsewhere in the square were four offshoots, with clear-vision glassene corridors going off at each ground-floor corner of the vast central mall. These led to different sections, four in all: a Parkland and Leisure Dome, a complex to train new recruits and a Medical Hospital Dome, plus numerous other buildings that were one and two storeys high. Cleaning techs, who had arrived from Enlopedia, were now doing the final cleaning and generally dressing the octagonal shape of Pella Square with decorative banners ready for the dayon of celebration to unfold. Above the square, on the second level, through the waist-high glassene- and-chromex partitions, personnel were hanging many different-coloured banners, saying 'WELCOME' and the like.

Back down in the square, Jan Barnford led his SSWAT officers in their blue armour into Main Complex, which he wanted them to patrol and which would be the right position for protecting Lydia and Darius Traun on their arrival. Everything smelt new in the atmosphere of the roughly three-square-milons-in-diameter complex. Jan broke away from giving orders to his men and headed across the square. As he went, so he noticed the smell of new construction mixed with the many fragrant blooms here and there in decorative containers en route. He wanted to make sure his men were in position for the first arriving flights, which would soon be arriving. He looked skyward through the clear glassene roof to see the twenty to thirty Quests and Transpo Launches already coming in to land, one behind the other. He looked forward as he went towards the Arrival and Departure Hall, where some people and aliens were already arriving for the big dayon ahead. Jan figured it was going to be the biggest security patrol headache he'd undertaken so far, beating even the opening of Enlopedia. Personnel were arriving to take up their new duty positions in the complex, in the many sections, in their designated uniforms of different colours. Medical personnel were heading towards the new Medical Hospital Dome to commence their new duties. They headed across Pella Square and down the walkway, that would take them to the Medical Hospital Dome. Many were glancing at signs on the walls of corridors telling them where they were to be on duty. Jan noticed the new Research Complex as he went, and the Hotel with over 300 units and a sign pointing to an outside sports building. Another sign pointed to the Apart-house and Domicile Area, where the new habitats belonging to many of the personnel, of both low and high rank, would dwell. He raised an eyebrow, wondering who would get one. Before him was his new Security Division Building, a building that had more floors than his last duty base. In covering four floors, this time it was catering for every kind of security and criminal matter on the planet and in the Universe. Jan figured it was a shame there was a threat hanging over such a beautiful dayon, but he was ready should anything unfold. His men were also ready. He acknowledged his men with a nod upon checking that they were where they should be in the entrance of the Arrival and Departure Hall. Jan knew who the threat was – Count Varon Vargon – and it made him mad, knowing he was back in circulation in a new version of the Carra Lair. It had amazed Jan how Vargon had slipped through the communications defences and had sent word of the impending threat. Both he and Darius Traun were taking the threat of attack seriously and something to be believed, hence the heavy security presence which would remain in place for the entire time of the opening ceremony, which Darius had refused to change because of Vargon's threat. He had firmly stated that he wasn't going to be intimidated by the Count at any cost. Jan was determined the ceremony would go successfully, and he was working closely with his chief.

***

Auran Amalthea Three came in to land and set down slowly and gracefully in the provided high-ranked area. Out from the Flight Complex came the boarding walkway with clear glassene roof. It slowly manoeuvred towards the cruiser's Docking-Bay doors and docked home, sealing a connection between cruiser and colony. Auran Amalthea Three was now officially on Pellasun Traun 2. The Docking-Bay doors opened.

First to emerge was Andory Paytern. She paused once out. Turning she thanked Tayce and the team, then hurried away down the walkway to meet her new bodyguard and escort, whom her father had shown her on the cruiser via Satlelink relay. Tayce was next off the cruiser. She immediately felt the Pellasun warm sunshine hit her face. She loved the feeling. It made her feel like she'd come home for the first time since she'd left Traun. The team began ferrying out behind her, including Twedor and Matt Loring. Tayce turned, ordering Amal via Wristlink to lock and secure the cruiser and to activate the intruder alarm system and head back into a stationary orbit just outside Pellasun until needed. If there was any sign of Count Vargon, she was to be contacted on Wristlink immediately and the whole cruiser was to go into Invis Shield mode. Amal agreed. Tayce told the team to feel free to spend the next houron looking around Pellasun, but advised them to meet up ten minons before the opening ceremony commenced. Everyone agreed. Turning, they walked away – that was apart from Marc and Dairan, who stood with Tayce, watching the others head off.

"Adam's up ahead," said Marc, looking in Adam's direction as he appeared at the beginning of the walkway exiting out from the Arrival and Departure Hall.

"He's walking towards us," said Dairan, looking past Tayce.

"Welcome to Pellasun Traun 2. Beautiful isn't it?" announced Adam, impressed by his surroundings.

"It's just like our original home world, Traun – right Marc?" asked Tayce.

"Oh, quite," he replied, glancing about at the impressive far-reaching views through the walkway's clear half-domed-shaped roof and full-length sight panes.

"I came to meet you, Tayce. Your father at the moment is in a closed meeting with Chief Barnford discussing Count Vargon's threat of trouble. Your father gave me the de-locking key to your bornday present – your Domicile. He figured you'd like to look over it whilst waiting for him to finish," suggested Adam.

"All right. Can you show us the way?" asked Tayce as she didn't know which way to go.

"Sure! Follow me," advised Adam, beginning back down the walkway.

Marc, Dairan, Twedor and Tayce followed Adam along the walkway back into the Arrival and Departure Hall, on out through the complex into Pella Square. Personnel who had travelled from Enlopedia to work on Pellasun Traun 2 greeted Tayce, Marc and Dairan en route. They knew many of them by sight.

Marc looked around in thought, noticing a very strong presence of security patrol officers in their blue Platex armour – not the casual uniform they patrolled in on Enlopedia. He could see they were ready for suspected trouble. He glanced at the many points of interest as he went, thinking Pellasun Traun 2 was very much like Traun, his old home world, had been – beautiful. Twedor walked closely beside Tayce. She had hold of his metlon hand as they crossed through the bustling crowd, toing and froing in the centre of Pella Square, just in case he got caught up in the middle and was pulled away.

Marc paused.

"Do you mind if I catch you two later?" he asked. "I want to have a look around this place."

"No of course not. Go ahead – we'll see you later," replied Dairan as Tayce was talking with Adam.

"Don't spend all your allowance," said Adam, laughing.

"Try not to – see you later," replied Marc, laughing, heading off in a different direction to mingle with the crowds heading towards the many purchasing centres.

Music could be softly heard – the kind heralding a joyous occasion being celebrated that dayon. Flags were blowing slightly from the sudden breezes ebbing in when doors were opened. Tayce and Dairan followed Adam on what seemed like an endless walk. They exited through silver-toned steelex-and-glassene doors, going out into what was warm sunny daylight, and continued walking along a walkway that would take them towards what was termed the Habitat District.

Adam's Wristcall pager sounded. He was wanted immediately. He raised his wrist and checked the display. He was needed back at his desk. Tayce looked ahead, suggesting they go on and find the domicile. Adam pointed up the path and advised them to keep going for another ten minons or so. They wouldn't miss it. It was the first domicile of modern architectural splendour to come into view. Both Dairan and Tayce nodded understandingly and continued on. Adam turned, heading on back to his duty and to Admiral Traun. Twedor looked about, taking in the daylight and sunny surroundings – something he'd never had the chance to experience when they'd visited daylight worlds in his old dayons as a guidance and operations computer. This was different and he was pleased he could experience it. This would become normal for him – being on a real planet he could class as his second home from the cruiser. On Traun, where he was constructed, he only heard what the outside surface was about whilst under construction. It was amazing what he'd been missing, he thought.

***

He was someone that had watched them arrive at Pellasun Traun 2. He was also someone Tayce had rescued during this last voyage. At the time of rescue he had no recollection of who he was, but he resembled someone everyone knew on the team in the first voyage. Now he'd been cured and was back to normal, knowing who he was and also his new place of residence. He was working on Pellasun Traun 2, or PT-2 as the planet was coming to be known by young cadets and the like. They felt saying Pellasun Traun 2 was too much of a mouthful and had started a shortened version with a slight twist in circulation, as it was much easier. He was working undercover for all the wrong reasons, even if he didn't realise it, for an evil enemy Tayce knew well. He thought he would get a good reward for his work, as it had been classed as important. He was doing wrong. He stayed just out of sight, following Tayce, Dairan and Twedor along the grey walkway. This someone had a familiar look about him – one Tayce had found hard to cope with upon rescuing him on Auran Amalthea Three in deep space. His plan was working well. All he had to do was distract Dairan and get him away from Tayce inside the domicile. He knew Matt Loring was Dairan's brother as he'd heard Matt in conversation earlier with a female of the Amalthean Quests team announcing he didn't want to crowd his brother's style and had let Tayce and Dairan spend some sharing time alone together. This someone with familiar looks, but working for an evildoer, was none other than Joshua Landorz. But why was he working for the being he was working for? Something wasn't right.

***

On seeing her new planetary domicile, Tayce gave a look of awe. The number on the modern construction of silver-toned steelex, marblex-effect stonex and glassene matched the number on the de-locking key. Dairan raised his eyebrows, impressed. The domicile was what anyone might expect considering Tayce was the Admiral's daughter. Dairan's Wristlink bleeped. He raised it and depressed Comceive. The voice on the other end was an official-sounding one. It requested him to go to the Security Division Building, where they had one Matt Loring in custody. Would he go in the next fifteen minons and confirm that who they'd apprehended in Pella Square was in fact who he claimed to be? Dairan sighed, then agreed. Angrily he ceased communications, thinking it was his first official duty and Matt had to go and screw it up. He was far from pleased. He was totally unaware that it had been an elaborate set-up.

"Problem? You look far from pleased," said Tayce, noticing his dark angered look.

"I can't leave him for ten minons before he does something stupid," said Dairan angrily.

"Matt? What's the matter? What's he done?" asked Tayce, looking at him questioningly.

"Yes, Matt. That was security. They've apprehended him, or so they believe, in Pella Square. They want me to go and confirm it's my little idiot brother," replied Dairan, far from impressed at his brother's behaviour.

"Are you sure it's Matt?" asked Tayce, giving him a questioning look, surprised.

"That's what he said. The officer wants me to go and identify him," replied Dairan, pacing, agitated.

"Hold on. Marc's out there – I'll get him to go and do it. The way you're feeling right now, I can see you both ending up in a holding cell together," said Tayce, realising it was just what would happen.

Tayce raised her Wristlink, contacting Marc. He soon answered with Pella Square sounds in the background. Tayce walked up the bloom-bordered pathway to the entrance of her new home, asking him if he would check something out. Marc listened as she explained about Matt. He agreed to her request, informing her that he guessed the Security Division Building was his next point of interest. With this he ceased communications.

Tayce turned, looking at the slot by the entrance to slip the de-locking key in. Pushing it home, she then keyed in the number on the accompanying dial and pushed 'activation' to release the entrance lock. It soon triggered the mobilisation process of the domicile, including internal operations and functions. The grand entrance steelex-and-glassene doors opened inwards. Twedor walked in first, followed by Tayce, then Dairan, his mind still on Matt and what he'd done. Once inside, the air was warm and they were met by beautiful furnishings of smoked glassene and shiny chromex with matching cream leatherex seating. The floor was carpetron tiles in a navy shade, which looked to be soft but hard-wearing. The main shutters on the far wall began to part, drawing back to reveal full-length breathtaking views as far as the eye could see, through four large glassene sight panes.

"This is beautiful. Mother must have remembered my favourite decor from Traun. What do you think of my home?" she asked, turning in a showy way, gesturing, pleased, looking up at Dairan.

"Come here and I'll let you know," he said, pulling her towards him swiftly and giving her a mischievous smile.

"Well?" she persisted as she landed in his arms.

"It's you – it's beautiful, elegant and pleasing to the eye," he replied, looking at her with a teasing look in the same eyes that had been angry moments before.

"Seriously? Really?" she continued, pleased.

"Yes, seriously," he said in a whisper, lowering his head to kiss her.

"Someone's approaching this residence," announced a straight-laced male computerised voice, which seemed to fill their surroundings.

"Who said that? Hardly polite, was he? Someone forgot to install politeness as part of his programming," spoke up Twedor, glancing around the open-plan area of the living part of the domicile, looking for the source of the odious sound.

"We'll have to work on that announcement system, won't we, Twedor?" agreed Tayce, laughing.

"You bet," replied Twedor, disgusted.

The entrance doors played a tune of light notes to signify someone had arrived at the domicile entrance. Tayce gave a voice command to answer the door. A few minons passed. Dairan waited beside Tayce, having let her go. Joshua Landorz entered the hallway and came into view, though he wasn't expecting Tayce to be with Dairan. He knew his plan and orders had been ruined when he saw Dairan still present. He tried to hide his disappointment, but wondered how he was going to rethink his plan in order to get Tayce alone.

"Mr Landorz, come in. What's this visit in aid of?" asked Tayce, surprised to see Tom's clone again.

As Joshua was about to answer, Dairans Wristlink sounded. He turned away, answering the call. It was Marc again. This time he began explaining a somewhat strange story. Matt had been apprehended, but it wasn't what was thought. He just hadn't understood the laws on PT-2. He was innocent, but the end result was the officer wouldn't release Matt without a member of his family coming forth to identify him and talk with him over Matt's behaviour. Dairan sighed. He really wanted to share some rare off-duty time with Tayce. So far, what with Matt and now the unexpected visit of Joshua Landorz, it was quickly looking like it wasn't going to happen. As Joshua and Tayce stood talking, Dairan suddenly sensed there was something he didn't trust about this unexpected visit from Landorz. He secretly used his Wristlink to scan his vital signs and they were showing far from normal levels of adrenaline, as if he was apprehensive about something. Dairan knew he didn't want to leave Tayce with Joshua, but he had to clean up the misunderstanding Matt had got himself into. He suggested Twedor walk him to the entrance. Twedor looked at Dairan, who winked at him. From this, Twedor picked up on the fact that Dairan wanted him to play along and do as requested. Tayce let him and Dairan go. Matt was giving him real unwanted grief and the sooner it was resolved the better. She watched him walk down the hall with Twedor, then, after a brief word with Twedor, continue on out through the entrance.

'At last!' thought Joshua. He didn't have to change his plan and orders after all.

Twedor eyed him suspiciously, Dairan was right: there was something creepy about this Tom clone.

Tayce turned her attention back to Joshua.

"I'm here, Captain, because I want to talk to you. I have something to ask you," he began innocently, then walked towards her.

Tayce noticed his features suddenly turning from pleasant to unpleasant. The nearer he came to Tayce, the colder his features turned. She tried to pick up on the sudden change in the way he was behaving and guess the reason for it. Twedor activated his Slazer finger, ready to protect his mistress. Joshua stopped before Tayce, looking at her unemotionally. She felt slightly unnerved and immediately noticed his eyes take on the same glazed look Dairan's had during the voyage, when Count Vargon had placed in his mind the thoughts to kill her.

'Not again!' she thought.

She went to back away, but he quickly grabbed her roughly by the upper arm.

"Don't make any fuss, Captain. You are to quietly come with me or the Romid will be destroyed," he said, quickly putting her in a restraining hold. Showing hostility as he did so.

"Joshua! What are you doing? Let go of me. Stop this!" ordered Tayce in cold commanding reply, fighting Joshua, trying to break free. She could suddenly see who was controlling him and she didn't like it. Vargon was back somehow and using Joshua this time as his latest pawn to get rid of her.

"Relax, Captain, and you'll be returned unharmed."

He held her tightly whilst she continued to try and break free.

"Twedor, do something! Help!" begged Tayce. She didn't like this situation.

Twedor didn't need telling twice. He opened fire and shot Joshua in the lower spine with a stun shot. Nothing happened for a few cencrons, but then he released Tayce and dropped to the floor. Tayce stepped out of the way. He was unconscious.

"Thanks, Twedor," said Tayce, stepping over Joshua's lifeless form.

"What's his game? Dairan said he didn't trust him – that's why he wanted me to watch over you," announced Twedor.

"Let's get out of here before he regains consciousness," said Tayce, glancing back.

They both ran for the entrance, ordering the in-domicile computer to activate the doors. They opened before them and they ran out into the daylight to find security. As luck would have it, Jan Barnford was walking towards the domicile, down the path, having finished his meeting with her father. Upon seeing him, she ran to him, leaving Twedor watching the entrance in case Joshua regained consciousness and came out.

"What's up? You look frightened. You're shaking. Take it easy. Tell me," he demanded, concerned.

"Inside – Joshua Landorz. He tried to kidnap me. It was as if he was possessed by the same force Dairan was under when Vargon took over his mind monthons ago," explained Tayce.

"What! Stay here," said Jan, sounding like the true top security chief he was.

Jan took out his Pollomoss handgun and continued on up the path, going through the open entrance of the domicile. He immediately contacted two of his officers over his Wristcall as he went, telling them to head over to the Traun domicile immediately. Jan walked slowly into the Living Area, his gun primed and ready to shoot Joshaua again should he be getting to his feet. But as he walked in to full view of where he suspected Joshua would be, there was no sign of him. Jan decided to check around, still keeping his gun primed in case of sudden trouble. Nothing. There was no trace of anyone, let alone Joshua Landorz. Jan was suddenly thrown into alert by a muffled scream from outside. It sounded like Tayce. He ran back out to see a yellow shaft of light, a disappearing Tayce, and Twedor lying on the path. A security patrol officer quickly stood Twedor back on his metlon feet, then looked into the exasperated and angry features of his chief, noticing he was far from amused. Marc, Dairan and Matt came into view, running up the path, having seen the shaft of light materialise and disappear again.

"I've just got word from Amal that she couldn't contact Tayce. Vargon's in orbit on the Carra Lair," began Marc.

"What's been happening? Where's Tayce?" asked Dairan, noticing the open entrance of the domicile.

"Are you familiar with a Joshua Landorz?" asked Jan, straight to the point.

"Yes, he was here just before I left to go and sort a problem out," replied Dairan, recalling the fact.

"It seems that, just after you left, this Landorz tried to kidnap Tayce. Twedor shot at him and Tayce came out to meet me coming up the path, thinking Landorz was still where he'd dropped inside. I went to check he was still unconscious, only to find no trace of him. Then I heard a muffled scream out here, and came running out to find Tayce being transported off the path to God knows where, through the shaft of light," explained Jan.

"Landorz could be working for Vargon, then. It seems like one of Vargon's dirty tricks," said Marc, shaking his head in disbelief, thinking it looked like Tayce was facing Vargon all over again.

"Can we be certain it's him?" asked Dairan, wondering if it was Vargon or someone else.

"I know a way we can check," suggested Jan.

"I'll lock the domicile and catch you two up," said Dairan, heading towards the entrance.

Jan, Marc and the two security patrol officers began back down the path towards the colony's Main Complex. Jan's concern was that the opening ceremony would be under way in just on twenty-five minons and Darius Traun was expecting to see Tayce present with the whole Amalthean Quests team. As it stood, that wasn't going to happen. Dairan and Twedor ran up to join both Jan and Marc after removing the de-locking key and deactivating all the internal functions of Tayce's new home. They were all wondering where Tayce had gone to.

***

Off PT-2's surface, Auran Amalthea Three was situated, with Amal waiting for further orders.

Everyone entered back through the Main Complex doors. Inside, people and aliens were now heading to the main Ceremonial Hall to take up their watchful positions for the ceremonial opening of the new base to begin. Dairan and Marc wondered how they were going to break the news to Darius that Tayce had been abducted by Vargon, if he was responsible. Lydia was the first to spot them and she immediately looked about for Tayce. Jan cursed under his breath. He'd hoped to have kept the fact Tayce was missing from her just a little longer, or just until it had been confirmed that Vargon was the one who had abducted her daughter again. Marc suggested he stall her with an excuse whilst Dairan headed to the Security Division Building to find out the truth. He knew it would buy them some time. Matt, at Dairan's request, went with them, as he wanted to keep an eye on him.

***

Tayce sat in a room she'd been in before, and she knew it to be one of Varon Vargon's holding cells. She sighed, exasperated by the fact that the bastard had done it again – abducted her. She was fed up with the barbaric bastard using her as a pawn in his threats against her father. The cell door opened and in walked two of Vargon's officers. They went to take hold of her to stop her escaping during escort to their leader.

"Don't bother – I can do this. It's not like it's the first time," retorted Tayce as she began towards the entrance.

"Our leader wants to meet with you. Move!" commanded one of the two ordinary-looking officers.

"I want to meet with him too," said Tayce, fed up with being abducted and used as a pawn. She walked from the holding cell in an angry way under the watchful eyes of the two officers. They were of average height and build, dressed in the sort of heavy black combat attire that would normally be worn by military. It made her realise that not only had the Carra Lair been improved, but so had Vargon's officers' code of dress. But Vargon wasn't the only one to have improvements; so had she. She was more than capable of taking on the likes of him this time around. She was taken along the familiar corridors to reach the Operations Deck – somewhere she hadn't planned on being again. Her mind was already thinking of a way to escape and head back to the surface of Pellasun and warn her father. As she went, she also checked the corridor walls for a Slazer emergency store. In time they rounded the corner of the doorway-type entrance that lead them on to the Operations Deck. Tayce's features turned from near furious to downright furiousness on seeing the man that filled her with coldness and hate. She held a cold, plain, no-nonsense look as she approached Vargon.

"Before you start giving your stupid speech, Vargon, save it. I'm not interested. What am I here for this time? To play your stupid games over Father? Joshua, I'm surprised at you trusting this bastard. He'll only do you wrong, and when he grows tired of you he'll torture you till death. Right Vargon?"

“I was going to welcome you back aboard. I can see you haven’t changed – as sharp as ever. You remind me of your father, Traun,” replied Vargon, unmoved by her outburst.

“This time will be different from our last encounter, believe me” said Tayce angrily.

Vargon paused before her, like he had the last time she had been on the Carra Lair, only this time she had more power ability to fight against anything he tried on her. She didn’t seem to think there was any time to waste. So she began silently concentrating, giving him a demonstration of just what she could now achieve. Without warning, Tayce quite unexpectedly began with her power force, lifting Vargon up off his deck floor. He glared at her coldly, wondering what she was trying to do. Tayce, with her powers, spun him around, encasing him in an energy field and threw him through the air with force and speed, bringing him crashing down in between the operatives’ desks. He quickly pushed his men aside and struggled, displeased, to his feet, straightening his uniform. Blood was trickling from his temple, with eyes of powerful angriness directed at Tayce, incensed that she’d managed to catch him off guard.

“What’s the matter? Didn’t you like my demonstration? What I just did was a warning to leave me alone. Now, if you’ll excuse me, I have somewhere to be and it’s not here for you to use as a pawn against my father.”

With this, Tayce dodged the officers who had brought her before their leader, each being going in a different direction and nearly colliding with the walls in the process. She ran back to the entrance and out into the corridor, off in search of a way to get back to the surface of Pellasun Traun 2.

“Stop her. Don’t let her escape. Stun her if you have to. I want her back here,” said Vargon, angered beyond words.

He figured that if she wanted to play power games, then he would give her the chance. Next time he would be ready to match her. He was looking an idiot in the eyes of his men – something he wasn’t going to tolerate. He was Count Varon Vargon – no one had topped him, ever.

The officers he’d yelled at to race after Tayce took to their heels and did as ordered, their weapons set to stun. After all, their leader wanted her alive.

Tayce glanced back over her shoulder in the distance as they rounded the entrance. She ran down the steps to the next level, going down two at a time. She knew she wouldn’t be able to use her ability too soon; but even if she could, she wasn’t going to waste her energy, so she began looking for a weaponry store to retrieve a handgun. One caught her eye on the wall at the bottom of the steps. She hurried and grabbed a gun, setting it to ‘disintegration’. Where did he steal these from? she wondered. Pollomosses! Tayce glanced back over her shoulder once again for another sign of the pursuing officers. They weren’t in sight. This gave her time to call on her Wristlink and get backup help. But as she looked forward, he was there.

"I don't think so, young lady," said Joshua Landorz, coldly stepping into view.

"Landorz, you idiot, you'll pay for what you're doing. My father will see to it," said Tayce coldly.

"You're coming back with me," he said, looking down at her.

"That's what you think. You could have been someone or something; instead you let this criminal give you false hope. Well, here's what you get for believing in beings like Vargon," said Tayce, feeling both angry and sorry for what she had to do.

But there was still hope for Joshua. He had his head turned by Vargon, that was all, and that could be put right if she could turn him against the bastard.

Tayce lifted the gun pointing it in Joshua's ribs and pressing the trigger. Joshua looked at her, grimacing in pain, then dropped to the floor right before her. Tayce continued with making contact with the others via Wristlink. Pressing Comceive, she managed to get Amal.

"Amal, this is Tayce. I'm on the Carra Lair. Transpot me and one other over to the cruiser now," ordered Tayce.

"I am adjusting block-out interference and undertaking your request as you speak," confirmed Amal.

"Hurry, Amal, before I'm joined by unwanted company," said Tayce, watching out for the pursuing officers.

Just as the pursuing officers came into view, Transpot took on around Tayce and Joshua and they vanished from the area at the bottom of the steps she'd come down earlier. On the way to Auran Amalthea Three. Tayce now knew Joshua had been brainwashed in the same way Dairan had been, judging by his unusual behaviour towards her and his glazed expression. Now it was time to put it right. She hoped he didn't remember her shooting him when he got his own mind back. In a way she felt sorry for Joshua. It had been the second time he'd had his mind played with since she'd first known him.

***

Down on PT-2, Jan and Dairan had had their fears confirmed. Vargon had used Joshua Landorz to abduct Tayce. They were now on their way through the thickening jostling crowds to deliver the news to Darius. News they knew somehow Darius wouldn't want to hear. Matt, who had been with them, turned and apologised. He felt the whole mess was his fault. If he had just stayed calm instead of reacting angrily to being reprimanded for breaking a rule he didn't know existed, letting his temper get the better of him, Dairan would have been with Tayce to stop her going through the turmoil of the abduction at Landorz hands, and she'd also be present for the opening ceremony. Dairan turned, seeing his younger brother's apologetic face. Then he looked to where they were heading towards the gathered Amalthean Quests team, Darius, Lydia and Marc. Upon coming to a pause, Jan requested a private word with Darius. Both men stepped to one side. Lydia glanced over, looking questioningly and uneasily at Darius and Jan, who were in discussion. They turned, but just as they did, to their utter startled surprise Tayce was walking calmly towards them. Lydia turned her head to see what was grabbing their attention so surprisingly and strongly.

"Tayce, oh my God! Are you all right?" asked Lydia, rushing forth to her daughter, concerned.

"Are you sure you're OK, darling? He didn't hurt you? Because if he did…" backed up Darius, studying her, also worried Varon Vargon might have hurt her in some way again

"I'm absolutely fine. Vargon won't be bothering me any time soon. Mother, I'll explain more later. Let's get the team together," said Tayce, glancing around to her team, trying to put her mind on what was about to happen in the opening ceremony.

"Marc, take command. I want to have a quick word with my daughter here," ordered Darius, putting his hands gently on Tayce's shoulders and guiding her to one side discreetly for a chat.

"But, Father!" Protested Tayce as Darius guided her to an area where they could talk out of earshot.

Jan sauntered over to be with father and daughter. He wanted to know what Tayce had to say, so he could in turn instruct his men to prepare for either space protection against Varon Vargon or a full-on ground attack on the colony. Tayce, Darius and Jan stood in discussion about the best plan of action after what Tayce had seen on the Carra Lair.

"Tell me," prompted Darius, studying Tayce.

"Vargon used Joshua Landorz and he had him abduct me outside my domicile. Of course I found myself in the usual unwanted surroundings of one of Vargon's cells. I was brought before him, but not for long. I managed to escape. I was all for finding a weapon to protect myself, which I did. Then Joshua was in the way. He'd been brainwashed by you know who, just like Dairan had, so I stunned him. He's now under maximum surround security on board the cruiser under the watchful eye of Amal," explained Tayce.

"Do you think it's wise to let him be on board alone, considering?" put Darius, a little concerned.

"Don't worry. Amal's excellent at keeping him where he is. She won't let him go walkabout, I can assure you," assured Tayce.

"Did you find out what Vargon's plans are?" asked Jan, interested.

"Let's put it like this: he's in orbit and you can bet it's a threat, like the one against Traun, to be taken seriously, with him where he is with what he has in possible ambush material. After all, before I managed to escape he was planning to use me against you again," replied Tayce.

"Jan, make it discreet, but get that attack and protection fleet ready in orbit of this place," ordered Darius.

"Right! I'll do it now," replied Jan.

Then he turned, walking away to carry out Darius's orders.

"Come on, young woman, we've a colony/base to open," said Darius, slipping a fatherly arm around Tayce's slim shoulders and guiding her on back to meet up with the others and Twedor.

***

Vargon on the Carra Lair was furious beyond words. He was shouting his orders at his crew for a full-on attack on Pellasun Traun 2 that, if successful, would wipe out of existence those thorns in his side the Trauns. Then the pathetic Amalthean Quests team would be out of his life forever, enabling him to do whatever he pleased in the Universe, to whomever he wished to strike at. His officers ran here and there in the attack-force uniforms, going to their fighter ships ready to depart from the Carra Lair on their leader's orders to do so.

***

Back at Pellusun Traun 2 the ceremony had begun with Darius taking to the stage. He walked to the Pella Square entwined fountain and to a control box on a podium that would relay a signal to the operations system and activate the fountain for as long as the colony stood in operation. He paused and began a speech as Admiral of now two bases in space. Everyone, including the Amalthean Quests team, sat giving him their full attention.

"Todayon is the beginning of a new type of headquarters base - one that brings together the daylight world that we presently stand on, Pellasun, and a world that was similar in beauty to this. That world was Traun. It is hoped that all who work on, live on or visit this planet will enjoy the hospitality, friendships, prosperity and stability that so far Enlopedia has prided itself on. For visitors, it is hoped our hospitality will encourage you to return again, or to pass word to enable your friends to visit here. Pellasun Traun 2 is a law-abiding headquarters base and it will continue many of the fine traditions, ideas and duties that Enlopedia does as its sister base in this current time. Pellasun Traun 2 - or, as I've heard it called already todayon, PT-2 - is your base. Treat it well. Look after it, so when todayon's young reach their senior leisure years they will have something to hand to their young and tell them of this dayon, when it all began. I hereby declare Pellasun Traun 2, or PT-2, open. Enjoy!" said Darius, pressing the control switch to start not only the fountain, which had been stopped for the opening speech, but functions all over the colony that would continue for the duration of the colony's life.

Music and merriment began with the march past of the Amalthean Quests team, beginning with Tayce, Marc and Dairan with Twedor behind. Then came Matt and the others, with Professor Maylen. Spectators cheered and clapped as the team passed, followed by other teams representing Enlopedia in their official uniforms. It was turning out to be a colourful spectacle, to be truly enjoyed and treasured by all. Tayce's thoughts were on Amal and what she might be finding out about Vargon's motives and next move. She wondered would he make that next move, even though Jan's protection fleet was out in orbit over the base, whilst the ceremony was in full swing?

After they had all passed the spectators, and come to the end of the march past, Tayce turned away to contact Amal on Wristlink. Dairan looked after Twedor and Marc talked with the others about what was happening around them. Tayce could be seen in conversation for some time, and her mother wished that just for a while her daughter would switch off and enjoy the opening ceremony. Lydia grew concerned about what was happening. She knew Tayce would do anything to help in stopping Varon Vargon making a full on attack on their present surroundings. She continued to watch Tayce, interested, as she finished her Wristlink conversation and stood in discussion with Marc and Dairan. Tayce explained to Marc and Dairan that Amal had informed her the latest scan on the Carra Lair had turned up the fact Vargon was getting ready to put his army into fighters, meaning only one thing.

"I'm going back to the cruiser to be ready," said Tayce without further word.

"Are you sure you don't want me to go? Your father may need you here," put Marc seriously.

Tayce stood in thought. She wanted to go back to the cruiser, but she didn't want to let her parents down on the special dayon that was happening. Marc suddenly came up with an idea that solved her problem. He went back to the cruiser and got everything under way. The moment Vargon moved on his threat to attack, then he'd have Amal transpot her back aboard. Tayce thought about it, then agreed. He began to move away. Professor Maylen watched him go in urgency, wondering what was unfolding.

"Professor, I have a favour to ask. I know todayon is a special one, but do you remember what happened to Dairan when Vargon made him want to kill me?" put Tayce.

"Yes, only too well. Problem?" asked Adrien.

"Joshua Landorz is on Auran Amalthea Three right now. Vargon has carried out the same procedure on him as he did on Dairan. I'd like you to help him. Return him to what he should be," asked Tayce.

"I'll need medical help. My Enlopedian team are around here – I'll find them and take Donaldo, if I may?"

"Right with you, Professor. Treketa, you stay with Tayce," said Donaldo.

"If you're sure you don't need me?" replied Treketa, beside Tayce.

"Positive," replied Donaldo, wondering if Tayce wanted otherwise.

"No, it's fine. You go, Don," said Tayce, picking up on his thoughts.

Professor Maylen and Donaldo continued on across the square. Dairan turned, drawing Tayce's attention to her mother and father heading on into the banquet held in honour of the visiting delegates. Tayce called the remaining team around her, to follow. Twedor walked down at her side, whilst Dairan discreetly ordered Matt to mind his p's and q's whilst they were going on in. Matt nodded. He'd done and said enough in getting into trouble. He figured he'd just speak when spoken to – that way he couldn't go wrong. Everyone mingled, going on into the Ceremonial Hall until they were out of sight and the doors had closed, guarded by security patrol officers of Jan's team armed for any sign of danger.

***

No sooner had Marc arrived back on board the cruiser with Donaldo and Professor Maylen than he went straight to Organisation, whilst Professor Maylen went to his lab to pick up what he needed to examine Joshua Landorz. He informed Donaldo that he'd meet him down in the holding cell, where Joshua was. Donaldo checked with Amal to discover where Joshua was and halted Adrien halfway down the corridor to inform him that Joshua was in fact in the MLC under force-field restraints on the highest setting. Donaldo continued on to the MLC, thinking back on what they'd done in discovering what had happened to Dairan when Vargon almost made him kill Tayce a while ago.

Marc meanwhile was reaching the top of the Level Steps and heading along into Organisation to see what could be done to thwart the attack Vargon was thinking of unleashing on PT-2. Upon entering the centre, Amal greeted him.

"What's the latest, Amal?" demanded Marc, looking out through the main sight port at Vargon's vessel.

"Varon Vargon has given orders to his men to prepare for launch. The security protection fleet from Pellasun Traun 2's surface is in a stationary orbit, prepared to protect the surface," informed Amal.

"This is getting serious. Has this happened in the last half-houron?" Marc asked.

"Less than that," replied Amal.

"How many fighters from the surface are in place?" enquired Marc, listening.

"Ninety, equally spaced for maximum protection," replied Amal.

"Amal, stand by for orders. I need to talk to Tayce," ordered Marc.

"I'll be standing by when you require more assistance, Marc," replied Amal.

He raised his Wristlink, contacting Tayce back down on the surface. He had an idea he wanted to explore, but he figured Tayce would want what was important, and that was to stop a similar bombardment weapon-wise from the one Vargon had unleashed on their old home world. He would run it by her none the less. He waited as the tone sounded for Tayce to answer his communication.

Tayce finished speaking with Empress Tricara on PT-2 and walked out into the conservatory area. She made sure she was safely out of earshot and out of sight of prying eyes. She raised her Wristlink, pressing Comceive. Marc's voice came through on the other end, asking her jokingly why the long delay? Was she enjoying herself?

"I was in discussion with Tricara. Fill me in on what's happening up there. What's Vargon up to?" asked Tayce.

"Amal's just informed me that he's preparing to send out his men in fighters," replied Marc over the Wristlink.

"I'm coming back—" she began, but he cut her off in mid speech.

"Hold on – I have an idea. And before you say this is your cruiser, hear me out – you might like the idea – please."

"All right, I'm listening," replied Tayce, giving him her full attention.

"In order to do what I have in mind, I need Phean, Nick, Craig, Lance and Aldonica. I want to put our Quest shuttles/fighters out to help the protection fleet, also leave this cruiser under Invis Shield and inform Jan I'm in orbit to sink home the final blow to Vargon if he needs it," explained Marc.

"Great idea, but I'm still coming back with the others," persisted Tayce.

"No, there's really no need – honest. I can handle this and, besides, if any of Vargon's men do like they did on our old home world you're going to be needed to help," pointed out Marc, remembering how the ground attack happened so fast on their old home world, Traun.

"All right, I trust you to finish this before it gets out of hand. I'll tell the others to leave now," replied Tayce, ceasing Wristlink communications.

Tayce, on ceasing communications, walked back into the Ceremonial Hall to find the rest of her team Marc wanted back on the cruiser. Darius noticed his daughter looking around in a searching kind of way as he stood in discussion with a planetary ambassador who was interested in signing the new Treaty of Pellasun. Darius was curious to know what was unfolding. He decided to let Lydia continue in discussion with the Ambassador and excused himself. Craig, Nick, Aldonica, Lance and Phean, who'd been talking with Tricara, accompanied Tayce to the main entrance. Here they talked for a few minons more then left the hall. Jan Barnford noticed the sudden gathering of some of the team and Tayce whilst talking with an interested off-world dignitary about security in the present dangerous Universe. Tayce turned to find her father behind her, looking questioningly at her. She glanced around the top-ranking officials, knowing she couldn't say what she had to say in earshot of them. She didn't want to raise alarm and panic.

"I need an urgent quiet word, Father," asked Tayce discreetly.

"All right, let's go outside," he agreed, beginning away to the entrance to the conservatory.

Jan, seeing what was unfolding, broke away from whom he was talking to and followed in case it was a security matter he needed to know about. Today he felt his job was a nightmare, trying to keep everyone on the colony/base safe whilst trouble seemed to be brewing in the sky above them. He sighed impatiently as he exited the Ceremonial Hall, out into the conservatory. Dairan stood back waiting with Twedor as father and daughter discussed the problem above their heads, in orbit. Darius listened, finding the situation becoming like a copy of what happened on their old home world, Traun.

"What are you going to do?" Darius asked Tayce.

"Marc at present has the situation in hand back on board Auran. I've just sent some of the team up to prepare to fight in Quests. I would put your men on alert, Jan. Vargon's given the word for a full-on unprovoked attack. I'm going outside with the remainder of my team that are still here on the surface. We're going to start looking about for any slip-through ground warriors," explained Tayce.

"I'm notifying my men to be on standby. It's almost time to act," said Jan in the true tone of chief.

Darius watched Jan stride away towards the back entrance to the Ceremonial Hall to leave and commence his orders. Tayce suggested that until it was certain there weren't any surface attackers it would be a good idea to keep the high-ranking dignitaries entertained in the Ceremonial Hall. Darius nodded, agreeing. He could see her point was a good one.

"Good luck. Don't let him get through if you can help it. Be careful at all costs," he said, concerned.

"I will. Just stay safe," replied Tayce, calling the remaining team, and Twedor, and beginning away to the square.

En route Tayce informed Matt he could help in this Quest. He would work alongside Dairan in looking out for Vargon's warriors. Matt nodded eagerly. At last, he thought, he was going to do something good in his brother's eyes as he knew how to handle a gun.

***

Upon the first members of team transpotting back aboard Auran, Marc met them upon arrival, telling them their next orders. They were to head to Quest shuttles/fighters and be ready to launch on his word. They were going to assist the protection fleet above PT-2. The team – Lance, Craig, Nick, Phean and Aldonica – turned and ran to the Level Steps to head down to the Flight Hangar Bay. Marc walked to meet Adrien Maylen, who exited the MLC on his way to see him. Marc listened intently as Adrien explained that Tayce had been right: Joshua Landorz did have his mind tampered with by Vargon. But he would be back to normal once he'd been moved to Enlopedia or the new facility on PT-2 for the intricate treatment. Marc nodded in understanding, informing him that he was heading back to Organisation, and the moment he'd got the Quests under way for the protection duty he would see about a medical team on PT-2 and have them standing by. In the meantime Joshua Landorz would have to be kept under sedation. Adrien agreed, nodding. Turning he headed back to the MLC.

Marc broke into a sprint as Amal announced over the Revelation System that Vargon was launching the first fighter wave of attack. On this, Marc raised his Wristlink, pressing Comceive.

"Amal, give the order to the team to launch immediately," said Marc in true command.

"Giving orders now, Commander," obliged Amal.

Marc ran up the Level Steps two at a time, back to Level 1. As he went he contacted Tayce via Wristlink on the PT-2 surface, warning her that Vargon had launched his attack fleet. Tayce could be heard acknowledging receipt of the information and advising him to keep her informed. Marc agreed as he rounded the top of the steps heading in the direction of Organisation. Upon seeing the startling sight of the Quests and the protection fleet joining forces through the main sight port as he entered the centre, he realised at least there was a warning in time for the people to act to protect themselves on this new Traun world.

He crossed to the main sight port and stood watching the developing scene of Vargon's Carra Lair and fighters, like a black evil vapour closing in on Pellasun Traun 2 and the Quests and protection fleet. There was an onslaught of firepower exploding in spectacular fashion on both sides. It was almost too blinding to watch this conflict between good and evil. Weapon fire bounced off the hulls of both the Quests and the protection fleet. Marc gave an impressed look at some of the tricky manoeuvres performed by the team and the protection fleet, just to stay ahead of the manoeuvres being pulled by Vargon's attacking fighters. He ordered Amal, the moment it looked like any stray fighters were thinking of breaking through to the surface, to open fire and take them out.

"Your orders are confirmed," replied Amal.

Marc watched intently as the Vargon's warriors' fighters blew up in spectacular fashion, sending out an array of explosive brightness. Over his shoulder, he ordered Amal to contact the medical team in the PT-2 Medical Hospital Dome and inform them there was a patient wanting mind-correction treatment by Professor Maylen's request. Amal began the request whilst Marc watched the battle raging in front of him through the main sight port. Vargon's Carra Lair was now surrounded by fighters from Auran Amalthea Three and the attack fleet from the surface in an onslaught of attacking weapon fire. The last few straggling fighters fought alongside the Carra Lair to try and protect it, but they were taking on some heavy firepower.

***

Tayce, Treketa, Matt, Twedor and Dairan walked out into the warm sunshine from the square. They looked skywards, watching for any sign of emerging fighters with an interest in attacking their present surroundings. But there wasn't any sign except the odd flash in the sky from the battle being raged in orbit above. Jan Barnford was looking through hand-held viewers for anything suspicious on the horizon looking like it was heading in their direction. His ground officers ran out now dressed in their blue Platex armour carrying Slazer mini cannons, taking up positions on the outside target sight points, around the colony, ready to repel an attack. Tayce suddenly caught sight of a suspicious-looking character. He was looking lost and guilty, both at the same time. As she watched him further, it seemed he was trying not to rouse suspicion in a strange way, which just made her watch more than ever. Dairan saw what Tayce was watching. Slowly she drew her Pollomoss Slazer, letting the shifty character, who was dressed in a Questa Enlopedia uniform, go on in through the glassene-and-steelex doors into Pella Square. There was something familiar about this being, she thought. She wasn't waiting any longer. She called the others and ran back into Pella Square. Looking for him once inside, she saw he was heading across Pella Square in the direction of the entrance to the Ceremonial Hall.

"There's something not right about him," said Dairan in whisper, coming alongside Tayce.

"He's heading towards the Ceremonial Hall," said Treketa in near whisper also.

"Twedor, scan him. Find out who he is before he enters the hall – quickly," ordered Tayce.

"Scanning now," replied Twedor.

"Hurry up," demanded Tayce, raising her gun and taking aim.

"Vargon warrior," replied Twedor, quickly, to the point.

Tayce ran on so she could get a clean shot. She took aim, considering that Jan's officers, who had been present inside the entrance, had gone outside. She was glad the members of her team were following on. The warrior reached the entrance doors to the Ceremonial Hall. The others slowly came forth, keeping low.

"You! Hold it right there! Don't move," shouted Tayce.

As Tayce raised her Pollomoss a Slazer shot rang out behind her, just to the side of her. Unfortunately for Twedor, he was clipped by the shot, which sent him on to his back and sliding across Pella Square, which was now almost empty of crowds. He couldn't do anything about stopping. He slid straight into the back of the suspicious being. He turned, glowering down at Twedor through the slits in his mask. Twedor could see the motionless dark eyes of the warrior and knew just what he represented. Without further word, he managed to manoeuvre his Slazer finger, setting it to 'stun', and shot him. The big-built Vargon warrior dropped to the floor yards from the entrance to the Ceremonial Hall. Out of nowhere two of Jan's officers ran forth and hauled him away for interrogation when he came round. Another officer came forth and retrieved his ID, weapon and communication device. Crossing, he handed the items to his chief, who was now in Main Complex. Twedor was stood back on his feet by Matt Loring.

"Close one, don't you think? I apologise for my officer's gunshot. It was a near miss for Twedor, but he is OK, isn't he?" confided Jan to Tayce, glancing at the stunned warrior being hauled away.

"Yes, he's just clipped, that's all. It was the force more than anything. I had my suspicions outside regarding the warrior when I saw he was acting suspiciously. Twedor did the rest. A few more cencrons and if we'd missed him, he would be raining terror down inside that hall right now," replied Tayce, much relieved.

"Yes, your father would be looking at an assassination attempt, that's for sure. Well done, both of you," said Jan, impressed.

"All in the line of my duty to protect when necessary," replied Twedor, far from amused that he'd nearly met his doom before a Vargon warrior.

"What do you think are the chances of more strikes by Vargon's warriors on the surface?" Tayce put to Jan.

At this moment Tayce's Wristlink sounded. She raised it, activating it for whoever was on the other end to speak. Marc's voice came through. He announced that the Carra Lair was dangerously close to the surface of Pellasun. Tayce gave a command to open fire – all weapons. Marc could be heard agreeing. Communications ceased and Tayce lowered her wrist, turning to ask Jan to inform her father that she'd be back. It was time to return to Auran temporarily. Jan nodded in total understanding. Tayce raised her Wristlink, ordering Amal to Transpot her. Jan watched as the Transpot's aura removed the team from the complex. He then walked off in search of more intruders and to pass on to Darius what Tayce had asked.

***

Back on Auran Amalthea Three, no sooner had Tayce materialised in the Transpot Centre with the others than she broke into an urgent sprint, followed by Dairan, Matt and Twedor, out of the centre and on up to Organisation. The cruiser was experiencing being caught up in the crossfire, being occasionally jolted by rebounding weapons fire as it hit the defence shield around the hull, bouncing off. Dairan, as they went, steadied himself and Tayce a couple of times en route. Treketa went back to the MLC to see how Donaldo was coping with Joshua Landorz, who was waiting for transfer to the surface of Pellasun by the medical team when the fighting was over. Tayce soon ran into Organisation followed by Dairan, Matt and Twedor. She demanded an immediate update on the situation as she came to a pause beside Marc.

"Vargon has advanced into a position to do damage to PT-2 on the surface. According to Amal, we're starting to join in the attack like you've ordered," informed Marc.

"Amal, scan for the central Operations Deck on the Carra Lair and target it," ordered Tayce, taking command of the situation from Marc.

"Scanning now," replied Amal in her elegant female voice.

“What are you going to do?” asked Marc curious.

“Do what Aldonica would do – drop PolloAld bombs aboard that vessel and blow it up once and for all. I’m not losing my parents again and letting Varon win for the second time in my life, when it comes to planetary possession. Not if I can help it,” said Tayce in a bitter and angry way.

“The central Operations Deck is at present vulnerable; shields seem to be depleting for some strange reason around the whole battleship,” announced Amal.

“Really? Open fire when fully unprotected, Amal,” ordered Tayce in a cold tone with no signs of emotion on her face.

“Firing now,” replied Amal, to the point, unleashing immense firepower from the cruiser.

Everyone watched as a constant bombardment of cannon fire hit the Carra Lair. In the cencrons that followed, explosions erupted, sending out debris as far as the eye could see. A slight smile crossed Tayce’s features as she knew this war of possession was one Varon Vargon hadn’t won. But, as much as she liked to think so, the galactic question was, was Vargon finally gone or had he miraculously escaped like he’d done numerous times before, leaving his crew to perish? Nothing new if he had! Tayce recalled the team from fighting out in the Universe, ordering them to return to the cruiser. At least Pellasun and its new base, PT-2, was safe. She watched as the protection fleet turned and headed back to the surface.

Tayce turned to Marc. “Let me know the moment the Quests are back. Then take this cruiser in to land on Pellasun,” said Tayce, heading towards the DC doorway.

“Sure – of course,” said Marc, pleased at the outcome of what could have been a total annihilation of a new base and the deaths of innocent people, including the Trauns.

“Marc!” said Tayce, pausing in the doorway.

“Yes.” He turned towards her.

“Your idea turned out well in the end. Great work,” praised Tayce.

“It was quite good, wasn’t it? Thanks!” he replied with a warm smile.

He turned back to the main sight port, watching as the team in their Quest shuttle/fighters flew back to the Flight Hangar Bay. After a few minons, Amal confirmed the shuttle/fighter team were back on board. Marc then ordered her to take Auran Amalthea Three back in to land on the Pellasun surface. Dairan stood in thought, wondering, like Tayce, if it was the last they would ever see of Count Varon Vargon.

***

Auran Amalthea Three descended back to the surface of Pellasun and PT-2, following on behind the fighters from the protection fleet. The team would cleanse and change for the evening celebration, knowing they were off duty for the remainder of the dayon of the opening ceremony. They had total relaxation in mind and no threat to worry about – whilst being on Pellasun, anyway. As for Vargon, had he gone this time for good?

11. Twedor

Auran Amalthea Three remained on the surface of Pellasun for the duration of the night hourons. Andory Paytern, the Councillor's daughter and singer, entertained everyone for the special celebratory evening, giving a full concert in the Ceremonial Hall. Dairan and Tayce had decided to stay in the domicile overnight. Marc had offered to take charge of the cruiser to make sure the team were all back on board by the midnight houron, ready for the next dayon's departure.

***

It was 2300 hourons. Tayce and Dairan had decided to call it a dayon and slipped away to the domicile. They exited out into a near-empty square. Tayce glanced about as they began to walk, thinking it was hard to imagine that less than five hourons previously Varon Vargon had caused another threat, causing chaos on the surface and attempting to destroy the new PT-2 Headquarters Base. There were a few stragglers that had been in the square and were soon heading away to their habitats and vessels. Purchasing centres for various wares and equipment for space travel had their lights shining in the sight panes. Dairan slipped his arm around Tayce's slim shoulders and they looked at each other in an affectionate relaxed way. Twedor looked up at them as he walked along beside them. He realised this night was going to be one where his mistress and Dairan could finally relax away from the cruiser.

Suddenly their moment of tranquillity was shockingly halted. Without warning he stepped into their immediate path, holding a Slazer pointed at them with a look that said he wasn't afraid to use it. He was of average height and of average looks.

He began coldly and aggressively: "Hand over the Romid – now."

"What! Who are you?" demanded Tayce, pulling Twedor behind her.

"I've been tracking this Romid for some time. Hand him over or I'll take him by force," he said, continuing to hold the gun pointed at them both.

"No, Twedor, stay where you are. This Romid is the property of Enlopedia Headquarters Base, so I don't know why you think he should go with you," said Tayce, adamant, refusing to let Twedor go, not in the least bit intimidated by this outlaw just because he was pointing a gun at her.

"Look, mate, this base is crawling with security patrol officers. This Romid is not for the claiming by anyone – even the likes of you. He's the design of Officer Bream and resides with my captain here, so do yourself a favour and go before I get the attention of that officer over there, who is at present watching you," backed up Dairan, stepping in between the gun and Tayce, looking darkly at the outlaw.

"You said the one person who is to blame for all this, so hand me the Romid and I'll be on my way and leave you in peace, unharmed," continued the outlaw under the watchful eye of one of Jan's officers who was growing suspicious about what was unfolding.

"No chance," replied Dairan. He didn't like this creep and wanted to drop him to the floor.

"No, don't, Dairan," said Tayce. She could suddenly sense trouble.

Too late. Tayce tried in vain to intervene and was knocked out of the way. Dairan tackled the outlaw to the floor of Pella Square before he got the chance to shoot Tayce and abduct Twedor. A fight quickly broke out between the outlaw and Dairan to gain possession of the Slazer weapon. The security officer came forth from the other side of the square, but it was too late. A single shot rang out, filling the air. Then, a few moments later, it was like time had stopped for Tayce. The air was filled with a deathly silence. Tayce gasped, thinking the worst, forgetting about protecting Twedor, who was out in the open. Dairan and the outlaw stopped in mid roll on the floor. To her horror, the outlaw pushed Dairan off and pulled free. In a split cencron he was on his feet, grabbing Twedor, and then he disappeared in a Transpot kind of way. Dairan was silent, not moving, face down. Tayce crossed, dropping to her knees beside him in sheer horror, thinking the worst – he was dead.

Over by the entrance to the Ceremonial Hall, Donaldo, Treketa and Lance had walked out. just in time to see the outlaw grab Twedor and disappear. Donaldo left Treketa and ran forth in urgency. Lance followed to support Tayce and get her up off the floor as the security officer called in to report what had happened. Lance looked at Tayce, realising what she might be thinking. This was a repeat of Tom Stavard all over again, except this time Tayce hadn't legally committed herself to Dairan.

"No, God, please, not again, not like this," said Tayce, fearing the worst, tears streaming down her delicate cheeks as she looked down at Dairan, thinking the inevitable had happened.

"It's all right, Tayce. Take it easy – Donaldo will sort it," reassured Lance, putting a friendly comforting arm around her for reassurance.

"No, it's not all right. I don't know who he was, but he's stolen Twedor. He said something about he'd been searching for him for quite some time. Please, don't let Dairan die like Tom. He was only protecting me," she said in Lance's hold, upset and crying.

Donaldo crouched down beside Dairan and felt his pulse. Once he'd established that Dairan was still alive, he turned, ordering Treketa to go and get an Emergency Crisis Team and hurry.

"Dr Tysonne, allow me. It's the least I can do," said the security officer, raising his Wristcall.

From the Security Division Building briskly walked Jan Barnford and two of his officers. Tayce looked at Jan coming forth with sudden alarm. In no time he was present and wanting to know what had happened. He'd heard a Slazer shot. He looked down at Dairan, then at Tayce, seeing her distraught.

"You heard the gunshot, then why didn't you investigate? You left your man here to take care of the whole situation. Twedor's gone – he was kidnapped by some outlaw who claimed he'd been tracking him for some time. Dairan did what you should have done, and now he's injured. Thanks, Jan," retorted Tayce, angry, fighting back the tears.

"You two spread out and take a look," ordered Jan, ignoring Tayce's outburst, but he understood it.

"You're wasting your time. He left via some kind of Transpot," said Tayce coldly, still angry.

Jan turned away, raising his Wristcall, ordering an immediate air scan of Pellasun for any signal or any sign of a vessel leaving the surface, as there wouldn't be many leaving legitimately, and he asked for the signal of Twedor to be traced. Suspicious spacecraft were to be stopped from leaving orbit at any cost. He lowered his Wristcall as the Emergency Crisis Team arrived.

Donaldo explained what had happened. The team took over from him and continued his medical care. Out of the Ceremonial Hall came Lydia and Darius. At first they were unaware of what was going on in the centre of the square, until they looked ahead. Lydia gave a look of utter alarm and concern upon seeing who was on the floor and the Quest team members all stood round. Darius walked to his daughter's side, watching Dairan under the care of the team, who were readying him for moving him to the Medical Hospital Dome. He then looked at Tayce.

"This creep came out of nowhere, Father. He was human, dressed in some kind of outlaw attire. Dairan tried to stop him. He said he had been tracking Twedor for some time. Now Twedor's gone. He grabbed him. Please, Father, help Dairan," said Tayce, now breaking down from the shock of what had just unfolded.

"I want every available officer skywards looking for this outlaw. Twedor is a very important Romid – you don't need me to tell you that. Make this your immediate priority, Jan," ordered Darius in a true Admiral's commanding tone. He didn't like seeing Tayce in the state she was in.

"Yes, sir, couldn't agree with you more. I'm already right on it. I have an air scan under way," replied Jan.

The Emergency Crisis Team were in the final stages of preparing to rush Dairan off to the Medical Hospital Dome. Darius ushered Tayce forward gently, suggesting she go on. Lance offered to go with her. Darius nodded in total agreement. Lydia watched Tayce walk away in Lance's care. She recalled the dayons passed when Lance and Tayce had been growing up together. They'd always found time to be there for each other when Jonathan went to Traun and brought Lance with him. It was good to see their friendship hadn't changed. Darius and Jan stood in discussion over what steps could be taken, besides the current air scan, to get Twedor back to where he belonged. Lydia turned whilst they talked, asking Donaldo to go and inform Marc back in the Ceremonial Hall. Donaldo agreed wholeheartedly. He informed Treketa and headed back into the hall. Lydia felt the whole dayon had been one of great pressure, and for her daughter it wasn't over yet. In no time at all Marc was leaving the Ceremonial Hall. As he walked across, so his features conveyed that he was greatly concerned. Jan finished his conversation, informing Darius that if he found out anything he'd contact him at first light. Darius nodded. Jan acknowledged Marc, then hurried away.

As Jan walked on across back to his building, he began thinking about the next steps to trace Twedor. It was hard to believe he could ever have guessed his first real case would involve a kidnapped Romid, let alone Tayce's Twedor. Marc paused before Lydia and Darius, ready to listen to the full story of what happened. Donaldo, who had walked back out with Marc, let him continue and headed away with Treketa to go back to Auran Amalthea Three. Darius began explaining the whole recent scenario of the past houron with Dairan, Twedor and Tayce. As Darius explained, so Marc's normally handsome features took on an alarmed look and he shook his head, giving a disgusted look. When Darius finished, Marc raised his Wristlink activating Comceive. Lance answered at the other end.

"I'm on my way to be with Tayce I want you back on Auran. I want you in command."

Lance could be heard agreeing over the Wristlink. Darius knew he could leave Tayce in Marc's care, knowing he'd do just this – look after her.

Before leaving Marc, Darius began: "Get her to rest at any cost," he ordered in a gentle ordering way.

"Of course – don't worry," assured Marc.

Marc knew he would have a job trying to make Tayce do just this. She'd be like a wound-up spring, wanting to find Twedor like yesteron. Without a further word, Darius guided Lydia off to their new residence whilst Marc walked off in the direction of the Medical Hospital Dome. This first visit to the lovely paradise world of Pellasun had been dogged by nothing but trouble, and if it had been anywhere else they wouldn't have wanted to visit it again. Marc noticed, as he went, how strong security was once more. In terms of numbers it was somewhat along the lines of how it was when Varon Vargon had threatened to wipe out their surroundings.

The Medical Hospital Dome entrance of glassene and steelex in a modern design came into view. Marc glanced at his Wristlink time display. It was almost the midnight houron. It had been a long eventful dayon and now that it was a matter of minons into tomorron he had a feeling tomorron was going to be just as eventful as that dayon had been. As he approached the doors to enter the dome he took a deep breath and got ready to resume command in helping Tayce. The doors drew apart in front of him. The overhead sensor picking up his presence. The warm sterile atmosphere came out to meet him as he walked into the foyer. Lance soon walked to meet him, seeing him enter. Marc paused, meeting him mid floor.

"Where's Tayce?" asked Marc, glancing about the foyer and waiting area for a sign of her seated, waiting.

"She's through there, waiting for news. They've taken Dairan straight in. It's just a matter of time. Dr Carthean's on the case. I know Tayce could do with your support right now," said Lance confidingly.

"Sure! Thanks for remaining with her. You go on back to the cruiser. I'll see you first light. Make sure everyone is back on board when you return," ordered Marc, glancing at his Wristlink time display, seeing it was midnight, which was when he had asked for everyone to be back on the cruiser.

"Let us know how Dairan is at first light," suggested Lance, glancing back to where Tayce was sitting.

"Yes, will do," replied Marc, deep in thought as he glanced to where Tayce was sitting alone.

Lance left Marc to it and headed on out through the entrance, off back to the cruiser, hoping Dairan was going to pull through. Marc casually walked across the vast foyer and on into the secluded waiting area. Tayce was now standing with her back to him, looking out into the illuminated landscape of Pellasun's surface. Marc carefully sauntered up to her. He reached out on coming to a pause just behind her, putting a reassuring hand on her shoulder and squeezing it gently, letting her know he was there for her.

"I'm all right, but I'm also angry," she said, then turned to face him with tear-stained features.

Marc pulled her into a comforting and reassuring hug. She suddenly broke down, resting her head on his uniformed shoulder, glad he was there for her.

"You have every right to be. Both Dairan and Twedor mean everything to you," said Marc understandingly.

"Twedor has been there for me since his first dayons as a guidance computer, Midge. It wouldn't be the same without him around," replied Tayce confidingly.

They stayed together for a few minons. Marc understood where she was coming from. She suddenly let him go, remembering what had happened during the episode with the Green Tempest Keeper. But she soon realised she was being silly. That had been put to rest, thanks to Adrien Maylen. She was glad, when she thought about it. Otherwise they could never be close again like they were at that moment. She sat down, her mind on how Dairan was doing, wondering if he would pull through and what they could be doing to him. After a long period of time that seemed like it would go on forever, Dr Carthean walked towards them.

"Tayce, Dr Carthean's coming," said Marc discreetly.

The Doctor smiled kindly as she entered the waiting area and saw Tayce looking concerned.

"How is he? Is he going to pull through? Please tell me he's going to be OK," asked Tayce, almost too afraid to ask.

"Dairan's going to be fine. It would, however, have been a different story if we hadn't recently installed the latest piece of equipment to take care of his kind of injury. Whoever shot him nearly killed him. The shot scratched the wall of his heart, but because we have our new equipment, a hand-held healing and penetration device, we were able to repair what had been damaged. He will be up on his feet by the middle of tomorron. We'll be watching him in the following hourons – just a precaution though," expressed Dr Carthean.

"When will he be well enough to return to normal duty?" asked Tayce casually.

"Give him roughly forty-nine hourons until he can be discharged. I'm going to speak to Dr Tysonne to get him to do extra monitoring for a further weekon, but his injuries are nothing to worry about," said Dr Carthean.

"Thank you for what you've done, Doctor," said Tayce, appreciative.

"I just want to see Dairan back on his feet. He's lucky he's made of the tough stuff. In the meantime, Tayce, get some sleep – you look like you need it – and come back in the mornet," said Elspeth.

"Good advice, Doctor. Come on, Tayce," said Marc, guiding Tayce on over to the waiting-area entrance.

Tayce didn't protest. She was tired and willingly went with Marc. Dr Carthean followed on out, going back to duty and to make her first check on Dairan of the night hourons. She watched both Marc and Tayce head back into Pella Square, thinking that the Amalthean Quests team had been hit by their fair share of trouble so far this voyage. She headed towards Dairan Loring's short-stay room.

***

Once back in Pella Square Tayce began to feel uneasy. The whole recurring scene of Dairan being shot flashed through her mind without warning, and with such force that it made her wince and a shiver run through her. Marc slipped his arm around her shoulders, just like any true friend would. He understood how she was feeling. Both Twedor and Dairan had been wrenched away in a moment of madness by some outlaw. Both meant a lot to her. Where was the little Romid? wondered Marc. Why had the outlaw seized him like he had? It puzzled him. He always thought Twedor was owned and designed by Craig Bream. Why should someone else want him? It wasn't making sense. He continued to think about the situation seriously as he went.

"Why do you suppose Twedor was grabbed?" asked Marc gently.

"Funny you should ask, but I'm thinking the same thing now. It is somewhat bizarre," replied Tayce.

"What are your thoughts on it?" asked Marc casually.

"Midge had the main characteristics of Twedor, and the new Romid body design is Craig's, but in any case I wouldn't think anyone would to want to steal him. It doesn't make sense," said Tayce, finding it really strange.

"Did Craig put the necessary documentation in when designing Twedor at the beginning of the second voyage?" put Marc, wondering if he'd forgotten.

"I believe so, yes!" replied Tayce, thinking back.

"When I come to think about it, I remember your mother approached me with the idea of converting Midge, saying Craig did have ownership of the outer casing. She asked could he go ahead and take Midge and turn him into Twedor?" explained Marc, recalling the fact as he walked.

"Why don't we see if Amal can throw any light on what's happened to Twedor?" suggested Tayce, eagerly heading off to the cruiser despite the fact that it was past midnight.

"I don't think so. You need a good night's sleep and I have orders from Dr Carthean and your father to make sure you do. I think we'll go this way," he said firmly, guiding her on in the opposite direction, away from the cruiser, towards her new domicile.

She looked up at him almost smiling. He wasn't going to let her win. They continued on and soon exited the complex, heading off towards the domicile. The night was relatively cool after the heat of the dayon. There were stars twinkling above and a gentle planetary breeze was blowing. The odd young-to-mid-aged group member or couple off duty walked by occasionally en route to wherever, nodding in greeting or voicing an acknowledgement to Tayce as they passed. A few minons later Tayce turned, seeing the entrance to the domicile, and soon walked up the path towards it. Marc followed and suggested he enter the domicile first, considering the kind of dayon they'd endured. She was too tired to argue. After activating the in-house computer system the entrance doors opened.

Tayce, even though it was her home away from space, felt apprehensive about entering, considering what had happened earlier that same dayon regarding Joshua. Marc walked in, and as he did so the in-domicile lighting came on to a natural setting. Tayce followed on after he gave the all-clear to do so. The entrance doors closed behind her. Marc turned to see the look on her face conveying that she missed Twedor and Dairan. He gave her an understanding look. She and Twedor had been together for a lot of yearons. He had always been there to watch over her. The atmosphere seemed strange with neither present. Tayce paused at the foot of the winding chrome-and-smoked-glassene staircase.

"I'm turning in. See you at first light. Help yourself to anything you want. Make yourself at home."

"Try and get some sleep. I know it's not going to be easy, but you need it," he kindly suggested as she began up the winding staircase.

No sooner had Tayce begun on up the stairs than she came over all dizzy and collapsed. As she did so, she called out to Marc. When she began to drop, Marc almost flew up the stairs in urgency, catching her in mid fall. He scooped her up in his arms and carried her gently but supportingly on up to her and Dairan's elaborate Repose Centre. Upon reaching the top he continued along the landing into the centre, where he crossed to the luxurious double bunk. Pausing once there, he placed her down gently, thinking this wasn't the first time he'd done this. Despite the fact that she was his captain and very close friend, he still felt at times she was still that naïve Traunian kid he'd had to take care of back in the Traunian dayons. It was funny how things never changed. He removed her boots, throwing them to the side of the Repose Centre, then pulled the heavy silkene coverlet up over her to keep her warm. She moaned and turned over. He knew this to be a sign she was OK and she'd merely fainted due to the dayon's exhausting events. He headed on back out of the Repose Centre, back down the stairs to grab himself a much needed cup of refreshing Coffeen before relaxing on the soffette and grabbing the last of the night houron's sleep. It was roughly four hourons before daylight.

***

It was 08:00, first light of a new dayon on the planet's surface. Already vessels were arriving to do business or leaving and heading back into space from being at the opening ceremony the dayon before. Various shapes and sizes of craft, in different designs, some menacing and some interesting, were manoeuvring into landing positions or lifting off and heading through the sky into space. Darius Traun could be seen through one of the sight panes of his new chambers shaking hands with an important-looking being in a way that conveyed it had been nice to meet him at the opening ceremony. They had been in an early mornet meeting discussing business. Elsewhere Matt Loring had been summoned to attend a meeting with Admiral Traun. He was walking across Pella Square in the company of Adam Carford, who had been sent to escort him. Panic and nervousness were filling every inch of his existence – he didn't know what the meeting was about and also he was awed by the fact he was facing Darius Traun. He to Matt was the big chief. He wanted to ask Adam why he'd been sent for, but was too afraid to ask. Adam glanced at Matt. He could understand his apprehension about meeting his superior, but there was nothing to be concerned about. His chief was going to offer Matt a chance to train on Pellasun at the training complex, to become a first-class officer like Dairan. But he didn't want to spoil the surprise – it wouldn't be right. He'd been given his orders to merely escort him to his chief.

In the domicile Tayce came down the stairs looking every inch the true beautiful refreshed captain and leader she was. She turned, walking to the open-plan Refreshments Area to see Marc sipping a cup of refreshing beverage. He turned, taking a drink and handing it to her.

"You look better this mornet," he said casually.

"I feel better. Please let's not have a repeat of yesteron todayon, what with Vargon's threat and now Dairan and Twedor," she began in between sipping the drink in her hand.

"Let's hope not. I've already had some good news. Dr Carthean called. She said Dairan's got the all-clear to leave her care later. Lance also called. He said he's been on duty since 06:00, tracking Twedor's signal via Amal's high-frequency link-up," said Marc, glad to see a little relief in Tayce's somewhat thoughtful and worried features.

"Did he find anything?" asked Tayce as she finished the drink.

"Yes, Twedor apparently is at a high-security criminal court colony called Admiran 4. According to Amal he's complaining about being swiped without permission," informed Marc with a slight amused smile.

"So that's our next destination. When are we getting under way?" asked Tayce, feeling eager to get going.

"I've already ordered Amal to plot the quickest route. There is one more thing."

"What?" asked Tayce, wondering just what he was going to say.

"Jan Barnford said he'll be along for the ride, as representative of both Enlopedia and PT-2 security and crime divisions to make a case that Twedor was stolen," replied Marc.

"He *was* stolen. Jan would be useful, especially if they start getting awkward about just who owns Twedor," said Tayce, thinking about the idea.

"You ready to leave? It's coming up to 08:49. Your father wants to see us, as you know, and we have to pick up Dairan en route," said Marc, putting his empty cup in the in-house incinerator recycler and heading on across to the Living Area.

"Yes, just let me put the message for clean into the Domestic Complex and key in the code for shutdown when we leave," said Tayce.

Tayce put the utensils from the first meal of the dayon into the incinerator, then crossed to the domicile's computer panel in the Domestic Area. Soon she'd done what had to be done and joined Marc, leaving the domicile for the walk to the Medical Hospital Dome to collect Dairan. Outside the domicile, after security was in place and everything was locked and secure, they both headed away down the path to join the main route back to PT-2's Main Complex. Tayce paused and glanced back, thinking what a time it had been for the first time in her own home. She came back to the present, walking on with Marc, who had stopped to wait for her.

***

Dairan was up and dressed, looking every inch the handsome man he was. He stood looking out of the almost wall-to-wall sight pane, watching the rise of the new second dayon of their stay on PT-2. Personnel could be seen working away in their every-dayon duties to keep the new colony moving. There were people walking and some were already in conference in the Parkland below. Just across the Parkland, garden techs checked and maintained the flower beds and trees, etc. Dairan thought to himself that one dayon, with or without Tayce, he would come and live on Pellasun. He felt it was somewhere he could settle down when his space-worthy dayons were through. The door of the short-stay room behind him opened. In walked Dr Carthean. Dairan turned.

"Sorry to keep you waiting. My last patient was determined to leave, even though he wasn't fit to do so. I'm pleased to tell you you can return to normal duties. Everything has healed. You'll be fine," she said in her usual doctors pleasant tone.

"Thank you, Doctor. What happened? All I remember was trying to stop this outlaw taking Twedor."

"You nicked the wall of your heart, but with the new treatment we have here, and our excellent surgeon, it's like the incident never happened. You're lucky!" exclaimed Dr Carthean.

"I guess I am. Thank you again," said Dairan, thinking he wouldn't be where he was if the technology to heal him wasn't there. He would have lost Tayce and the life he'd come to love.

"I urge you next time you feel like heroics to think of the outcome. You may not live to tell the tale," suggested Elspeth with a grin.

Dairan nodded, fully understanding. She had a point. Maybe he should have thought of his actions before doing what he'd done.

Behind them the door to the short-stay room opened and in walked Tayce and Marc. Tayce paused, wondering if she was intruding on Dr Carthean's visit with Dairan. Dr Carthean stepped aside, seeing Tayce, and happily announced that Dairan was free to leave. She had other patients to attend to. With this, she excused herself and walked from the room. After she'd gone Dairan reached out, pulling Tayce into a hug. She tried not to hug him too tight in case he was still sore.

Dairan let her go gently and began: "Has there been any further news on Twedor's whereabouts?" he asked, interested.

"He's been discovered on a criminal court colony called Admiran 4," replied Marc.

"Amal has plotted a course to take us there just as soon as we're back on board," said Tayce.

"Ready when you are," replied Dairan, eager to get going.

All three walked from the short-stay medical room back into the corridor. Marc's Wristlink sounded on his wrist. He raised it, pressing Comceive as they went. It was Lance and he had an update. Marc suggested he compile a report and have it ready for when they arrived back aboard later. They would be back in roughly an houron. Lance agreed, signing off. Tayce glanced at Marc in a questioning way.

"Lance has more information. I told him to compile a report for our return," said Marc.

"Right! OK – good idea," said Tayce.

***

Darius Traun was in discussion with Matt Loring about his proposal that he make something of his life. Adam stood by, ready to make all the necessary arrangements and escort Matt to the Pellasun training facility, as he had agreed to the proposal that had been put forth. The entrance doors soon parted and Tayce, Marc and Dairan walked in. Upon Dairan seeing Matt present, standing before Admiral Traun, he gave a look as much as to say, "What's he done this time? It has to be serious." Matt turned to see his brother's far from pleased questioning look. Darius saw Dairan looking at his younger brother and quickly quashed Dairan's suspicion Matt was in trouble, by announcing that he'd offered Matt a place training to be a first-class officer at the Training Complex: he just needed the necessary permission from Dairan or another member of the Loring family, such as one of his parents, to let it happen. Dairan stepped in and gave permission. It was his responsibility in the absence of their parents, him being the older brother. Darius immediately turned to Adam and gave him orders to take young Matt to begin his new life.

"Good luck, Matt. Do well and you could return to Auran," said Tayce.

"Yes, little brother, keep your head, study well and keep out of trouble," said Dairan in an advising way.

"Next time we see you we want to see you've done well. Good luck," said Marc.

"Thanks. I'll try."

Dairan watched Matt leave and it kind of reminded him of his early dayons when he started out. Sometimes he thought maybe he was a little hard on Matt. But he wanted to see him achieve something with his life. Maybe this idea of the Admiral's was just what would turn him into what he was ideal at, other than being just one of the gang back home. As soon as the entrance doors closed, Darius asked Tayce if any progress had been made towards tracing Twedor.

"Lance has so far discovered Twedor is on Admiran 4," said Tayce.

"Admiran 4? That's a colony that has only been in operation for about four yearons. It's built on an old space platform. They specialise in breaches of contract, including design copyright," said Darius, curious.

"But that can't be right. Why should Twedor be taken there? It doesn't add up. As you know, Father, Midge had the central characteristics of Twedor," said Tayce, finding the whole situation still strange.

"You're right. Midge was registered to Marc here and commissioned by myself in the early dayons, but I fear it's his new outer casing that's the problem – what he is now. I think you need to question Craig Bream," advised Darius, thinking Tayce's design had something to do with the situation.

"Father, if there's nothing else, we'd like to head back. Say goodbye to Mother for me. See you soon," said Tayce, giving her father a goodbye hug.

"You just let me know when you have Twedor back where he belongs," he replied gently.

"We will," promised Tayce.

"Oh, Dairan, nice to have you back with us," said Darius with a warm smile.

"Thank you, sir. It's good to be alive. I'll take care next time," replied Dairan casually.

"All right, go and find Twedor," said Darius, ushering everyone out.

He watched Tayce lead the way from his chambers on the return walk to Auran Amalthea Three. He was hoping she would be successful in getting Twedor back where he belonged. Lydia came in from the other Officette from her meeting, missing the team by a few minons. Darius explained that Tayce and the others had gone back to the cruiser and had said their goodbyes. Lydia felt disappointed she'd missed them. She had wanted to inform Tayce that she'd heard from Joshua Landorz, who was back to his normal thinking self and wanted to thank Tayce for her understanding of what had happened to him during the episode with Vargon. But it could wait, she guessed until next time they were in communication with each other. She began gathering her Officette Porto Compute notes and disks containing the data that had been discussed. There was little time left before she returned with them to Enlopedia under extreme security.

***

The team a while later stepped back aboard the cruiser, including Professor Adrien Maylen. Even though he felt PT-2 was the ideal world to spend the rest of one's dayons on, he'd grown used to being part of the Amalthean Quests team. He only just made it on board before departure, after everyone else had already boarded. He headed straight up to Organisation to give Tayce an update on Joshua Landorz. Amal, after doing a crew recount, confirmed that all but Twedor were aboard, then she put the cruiser into operation, destined for Admiran 4. The cruiser lifted up off Pellasun, leaving behind the PT-2 Headquarters Base, heading back into the sky and on into the vastness of the Universe, leaving behind the natural daylight for a while.

***

Lance stood up from his seat upon Tayce entering Organisation. He waited as she checked they were heading on their way to Admiran 4. Then he continued on into the DC behind her with the information he'd found. Dairan stayed with Marc on duty in Organisation. He decided to check out the layout of Admiran 4 on the star-chart podium after he'd made a request to Amal for it to be displayed. Jan Barnford entered Organisation, having boarded on Pellasun just before Professor Maylen. He walked on through to see Tayce in the DC. He entered just as Tayce sat down behind her desk. Crossing, he came to a pause by the sight port at ease. Looking out into the now passing stars, which were ebbing away behind the cruiser into yonder.

Tayce looked up at Lance, who was now stood before her desk. She took the disk-chip information as he explained that he'd downloaded the finer points in preparation to visit Admiran 4. Turning, Tayce placed the disk chip into the reader and activated it. The first image frame that appeared on screen was of a cold, calculating-looking woman with short mousey-coloured hair and eyes that were icy slate grey. There was a certain no-nonsense military look about her. Jan gave an unbelieving look at who he was staring at. He shook his head in disgust and sighed exasperatedly.

"Not her!" he openly said without thought.

Lance and Tayce looked at one another, then Jan, wondering what it was he felt so disgusted about.

"Is there something we should know about?" prompted Tayce, looking at him questioningly.

"Did I miss something in research? I thought I covered it all," said Lance, looking worried he'd missed something vital, judging by the look of disgust on Jan's face.

"No, it's just a good idea you brought me along if you want Twedor back," replied Jan seriously.

"Why, what do you know that we don't?" asked Tayce directly.

"That woman is someone you could say goes all out to break every rule in the rule book. She's been known to make a few of her own too, if it is to her advantage to do so, and to cover up when she feels the need. She's not to be trusted. Goes by the name Officer Lathanual," said Jan, disgusted.

"I don't care who she is. She has something that doesn't belong to her, or the outlaw who took him, and that's Twedor, and I want him back," said Tayce, angry.

"Quite! I think we need to talk to your tech officer," replied Jan, to the point.

"No time like the present. Lance, get Craig in here," requested Tayce.

"Right!" replied Lance, turning and heading back out into Organisation.

Tayce waited, as did Jan, only he was still angry to think he had to deal with a woman he'd like nothing more than to dump on a remote planet without life support. What she stood for, in his eyes, was her own kind of law and not the genuine kind. Craig soon sauntered in looking unsure of what was wrong or what he was wanted for. He looked at Jan, wondering what law he'd broken, judging by the look on Jan's face. Jan just looked at him in a no-nonsense kind of security-chief way as if he was summoning him up.

"Sit down. We have have something to ask you," asked Tayce seriously.

"Of course. Have I done something wrong? Is there a problem connected to Twedor?" asked Craig.

"What makes you ask that?" demanded Jan in the true interrogation tone he used as chief.

"Jan, I will ask the questions. No one is under interrogation here," said Tayce in her true tone of command.

Jan looked away. He knew he couldn't say anything – he was on Auran Amalthea Three, not in his Officette on PT-2, though he thought Craig wasn't being truthful.

Tayce activated the wall Sight Screen and an image of the outlaw that had abducted Twedor flashed up. Craig looked at the image and found himself looking at a man he used to consider his buddy and mentor. Someone from back in his tech training dayons who had taught him all he needed to know to create intelligent life, such as Twedor.

"This is the considered outlaw that abducted Twedor and almost killed Dairan. I can see you know him. Care to explain?" asked Tayce. She could sense Craig was shocked at seeing the person on screen and surprised at the same time to be seeing all over again someone he once knew.

"He's Retura Davin, though he never used to look like that. He was a lot smarter, also a good friend too," said Craig, finding his once friend's appearance somewhat shocking.

"What's he want Twedor for?" asked Tayce, straight. "He said he'd been tracking him for some time when we encountered him in the square yesteron."

"He shouldn't be – he has no cause to," replied Craig, surprised at the fact.

"Why do you think he'd do this? After all, you say you were once friends, Officer Bream. We need to know because in roughly one houron we'll be at Admiran 4 and we've absolutely no intention of leaving without Twedor," expressed Jan to the point, still taking the interrogation approach.

"I'm sorry, Chief, I don't know what to say," said Craig, looking up at Jan.

Tayce didn't stop Jan this time. He was right: everything Craig knew about this Retura Davin of old had to be put out in the open. After a few moments of silence, Craig began to describe how Twedor's design came into being. It had been in the early dayons of his training. They'd been set a project to come up with an outer-casing design for a small intelligent robot-type three-foot Romid. It had been a joint venture between himself and Retura, except after the course was finished the design was left on the shelf. Later he took it and modified it further, and Twedor's outer casing was born. When Craig left the Training Complex he kept the design as no one seemed to want it.

"So what happened to this Retura Davin?" asked Jan.

"I never saw him after the course. We kind of lost touch. He said the design was mine if I wanted it – after all, I'd progressed further with it. He'd gone as far as he could with it anyway. I didn't see any harm," replied Craig, remembering.

"Did he sign ownership over to you, to confirm he wanted you to have it and that he'd have nothing more to do with it?" asked Jan, forming a picture of what had happened in his mind.

"I didn't think anything more of it. He didn't want it and I thought it was perfectly all right to take it. After all, he just walked away from it and disappeared. I figured I could do more with it. I felt it was a waste to let it go. I checked at the time if anyone else wanted it; no one wanted the design, so it became mine, but before I converted Midge into Twedor I filed the essential paperwork and I did try and find Retura," replied Craig.

Jan and Tayce both glanced at one another. Tayce sighed. It looked like a case of design theft without Craig realising what he'd done, even though at the time it didn't seem like it to him. Craig had been taken for a ride, being an innocent young tech cadet. Now it was time to put it right.

"You're picked to come to Admiran 4 with us. You'll have to tell your side of what happened in all this. In the meantime I'm relieving you from duty. I want you to go back to your console and get any records of the construction of Twedor's outer casing in your student dayons and when you worked on him on your own – all the details you filed to make him official, anything, and download it," suggested Tayce.

"Believe me, I didn't steal Twedor's design, Tayce, honestly. The complex where I did my training was going to put it in the waste-recycling system after it had been on the shelf a monthon if unclaimed," said Craig as he rose to his feet.

"We'll get this sorted. We'll have the truth. I'd rather believe you over some outlaw. You've always proved yourself to be an upstanding part of this team and I have no cause to think otherwise," said Tayce sincerely.

"Thanks. That means a lot. I'll go and see what I can come up with," said Craig, pleased to hear Tayce believed in him. He felt a total idiot for falling for such a dirty trick by his once friend.

As he walked from the DC Tayce found herself wishing she hadn't taken him off duty in case there was an emergency. But Craig needed time out in order to retrieve information from his past – they needed to get Twedor back. He needed to have his full concentration on the matter. There was also an even more serious side to dropping him from his duties. Craig had suddenly gone from being tech officer of the cruiser to being accused of stealing a design, and it was right he should be removed from duty until the situation was cleared up. Jan looked at her, understanding her awkward situation. He knew how Tayce felt about her team. Each member was special in their own way with what they brought to the concept of Amalthean Quests, and when it came to a situation like the one they were in then she would do what she could to get to the bottom of it and set it right. Jan suggested they continue to study Admiran 4 to find out what other nasty surprises lay in store for them and Craig.

***

Thirty minons from Admiran 4 the Organisation Sight Screen suddenly activated, flashing into life. Towards the centre of the screen was a cold, official, no-nonsense bald and plain-looking humanoid male. He looked into the screen like he was taking a good look around the Organisation Centre with a scrutinising eye of suspicion. Marc turned, giving a taken-aback eyebrow-raised look of surprise. Dairan looked where Marc was looking and called Tayce from the DC. The humanoid male in his late forties was not the least bit interested in Dairan; he was waiting for answers. He was more interested to know what Auran Amalthea Three was doing in her current orbit. Tayce briskly walked from the DC and came to a pause beside Marc in the centre of Organisation.

"Am I addressing the leader or captain of the vessel in the vicinity of this base? If so, state the reason for your business before entering the access point of our sector, or I will be forced to take drastic action to deter you from coming any closer," he demanded, sounding just as cold as he looked.

"I'm the captain of this vessel. We have business on Admiran 4 which cannot be divulged for legal reasons. All we can say is it's of an urgent top-priority nature," replied Tayce, just as cold.

"I cannot permit your vessel to dock unless I know the nature of your business," he persisted.

Jan walked up behind Tayce, discreetly suggesting he handle this access-point authoriser. Tayce nodded, only too happy to let him try. He stepped in front of her and came to stand at ease, like the true security chief he was. His whole body and look matched that of the being on screen, straight and stiff.

"I'm Security Chief Commander Barnford of Enlopedia. This team and cruiser have Enlopedian clearance to proceed by Admiral Traun's authorisation to sort out a misunderstanding. Now, if you don't want Admiral Traun of Enlopedia to report to your superiors that you're not being cooperative to one of the Universe's well-respected crime-orientated teams—" began Jan, but he was quickly cut off by the being on screen.

"You are hereby granted permission," blurted out the bald authoriser in a hurry.

Jan lowered his head, smiling a rugged amused smile as the screen went blank. Lifting his head, he turned to inform an amused Tayce that the matter was sorted. They could continue to docking.

Marc and Dairan exchanged glances of amusement at the way in which Jan had made the being on screen quickly do what was asked. Tayce turned, ordering Kelly to take the cruiser into docking.

***

Admiran 4 came into view, looking somewhat squashed and round in appearance, rather like a stepped-on ball. It was spread out in all directions. Modern in construction, large dome-shaped modules were linked to flat one-storey buildings. The slightly smaller one-storey buildings were triangular-shaped covering vast areas. Clear-vision walkways with clear domed roofs linked all the modules and buildings. The whole base was slate grey in colour, uninteresting to look at, covering a vast diameter of four milons across. Vessels of all shapes and sizes came and went from Docking Ports which protruded out from the central main point of the base underneath. It was busy, just like a continuing rush houron at Enlopedia or PT-2. Admiran 4 had life support fit for normal working and habitation for the many criminals that were held there after trial for transfer to wherever they would serve their sentences. This was a base that wasn't going to prove a walk through the Parkland for Tayce, Jan and the team, going over to get Twedor back where he belonged.

***

Tayce picked her Quest team: Craig, Marc, Jan and Phean Leavy for his ability to read the motives of Retura Davin, to see whether he was trying to hide something in regard to Twedor. Tayce didn't want a large team. This was not an exploratory Quest; it was merely to get Twedor back. She checked everyone was ready then began towards the Organisation entrance. Marc placed Dairan in command, ordering him to stand by. Dairan nodded. Nick called out that he'd stay in contact. Marc agreed, following on behind the others going on out of Organisation as Auran Amalthea Three ebbed into the final moments of docking at the Admiran 4 base.

***

Craig Bream having been requested to find any evidence to support his side of the ownership argument over Twedor, left his quarters, heading along to the Level Steps to go up and join the Quest team. In his mind he wondered why Retura Davin, his old buddy from their training dayons, had suddenly done what he'd done, in abducting Twedor and deciding he wanted Twedor back. Was he getting back at him because of what Twedor had become – the first of his kind? He reached the top of the Level Steps and saw Tayce and the others waiting by the

Docking-Bay doors. He hurried and apologised for keeping everyone waiting, but he now had all he needed and was ready. He braced himself, knowing in his mind that, even though he was innocent, this particular Quest wasn't going to be an enjoyable one. Twedor was at stake. If he had to be handed over permanently, who knows what Retura Davin would put him to use as!

"Craig, a piece of advice: whatever happens when we set foot on this base, don't react. Let us handle the situation, along with Chief Barnford here, until your evidence of ownership is brought into consideration," advised Tayce, to the point. "Understood?"

"Yes, fully," replied Craig seriously. He just wanted an end to what was going on.

The Docking-Bay doors opened upon docking completion with Admiran 4. Rowdy noise filled the air mixed with abusive language from freshly arrived criminals. Tayce and Jan walked out down the walkway, first to head into the central area, followed by Phean and Craig. The noise came from the end of the walkway and was growing louder by the minon as they walked towards it. They stepped out into what can only be described as a processing area. Criminals, including whole gangs of jostling uncooperative aliens, were fighting against the rough stern handling of the Admiran law officers. There were aliens in strange guises, with weird complexion colours and odd-coloured eyes that were part of their normal make-up. It was not a place for the faint-hearted. They eyed the Amalthean Quests team,with interested evilness. Tayce paused, trying not to appear nosey or intruding, but was surprised by the many criminal races there were present, most of which she hadn't seen before. Suddenly a loud male voice bellowed in their direction. It made Tayce flinch, which was something she rarely did.

"Ma'am, you and your people don't belong here. What's your business?" yelled a military-looking male on the far side of the area.

Tayce, somewhat shocked by the commanding outburst, turned in the direction it came from. He was wearing a dark-grey uniform with the Admiran 4 emblem, 'A4', on the right upper side of his jacket. Big-built and strong-looking, he marched forth, frowning at Tayce and the others. There was no welcome smile expected on his features any time soon. He was official to the core. He sighed impatiently as he came to a stop before her and Jan. Tayce noticed his eyes showed no kindness. He had obviously seen his fair share of criminals and lawbreaking activities, making him nothing else if not official. Phean thought to himself that this rule keeper was probably summing them all up in the same way most criminals were scrutinised in their current surroundings, despite their smart attire and their legitimate reason for being there.

"As I said, you people don't belong here. State your business or leave. We don't need sightseers here," he began coldly and thoughtlessly.

"I'm far from being a sightseer. We've come to claim back property that's rightfully ours. You have a Romid here that was brought in via very unlawful means," began Tayce.

But she was cut short by the officer before her, now almost towering over her in an intimidating way. Not that it bothered her.

"Name?" he barked in cold reply.

"Captain Traun of the Amalthean Quests," replied Tayce.

"We have a name that was given to us – Retura Davin. That's the reason we're here," spoke up Jan in his official tone. He could see Tayce was growing fed up with the attitude this officer was showing her, considering she wasn't there as a criminal.

"Wait!" replied the officer abruptly, and he checked his hand-held device.

After checking, he gestured to a seating area just across from them. As they crossed, Tayce gave the officer an unimpressed look, conveying that she was far from amused by his volatile behaviour. Phean read Tayce's thoughts and discreetly announced that he'd encountered worse. As Tayce waited, so her thoughts drifted to Twedor and how he was coping in all the current unnecessary mess. Where was he? she wondered. After what seemed like ages, out of the corridor's end doorway came a thin, tall humanoid woman with the officer they'd been dealing with. She seemed to be reprimanding him in a stern way as she came towards them. Jan recognised her from the image on the Porto Compute back in the DC. She came to a stop just a short way away from them. Jan glanced away, feeling a feeling of disgust.

"Which one of you is Captain Traun?" she demanded, almost looking down her nose as she said it, glancing along the line of the seated team and Jan.

"I am. You are?" demanded Tayce without politeness, rising to her feet.

"Case Officer Lathanual," announced the officer in a cool to-the-point tone.

"Where's my Romid? I demand to know," asked Tayce. She could see she was an equal match for this case officer before her, in coldness.

"The Romid in question is perfectly safe, Captain, and as soon as this case is sorted the rightful owner will be awarded ownership," replied Officer Lathanual, continuing to look down her nose at Tayce.

"I am the rightful owner. I have Officer Bream here to submit evidence for his side of the case. Believe me, Officer Lathanual, when we're proved the rightful owners there are going to be repercussions over what's happened to bring us here following the abduction of my Romid," said Tayce commandingly

"Are you prepared to give your side of events freely, Officer Bream?" asked Lathanual, brushing her long hair away from her face.

"Yes, ma'am, I am," replied Craig, to the point.

"Then you had better follow me. Come into my Commission Unit, where I can discuss further what is required regarding the forthcoming case," replied Officer Lathanual, turning and leading the way back off up the corridor she'd come down, walking in a precise and elegant manner ahead of Tayce and the others.

Marc and Jan exchanged raised-eyebrow glances, unimpressed by Officer Lathanual's upper-class officialdom. Jan knew better where this woman was concerned. He was watching her attitude towards Tayce and the case and considering the last time she and he had met. It was because of her misconduct in the case of a young up-and-coming officer who had been wrongly accused and underhandedly sentenced to an unfortunate death. It was discovered too late that the young officer in question should not even have been convicted at all. He'd been in the wrong place at the wrong time and had been framed. He'd been put on trial and sentenced to an unnecessary death. He'd been the victim of a very immaculate set-up, even though he'd been innocent. Jan felt angry at what had occurred. How smugly Lathanual had walked away after what she'd done. If he'd been over her as her superior, he would have had her kicked out of her current position.

They all entered through tall doors into what can only be described as a vast plush light and modern Officette. Officer Lathanual crossed to her desk, which seemed to almost be the focal point of the Commission Unit. Both Marc and Tayce sat on chairs in front of the desk. Jan didn't know how to keep a straight face, seeing Tayce and this Officer Lathanual opposite each other, both showing their rank and cold tolerance of each other. But Jan knew whom he'd put his confidence in in a moment of trouble and it certainly wasn't Officer Lathanual.

"Captain Traun, your Romid – his design has been stolen. That's the case being brought by Mr Retura Davin. He claims your officer here has taken the Romid's outer-casing design and used it to make an upgrade to your former guidance and main operations computer and named him Twedor. In fact you, Captain, have been using something that doesn't belong to you, according to this report filed before me, but I understand you have brought other evidence and the other party involved in this situation here todayon to tell his side of the story. I will have an assistant take your Officer Bream to give him a sensory truth test and his evidence will be taken into account," explained Officer Lathanual.

"Only if accompanied by Chief Commander Barnford. You have your rules; I have mine," said Tayce, and she wasn't prepared to discuss it.

Upon hearing Jan's name, Officer Lathanual glared at him across the desk, recalling the last encounter she'd had with him and at the hands of her superiors. She looked away, ignoring his cold look of suspicion towards her, and she immediately gave her permission for Marc instead to accompany Craig. Jan gave a look that said it all: she was hiding something again. If she was, she hadn't better. Phean began reading Officer Lathanual's mind, finding out just whom she really wanted to have own Twedor and seeing if she was going to benefit from it or not. The doors soon opened. In walked Officer Lathanual's assistant in the same grey uniform of the Admiran 4 colony. He just looked like all the rest, austere to the core. Officer Lathanual ordered Craig to go and give his evidence. Marc rose to his feet ready to go with him. He looked at Officer Lathanual, trying to make her out. There was something not right about her, like she was hiding something very convincingly; but what, he couldn't quite put his finger on. All he could see was that she seemed to be pretty uncomfortable about Jan's presence.

As the doors closed behind them, so Tayce began: "I want to see Twedor, my Romid. I understand he's part of this case, but I still want to see him," requested Tayce. She wanted to see he was in one piece, as he should be.

The request caught Officer Lathanual off guard. She sat in thought for a few minons.

"I will escort you now if you wish, but please keep in mind that seeing your Romid will not change the fact the law decides who he will return to once the case is through and not you, Captain."

"I'm aware of that, Officer Lathanual; but if I don't see him, then how do I know he's here? Just because you say he is? For all I know a team of technicians could have tried to dismantle him," pointed out Tayce with a plain look.

"Captain Traun, we don't do things like that on Admiran 4 without good reason," replied Officer Lathanual in a tone that said she didn't like Tayce's accusation.

"That's good, then. Shall we go?" asked Tayce, giving Officer Lathanual a look as much as to say, "Prove it!"

Lathanual could see Tayce was becoming dissatisfied over the handling of Twedor and Retura Davin's claim that the outer casing was his. But she owned Midge, who was part of Twedor, and there was no disputing it. If Retura Davin won, against all odds, then all that was Midge would have to be downloaded somehow to be returned to Enlopedia to be designed in a new form. Lathanual, under the watchful eye of Jan, began walking over to the unit entrance. Jan and Phean could see the cool exchange that was brewing between Tayce and Officer Lathanual and turned to head on out behind. As Tayce walked with Phean a slight way ahead, Jan reached out and grabbed Officer Lathanual by the upper arm. As she looked at him, he warned her discreetly that if she messed up this legal situation he'd make sure she never worked for any legal organisation on any colony in space again. Did she understand? Lathanual pulled her arm free, giving Jan a look of pure annoyance. But she wondered if he would do what he'd promised. Tayce looked from Jan to Lathanual, wondering what was being exchanged between them. He dismissed her questioning look, glancing away as he followed on up the corridor, heading to where Twedor was presently being held.

Suspended in the middle of a large centre for technology, on a type of silver-toned crane in a harness, was Twedor. He was surrounded by four security officers primed with hand-held weapons and a force field. No one could have stolen him even if they'd wanted to. He was active, but on standby mode. During this time, the Admiran security watch were unaware that he was in contact via high-frequency link-up with Amal. They'd linked the moment Auran Amalthea Three had come into orbit. He could look about his environment, even though he found it quite uninteresting. There were various pieces of technical equipment and large machinery.

The entrance doors drew apart across from him. First into the technical facility walked, much to his delight, his mistress. Twedor looked at Tayce. He wanted to say something, but figured it would be unwise with the heavy security presence. Without warning, Officer Lathanual's communication device sounded the alarm signal. The officers surrounding Twedor suddenly increased the force field around him. It became brighter to an almost glare.

"What's going on?" demanded Tayce.

Officer Lathanual ignored Tayce and moved out of earshot to answer the communication. Phean used his hearing power to make out what the sudden alarming situation was that was unfolding. Jan and Tayce exchanged serious concerned looks, wondering what was going on. In no time at all Officer Lathanual had finished her call and turned to walk back to Tayce.

"I'm waiting, Officer Lathanual. Why has the force field suddenly increased around Twedor?" asked Tayce, alarmed.

"Captain, I want you to return to the Commission Unit. We have a situation that affects your Romid here and the case for ownership. I will return to the unit just as soon as I know what's happened," explained Lathanual, heading back to the entrance in urgency, ignoring Tayce.

"One minon, Officer Lathanual. Just what is happening?" demanded Jan, stepping out from behind Tayce.

"I'm not in a position to divulge just yet. Please bear with me," she replied, straight to the point.

Jan wondered if she was or wasn't and just wasn't going to say. He didn't trust her. A security officer guided Tayce and the others back to the Commission Unit. Tayce glanced back at Twedor, who strangely enough was watching her walk on out. She felt like she was leaving a friend behind, never to see him again – he had always been a friend. Twedor watched until his mistress was out of the technical facility and he was on his own again. He hoped he'd see her again, he thought.

***

He lay in the room he'd resided in since arriving on Admiran 4. It was furnished, but sparsely. He was either unconscious or dead. Security had been alerted to the fact. When a cleaning tech had called to clean, the cleaning tech had thought he was dead. Someone or something wanted him gone for good reasons. But the strangest thing was that this was an act of unusual violence. It had to have been carried out by an intruder or an inside person. Also had Retura Davin killed himself with his own Slazer weapon? No one had witnessed what had happened and no one had been seen leaving the room. A security officer of high rank and a medical attendant entered the room. The pretty female medical attendant, upon reaching Retura's body, crouched down, checking whether he was in fact unconscious, or dead, as first reported. A few cencrons elapsed and she turned her head, shaking it at the nearby security officer. Upon standing, she announced that a Slazer weapon strike was not the cause of death, as first thought. Something else had ended Retura Davin's life. There would have to be an internal body scan to find the cause. Officer Lathanual soon arrived in the open doorway.

"Looks like that case for ownership is over. This is Retura Davin, your claimant," explained the young female medical attendant.

"Not quite. I want the cause-of-death report brought to me in an houron," ordered Officer Lathanual.

"Come off it, Officer Lathanul. He's as dead as anyone can be when they are not living. There is no case. Let it drop. All evidence there was in this case is null and void, and the main reason is before us. Let the Romid and the people that came here to claim him go. Give him back. You know as well as I do that Davin has no heirs to pursue the claim he made. He was a loner, according to his records," said the security officer.

"Yes, you're right, and it would get that Chief Barnford out of my sight," said Lathanual, agreeing.

"Then take some advice from someone who knows you well: let it go," he sternly advised close to her.

Whoever this officer was, he was above Officer Lathanual in experience and authority. He, unlike some of the solemn-faced officers, was quite good-looking. He was older – in fact he had platinum-grey hair. He was somewhere around his mid fifties, tall and broad. He made Officer Lathanual look small. He looked at her with serious green eyes that conveyed he was serious about making her drop the case; otherwise he would take steps to make her do so. She turned and walked on back to the Commission Unit, not looking back at the threatening officer. She was feeling somewhat angry at the sudden unexpected outcome regarding Retura Davin. Two things that still bothered her were who did kill Retura Davin and why? She took her communication device out of the top pocket of her suit and activated it. She reluctantly gave the order to have Twedor brought to the Commission Unit. As she walked the final yards, upon her order being confirmed, she lowered her device and sighed. She knew the look she'd get from Chief Barnford when she entered the unit would express that he was glad she'd lost this time around. But she could take it.

***

Twedor was immediately lowered to the technical-facility floor, much to his relief, then taken out of the force field and harness and guided by two male burly-looking Admiran 4 security officers. On the way out, on his way to the

Commission Unit, Twedor had no idea of what was happening. After all, they could be taking him on his way to be dismantled and he'd never see Tayce or the team again. He looked at a corridor wall sign and, much to his relief, he realised they were not heading to the Dismantling Centre. This made his outlook look optimistic, he thought.

***

Officer Lathanual braced herself outside the Commission Unit before entering. She was trying to push to the back of her mind her disappointment about what had happened regarding Retura Davin. She hated losing. She finally entered to find Marc Dayatso and Craig Bream looking somewhat puzzled, as was the rest of the team, about why they'd all been returned to their present surroundings. Tayce looked at Lathanual in a questioning cold manner as she walked around the back of her desk. She paused, standing, ready to deliver the news she didn't want to give. She wanted to win this case.

"What's going on? Wasn't my officer's evidence good enough? Why were we ushered back here?" demanded Tayce, becoming angry.

"It would appear there now seems to be, for some uncertain reason, no case for ownership by Retura Davin over your Romid, Captain. He's being returned to you. As far as Mr Davin goes, he's been removed from any further ownership claim over the Romid and all evidence on his side, has been withdrawn against you and Officer Bream," she explained, to the point.

"What's to stop him coming after the Captain's Romid again any time soon?" asked Jan, unsure of what had unfolded, though he could sense something wasn't right.

"That won't happen, Chief Barnford. About an houron ago in the Habitation Section, an alarm sounded. Mr Davin was found dead in his quarters. The cause is not yet known, but I have been ordered by my superior to close the case and return the Romid to you, Captain," replied Officer Lathanual.

"So where is he?" asked Tayce, eager to get Twedor back where he belonged.

At this moment the Commissions Unit doors opened. Everyone turned. Twedor entered and went straight to Tayce, glad to be back with her as her long-standing escort again. Officer Lathanual suggested she escort everyone back to the entrance, where they first arrived. Tayce put her hands on Twedor's shoulders, guiding him over to the unit entrance. The doors opened. Everyone, including Officer Lathanual, walked out and down the corridor. Jan, halfway down, dropped back to talk to Officer Lathanual discreetly, so the others couldn't hear what was said. They all walked out into a near-deserted reception area, going over to the walkway that would take the team and Twedor back to Auran Amalthea Three.

"Captain Traun, a moment before you leave," asked Officer Lathanual.

"Yes," replied Tayce, pausing, turning back for a moment.

"I hope your time on Admiran 4 was not an unpleasant one and that you understand protocol had to be followed where your Romid was concerned. He's quite unique. I hope you have him for many yearons to come. It's been an honour to meet you. I had no idea we are on the good side of justice together, fighting for what's right," said Officer Lathanual, stretching out her hand for Tayce to shake.

"Officer Lathanual," said Tayce, grasping Officer Lathanual's small, slender hand and shaking it.

Tayce walked on aboard behind the team, guiding Twedor, who waited for her. Officer Lathanual walked away, returning to her duty and moving on to the next case: to find out who really did kill Retura Davin and why. She paused, hearing Auran Amalthea Three depart and turned to see it leave. It was a case of here one minon, gone the next. She continued on down the corridor.

12. Phean's Dilemma

Jan Barnford felt Retura Davin's sudden demise was too convenient. So he'd informed Tayce the moment he arrived back on PT-2 that he was going to look into it further and let her know what might have truly happened. As far as Twedor was concerned, there was nothing else to resolve and there would be no more trouble for the little Romid. He was definitely Tayce's and Craig Bream's. Jan was picked up quickly by Patrol Cruiser and was on his way back to PT-2 to resume his duty within two dayons of leaving Admiran 4.

***

Almost a weekon from Jan's departure, Tayce had decided to keep up her new ability training by request of Phean. It was also a chance for both of them to flex their abilities. Phean had so far taught Tayce many new skills during their time together, since the beginning of the voyage. In this current training session Phean was teaching Tayce how to use a single ball of pure energy to put anyone, just by thought alone, under her influence, to make them do what she wanted them to do. Both were enjoying the training, laughing as Tayce got the hang of honing the new skill for use, having a few near misses. Without warning, both Emperor Honitonia and a guard from the Realm of Honitonia arrived. Tayce and Phean, a little surprised by the sudden arrival, stopped the training session and turned their attention to an annoyed-looking Emperor plus the white suited guard beside him.

"My visit it not a social one, Tayce. Phean, you are required to return under arrest to the Realm of Peace" ordered the Emperor plainly.

"Why?" asked Tayce, shocked at his request.

"I will show you," said Phean, placing the reason why in Tayce's mind for her to see.

The Emperor's guard walked forth and took hold of Phean in a restraining grip. Tayce was far from pleased. This was her cruiser, not the Realm of Honitonia. How dare a member of the Emperor's guard just think he could come aboard and arrest one of her team without her authority. Then she saw what Phean placed in her mind and the reason why he had to return the way he was. It was for a crime he'd carried out on her behalf and it involved Twedor on the last Quest on Admiran 4. He had to pay the price for breaking the Empire ruling, that no joined member of the Realm of Peace may intervene in spacial matters – i.e. probing the mind of someone to gain knowledge, or terminating life without good reason.

"Retura Davin – did you kill him, Phean?" asked Tayce, giving Phean a surprised look.

"I'm guilty of the actions as stated. I wanted to help you. I know what Twedor means to you," he said, trying to make her understand he'd done what he had because he wanted her to win.

"Oh, Phean! What's going to happen to him, Emperor?" asked Tayce, not liking the fact that the Emperor's guard had such a restraining hold on Phean. She wondered if she'd ever see him again.

"He will answer for his intrusion into the mind of another and the other breach of spacial law. Then he will be returned to you," said the Emperor plainly. He could see Tayce was somewhat disappointed by what had occurred. She felt Phean had been an idiot, to say the least, even though he thought he was doing good by helping her keep Twedor.

"What does it entail? He may be a member of your Realm, but he's also a valuable member of this team and as such, being his captain, I have a right to know," pointed out Tayce.

"Not in this instance. The Higher Minds have forbidden you to know anything of the punishment," replied the Emperor.

"Well, that's not good enough. Like I said he's a member of my team and I have a right to know," said Tayce in a annoyed tone.

"Tayce, don't make me have to reprimand you for interfering in Empire matters where it is forbidden. You're not allowed to know," warned Honitonia, still angry with Phean.

"You reprimand me! This is my cruiser – I won't stand for this. If he did something wrong, then it's not only your business; it affects me as well," said Tayce, not giving in.

Emperor Honitonia didn't want to reprimand Tayce, but, in order to make her stay out of what had happened, with the raising of his right hand, and without thought about what he was doing, he lifted Tayce up off the practice mat with his powerful force, encasing her in a brilliant yellow punishment force, and threw her across the centre. She impacted into the area where workout equipment was stored and dropped unconscious to the floor, still in the yellow energy force. Phean was horrified to think the Emperor would do such a thing. He called over to her as she lay with her head on one side, out cold. He could see she was injured and wanted to help her. But before he had the chance to find out how badly she was hurt, he was removed from the cruiser in the grip of the Emperor's guard, in the Telepathian aura of transportation, along with the Emperor. Who was looking at an unconscious Tayce as he vanished, not pleased that she'd made him do what he had.

The Armed Combat Centre was almost empty for a few minons. Then, a few minons after that, the doors opened. A male figure walked in, throwing a couple of mid-air combat strikes into nothing, not really taking in that he wasn't alone in his present surroundings. As he turned to aim in another direction, into nothingness, so his sight caught her slim figure sprawled on the floor, now free of the yellow energy force, in the equipment area, not moving. He raised his Wristlink, sounding the emergency alarm, pressing Comceive and hurrying towards Tayce. Donaldo answered.

"You'd better get down to the Armed Combat Centre. Bring your Medical Crisis Kit. It's Tayce. I don't know what's been going on here, but she's injured, out cold," said Lance.

"On my way," said Donaldo into the Wristlink from MLC.

Lance ceased communications, then got down to carefully lift Tayce up into a comfortable position. He wondered what had been going on. The last he'd heard, she and Phean were taking power-endurance practice. What had happened? Where was Phean?

The doors opened to the centre, and Donaldo and Treketa came running in with a Medical Crisis Kit and Hover Trolley. Treketa activated the Hover Trolley, watching Donaldo help Tayce. After a few minons Donaldo had Lance move Tayce. He carefully scooped her up, going into a standing position, turned and placed her gently down on the Hover Trolley.

"What happened here? According to my Examscan reading her brain is in some kind of suspended state," said Donaldo, guiding the device all over Tayce, checking the reading was right.

Both Lance and Treketa exchanged concerned glances. After a couple of minons, Donaldo suggested they move Tayce to the MLC, where more tests could be run to determine what was happening with her. With this, Tayce was taken away on the Hover Trolley, on out of the Armed Combat Centre and off to the MLC. Lance watched them go and raised his Wristlink. Activating it, he informed Dairan of what had happened. Once done, he returned to his off-duty combat practice, still wondering where Phean had disappeared to. His thoughts were still on what could have unfolded in his present surroundings. He continued to do his mid-air strike practice punches.

Dairan ran out of Organisation, thinking to himself he wished he'd made Tayce change her mind in continuing the power-ability practice with Phean that mornet. As he'd noticed of late, Phean had been acting somewhat strange ever since returning from Admiran 4. He'd had a hunch it had something to do with the mystery surrounding Retura Davin's sudden death. He'd often wondered how he had died, and he'd noticed a couple of times when the subject had come up Phean's features had taken on a look of total unease. Now Tayce had been hurt. Just what was going on? he wondered. He ran down the corridor and down the Level Steps two at a time, as fast as he could go, in order to find out just what had happened to Tayce.

***

Emperor Honitonia was far from pleased with both Tayce and himself. He understood her point of view regarding the fact that Phean was a true loyal member of her team. But he couldn't allow her to find out Phean's other side, at any cost. It was forbidden. The Emperor had acted to protect her, even though he had been forced to punish her as a result. It had been her persistence that had made him halt her so violently. He walked about shaking his head, hands clasped behind his back, disappointed by his actions towards Tayce. He was wondering how she was. A young female approached the Emperor dressed in a cream trouser suit with a stand-up collar and thin maroon decorative band running like a sash from her left shoulder to right hip. She was of slender build with shoulder-length brown hair and she was of exceptional beauty, with blue eyes that sparkled. She could see her superior had a lot on his mind and was displeased with himself. She came to a pause like an obedient servant and waited. The Emperor sighed.

"Yes?" demanded Honitonia, not leaving, looking out at the landscape of the Realm in thought.

"Sir, Phean Leavy is refusing to continue the treatment unless he knows the Traun female is safe," explained the young woman.

"Tell Phean she has been temporary rendered helpless. There will be no damage or side effects. Also tell him if he does not continue I will remove him from Auran Amalthea Three permanently," said Honitonia without turning to face the young woman.

"Yes, sir, of course, sir," she replied politely, then bowed obediently.

With this she turned and began to depart from her superior's surroundings. She found his orders a bit harsh, but it wasn't up to her to question him. The Emperor continued pondering over Phean's future, looking out across the Realm landscape. He'd given him some of the late Tom Stavard's memories, knowledge and experiences – enough to make him fit in with the Amalthean Quests team – and was wondering if he'd done the right thing considering what had taken place. It was the first time something like it had been done. He also wondered whether it had been a good idea to link him with Tom Stavard's past in the first place if he had to keep reprimanding him for overstepping the mark each time and hauling him back to the Empire to answer for his actions.

***

Phean Leavy, in the Realm of Peace's analytical chamber, lay on a white mouldable leatherex table. Above him was a white pulsating orb that was descending slowly to the required level – just above Phean's forehead – controlled by the Empire of Peace medical tech, now standing to the right of Phean in an aqua-coloured suit. Nearby screens would display the findings to reveal what had caused the leakage to let Phean break the rules of the Realm, to interfere in life and spacial affairs. He was forbidden to break these rules using mere thought. Phean felt great apprehension as to what he might unexpectedly feel during the process. This was the first time he'd been linked to the past of someone in the Realm of Peace. Much to his relief, he felt nothing as the probing began. His whole body had suddenly been rendered numb.

***

In the MLC aboard Auran Amalthea Three Tayce suddenly woke without warning on the medical bunk. She sat bolt upright, shocking Treketa, Dairan and Donaldo. Donaldo guided the Examscan over her just to make sure she was fine. The reading came back, much to his relief, 'normal'. Tayce pushed the Examscan away and slid to the ground, proceeding to the middle of the MLC, where she paused and began to leave the centre, much to everyone's surprise, using her telepathic ability. Dairan exchanged looks of concern. He decided to try and join Tayce, so ran across and jumped into the aura of travel, grabbing Tayce around the middle. Within a few cencrons both had vanished into nothing. Donaldo crossed to inform Marc what Dairan had done with Tayce. It had been quite unexpected. He wondered just what would happen when they both arrived in the Empire, with Dairan not being gifted.

Nick Berenger, in Organisation, turned at communications, informing Marc of what had occurred in the MLC. As he stood watching the course unfold to their next port of investigation, Bellatrixan, Marc listened. He turned, looking in Nick's direction, finding what had been said somewhat worrying, considering Tayce had only gone to practise her powers. One thing was for sure: he now realised he was in command for the Quest ahead to the planet surface. Lance now cleansed and changed into a clean uniform, walked back into Organisation to take up his research position.

"Any news of Tayce? Is she going to be all right?" asked Lance as he headed to his seat.

"Oh, she's fine – back on her feet. Now she's gone after Phean, and, what's more, Dairan's gone with her too," said Marc, finding the whole thing crazier by the minon.

On these words, a blinding flash happened in the middle of Organisation and Dairan was flung out on to the floor. Marc turned, putting out his hand to help Dairan to his feet. Dairan grabbed it, rising until standing.

"Guess you're not allowed to be there," said Marc, meaning the Empire.

"It certainly looks that way," agreed Dairan.

"What's Tayce up to?" asked Marc, curious to know just what was going on.

"She came awake in the MLC, said she was fine, slid from the bunk, crossed to the centre of the MLC and started to use her power ability to travel to another place. I ran and jumped in, joining her in going where she was heading, to try and help, but I ended up back here. They threw me back," explained Dairan, surprised he had been sent back so abruptly.

"Something has always made me suspicious about Phean Leavy. It's as if he's been hiding another side. No one is that calm all the time," said Marc, assuming something was adrift with Phean.

"He's been acting strange for almost a weekon, ever since he returned from Admiran 4. Something he did over there he's obviously answering for now, judging by his sudden disappearance," said Dairan.

"You didn't say anything, then, to Tayce about your suspicions?" asked Marc, taken aback that he hadn't.

"I thought whatever it was Tayce would find out, considering they're both gifted," replied Dairan casually.

"I suppose as always all we can do is wait and see what will unfold. Tayce has obviously gone to the Realm to sort out what's suppose to have happened," said Marc.

"Yes, quite!" replied Dairan, wondering just what Phean had done.

Both men crossed to discuss the points needed to be considered in the Quest to Bellatrixan. Their present course would bring them into orbit around the destined port of call in roughly a dayon. But what the team hadn't foreseen, or anticipated, was that there was a mysterious field heading towards them in their line of travel. It hadn't been downloaded in the journey information as it was so small. The readings to be picked up from the field would not identify it as a possible hazard.

***

A young female walked towards Tayce in the Honitonian Realm of Peace. It was the same young woman that had approached the Emperor earlier over Phean's behaviour. She'd been sent to assist Tayce. Tania Australison was her name and she introduced herself as such. Tayce ignored her, trying to look beyond her for any sign of Phean. She had no intention of leaving without him.

"Captain, our apologies for sending Dairan Loring back to your cruiser so abruptly, but he's forbidden to be in these surroundings. The Emperor wishes to meet with you. Please follow me," she requested softly.

"I want to meet with him too. How's Phean? What's happening with him?" asked Tayce, still trying to see any sign of him as she followed Tania.

"I'm not allowed to express my thoughts on this matter. The Emperor will explain," replied Tania, refusing to divulge anything.

Tayce sighed as she and Tania headed into the Realm's swirling vapour, which was now at knee height. A white building loomed up. Tayce tried hard to reach Phean with her mind, calling out to him, but she got back nothing. Where was he? What were they doing with him? Time in the Realm moved more quickly than normal spacial time and she also wondered what was unfolding back aboard the cruiser. Tania led the way into a cream-coloured room once they'd entered the white building. It was furnished in modern elegantly designed furniture. The Emperor turned and looked at Tayce as if he was about to lecture a student. Then his features mellowed and he gave her a slight smile.

"Determined to be here, aren't you?" he began, clasping his hands behind him.

"I'm here for Phean. I want to take him back and I don't intend to leave without him," stated Tayce.

"And you won't have to. He is enduring the final stages of his correction treatment," replied Honitonia calmly.

"What happened? What made you do what you did?" demanded Tayce. "You could have killed me?"

"I personally had nothing to do with having young Phean arrested. I was what you call merely following orders from the Empire's Higher Minds; and as for me nearly killing you, I had to stop you from interfering with the plans the Empire's Higher Minds have for Phean. You wouldn't have died – what I did was a mind stun. Now, you undertook a Quest a weekon ago and it ended in somewhat mysterious circumstances, did it not?" asked the Emperor, walking around the ornate desk to come before her.

"Yes, but what does this have to do with Phean?" asked Tayce, interested.

"Phean used his mind to transfer a power surge to kill the being known as Retura Davin, leaving no trace of what he'd done," explained the Emperor to a surprised-looking Tayce.

"You expect me to believe Phean killed Retura Davin! I can't. He doesn't have a bad streak in him," replied Tayce in utter disbelief. She couldn't believe what the Emperor was saying.

"Phean as a being – No, I apologise… I should explain: the person who is joined with Phean made him undertake the murder," expressed the Emperor, pacing about in thought, working out what he was going to say next.

"I'm not with you," said Tayce, somewhat puzzled.

"Let's take, for instance, Dairan. He was controlled by a force when he was under that Vargon character's influence. Well, Phean is linked to someone that controls him from another Realm, only it went wrong and he murdered the being Retura Davin. Let's just say, as you'd no doubt term it, someone else pulled the strings. But it's been sorted now and what you've heard will not leave this Realm, is that understood?" asked Honitonia.

"Yes, but what do I tell Chief Barnford? He's still investigating the matter with Officer Lathanual."

"We'll handle the situation from here. No more action will be taken on the matter," said the Emperor without a further word.

They continued to talk about Phean and what had happened while Tayce waited to take him back to the cruiser. As they did so, Tayce was totally unaware of the unfolding situation back in normal space, where it was the mornet of the next dayon since she'd left.

***

It was light misty grey in appearance as it swept almost invisibly up to Auran Amalthea Three as she travelled the last milons to the planet of investigation, Bellatrixan. This was a vapour-orientated phenomenon with a hidden agenda. It covered the best part of two square milons like a blanket. It was undetectable by any vessel's scan. Right at this moment Auran Amalthea Three and the Quests team were in its powerful and evil sights.

***

Dairan downed the last sips of his early mornet Coffeen, unaware of what was unfolding as he sat at the table in the Leisure and Refreshment Centre. He and Marc had been in discussion during the first meal of the dayon about whether Tayce would be back in time to take part in the planetary investigation of Bellatrixan. He rose to his feet and proceeded to the waste incinerator, discarding his cup and utensils. Marc soon joined him, doing the same. Dairan hoped Tayce was back this dayon, as he missed her especially during slumber times, when he turned over and she wasn't there beside him. Both men soon walked from the centre, heading on out up to Organisation in continued discussion about Phean and other subjects.

***

Lance seated himself at his research console, ready to study any last-minon updates that could have come via Satlelink relay during overnight sleep time. He glanced at Craig, who had Twedor by his side, commenting on the fact that it didn't look like Tayce was back. Craig nodded, then began his usual mornet systems and operations check of the whole cruiser – something he'd done regularly since returning to the Universe after the ambush at the beginning of the current voyage. Marc and Dairan entered Organisation, followed by Kelly, who squeezed past when they came to a pause in their talking, finishing their conversation before getting ready to pick the Quest team. Marc walked on across the centre to the DC. He was about to step inside when the field-type phenomenon began engulfing the whole cruiser. He began to feel the most amazing weakness and dizziness both at the same time. Within minons he'd dropped to the floor just inside the DC doorway. Kelly, Lance, Craig and Nick each felt the force of what was engaging with the cruiser and fell under the same influence as Marc. Twedor reached out with his metlon hand and prodded Craig to see if he was out cold, slumped over his console. Twedor felt a case of déjà vu, remembering the last time he had to take control of his surroundings, which was during the Space Triangle phenomenon. It was looking like it was going to be him and Amal in charge all over again. What should he do first? he wondered. He walked over to Kelly's position and reached over the console, pushing the button for Amal to take overall command. How he wished Tayce was back and not in the Realm of Honitonia. He turned to catch the sight out of the main sight port and shrieked, a horrific electronic sound of alarmed panic. The cruiser was heading straight for the planet of Bellatrixan through the strange field at an amazing speed. As if someone had answered his prayers, two blinding blue illuminative auras materialised in Organisation.

"What the! Oh, my God! Amal, evasive manoeuvres immediately – now!" commanded Tayce in sheer horror at what was happening.

In a matter of moments they would hit the atmosphere of Bellatrixan at terrific speed, which would cause complete engine failure and they would plummet to the surface like a stone, destroying the cruiser and killing all aboard.

"Captain, I am unable to change course. I am locked in without ability to cancel the course," replied Amal.

Just as Amal said her words, Tayce and Phean began to submit to the same dizzy and weak feelings the others had succumbed to before dropping to the floor and becoming unconscious. Both dropped, much to Twedor's surprise, but Tayce fought against the feelings, using her ability to stay conscious. Otherwise she would have lost the cruiser on the surface of Bellatrixan, as well as losing the lives of herself and the whole team. She slowly hauled herself back on to her feet, fighting against the immense force to put her out cold like the others. She was quickly joined by Phean, doing the same. He wondered, as he looked around him at the silent sprawled team, whether they would let him stay when they awoke, when they found out he'd caused the mysterious death of Retura Davin on Admiran 4. But maybe Tayce wouldn't say anything and it could all be forgotten.

"Get Kelly out of her chair. Let's see what we can do to break out of this dive towards Bellatrixan. I'm not losing this cruiser," ordered Tayce as the cruiser continued at breakneck speed in a dive.

Phean, on Tayce's command, lifted Kelly carefully into a standing position from being slumped over her console and slowly guided her to the DC steps, sitting her down and leaning her carefully against the wall. Tayce crossed and sat down at Kelly's console, looking over the course, displayed in colours, to see if there was a reason for the sudden lock in their course. Twedor crossed to her side, watching.

"Twedor, link with Amal. Analysis mode, please," commanded Tayce.

"You've got it," said Twedor eagerly, beginning to link up with Amal via high-frequency signals.

He linked to Amal and went straight into analysis mode to find the cause of the locked-in course, without the ability to change. He went deeper into Amal's systems and discovered that what was stopping the ability to change course was the mist phenomenon. The mist was washing over the whole cruiser and was at that moment holding them in its powerful grip. Twedor went deeper still, discovering that the mysterious phenomenon had cast its powerful control over everything operational, rendering cruiser-wide operations inoperable. They were flying blind and were out of control in a dive towards Bellatrixan. He immediately began finding a way to bypass what had been done and to gain back operation of the cruiser as Tayce continued trying frantically to gain control too, keying in many commands to break the hold.

"I hate to tell you this, but we're goners, Tayce," said Twedor as he tried hard to help her gain control.

"That's not what I want to hear now, Twedor," said Tayce, not pleased, continuing to key in possible override codes.

"We're engulfed by a strange phenomenon and it has a grip on our course even I can't break," said Twedor, breaking his high-frequency link with Amal, finding, much to his disappointment, there was nothing he could do.

Phean looked out through the main sight port. Something had to be done soon or they'd all perish, he thought. He knew of a possible way, but it would mean nearly exhausting himself of every ounce of his abilities. He thought about it, then decided that as Tayce had been there for him at the Realm, it was his time to help her. Besides, it would look good later in his defence, if and when the others found out what had happened with Retura Davin. Phean placed a friendly hand on Tayce's shoulder.

"Let me take care of this – it's the least I can do. You were there for me at the Realm," said Phean in his soft tone.

"Are you sure? You've just come out of treatment at the Realm – let me help," said Tayce, concerned that he wasn't up to full strength.

"No! I have a higher degree in what I want to do; you'll be killed," said Phean, sounding firm for the first time.

"Yes, but you could be too. You'll be exhausted – it's too soon," insisted Tayce in true concern.

"Trust me, I'll be fine. And if I'm not, well, I will have saved this team and you, and that will look good in the Emperor's eyes, won't it?" he said jokingly.

"Yes, but…" replied Tayce.

She didn't like to think after going to the trouble at the Empire she could lose him. He'd taught her a lot regarding her abilities.

"Twedor will look after you," he assured her.

"Yes, Phean," said Twedor, stepping up beside Tayce.

Phean closed his eyes, concentrating on the overall dimension of the cruiser in his mind. He travelled to every furthest point, forming a picture in his mind and at the same time creating a power ball of pure energy in his hands. It soon glowed to a bright-yellow brilliance, then burst out, spreading throughout the cruiser, engulfing it. Slowly Phean brought the cruiser to a slow descent with every ounce of his ability. Tayce watched him, extremely worried as the sweat began appearing on his forehead and his breathing became difficult. He stood facing the sight port, silent, seemingly unemotional apart from the rapid eye movement behind his closed eyelids. Auran Amalthea Three was slowing down and levelling off, heading to the surface of Bellatrixan at a better landing speed, enabling Amal at last to gain enough control with help from Twedor to lower the landing gear and set her down normally on the surface. Tayce watched and, the moment it looked possible, she ordered Twedor to assist Amal with the landing on Bellatrixan.

Phean had done what he'd set out to accomplish, and that was to stop Auran Amalthea Three crashing into the Bellatrixan surface. He felt drained and almost collapsed as he came back to normal. His features were strained and wet with strained perspiration. Tayce quickly came to his aid, steadying him, thanking him. She guided him in a caring manner towards the DC. Kelly was regaining conciousness. She sat up slightly miffed, wondering why she was sat by the entrance to the DC and not in her seat. She quickly moved aside upon seeing Phean in Tayce's guiding care, walking into the centre past her.

"What happened? Is he all right?" asked Kelly, seeing Phean extremely exhausted.

"Kelly, do you feel up to getting a beaker of Plicetar for me?" asked Tayce as she lowered Phean to sit down on the soffette with her support.

"Sure! of course," she replied, forgetting the fact she'd only just woken from the forces of the phenomenon, and went after the drink.

"You sit there. I could call Donaldo, but I'm not sure if he's regained consciousness yet," said Tayce, not quite sure of what to do for the best. She didn't like the way Phean looked.

"I just need to rest. Tayce... I'm sorry," said Phean.

He'd put her through a lot in the last couple of dayons.

"You have nothing to apologise for. You've just saved us all from an untimely death. Just forget it," replied Tayce without further word, watching the slow awakening of the team getting back to their feet. Kelly soon ran back in with a beaker of Plicetar. This was water containing reviving and nourishing molecules.

She crossed, handing it to Phean, then stepped back, announcing, "Everyone is getting back on their feet out there."

In through the DC entrance Dairan and Marc came, straightening their uniforms after being on the floor out cold. They quickly paused, noticing Phean resting, looking somewhat shattered.

"Phean, I want you to rest in your quarters to regain your strength. If you feel ill, check in with Donaldo on the way," ordered Tayce concerned. "Is that understood?"

"Yes, thank you," said Phean, rising to his feet and walking from the DC.

"You're back. What happened over at the Empire?" enquired Marc, giving Tayce his full attention.

"I noticed we've landed, finally. I'll get the Quest team ready," volunteered Dairan.

Tayce nodded to him, then walked to the sight port and looked out on the Bellatrixan landscape. There was no sign of the phenomenon that had almost cost them their lives. The view was now of blue hazy sky, green clouds and hills. Marc hit the door-closing mechanism panel. The doors closed, sealing off Organisation. He sauntered over towards her.

She began by telling him there was something she had to say and that there was a reason behind the mysterious circumstances of Retura Davin's sudden death. Marc looked at her questioningly, waiting. She continued, relating that she'd noticed just after the Quest to Admiran 4 that Phean seemed agitated every time the question of who killed Retura Davin surfaced.

"That much I'm aware of, but why the visit to the Realm of Honitonia at such short notice?" asked Marc, curious, giving her his full attention.

"I decided to take it further after I woke from being reprimanded by the Emperor, so I headed to the Realm. There I learned that Phean was being punished and undergoing treatment for overstepping the mark. Having been linked to someone from the Realm of Peace, he'd acted on a past memory from that person, killing Retura Davin because he wanted to take away Twedor. The way in which he did it, which leaves no trace, is forbidden. So now you can guess how Retura Davin mysteriously died: because of Phean's actions using his mind and motivated by linked memories."

"So what happens now? Considering he's back here, is he cured?" asked Marc, slightly concerned.

"He's fine now. He's been treated by the Realm. What made him do what he did has been rectified. Emperor Honitonia assures me this could never happen again. I feel what is done is done. When we arrived back here and you and the others were unconscious, we found this cruiser nosediving at immense speed towards the surface of this planet. Phean used his powers – he single-handedly used his mind to pull this whole cruiser to a slow descent and save us from being killed. I feel we should let go what Phean did and carry on as if nothing happened on Admiran 4. It's something that only you and I will ever know the truth about," said Tayce.

"But Jan's still investigating what happened," said Marc, thinking about the fact.

"He'll soon close the investigation when he finds nothing, and I don't want this taken any further. It's between you and I – is that understood? The Emperor said he would handle it," replied Tayce finally.

"All right, but are you happy to keep him on the team considering what's unfolded?" asked Marc, curious.

"Yes, of course," replied Tayce positively.

"I'm sorry, Tayce, but I feel he needs to be watched for a trial period. I know he's always volunteered eagerly to help in moments of need, and I must admit I'd like him to remain as part of the team – he's always been there when we've needed him – but it makes me feel uneasy. If he should suddenly relapse, you'll have another problem. You said you want to keep it between you and me, but Lance and Dairan both know what's gone on; so does Donaldo and Treketa. They might not trust him if they find out," put Marc, uneasy.

"Then what do you propose?" asked Tayce calmly. She always welcomed his input.

"Let's do this Quest and discuss it later in a meeting, see how he behaves during it and talk with Lance, Dairan, Treketa and Donaldo. If they're happy for it to be let go, then so be it," replied Marc.

"All right, I'm all for that. I'd like nothing more than for everything to return to normal," replied Tayce.

Marc crossed back and hit the doors' mechanism panel, and the doors began to open, back into Organisation. Dairan announced that the team were ready to go on the Quest. He further informed everyone that it was just a planetary investigation and portable oxygen containers should be used as the air was not termed breathable for long periods of time. Also eye shields were to be worn as the brightness of the planetary sun would destroy the sight of everyone going if protection was not worn. Tayce was a little unhappy about this Quest. From what she was hearing, it looked like the utmost care would be needed when on the surface.

"Right, let's get going. We're not staying long. I'm not happy with the conditions we'll be under, down on the surface," said Tayce in the true tone of leader, heading towards the entrance.

Soon she left Marc in charge and began on out through the entrance of Organisation with Dairan, Lance and Kelly. On the way down the corridor Tayce suggested they take their Pollomoss handguns just in case, though they hadn't detected any trouble on the scan of the planet's surface. They checked their weapons were fully charged as they went. A while later, when the team had picked up their eye shields and oxygen containers and had arrived on Level 2, Phean Leavy was stood waiting, looking no different from how he always looked, totally calm.

"I thought I ordered you to rest," said Tayce in true concerned tone.

"If it's all right, I'd like to go with you so I can do some plant study for the Lab Garden Dome," he expressed.

"As long as you feel strong enough now. I don't want you collapsing outside," replied Tayce seriously.

"I'll be fine – honest," he assured her calmly with a reassuring smile.

"All right, but if you show any signs of fatigue I want you to return to the cruiser. Is that understood?"

"Will do," he replied.

They all continued on to the Docking-Bay doors. Tayce raised her Wristlink and contacted Marc, informing him that Phean was going along with them on the Quest. Marc could be heard, after a brief pause, acknowledging this. Then she signed off. The small Quest team all paused at the cruiser's entrance. The doors soon opened and the Bellatrixan daylight rushed in. The small Quest team put their eye shields on and made sure they had their oxygen containers in place.

"Phean, you work with Kelly and Lance," ordered Tayce. She didn't want him working alone.

Lance glanced at Kelly. He was still thinking about how he'd found Phean had vanished and Tayce lying unconscious in the Armed Combat Centre. He was wondering what had really happened during Tayce's power session. Would Phean try something again and jeopardise the current Quest? He'd be keeping a suspicious eye on him. They all walked down the walkway into the warm, sunny Bellatrixan atmosphere.

Once on the surface, they looked around at the vast panoramic rocky and green terrain. Kelly began recording the surrounding planet on the portable Vid Cam, to view later. Dairan raised his Techno Viewer and began looking into the distance. He announced there was a lake in the distance about forty minons from their current position. He handed the Techno Viewer to Tayce so she could see. Lance suggested they head off to the right, where there seemed to be a group of rocks, trees and other vegetation worth studying.

"Stay in contact. Don't go too far or near anything if you're not happy investigating it. Remember, if it looks suspicious then leave it alone – it's not worth dying just because curiosity got the better of you. Also remember we're not staying long," ordered Tayce.

"I'll make sure they behave, Tayce," said Kelly, following on behind Lance and Phean.

"Thanks, Kelly," replied Tayce, glad she could rely on her to be the sensible one of the small group.

"Let's take a look at that lake not far from here," suggested Dairan eagerly.

Lance, Phean and Kelly walked away to do their research whilst Tayce and Dairan let the Docking-Bay doors close and headed on in the direction of the lake. Lance glanced back as Kelly caught up with him.

“There’s a real bond building between those two, if you ask me,” said Lance, glancing in Dairan and Tayce’s direction as he went.

“It certainly looks that way, and who can blame them?” replied Kelly, looking in the same direction, watching Tayce and Dairan head away into the near distance.

They went on to catch Phean up. Tayce and Dairan walked down a powder-blue path of soil and rocks to the lake, which was filled with white cloudy-looking water. It stretched for milons into the distance. Coming to the near edge, both paused, looking around at the strange landscape. Dairan used the Techno Viewer. Tayce looked at the trees of various yellows, purples and an olive colour.

“Why the closed DC doors earlier, or is it top secret?” asked Dairan casually as he scanned the view.

“Marc did it. We were discussing Phean. You’d better brace yourself: after I regained consciousness in the MLC I couldn’t wait to get to the Empire Realm as Emperor Honitonia had showed up during my power practice and arrested Phean. I wanted to find out why. I discovered that Phean is linked to a mysterious being in the Realm of Peace, and he was responsible for the mysterious demise of Retura Davin. Emperor Honitonia explained that Phean had been arrested for an act he’d carried out without Realm permission. Phean used his mind so that no trace could be left in killing Retura. But before you say anything to blame him, you have to know that Emperor Honitonia has corrected what happened and has assured me that Phean won’t ever do it again. Something had gone wrong during the original linking process.”

“But what makes them think he won’t?” asked Dairan, still looking through the Techno Viewer.

“Between you and me Emperor Honitonia has someone keeping an eye on Phean, in the next six monthons, in case he tries it again and then he’s hauled back to the Empire for good,” assured Tayce.

“But in a way Phean wasn’t responsible surely, the being he’s mysteriously linked to is?” put Dairan lowering the viewers, looking at Tayce questioningly.

“I’m glad you see it that way, because that’s my thoughts exactly,” replied Tayce, pleased to know he felt the same as she did.

“What are you going to do with him?” asked Dairan walking up to her.

“I want him to stay as a continued member of the team, I feel he’s proved himself valuable up until this latest situation, but he’s been cured and what is done is done,” said Tayce seriously.

“If it’s any help I reckon the others will look at it like you do, if they find out, they won’t find out from me though, what about Jan, he was investigating Retura Davins death?” put Dairan

“The Emperor said he’d handle it. no more would need to be done and in time when Jan draws a blank, he’ll shut his investigation down, where it will stay, buried forever,” replied Tayce.

"Shall we look around," suggested Dairan changing the subject.

"Sure! let's," replied Tayce.

Both began walking off along the waters edge discussing the ups and downs they'd endured in the current voyage so far. Dairan began, it seemed strange their enemy was keeping quiet. Tayce glanced to him. He met her questioning expression of who he was referring to.

"Vargon," said Dairan, without further word.

Tayce nodded, he was right, ever since Marc sent Varon Vargon running when he made his threat of attack over Pellasun Traun 2, he'd stayed away. It made her wonder what the evil bastard was planning somewhere for next time. As she was sure there would be, a next time. Dairan certainly had her thinking about Vargon and when he would no doubt strike again using the latest stolen mode of flight and some unsuspecting group he'd brainwashed to work for him again.

Dairan glanced around, then reached out, pulling Tayce towards him swiftly. She wondered what he was looking for. There was no one around other than the rest of the Quest team, so she thought. She wondered if he was beginning to be affected by the planet's atmosphere, making him act suddenly romantic. She looked up into the warmth of his brown eyes questioningly. To her surprise he looked over her shoulder and quickly dropped her to the ground without thought.

"Dairan, what are you doing?" protested Tayce, losing her balance and dropping into the long grass.

"Not what you're thinking. Stay down," he ordered, seeing she thought they were going to have an unexpected moment of intimacy.

"What's wrong? What is it?" she demanded in an urgent whisper, crawling into a position from which she could see.

Just as Tayce answered, a missile sailed over them a tremendous speed. They were not alone on the surface after all. Dairan took out his Pollomoss handgun, as did Tayce, and they crawled away through the long grass towards some trees and rocks that were large enough to hide behind. Once behind the rocks, they slowly peered out. Dairan used the Techno Viewer, setting it to anti-glare so they couldn't be detected from the reflection in the glassene from a distance. Tayce raised her Wristlink, contacting Lance in the other group. He answered, sounding as if he was whispering. Tayce ordered him to take what research specimens he'd got and make his way back with the others to the cruiser. She didn't know how, but they had just outstayed their welcome. Then she contacted Marc via Wristlink, ordering him to lift off when Lance and the others were back aboard. They were no longer welcome on Bellatrixan. Dairan glanced at her in surprise as he returned Slazer fire, wondering just how Tayce thought they were going to get back on board. Tayce continued to return Slazer fire, which was coming rapidly in their direction, ignoring his stare. Without warning Tayce saw the chance and went for it. She took to her heels, returning fire, and yelled at Dairan to follow on. As Dairan did, he was shot in the shoulder.

Tayce paused, ordering Marc via open Wristlink to Transpot. He could be heard agreeing. Auran Amalthea Three began lifting up off the surface, returning fire in the direction the attack was coming from on the surface as the landing gear retracted back home. Within minons the usual Transpot blue swirling aura took on around Tayce and Dairan, removing them from the planet surface to the safety of the cruiser, out of danger.

***

Donaldo, upon Tayce's emergency medical request, was standing by in the MLC. Treketa prepared the exam bunk ready for treatment, to examine Dairan and take care of him upon his return. The centre doors soon opened and Tayce entered, supporting Dairan. Treketa hurried to help. Both women helped him on to the bunk. He began complaining about seeing double and having the most amazing headache he'd ever had. Donaldo immediately ran the medical Examscan over him, then glanced at the reading. He couldn't believe the erratic levels he was seeing. Everything in Dairan's body was all over the place. The function readings were far from what they should have been for a person sustaining a normal Slazer wound. Without warning, Dairan lapsed into unconsciousness and fell back on the bunk, quickly being steadied into a lying position by Treketa and Tayce. Donaldo immediately grabbed the nearby Comprai Inject Pen and loaded a cartridge of purple liquid, then immediately administered it to Dairan's upper arm. Looking at the overhead vital-signs readings on the overseer screen, he waiting for the levels to return to near normal.

"What was it you gave him? Did it work?" asked Tayce hoping so.

"It should bring his heart rate back to normal – at least I hope it will," said Donaldo, continuing to watch the overhead screen.

"What's happened?" asked Tayce, growing concerned. "I thought he was only injured through Slazer fire."

"Believe it or not, this is not the first time this type of wound has come before me. It's caused by a new kind of weapon – well, it was the last time I encountered this kind of gunshot. It first appeared when we did fieldwork for the Intergalactic Medical Colony. This kind of weapon causes its victim the most horrendous side effects. It fills the whole body with a toxin that starts to shut down the body's systems one by one in a drastic way, as it's currently doing in Dairan. The treatment should be administered within one houron or the whole body implodes and it's goodbye Universe to whoever is suffering from it," explained Donaldo.

"My God! Who would design such an evil weapon?" asked Tayce, looking from Dairan to the overhead screen.

"Let's put it this way: you wouldn't want to make friends with them," replied Donaldo, gesturing to Treketa for another treatment vial, ready to insert into the Comprai Inject Pen and administer.

"Don't worry, Tayce – Dairan's lucky we're here and have treated this type of wound before. He'll be back to normal in a couple of hourons – right, Don?" said Treketa reassuringly.

"Yes, absolutely. As you can see, it's taken a little longer than anticipated, but his heart rate is descending to normal and it's holding. You can leave him with us if you want. He'll be fine," said Donaldo, confident that Dairan would be all right.

"You sure?" replied Tayce, reluctant to do so even though she totally trusted Donaldo.

"Yes, Treketa will call you," he assured.

"All right, I'll be in Organisation, finding out who did this," assured Tayce.

As Tayce turned to walk back to the MLC entrance, the doors opened and Phean and Twedor stood there, about to walk in. They backed out into the corridor as Tayce walked out to join them on the walk down the corridor. Phean announced that he'd heard what happened just after himself Lance and Kelly managed to get back aboard, before take-off. Hence he was there to see if Dairan was going to be all right. Tayce nodded. She knew deep down there was no way she could even think of letting the Honitonian Empire take Phean back after the trial period, even if they wanted to. He was caring and was too good a team player when she needed him. They walked as far as the Level Steps, where Tayce paused. She turned, explaining that she was about to hold a meeting in the DC over his future on board and it was up to him whether he wanted to sit in and hear points being raised on what he'd done and whether the team wanted him to stay. Or he could go to the Lab Garden Dome and continue the duty he was doing before the Quest started and she'd call him to the DC later for the outcome. Phean thought for a minon. He knew that, whatever was going to be decided, it wouldn't matter if he was there or not. What would be would be.

"It's fine – I'll head back to the Lab Garden Dome. I've some specimens from Bellatrixan to check out," he replied casually but sadly.

"All right, I'll call you later. I want you to stay no matter what," said Tayce.

But this matter involved others, whether they would feel happy if he remained (considering he'd acted on the spur of the moment without thought) and whether they could trust him and forget what happened to Retura Davin.

Phean nodded, then turned and headed away, leaving Tayce and Twedor to head on up to Organisation. Tayce could see Phean was prepared for the worst outcome regarding the decision, but she was going to do her utmost to make sure the team saw it from her point of view and that they knew it had been out of Phean's control.

Marc was watching the scene through a sight port as the cruiser left the surface of Bellatrixan, still under weapon fire. Lance had run a scan to find out where the firepower had come from. He brought a magnified image to the screen, pinpointing the exact location with a pointer. Marc couldn't believe it when Lance drew his attention to what he'd found. Pirates – eighty or so plus their super weapon-orientated vessel – were hiding just behind the far hill, beyond where Tayce and Dairan had been at the lakeside.

"Amal's archives identify this band as being in the same class as – would you believe it? Fatashia. This is an all-male group, but they belong to Fatashia's ancestral line. They seem to have the same type of upper torso and head as she had," explained Lance.

"Perhaps this lot got fed up with her female rules and decided to break away from her. What happened to her anyway?"

"Tayce went searching for her in her domain when we rescued Kayleigh and Pia Starkern and that's all we know, Tayce won't say anything about what happened," replied Lance.

At this moment Tayce walked into Organisation and across to Marc. He looked at her, then at the screen in front of Lance, showing the image of a male version of the Cartarcan Pirates.

"You want the good news or the bad news first?" asked Marc.

"Let's hear it," said Tayce without a further word.

"Your favourite female pirate has a male equivalent. They're the ones that attacked us and you on the surface of Bellatrixan. They're also in the same age group as Fatashia. The good news is they've finally given up playing with us and gone off somewhere else," explained Lance.

"That's interesting," said Tayce, thinking about it and wondering why they'd suddenly disappeared.

"How's Dairan?" asked Marc, curious, hoping he was going to be all right.

"Extremely lucky in one way. Donaldo explained that he's encountered the same kind of wound from gunfire before, many yearons ago. He said this particular weapon has been known to destroy the person it hits. A message to the Intergalactic Criminal Punishment Life and Termination Colony is advisable, informing them there's a band of pirates using the kind of weapon that shot Dairan and a task team needs to be sent forth to stop it. Nick, accompany it with a medical report from Donaldo regarding Dairan, please."

"You've got it. I'll do it now," replied Nick.

"I want everyone for a meeting in the DC just as soon as you've all finished what you're currently doing."

With this announcement, and Auran Amalthea Three heading back into space, Tayce continued with Twedor on into the DC deep in thought about a male version of the Cartarcan Pirates being at large. Marc ordered Lance to store the information on the new band into Amal's archives and follow on for the meeting when that was done. Lance nodded. Marc turned and walked away on into the DC. As he entered he saw Tayce sitting in her high-backed swivel chair, deep in thought, looking out into the stars through the DC sight port.

"Did Dairan say what he thought about Phean?" asked Marc.

"He agrees that Phean's not to blame directly. Have the message and report been sent?"

"As we speak. I can't imagine they'll be eager to send out a task force. We've included Dairan's report and all the details of what the weapon can do."

"We've brought it to their attention and that's all that matters," replied Tayce.

Both continued to discuss what had happened. Roughly an houron later the team began ferrying into the DC for the meeting, which Tayce decided should include everyone as it would affect the whole team working with Phean and they would have a chance to air their concerns about trusting him. Treketa entered the DC minus Donaldo. She explained he'd stayed to keep an eye on Dairan, even though he was improving. He'd suggested that if there were any decisions to be made, she could take care of them in his absence. Tayce agreed, understanding. When everyone had arrived and were seated around the table (apart from Professor Maylen, Phean, Dairan and Donaldo) Tayce rose to her feet. Professor Maylen ran in, apologising, at the last minon. He explained that he'd been talking with Phean.

"This meeting is going to be brief, and what I have to say affects the whole team. A matter has come up which I feel must be decided by you all," began Tayce as she paced.

"This sounds serious. They're not disbanding this team again, are they?" asked Lance.

"No, Lance, relax. None of us are going anywhere. This subject involves Phean. You all know that Retura Davin died in mysterious circumstances and none of us can deny it's been on our minds, wondering who did it. Well, two dayons ago I found out who did the act that allowed us to keep Twedor," explained Tayce, pausing beside Twedor, resting her hands on his metlon shoulders.

"Good for him, that's what I say. That jerk Davin was the reason I was unmercifully hung from the equipment in that centre on Admiran 4, surrounded by a load of weapons," said Twedor suddenly, far from pleased.

"Quiet, please, Twedor," said Tayce.

"Not Phean – don't ask us to believe it. He hasn't got it in him to be a cold-blooded murderer," said Aldonica in total disbelief.

"In a way, I'm afraid so, but not in the way you would think – cold-blooded. Phean is linked to a mysterious being in the Empire of Peace. He's linked by thoughts and experiences that the being from the Realm of Peace holds, plus any other knowledge and memories. Because Phean could see I was going to lose Twedor here, whoever Phean was linked to influenced him enough to make him get rid of Retura Davin, using Phean's mind ability. There was no trace of who killed Retura Davin, but the Honitonian Empire discovered that a problem had leaked through to Phean. It has been rectified and they have assured me nothing like this will ever happen again. I want you all to sit and think for a few minons. Should Phean be allowed to remain as part of the Amalthean Quests team, considering what happened, that the problem has been rectified and that he's made up for his actions since by saving this cruiser?" asked Tayce.

The DC fell silent as Tayce walked back to her seat, leaving Twedor. Everyone sat weighing up the situation. Tayce hoped in her heart that her team would see the situation the way she saw it – that Phean was not directly responsible.

Lance was first to put forth a question: "What's to stop him doing it again?" he asked casually.

"The Empire have put in place procedures to withdraw Phean the moment they see it could happen. They currently are watching his actions for six monthons, but they have assured me, as I've just said, that it won't happen again," replied Tayce.

"I'd like to add I've just been in conversation with young Phean and he feels bad about letting everyone down, even though, as you've just said, Tayce, he wasn't directly involved," expressed Adrien.

"I'd also like to add something: that when we were all out cold upon Tayce's return from the Realm of Peace with Phean, they found this cruiser nosediving into the surface of Bellatrixan. None of us would be here if it wasn't for Phean using his power ability to slow and level out this cruiser," spoke up Marc.

"I look at it like this: from what you've told us, Phean is not responsible, he was doing something he was influenced to do. I say he stays and I for one am not going to think any more about it," said Kelly.

"You're right, Kelly. Me too," agreed Aldonica.

"Show of hands to agree to forget this whole situation and Phean stays," said Tayce.

Everyone raised their hands in agreement without hesitation, after what Kelly said, wanting Phean to stay. Nick added that Phean had been misused by an outside force and anyone around the table who had been faced with the same dilemma would probably have done the same. Everyone nodded in agreement, seeing Nick's point. Adrien clapped him on the shoulder, remarking that it was well said. Tayce made sure there were no more points to be brought up before closing the meeting. Everyone looked at each other around the table and stayed silent. With this, she closed the meeting. The team all stood and began walking on out. Adrien stayed. He wanted to talk to Tayce. She turned to listen.

"How's Dairan? I heard he was wounded by a Catronic weapon – deadly those things?" he said casually.

"He's slowly recovering. You've heard of the weapon, then?" asked Tayce.

"Yes, I had a patient in my clinic once whose side effects left him with a condition that affected his coordination for monthons. Though he received treatment to cure it, it played hell with his duty. He was a young first-class security officer," replied Adrien, recalling the fact.

"I guess Dairan's lucky," replied Tayce, realising he was.

"Yes, but you've got a good medical man in Donaldo. What will you do about young Phean and the fact I've heard Chief Barnford is still investigating the mysterious death of Davin?" asked Adrien, curious.

"The matter will be closed and it will go no further than this cruiser," replied Tayce seriously in the tone of true leader.

"Understandable – no qualms from me. He's a good team player," replied Adrien without a further word.

Tayce turned to look out through the sight port to watch the planet of Bellatrixan ebbing away into the distance. Adrien walked across the DC, leaving her standing alone with Twedor. Tayce began thinking about the current Quest and how it had been filled with dilemmas and the threat of a new weapon, which if it wasn't stopped, was sure to surface again more widely. It was strange to think that in a Universe so vast, weapons of immense power to inflict destruction and injury could just surface out of nowhere. But she knew that ever since she'd left Traun, wars and destruction hadn't ceased. They had just been hidden from sight. There would always be someone in power disagreeing with a judgement and rebels starting wars on just a word, objecting to a rule and perhaps weilding a new kind of deadly weapon. Phean, much to Tayce's relief, was staying, which she was glad of despite all that had occurred. He was her friend and Telepathian guide and she wouldn't want it any other way. She wondered just who he was linked to in the Realm of Peace. Maybe one day she would find out.

13. Prexan Forces, Part One

Dairan was back to normal health within a weekon. His only side effect from the injury at the hands of the Catronic weapon was sudden bouts of nausea that in time would fade, according to Donaldo. Lance had been trying to discover what had happened to the strange phenomenon that forced the cruiser to nosedive towards the surface of Bellatrixan. It had simply vanished after they'd landed, and he was trying to find where it had disappeared to. He decided to give up as he couldn't get a scan where it had vanished to and he'd already spent the best part of two hourons of duty research time on it. He decided to write something in the archives in case they came across it again, so they'd be better prepared if there was a next time.

***

The time was 21:59 by the Organisation wall time display. The team had all gone off duty for the dayon – all, that is except Dairan and Tayce, who were sorting the information from previous Quests, including planetary information, for the cruiser's archives. This was a duty they liked sharing. Because of Dairan's astronomy background, the exact facts could be keyed in. It was a duty they'd shared right from the beginning of the second voyage. Marc entered the centre. He'd heard they were still working late. Tayce hoped he'd brought refreshments, but he hadn't. He looked at what they'd been doing in updating the archives. Tayce glanced at her Wristlink time display, having finished what she had to do, realising how late it had become. They'd been so busy they hadn't had a chance for something to eat. It was nearly time to call it a dayon, she thought. She was feeling tired and hungry. Maybe they could stop off and get something on the way to their quarters. All three began in discussion over what had been accomplished to date during the current voyage. But what they didn't realise was that, as they did so, it was materialising in the corridor outside Organisation.

Small, round and glassene-like in appearance, like a large marble, covering just under two inches in diameter, it started to roll once fully materialised along the corridor floor, entering into Organisation. Pausing, as if it was summing up what, or who, was present, it rolled then paused again. It was like it was looking through a camera built within its form. It seemed to scan every inch, minon by minon, as it rolled this way and that, stopping intermittently and taking in the surroundings as a colour image.

Twedor came on sudden alert. His sensors were either playing tricks or he'd just seen something shoot past him at great speed across the floor. The small round marble rolled into the middle of Organisation and suddenly activated, growing in size to a large orb. It split in two and opened. Out of the centre rose and materialised a fully dressed tall human male. He had short layered dark brown hair, handsome good looks and the strangest of green eyes. Marc turned, startled by what was unfolding. The form spoke and, much to everyone's surprise, in fluent English.

"My Queen needs you two to serve her," he announced, and with a snap of his long, slender fingers, before either Dairan or Marc had time to react, both vanished in the blink of an eye, leaving Tayce shocked and speechless.

The Orb remained in the centre of Organisation. Twedor shielded himself from any feedback he might sustain from the power the Orb gave off as it took Dairan and Marc to wherever. Tayce stood for a few minons, thinking over what had just materialised. Twedor, when the being who had taken Dairan and Marc had disappeared, decided to investigate the Orb more thoroughly. He crossed, bent down and picked it up, scanning it for a few cencrons, running his own analysis. Tayce gathered herself together. Marc and Dairan had both been abducted by some unknown source that seemed to have a queen in charge. She thought, 'My Queen? What did the being mean? Who was she and just where exactly had Dairan and Marc disappeared to?'

Twedor prodded her.

"This thing serves as a transportation device, but there doesn't seen to be any indication of its origin," said Twedor, turning it this way and that.

Tayce realised this Queen had to have extreme abilities of a powerful kind, and she was growing suspicious. There was only one woman that came to mind when she heard the phrase 'My Queen', and she was supposed to have died in their last confrontation. Tayce hoped it wasn't her against all odds.

"Bring that thing with you and follow me, Twedor," said Tayce, heading for the entrance to Organisation.

He followed her, trying to keep up, taking the Orb on out of Organisation, heading off to Level 3. He could see by the way she was in a hurry, and the thoughtful look on her face, that she was determined to look into the mystery of the Orb and it's origin to try and find a way to get Marc and Dairan back from the Queen.

***

At 0900 hourons the next mornet, Lance walked into Organisation. He was always the first one on duty – besides Marc, who would always be there drinking his first cup of Coffeen of the dayon. This mornet Lance found it strange that Marc wasn't present, wondering if he'd got held up somewhere along the way. He ordered Amal to play back the disk showing the last evening on the main Sight Screen. Kelly and Phean entered just as it was about to play. Phean glanced around for signs of Tayce, but, upon hearing her on screen, soon paused and looked in its direction. Upon hearing the words 'My Queen' Phean turned tail, and before Kelly and Lance had a chance to ask what was wrong he'd run from Organisation. Lance raised his eyebrows, surprised by the way in which Phean had left them, thinking, 'What now?'

"Poor Tayce! I wonder who this Queen is?" asked Kelly, looking at the screen.

"It looks like she's going to need all of us for this one, when we can find her," replied Lance as the Vidfilm of the last night hourons ceased. It made him wonder what was materialising.

"I wonder where that being took them?" asked Kelly, deep in thought, crossing to her duty place.

"A place I wouldn't want to be in in a hurry. God knows why or what this Queen wants them for, whoever she is," replied Lance.

He crossed to his research position. He began thinking of possible ways he could try and help track the place Marc and Dairan had been abducted to via the Orb.

Without warning the familiar flash of Telepathian aura occurred in the middle of Organisation. Lance turned, as did Craig, who had just walked into the centre. Craig began enquiring where was Phean going in a hurry? He'd just passed him in the corridor running.

Emperor Honitonia, now fully materialised, stood calmly waiting for attention, wondering why Tayce wasn't present.

"I have some bad news. Where's Tayce?" said Honitonia in his usual precise tone.

"She's not on duty yet, sir," replied Lance politely.

"I am aware of this. I believe young Phean has gone to find her. I would have liked her here," said Honitonia calmly.

"Sir, do you know what's happened to Marc and Dairan?" asked Lance, having a suspicion he might, judging by his timely arrival, which generally meant something was wrong.

"Oh, I do, Officer Largon, but I have to tell Tayce first," expressed the Emperor with a sigh.

Silence filled the air for a while.

Tayce suddenly walked in with Twedor and Phean by her side. She paused upon seeing Emperor Honitonia, realising he was becoming somewhat of a regular visitor to the cruiser and for him to be present meant something was wrong. Twedor held out the glassene-like Orb to the Emperor as he approached him. He took it without so much as a thought and summed it up in an interested kind of way. Tayce looked at him, waiting, wondering.

"What's the reason for your visit? It's not Phean again, is it?" asked Tayce, hoping not.

"No, I have something of great concern to tell you. It's something that could jeopardise your, my, Phean's, Empress Tricara's and the Honitonian Empire's existence all over again," replied the Emperor seriously.

"Dairan and Marc vanished when that thing appeared and a dark-haired male rose out of it. The main thing that's bothering me is who is this so-called Queen? It's her, isn't it? She's back from the dead somehow," said Tayce, seeing the Emperor's features change as if he didn't know how to confirm what she feared.

The Organisation team members present stood looking on in the Emperor's direction with great interest, wondering whom Tayce was thinking of. The Emperor sighed and nodded, much to the team's annoyance. Tayce gave a disgusted look. Witch Queen Aemiliyana had risen from the depths of death, where she'd been hopefully placed for all eternity at the end of the second voyage, when she and Tayce had had their 'final' confrontation, when Tayce hoped the power arrows she drove into her, had ended her forever. But it was not meant to be. Lance shook his head – he couldn't believe the evil bitch was back.

"Why does she want Dairan and Marc?" asked Lance suddenly. He was curious.

"Lance is right – what does she want them for?" backed up Tayce, looking at the Emperor questioningly.

"Aemiliyana and who she's no doubt teamed up with know they are both important members of the team. Without them she thinks you're helpless," he replied, much to Tayce's surprise.

"So who's the idiot foolish enough to team up with the likes of her? Who brought her back from the dead? Who's she working with this time?" demanded Tayce, pacing as the Emperor went on explaining.

"It would appear he's connected to the one that came aboard. We're still trying to identify who. We know little as yet, but there's more to this set-up this time around than we first thought. The Realm are working hard to find out where the other being and the members of the small band she has put together originate from," replied the Emperor.

"Who else, we ask, is evil enough to work with the likes of her and resurrect her in all her powerful glory to get back at me?" replied Tayce, wondering just who.

Suddenly Nick, behind her, was receiving a communication over his Microceive. Of all the times he had to pick! It was from her father, Nick announced, and it sounded urgent. He was requesting an urgent word. Nick waited until Emperor Honitonia had finished discussing Aemiliyana's possible escape from eternity back to the present, restoring all she'd had before. Tayce turned to give him her full attention and he announced her father was on Satlelink, waiting to be put through to the DC. Tayce nodded. Nick continued to put him through. Tayce suggested to the Emperor that he speak to her father with her, as what had happened might be connected, knowing Aemiliyana. He obligingly nodded. He could see her point. Last time the Empire had been held to ransom by the evil witch of a woman, Empress Tricara was affected too. Both walked on over and into the DC to where Darius Traun was on the Sight Screen, looking far from pleased over something.

"Father, is this important? Right now I'm in the middle of something that's somewhat of a large problem," began Tayce.

"Emperor, we have a large problem here too," replied Darius, displeased.

"What is it, Father? What's the matter?" asked Tayce. She was picking up something so strong and bad.

"Would you believe Vargon's made another threat! When will that barbarian ever quit? This time he's teamed up with some powerful female. Your mother was in the inner chambers this mornet when this marble thing appeared and a young man emerged to deliver a message that in two dayons' time Count Vargon is intending to try and take possession of Enlopedia with this evil woman. Your mother has been thrown into total shock about it all," said Darius in a no-nonsense tone.

"If I may, Tayce, the woman that you speak of, Admiral, is Witch Queen Aemiliyana. She has escaped from where she was sent in her 'final' confrontation with Tayce here in the second voyage. We had hoped she'd met her doom. You could say, this is unfortunate for all of us," expressed the Emperor sadly.

"How bad is she this time? What's she capable of?" asked Darius, thinking on the safety of his Enlopedian people and Tayce.

"As bad as you could ever imagine with her, unfortunately. Any safety measures you have to protect the people of Enlopedia, Father, do them. There is an added concern in all this: she's had the same being arrive here out of the same type of transportation, and both Dairan and Marc have been abducted," explained Tayce.

"Admiral, take advice from someone who knows her capabilities, like myself and Tayce. She will stop at nothing – she'll use her power to the extreme. And, as you say, she is working with Count Vargon, which will make the situation a whole lot worse if he's as evil as you say he is," advised the Emperor.

Tayce stood in thought. She was thinking of a way in which she could somehow find Aemiliyana and rescue Dairan and Marc from becoming innocent pawns in her attack against Enlopedia on behalf of Count Vargon. Why couldn't Vargon do the decent thing and disappear off the face of the Universe for a change? she wondered.

"I want you to return to Enlopedia. Maybe you'll be able to help avert this threat that's about to befall the whole base," asked Darius, hoping.

"All right, you've got us," replied Tayce, letting the screen go blank and hurrying back out into Organisation.

The Emperor looked at her. He could see her thoughts so he knew she was thinking over a good plan of action.

"I will leave you, Tayce, but the Empire and I will be watching over you, should you need us. As you know, we cannot interfere in general universal matters; but when it comes to Aemiliyana, if you need our assistance we will assist in cencrons whenever you request us to do so and Phean will help too," assured Honitonia.

With a blinding flash Emperor Honitonia vanished, leaving Tayce stood in the middle of Organisation wishing Dairan and Marc were aboard and she didn't have to take command of this evil situation alone. Phean could see Tayce was worried. He crossed, putting a reassuring hand on her slim shoulder. She turned from looking out at the stars towards him.

"Don't worry – you'll do this. You did it in the second voyage. You have a much higher ability now and your powers are a lot more centred. You beat Aemiliyana once, remember, the last time with just a weapon. You're stronger this time around in your own abilities. She won't know what hit her," assured Phean.

"What worries me is what she'll do to Marc and Dairan. She has the kind of powers to turn any mind to her advantage to get them to do what she wants against me," replied Tayce.

"In their absence I'll work with you. You won't go it alone and you have the help of everyone else here too," said Phean, understanding how she felt.

At this moment Nick was staring at something, looking past them at the Sight Screen behind them. Then Tayce heard the familiar evil voice behind her – one she thought she'd never have to hear again in her life. Lance looked at Tayce then at the screen. Tayce turned to give Aemiliyana a cold far from pleased look. The Witch Queen glared back in all her made-up beauty and she didn't look a dayon older since the last encounter. Then he stepped up beside her, much to Tayce's utter disgust. Words failed her at the sight of Count Varon Vargon stood beside someone she thought was gone forever.

'Two criminals for the price of one,' thought Lance.

Aemiliyana announced her new partnership, as she put it, with a man who could conquer the Universe easily. Combining their powers and skills, everything that had been was restored. Upon seeing Tayce, Vargon informed her that she could think again if she thought she'd seen the last of him.

"We wish! I sense trouble with this double act," spoke up Twedor, looking at the screen beside Craig.

"No surprise that you're working together," said Tayce coldly, to the point.

"Then you'll be wise to stay out of what we've planned, Tayce Amanda," announced Aemiliyana as a combined warning and threat, feeling like she had the upper hand.

"I don't often offer advice to an evil Witch like you, but I'd be careful working with Count Vargon," warned Tayce.

She knew he wouldn't hesitate to put her back where she'd been retrieved from. It would happen in an instant if she didn't do what he wanted her to do.

"Your warning is nothing to impress me, Tayce Amanda. I have freedom. As for your two most important team members – especially the handsome Dairan..." said Aemiliyana in an almost gushing evil-desiring tone, teasing Tayce shamefully and provokingly as she walked around a newly brought to her Dairan, pretending his was the best body she'd seen in a long time.

Tayce told herself to remain calm, even though she felt otherwise. Her angriness neared the surface, waiting to erupt at any cencron. In time, she thought, they would come face-to- face again and it wouldn't be a moment too soon. But it would be Aemiliyana's end to end all endings.

Count Vargon ignored Aemiliyana's spiteful, revengeful playful and provoking manner. He suggested maybe Tayce should think about rescuing her parents, unless she wanted them to become victims of the unwanted takeover of Enlopedia when he and Aemiliyana's forces attacked, taking over their first base of many, in joint ownership, with help from two officers that would be very easily adapted to fool the highest-ranking of resisting personnel on Enlopedia.

Tayce, still trying to contain her anger, simply suggested he go ahead and try. But he needed to realise the personnel of Enlopedia weren't easily fooled, least of all her father. No more was said – the screen went blank.

Lance had taken steps, luckily for Tayce, to trace the communication and where it had emitted from. Within cencrons the information was beginning to appear on screen in front of him. Tayce turned to watch and study what he was getting. Phean looked as well, interested.

"Whatever destination comes up, transfer it to Kelly and lock it in. Forget heading to Enlopedia – we're going after Dairan and Marc before Vargon and that bitch do any harm that can't be reversed," ordered Tayce without thought, she felt so enraged.

"Are you thinking straight?" asked Lance surprised. "We don't know what we're up against yet."

"Aemiliyana will no doubt try her power tricks; and as for Vargon, it won't be something I haven't seen before and can't handle. I can assure you I'm thinking perfectly straight," replied Tayce, far from pleased. If it had been anyone else she would have reprimanded him for his outburst, undermining her, but she could see it was just concern.

"Before we put any course into action, don't you think it would be wise to check what kind of hi-tech weaponry they have in place. It might be a classic case of the old saying about the spider and the fly," replied Lance.

"Spider and the fly?" asked Phean blankly, not having a clue what Lance meant.

"It's an old earth saying from many centuries ago. It means you could be walking into a trap," announced Adrien Maylen, walking into Organisation, having overheard them as he came up the corridor.

Tayce turned and in a way was glad to see him. He was the oldest member of the team and she and the team were beginning to look upon him as a senior source of support and advice in low moments. He paused in the middle of the centre, glancing at Lance's research screen, announcing that if she needed his help then she could count him in. Tayce nodded, ordering Nick to get her father back on Satlelink and transfer it to the DC again. Nick agreed. She began walking back to the DC, telling Lance that the moment he found anything on the weaponry Varon and Aemiliyana had in their possession she wanted to hear it. Adrien watched Lance keying away, then walked on into the DC.

***

Aemiliyana in all her powerful prowess aboard her resurrected powerful fortress had had Marc taken away and placed in a holding chamber until she decided what she wanted to do with him, as she considered him her main prize pawn to use against Tayce. Before her, with all his handsome warm good looks, was Dairan Loring. She studied him as she paced around him. She looked at his pleasing physical appearance in the attire she'd had him put into of white satinex baggy trousers and nothing on his torso. She noted way in which he chose to ignore her presence, as though she was merely nothing, which she found quite amusing and alluring both at the same time. Meeting his handsome brown eyes, looking into them, she intimidated him playfully, making him enraged at her actions. It excited her to think he was falling for her. She laughed. Dairan found himself fuming enough to want to erupt and lash out and throttle her. But he couldn't do anything. She had rooted him to the spot with a powerful force. He shared Tayce's feelings over this evil bitch – and a manipulating one at that. If she had bewitching designs on him, she'd had it. He could see her for what she was. Aemiliyana reached out and stroked his face.

"I see it – the attraction deep within you. You can't hide it from me, Loring. I can bring it to the surface any time I wish," she said, looking into his dark-brown eyes, using her powers to go deeper, almost into his soul.

Using her searching powerful ability, she reached right into the most furthest sensual part of his mind and manipulated him to her satisfaction. Dairan realised it would make Tayce very uncomfortable if she knew what this evil bitch was doing to him right then in every possible way, though he was doing his utmost to keep it in check. What were her plans, he wondered, besides the obvious? Aemiliyana could read those thoughts, but said nothing. He found her powers too much and looked away abruptly in disgust. She laughed again – he was an enjoyable distraction.

"I told you before, I refuse to become one of your slaves and playthings. Find someone else to amuse you, Witch. You mean nothing to me and never will do," retorted Dairan, looking darkly at her.

"We shall see. You two, take Loring here and prepare him for the Obligation Chamber. Let's see how long you can remain resistant before I make you be under my command," she said, looking at Dairan, now back to her normal self.

"Let go of me. You'll pay for this, Witch. Tayce is more than capable of taking you on this time. She'll put you back where you belong, this time for good," shouted Dairan, fighting in the grip of two of Aemiliyana's men as they dragged him away.

"Silence!" retorted Aemiliyana and she threw a power ball of pure force at him, knocking him unconscious and leaving him to be dragged the rest of the way out of her sight.

Count Vargon had witnessed her act and said nothing. He crossed to a circular area where seated cream-robed operatives were all working towards the joint venture of their mistress and new master: to take the fortress to Enlopedia Headquarters Base for takeover by any means. He came to a pause beside Aemiliyana. She looked at him in a powerful tolerating kind of way, letting him know who was leader in the joint venture, even if he thought he was her equal. She was no fool. If she found out he was using her, he'd be done away with in the most torturing way despite whatever powers he might try on her.

Looking at her, it was clear to see she hadn't changed a bit. She still had the slender shapely figure, the evil and powerful dark coal-like eyes and she was dressed to convey who she was in a long flowing gown of cream and gold, with a high splayed- out collar. Her make-up was perfect. Varon studied her. She was older than she looked, he thought.

He advised her to tread carefully where Tayce Amanda was concerned. He recently had been fooled into thinking she was no match for him, but she had proven otherwise. Aemiliyana took it on board, but felt it meant nothing, refusing to be unnerved by the news. She began to pace about, thinking, then paused, turning, the cream gown sliding on the floor. She sighed deeply.

"I will consider your warning when Tayce Amanda arrives, and not before," she retorted at Varon, but she didn't like the thought that he could be right.

She continued on to the nearest operative – her assistant, Eltarin, the young sorcerer with amazing powerful potential. He had assisted in her escape from the place where she had been sent, supposedly never to return again. He stood waiting as Aemiliyana approached. He informed her that Dairan Loring was ready in the Obligation Chamber.

"Varon, you are in command. It's time to convert two special operatives to fight on our side. Dairan will serve me against Tayce Amanda," she announced, walking across the chamber with Eltarin, heading off to do what she was going to enjoy most: turning Dairan against Tayce.

Varon watched her leave the vast chamber, walking with elegant strides, her long cream gown sliding behind her until she was gone. He stood in thought, thinking over in his mind whether Aemiliyana was forgetting their real reason for being in the joint venture and the reason he'd let Eltarin bring her back with him: the takeover of Enlopedia Headquarters Base. Was she using their partnership to further her wish for a long-awaited revenge against Tayce Traun? he wondered. He hoped not, for her sake. He wouldn't allow her to jeopardise his goal at any cost. Their takeover of Enlopedia could come apart if she had ulterior motives. No, he couldn't allow it. She would have to be done away with if he got the slightest hint that this was what she had in mind.

***

Darius Traun and Chief Jan Barnford were on the Sight Screen from Enlopedia. Tayce had put her idea to them: that if Lance could get the exact bearings of Aemiliyana's fortress they could intercept it before she reached Enlopedia. Jan gave an impressed look, pleased by the thought. Even though Darius was also impressed by the idea, he didn't like the thought that Tayce was going to have to come face-to-face with Aemiliyana and Varon Vargon together. Plus Dairan and Marc were not able to assist her. He needed time to think about it. He said he'd get back to her in an houron, after the meeting with Enlopedia heads about the forthcoming possible unlawful takeover. Tayce could tell by her father's tone that he was concerned for her. Sure enough, she didn't want to come face-to-face with Aemiliyana or Vargon. But in order to get Marc and Dairan back from two of the most evil beings in the Universe she had no choice. Adrien stood at the end of the desk in silence as the screen went blank. He had to admit he shared Darius Traun's concern over Tayce's safety, knowing first-hand what Varon Vargon could be like, and having been told how powerful the Witch Queen was. There was cause for concern over Tayce's attempt to do what she was thinking of. Tayce turned in her swivel chair, seeing Adrien's concerned features.

"Tayce, I know this is a tricky situation, but I share your father's concern. Firstly, you're his only daughter. I wouldn't like any daughter of mine facing those two no-gooders, especially with the odds stacked against you. You're also captain of a very successful team. If you let this Witch Queen confront you again and you don't win, perhaps if your ability suddenly fails for some reason, think of how your father, myself and this team will feel without you," he said, straight.

"Your point is noted," replied Tayce calmly and casually.

She looked out through the DC sight port thinking he was right. The team would be without their leader. It would also herald the end of the Amalthean

Quests and her parents would lose her and be devastated. It might be enough to start a planetary war. But even with this in mind, she knew she had to get Dairan and Marc back. She had to go in.

Turning back to face Adrien, she simply began: "I have no choice, Adrien. As two of this team are in danger, risking my own life is a risk I have to take."

"Then take some advice: work with this team for as long as you can. Let them help you – and that includes me. If I had a daughter like you, I would be right there beside her, and that's where I want to be for you."

"Thank you. That's great to know," replied Tayce, pleased with his kind words.

One thing she'd realised was that having Adrien aboard was like having her father around. He was becoming a real true valuable friend. He could discuss situations on the same level as her father could, when they met up. He had yearons of knowledge and experience in space travel, etc., and it was nice to know he was present like a kind of mentor. They both walked from the DC out into Organisation. Lance turned, announcing that Aemiliyana's fortress was in real space again as it had been in the last encounter with her. Tayce, on this, leant on the back of his chair as he continued further, saying that Varon Vargon's contributions in the venture with Aemiliyana included a stabilising system to enable the fortress to remain in their real time. Also the fortress was equipped with Slazer cannons at strategic positions to do the most damage and provide the most firepower. Also there were fighters on board. Upon hearing this, Tayce knew these had to be yet another of Varons contributions as Aemiliyana's convenient partner in crime. She would never use fighter craft – it wasn't her style. Powers and explosives of the witching kind were more to her liking, and the more she could unleash and destroy with the better.

"How many fighters aboard? Any idea?" Tayce asked.

Lance scanned the probe information that was coming through and there it was: eighty fighters. Tayce saw it and knew Jan's men would have to be the special combat type. This was not going to be easy.

Nick turned at communications, announcing there was another call coming in from the Witch Queen. Tayce sighed, stood up and turned towards the main Sight Screen, giving the order to open up communications. Nick did as requested. The main Sight Screen flashed into life and Aemiliyana appeared with Dairan dressed in the same attire he'd been placed in before, looking more like an Arabian prince than her Lieutenant Commander and soon-to-be legal intimate partner.

"What do you want now, Aemiliyana? More threats?" demanded Tayce, plainly noticing Dairan in a state of semi-undress.

"I thought you'd like to see my latest recruit for the attack on Enlopedia when we arrive. Tell her, Dairan, who you serve now," ordered Aemiliyana commandingly, with glee.

"He looks like she's drugged him in some way," said Adrien discreetly over Tayce's shoulder.

"I serve only you, Your Majesty, and honour all that you stand for," said Dairan, like he had been programmed.

"Excellent! He's so charming, handsome and attentive, I may keep him," said Aemiliyana, knowing she was winding Tayce up.

"Is this supposed to impress me? You've failed. It's just another of your powerful play tricks that will soon be easily rectified. Now, if you've stopped wasting my time, I've things to do," replied Tayce.

"See you at the attack, Tayce Amanda," announced Aemiliyana, and she ceased communications.

"Bitch!" said Tayce in outspoken anger, though looking around she could see the team didn't blame her.

"She's quite something, I'll give her that," said Adrien, surprised by the cunning troublemaker.

"Nick, get me Aldonica online," commanded Tayce.

"Right!" replied Nick, doing as Tayce requested.

"Lance, keep working on that information coming in. I want the information on the stabilising system of that fortress and layout in case anything has changed. Craig, I want you to upgrade our weaponry power," ordered Tayce.

"Aren't you going to wait a while for your father's decision?" asked Adrien.

"No, I'm getting prepared, no matter what Father says," replied Tayce. She knew what she wanted to do.

"Aldonica is online waiting," announced Nick.

"Tell her I'm on my way down. Lance, you're in charge. Tell me if anything develops unexpectedly and inform me en route," said Tayce, walking from Organisation, Twedor hurrying behind her, finding it difficult to keep up. He wondered what his mistress was thinking of doing where Aemiliyana was concerned.

Lance watched her leave. He shook his head, thinking how Aemiliyana had overstepped Tayce's tolerance point and she was not prepared to take any more trouble from the Witch. He continued on with a much more in-depth search on the fortress. He would also help work out a strategy plan in case they needed it.

Marc Dayatso was assessing up his average-sized holding environment. It was just like the rest of the fortress – elaborate, futuristic and cream in colour with smooth marblex floors and stonex walls. High up to the right of him was a grid-type cover, leading to somewhere. He looked around for something to use to get a better look at what was behind it. There wasn't much – there was a bunk and a hard stonex seat. Watching in case anyone came, he estimated the height he'd need to reach it and how high the seat was, wondering if he could jump up from the highest point. It was possible, he thought, if he jumped and stretched, throwing himself at it. He turned to look in the direction of the clear entrance doors, then proceeded to step up on to the seat, going to the highest point, the arm, and reaching up. It took a bit of balancing. Then he jumped, stretching at the same time. He managed to pull at the cover, and landed back on the arm. Luckily it came away in one pull. It swung back away from the entrance, which he could see was wide enough to crawl through.

He jumped up again, throwing himself into the entrance and landing half in and half out. He found himself on his stomach and had to wriggle forward to get the rest of himself inside. Once in, he got into a position so that he could crawl onwards. There was an airflow coming from somewhere further up. He reached for the grid cover and pulled it shut behind him, crawling onwards. Voices could be heard in the distance. He listened intently. It was Aemiliyana and Varon Vargon in discussion. When he came to a junction, he listened intently again for a moment, trying to make out what was being discussed. Upon realising which direction the voices were coming from, he crawled on. He wanted to find a gun somewhere. He figured a corridor would be the ideal place to find a weaponry store or, perhaps somewhere near, the main armoury.

After crawling for what seemed ages, he reached a grid in what seemed like an empty corridor, a Level up from where he'd climbed in. He quietly pushed open the brown grid cover. It swayed back on the hinge. Peeping out cautiously, taking a look both ways, he couldn't believe his luck. Someone must be on his side, he thought, as across the spacious corridor was an emergency weaponry store. It looked like something that had been recently installed. It looked out of place. Was it one of Vargon's contributions? he wondered. What was Vargon hoping to get out of this partnership? he wondered.

Upon making one final check, he swung himself into a sitting position and jumped down. To his relief no one heard his boots hit the floor, so he hurried on close to the wall towards the weaponry store, listening all the time for any sign of Aemiliyana's guards. Reaching in, he retrieved a weapon. Examining it, he realised it was the very weapon Tayce feared would fall into the wrong hands – the Catronic weapon. The thoughts that were going through Marc's mind included 'Where had Vargon got his hands on this evil weapon so easily?' He looked at the setting dial – *1, stun; 2, kill; 3, disintegrate.* Marc pressed the key for '2'. He wasn't the kind to deliberately kill for the sake or fun of it, but if it meant he stayed alive then so be it. He began moving up the wide palatial-type corridor, the Catronic weapon primed and aimed ready for the first sign of trouble.

***

Aldonica lifted the Power Arrow Launcher out of the weaponry stand and placed it on the workbench, in the Weaponry Design Centre. She proceeded to begin opening up the arrow casing that would hold the cartridge of powerful destructive arrows, generally twenty-four in a cartridge. Tayce watched as she explained that as she wanted a more powerful weapon she'd have to upgrade the arrows from what they were currently set at. Tayce nodded for her to do what she had to to make the weapon more powerful than before. As Tayce began towards the doors to the corridor, she turned.

"When can this be ready?" she asked.

"Considering I won't have to change the launcher, only upgrade it slightly, I'd say about an houron," replied Aldonica, studying the arrows she had in her hand.

"Call me for the testing. We're up against the likes of Aemiliyana and Vargon this time around. That should give you some idea of how powerful I want the weapon to be. This, between you and me, has got to be her end – permanently. The more powerful upgrade you can achieve, the better the outcome," confided Tayce.

"Don't worry – it will be ready. Are you going it alone, to get Dairan and Marc back?" asked Aldonica, curious.

Before Tayce had a chance to reply, her Wristlink sounded. She raised it, pressing Comceive. Nick Berenger was on the other end, in Organisation. He informed her that her father was on Satlelink and waiting to talk with her urgently.

"I'll catch you later, Al. I'm on my way, Nick," said Tayce, ceasing communications.

Aldonica thought it unwise if Tayce was hoping to take on the likes of Aemiliyana on her own. She watched her captain and friend walk briskly from the centre, then went back to improving the power arrows and their launcher.

***

In the short time it had taken Marc to reach the area outside the main Operations Deck, he had dodged no fewer than five groups of guards, all dressed in combat attire with the familiar initials on the shoulder of: 'CVVWA'. It all came flooding back; all through the past monthons he hadn't thought of the incident that had almost destroyed the Amalthean Quests team and cruiser at the end of the last voyage. The same initials were on the uniform of the attacker that almost left him for dead. He sighed, realising he had to forget what he was thinking and focus. Aemiliyana's voice could be heard ahead and she was addressing Dairan. 'Dairan!' he thought. 'Surely he hasn't been turned into her latest mindless plaything!' He had to get him out of that bitch's clutches, but how? He looked down at the Catronic weapon in his hands, set to kill. Looking down the corridor, at this particular moment there were no guards coming. If he acted quickly he could get Dairan out. Otherwise, he thought, Tayce would never forgive him, if anything happened to him, considering they were both in this damn mess together.

What Marc didn't realise was that Dairan was under Aemiliyana's total domination. He stepped out into the wide-open entrance brandishing the Catronic weapon, briskly walking into the main Operations Deck and firing into the group of operatives to get Aemiliyanas attention. She shrieked. Turning, she glared at him in outrage with powerful dark eyes.

"Fool, how did you escape?" she blurted out coldly, her eyes showing their powerful potential.

"It was quite easy. Let's go, Dairan – we don't belong here," ordered Marc commandingly.

"Are you going to leave like Commander Dayatso insists, Dairan?" asked Aemiliyana as Dairan didn't move. She knew Dairan wouldn't.

"Come on, mate – let's go," said Marc, waiting impatiently, not understanding what was going on or why Dairan wasn't responding.

"I serve my Queen," replied Dairan casually, under Aemiliyana's influence, much to Marc's horror.

"What! What the hell have you done to him?" demanded Marc, with a look of rage.

"Calm yourself. Dairan is quite happy to cooperate in my little joint venture against Tayce Amanda, but you, Commander, can leave any time you like. In actual fact, I'll give you a hand as you are proving to be a strong risk to my perfect plan," announced Aemiliyana coyly.

Aemiliyana summoned Eltarin, and in a split cencron, before Marc had time to fire off another shot from the Catronic weapon in his grasp, Eltarin appeared and both he and Aemiliyana cast energy balls of sheer power at him. They hit home with tremendous force. Marc was bathed in a brilliant red-hot energy, which rushed through his body and dropped him to the floor. The Catronic weapon slid from his hold to land at the feet of the influenced Dairan. Aemiliyana went further, using her powers to remind Marc never to interfere in her plans again. One more strike rendered him unconscious, breaking three of his ribs and almost shattering every system in his body. She then returned him, using a powerful force, to Amalthea. Dairan watched his teammate without emotion, unmoved by what had just happened before his eyes.

Varon Vargon had witnessed the whole incident from the entrance. It pleased him to see Marc Dayatso being treated the way he was. But it also unnerved him a bit to see just how strong Aemiliyana's powers had grown, since her arrival back in space. He wondered if she could jeopardise what their venture meant, seeing her using this kind of powerful action. Yes, he had to watch her, he thought.

***

A while later on board Auran Tayce had finished her meeting via on-screen communication with her father and he had informed her that the meeting with leaders of his people had gone well. The heads of departments, etc., had all agreed to her proposal that she should try and cut the attack fleet and Aemiliyana off before they could reach Enlopedia. Chief Jan Barnford's men would be in the positions suggested, ready to take on the mighty fortress when it arrived in orbit. Tayce walked out into Organisation just at the moment Marc was literally dumped back on board from the fortress, materialising right in the middle of Organisation unconscious. Tayce was taken totally by surprise, as were the rest of the team. She rushed to his side, horrified to think he could be dead. Aemiliyana had tortured him almost within inches of his life. Nick announced that there was an incoming communication from the woman herself. Tayce was angry beyond words. She totally abhorred Aemiliyana and she had no doubt this call was to boast of her prowess, having taken Marc within inches of death. The screen activated and Aemiliyana appeared, almost filling the screen, looking smug about what she'd done to Marc.

"I see you've found your commander. Is he alive? I guess I got a bit carried away. I had to let him go with great disappointment. He was far from proving loyal, unlike your Dairan here" she said in tones of evil sarcasm.

"I'm looking forward to putting you back where you belong – for all eternity this time, Aemiliyana, with no escape – when we meet," said Tayce sharply, gesturing for Nick to cut communication.

The screen deactivated and Tayce attended to Marc. Nick informed Tayce he'd already contacted Donaldo, declaring a medical emergency, and he was on his way. In no time at all Donaldo came rushing through the open entrance with his usual Medical Crisis Kit, followed by Treketa with a Hover Trolley. Treketa gasped at Marc's injured state. Donaldo set down his kit and took out the Examscan, beginning to check Marc's injuries.

To everyone's surprise Emperor Honitonia suddenly materialised. Tayce looked up at him, coming to a standing position. He gave her a reassuring look. "Doctor, I will take care of this. Tayce is going to need Marc here," announced Honitonia, crossing to Marc.

Donaldo stood out of the way. Emperor Honitonia simply announced he meant no offence in taking over the healing of Marc's injuries. It would just be a lot quicker in the circumstances. Donaldo smiled. He wasn't going to argue with the great and powerful being that the Emperor was. He could see his point.

"You go right ahead," replied Donaldo.

The Emperor stretched out his hand, his palm facing down over Marc's still form. He began concentrating. After a few cencrons a shaft of healing and rejuvenating power force came from the centre of the Emperor's palm, without much effort. It entered Marc and after a while Marc's breathing began to return to normal. All the injuries he'd sustained began reverting back to normal, as they were before he was tortured at the hands of Aemiliyana. After a while the Emperor ceased his act, completing what he wanted to accomplish.

Donaldo guided his Examscan over Marc, and it gave him a perfect reading. Emperor Honitonia found it amusing, but said nothing. Marc opened his eyes, focusing for a few minons on his surroundings. Everyone present was pleased with the Emperor's help. Tayce crossed and helped Marc back on his feet. He looked at her for a few minons, then hugged her to him. Letting her go, he thanked the Emperor.

"My pleasure, Marc. You must tell Tayce here what you have seen. You are now, in fact, our vital pin, you could say, in disrupting Aemiliyana's plan. We are all interested to know exactly what she has aboard her fortress, with the help of that Count," expressed the Emperor.

"And you will," assured Marc.

"Tayce, he's all yours. We in the Realm will be viewing all progress in all this until it's our turn to step in and assist," said Honitonia.

With this, the Emperor vanished just as quickly as he had arrived. Tayce and Marc turned and headed into the DC. Tayce wanted to hear everything about the fortress interior before Marc headed off to get cleansed and changed, to feel more like an Amalthean Quests team commander than Aemiliyana's reject. He paused inside the DC. He could see by the look on her face that she was waiting for him to say something.

"I tried to get Dairan out. He's totally been changed by some force she's got him under. She's got him right where she wants him. He even stood by and let me be tortured without emotion" said Marc, surprised.

"Adrien reckons he's been drugged in some kind of way," replied Tayce.

"I heard her say, as they dragged me away, she wanted him placed in something called the Obligation Chamber. He was totally not the Dairan we know. When I went to try and rescue him, you can see what I got for my attempt to do so. He just acted blankly – he let her torture me," said Marc, finding it hard to believe.

"Sounds like her kind of treachery. It seems this so called Obligation Chamber is her key to converting minds to work for her and Vargon. What about the interior of her fortress? Has that changed?"

"After escaping, I noticed – and you're not going to like this – Aemiliyana and Vargon have the Catronic weapon. As for the fortress, there's no change in layout."

"What! She's got that weapon! Why am I not surprised?" said Tayce, giving a furious look.

"Yes, also somehow Vargon has another army. I did my damnedest to dodge a couple of groups on the way to try and rescue Dairan. He still has them wearing the initials 'CVVWA,'" explained Marc.

"The Catronic weapon bothers me. Father has to know their using it," said Tayce, concerned.

"It is worrying. Do you mind if I go and get cleansed and changed before I get back on duty?"

"You go ahead. Marc?"

"Yes, what?" he asked pausing and turning.

"I'm glad you're all right. We just have to get Dairan back now," replied Tayce, knowing the task wasn't going to be easy, but she'd fight to the death if she had to, to restore her team.

"Thanks. See you in a while," he said, giving her a reassuring smile and continuing on.

Marc walked from the DC, leaving Tayce in thought. She turned to the Telelinkphone by her side, lifted the handset and ordered Nick to connect her with her father urgently, on Enlopedia, and have his call transferred to the screen in the DC. Nick agreed. As she placed the handset down Adrien entered the DC, announcing that it was good to see Marc back and saying that the Emperor was quite a powerful being.

"Is it true Vargon's using that deadliest of weapons, the Catronic weapon?" asked Adrien.

Tayce was about to answer when the DC screen flashed into life and Darius Traun appeared, waiting for her to speak and say what she had to say.

"Marc's back – he's fine," said Tayce. She spared her father the details of what had happened to him.

"Have you a further update?" he asked in his true Admiral's tone.

"You're not going to like this, but Marc discovered Vargon's using the Catronic weapon and he has a new army with the same initials as before."

"It doesn't surprise me. He's notorious for everything that's bad about this Universe," replied Darius.

"How are things at your end?" asked Tayce, interested.

"Jan's readying his men and preparing for the onslaught of attack, and many of the sections and complexes are moving their personnel temporarily to PT-2 until this is all over," explained Darius.

"Good luck, Father. We're going to need it too," said Tayce, turning her attention to Adrien.

The screen went blank. Tayce asked Adrien if he'd ever heard of such a chamber as the Obligation Chamber. Adrien thought for a few minons, then said he hadn't, but if the results were anything like what Aemiliyana had done to Dairan then he guessed it had something to do with altering someone's mind to suit another's needs – in this instance Aemiliyana's. Tayce nodded in agreement. Rising to her feet, she walked back out into Organisation, discussing with Adrien just how massive this whole situation was becoming by the minon.

Once they were out in Organisation, Adrien crossed to the entrance to leave and Tayce found out how the journey to rendezvous with the fortress was coming along. Twedor noticed how Tayce seemed to be doing a good job in hiding her thoughts over Dairan, trapped under Aemiliyana's thumb. He believed that when both women came face-to-face it would be a situation to end all situations. But what concerned him was who would be the winner? Even though he knew Tayce was good in her new ability, he would be there for her should she need him, as backup to protect her. It was his duty.

14. Prexan Forces, Part Two

At Enlopedia Headquarters Base all non essential personnel were heading under instructed guidance to awaiting Patrol Cruisers and any other suitable means of transportation, to head temporarily to PT-2. In the arrival and departure area, men, women and childlings dressed in various off- and on-duty attire were concentrating as they went, wondering if they'd have a home to come back to. As soon as many of the transferring personnel reached PT-2 they would take up temporary residence and duty sharing with the present surface personnel. Chief Jan Barnford was stood in the square, watching the throng pass, thinking all this movement was because of one evil super-witch and a man that should have been shot ages ago.

She walked across E City Square. Adam was by her side carrying her overnight holdall. Lydia Traun was heading up to Auran Amalthea Three on a high-security Transpo Launch, which was waiting to leave just as soon as she'd boarded. She let Adam hand the holdall to Jan and headed back to Admiral's Chambers. Lydia looked at Adam walking away, hoping she'd see him and her husband again. Jan could see the uneasy look on her beautiful features as she took one last look at the now becoming empty square. He'd seen that uneasy look on Tayce's face many times before. It never ceased to amaze him how much mother and daughter were alike, in many of their expressions and ways.

"Shall we go – that's if you're ready?" asked Jan softly and casually.

"Yes, lets go," said Lydia in soft reply.

She figured what was about to happen was similar to Traun all over again, only this time Vargon had a powerful partner wanting possession of the current base. She was even more evil than Carra, his once joined partner. As Jan walked with her, Lydia asked him to watch Darius and make sure he was safe in the threatened attack that was about to unfold. After all, they only had one Admiral. Jan assured her he'd do his very best – he was assigning two of his top officers to escort Darius everywhere he needed to go during the upcoming danger. They soon reached the high-security Transpo Launch and a young smartly uniformed female courier took Lydia's holdall and walked back aboard. Lydia nodded to Jan, then walked on aboard. Jan's Wristcall sounded. He answered it, heading back to E City Square, talking as he went, leaving the Transpo Launch behind him preparing for immediate take-off.

***

On Auran Amalthea Three Marc walked into Organisation looking refreshed and ready to assist in the forthcoming unwanted Quest. He paused by Lance's seat, asking for the latest they'd managed to get on the fortress. Tayce walked from the DC, exclaiming that she was off to see the improvements Aldonica had done on the Power Arrow Launcher. Marc nodded, then continued to listen to what Lance had so far and offer any further points he thought of, which Lance keyed in. Nick turned at communications.

"Enlopedia have just informed us that Chief Traun has left and is on her way out, to stay until the situation is over," said Nick.

"All right," replied Marc, watching what Lance was bringing up on screen.

Marc realised, upon hearing Nick, that his former chief and friend thought he was playing it safe in sending Lydia out of harm's way, where he thought she would be safe during the attack. But he wondered if she would be any safer on board considering Tayce and the team were as much under threat as Enlopedia.

"She'll be arriving in roughly one houron," continued Nick.

Marc nodded, continuing on with Lance, sifting what they needed and picking out the finer points to consider in what they had to face.

***

Aboard Aemiliyana's fortress preparations were well under way for the taking of Enlopedia Headquarters Base. Aemiliyana walked briskly from her Grand Central Chambers into the main Operations Deck dressed in a black-and-purple body-hugging full-length suit, with matching high black-and-purple collar. She was wearing shiny black leatherex boots that were hardly fit for the purpose of taking over a base, with their high slim heels. Dairan walked behind her, still under her effortless command. He'd been in her private chambers for the duration of the night. What she had made him endure, knowing she would use it against Tayce when the time came, was, to her, quite a special and delectable experience. He looked somewhat shell-shocked. She paused, turning, and looked at Dairan, stroking his cheek, treating him like some beloved pet. He looked at her, his brown eyes showing no warmth, or their usual mysteriousness; he seemed lost of all soul.

"Sit Dairan by my side." She gestured as she went to her command chair.

Count Vargon watched her with Dairan. He was growing suspicious. She was enjoying Dairan's company just a bit too much. She was forgetting why they were in partnership to attack Enlopedia. He walked over and she gave him a questioning look. He began explaining, as she listened, that their officers were, as he spoke, preparing to move into attack positions, ready to face the Auran Amalthea Three, which was currently two hourons from their present position, between the fortress and their main prize – Enlopedia.

"Whatever happens, Tayce Amanda is mine," she stated point- blankly.

"You can have what you want just as soon as I have Enlopedia in my command. You'll be doing me a favour as once she's in your powerful hold she can be disposed of once and for all," he said with little emotion.

He looked at Dairan, wondering what Aemiliyana would do with him once the takeover of Enlopedia had been achieved. His mind moved to thoughts of his latest plan to get rid of the last members of the Traun family. It was a problem that had nagged him for the last five yearons of his life. The Traun family! A slight evil pleased smile crossed his features at the thought that soon he would be able to roam the Universe in peace without Tayce Traun trying to stop him. He headed to the entrance, leaving Aemiliyana in command. After all, the fortress was her vessel of sorts, even though he'd done modifications to keep her from returning to the Mid Dimensional Zone beofre their joint venture was through.

Aemiliyana turned to Dairan by her side: "Your precious Tayce Amanda, granddaughter of Alexentron Traun, will soon be no more than just a speck of space dust," said Aemiliyana in a catty way.

"As you wish, my Queen," said Dairan obligingly, motionless.

His mind was totally under Aemiliyana's command – she could get him to do whatever she so wished. She smiled, pleased that she had achieved the parting of Dairan from Tayce and would soon achieve the demise of Tayce Amanda for what she and Grandmaster Alexentron Traun had done to her.

***

Lydia, in the high-security Transpo Launch, soon came alongside Auran Amalthea Three, docking at the Docking-Bay doors. Marc had sauntered down to meet her as Tayce was with Aldonica, testing the new more powerful Power Arrow Launcher in the Weaponry Design Centre. He stood casually waiting by the Docking-Bay doors, thinking through some thoughts regarding the latest Quest. As the doors drew open, a warm rush of recycled air came forth, followed by the young female courier, to hand Marc Lydia's holdall. Marc tried to put a brave face on, with a warm welcoming smile, thanking the young courier. Lydia studied him. She could see he was hiding what they were all suffering at the present time of great uncertainty.

"How are you, Marc?" she asked, seeing his thoughtful expression.

"Fine, considering. It's Tayce I'm worried about. She seems to be pretending this Quest isn't fazing her one bit. It concerns me. Aemiliyana's out for further revenge and she has the added bonus of Vargon on her side wanting his hands on Enlopedia," he confided.

"Darius and Tayce are very alike – too much sometimes and you're not the only one to be concerned. I didn't like leaving Darius alone with just security to protect him, considering the past he and Count Vargon have. Jan assures me he'll keep him safe – make him a top priority. I also think that both Tayce and Darius would like to get rid of Vargon forever. You also have to understand that Dairan is over on that fortress and Tayce probably is trying her hardest to hold it together for his sake. Any slip-ups and she could lose this team, me and Dairan plus a lot more. She's probably thinking she has to put everything she can muster into protecting everything she knows. She, as you know, has a habit of thinking in a single-minded way and that's probably where she is right now. Don't worry," Lydia reassured him as they walked.

"I guess you're right. It's just..." said Marc, then he fell silent in thought.

"I know you care for her – you always have done – but she'll win through," assured Lydia.

"Yes, but the last time she came up against the likes of Aemiliyana she nearly was killed, and this time around Witch seems to have more to throw at her, including the likes of Vargon," replied Marc.

"You know this? How?" asked Lydia, coming to a pause, worried.

"First-hand. I was aboard the fortress. She sent me back near to death, and if it wasn't for Emperor Honitonia I wouldn't be here to tell you," replied Marc.

They continued on to the Level Steps. Pausing, she suggested she take her holdall and head down to the guest quarters. Marc agreed, informing her that she was in her usual quarters. Both parted. Marc went up to Level 1, back to check on the progress of the special attack fleet, which was guarding Enlopedia, taking up positions in a new orbit to defend Enlopedia against the arrival of Aemiliyana's fortress and Count Vargon's CVVWA fleet of fighters. Lydia walked on down on to Level 3, deep in thought. Her mind was on Darius, the situation that was unfolding around Enlopedia and her daughter's safety. It unnerved her.

***

Jan Barnford entered Admiral's Chambers. Adam and Darius were in serious discussion over the procedures for the remaining personnel if final evacuation had to be undertaken, should the detaining attack line not hold back the forces of Aemiliyana and Vargon. Adam was agreeing on various points and checking his next orders, which he had to make sure of. Jan stood at ease, listening. Adam acknowledged Jan, then walked on out. Jan waited until Darius had finished marking off the schedule of orders he'd given Adam.

"They just don't know what a hell of a mess they've caused, do they?" confided Jan.

"You're right on that one, Jan," said Darius, agreeing in reply.

"My Security Transpo Launch pilot, who flew Chief Traun out to Auran, informs me that she has safely been delivered."

"Good! At least I know she's safe. Good work, Jan. Are your men moving into position yet?"

"Yes. As we speak, eighty Quest fighters are on their way with my best top combat pilots aboard," assured Jan.

"It's shaping up nicely. It's a darn shame this whole mess had to materialise, but while that man's alive you know as well as I do that there will never be any peace for myself, Lydia, Tayce, or this base or PT-2 as long as those two are at large in this Universe. All we can hope is that this time we see them fall for good," replied Darius with a hint of optimism in his voice.

"Couldn't agree with you more. Vargon seems to have been putting you all through it with his threatening attitude the whole of this yearon, ever since the ambush on the Auran. Another reason I'm here: I have posted two of my SSWAT officers to escort you everywhere during this period. Even when you return to your residence, they will be posted outside, armed at all times," explained Jan seriously.

Darius nodded understandingly.

Jan's Wristcall sounded on his wrist. He asked Darius if there was anything else – he'd like to head back and continue preparations for the final attack. Darius nodded, praising him for what he'd achieved so far. Jan began walking over to the entrance. Pausing halfway, he turned, informing Darius that he was sending a team of SSWAT officers to back the Amalthean Quest team when they go aboard the fortress. Darius looked at Jan, knowing Tayce was not going to like the idea. He let Jan continue, knowing he'd soon feel Tayce's wrath if he tried to take over this Quest.

"Make sure Tayce gets top-priority protection on the fortress, if she needs it," asked Darius.

"You've got it, Admiral," said Jan.

He continued on out through the opening doors as they parted, hoping the action ahead of him was over quickly and everything would come back to normal. He raised his Wristcall, answering the call as the doors closed behind him.

In the Chambers, Darius found himself picking up the glassene orb that had delivered the threatening message earlier, studying it in thought, wondering how something so beautiful could start a journey leading to turmoil and their possible demise. He placed it back on the desk, continuing on with his last final preparations to meet the attack on Enlopedia, be it by man, vessel or warrior.

***

He looked at the identical creation which stood before him, with a look of immense admiration. It was like looking at a mirror image of himself, yet a silent one. The creator of the identical self looked from the original to the copycat version, seeing they were exact – perfect, he thought, in every detail. Vargon looked at his twin with great scrutinising interest. It was amazing. The Prexan forces had achieved replication of the smallest of fine details, especially around the eyes. His exactly reproduced features were so perfect that it almost made him shiver. Garnex, the creator of the perfect copy of Vargon, announced that the clone was called *Saron* and was ready when his master so wished for him to be put into action. Vargon turned to the thin, uninteresting-looking man in his late forties and ordered him to tell the clone to say something – a threat or some other sentence. He wanted to hear if he sounded convincing enough. To Vargon's surprise, Saron spoke word perfect, in the same cold, evil tone. An impressed smile crossed the real Vargon's features, which was rare at any time. The clone was exactly what he had planned. Garnex could see his master was pleased.

"Excellent! You've done a fine job, Garnex – truly convincing. I may keep you when all this is through, for another project I have in mind."

"Thank you, Count Vargon," replied Garnex, pleased.

Garnex found it pleasing to think his master wanted him for further work, as he had not had the chance on his old home world to succeed in his talent for making such creations. Vargon turned to leave, but before he did so he ordered that he wanted the clone Saron dressed exactly the same way as himself for an important mission, ready to go when he gave the word. Garnex nodded in utterly eager obedience. Vargon turned and walked from the lab, thinking his plan was looking decidedly good after what he'd just seen.

***

No sooner had Lydia dropped off her holdall in the guest quarters than Twedor arrived, expressing that Marc had sent him to escort her to see Tayce. Lydia gestured for him to lead the way. They both walked from the Guest quarters out along Level 3 to the Level Steps. Lydia watched Twedor, thinking how he had gone from being a mere guidance and operations computer in the corner of Amalthea One to his present intelligent mobile state of Romid and escort. Twedor meant the Universe to Lydia's daughter. They walked down until they were on Level 5, where Lydia could hear weapon fire from down the corridor. Both herself and Twedor walked along until they reached the Weaponry Testing Centre. Twedor entered first as the doors opened; Lydia followed. She paused silently, watching her daughter proudly in the Test Chamber, using the new improved Power Arrow Launcher with expert precision of aim and movement in a simulation of attack. Twedor began recording silently the scores of successful strikes to put in Tayce's record of combat qualifications.

"Chief Traun, welcome aboard," said Aldonica politely, coming out into the open from her side study area, checking the points she wanted to accomplish in the upgrade.

"Hello, Aldonica. I guess this is the end result of the new modification. It's good. I'd forgotten how good she is in a combat situation. She showed potential yearons ago on Traun," said Lydia with a slight pleased smile.

"Yes, Tayce wanted it good enough to take on Aemiliyana, with high intensity, to rid us of the Witch Queen once and for all. And judging by Tayce's actions and the readings I'm getting, everything is checking out fine."

Both women stood watching Tayce until the session was through. Tayce turned, surprised to see her mother present and watching. She deactivated the Power Arrow Launcher and stepped from the chamber. Aldonica took the launcher as Tayce handed it to her.

"Great work! It will certainly do what I want it to do," praised Tayce.

"I'll have it ready for you in roughly two hourons. Is that OK?" asked Aldonica.

"Yes, perfect."

Lydia and Tayce plus Twedor walked from the Weaponry Testing Centre, leaving Aldonica to complete her work. The finished weapon, with its increased power, was to be used against Aemiliyana. Both mother and daughter walked in the direction of the Level Steps in discussion. Twedor walked down at Tayce's side, listening, summing up what his mistress and Lydia were discussing. He could see Tayce was thinking about the Quest ahead, whilst Lydia was concerned for Darius back on Enlopedia.

"What made Father send you out here? Not that I and the team mind you being on board, but you'll be no safer here when things start happening than if you remained back on Enlopedia. He should have sent you with the others to PT-2," said Tayce, concerned.

"His idea was that should the worst come to the worst, and Enlopedia's destroyed, then I will travel to PT-2 and take overall control as chief of the whole base," expressed Lydia.

"He's not thinking it will come to that, is he?" asked Tayce surprised. "Tell me he's not."

"You know Count Vargon. He's proved unpredictable and certainly evil and vengeful over the yearons. Look what happened when the war over our home world occurred. Your father is not taking any chances, so here I am," replied Lydia, draping her arm around her daughter.

"Mother, I'm not being awkward about having you with us. It's just I don't want you being hurt or killed should this Quest fail for any reason," replied Tayce, knowing the inevitable could happen, as it did back at the very beginning of the voyage.

"If it fails, we'll all perish anyway. Are you worried it will fail?" asked Lydia, ready to listen.

"I'm going to give it my all. I have the Power Arrow Launcher, which is a lot more powerful this time. I want that Witch back where she belongs, never to return, and Dairan safely back here on this team," replied Tayce. Failing was once again the furthest thought from her mind.

"Do you think Dairan will be able to return to the team?" asked Lydia, curious.

"There's no telling what that Witch has done to him. Professor Maylen is standing by. I certainly hope so – I love Dairan, Mother, truly I do. I'd do anything to get him back to normal and out of that Witch's hands," replied Tayce.

Lydia hugged her daughter to her and said no more. She hoped, for Tayce's sake, that whatever Aemiliyana had done to Dairan could be reversed.

They both turned at the top of the Level Steps on Level 1 and walked on into Organisation. Lance turned, welcoming Lydia on board. Lydia paused by his seat, asking for the latest report. Lance keyed in a sequence of key commands. The Sight Screen flashed into life and an interesting scene appeared – one that signified that the start of something big in weapon power was about to unfold. The Quest 2s from Enlopedia were in formation attack mode, ready for the likes of the fortress and whatever else Aemiliyana and Vargon wanted to unleash. Tayce turned, finding the sight spectacular, to say the least. It was a battle in the making. She went about picking the Quest team, or was about to, when Marc suggested a quick discreet word in the DC – and that included Lydia. Tayce sighed. She was geared up to put into operation her own preparations for what they faced ahead. She followed on, thinking this had better be important – time was not for wasting. She wanted to go and get changed into her combat attire ready for the action ahead.

Once in the DC, Marc turned in mid floor. Lydia looked at him in a questioning way.

"Aemiliyana thinks I'm dead, right?" he said.

"Yes! The last time she saw you was out in Organisation, close to death. Where's this leading?" asked Tayce, wondering.

"Instead of taking a Quest team, I know how you want her dealt with, so how about I dress differently, disguise my features and personally deliver you with the Power Arrow Launcher to her?" he put to a surprised-looking Tayce.

"I can't believe you just suggested this, Marc? It's highly dangerous," said Lydia, taken aback that he should think of doing such a dangerous thing to her daughter.

"I'm surprised too. Hold on, Mother, where am I going to conceal the Power Arrow Launcher, Marc?" asked Tayce, wondering.

"I could conceal it under my disguise – maybe a dark cloak and discreetly hand it to you. It would get you right into the very heart of the situation; and once in, you get a head start on her and her guards, plus I can help in the situation and Phean could join us in disguise and help," explained Marc.

"If you want my thoughts on this, it's highly risky," said Lydia with a face that was worried.

Tayce thought about the idea for a moment. Marc was right – it would give her a chance to get Aemiliyana and then hand her over to Emperor Honitonia, eliminating one of the treacherous twosome. Lydia stood thinking the whole thing was extremely preposterous – anything could go wrong. But if Tayce wanted to do it then she knew there was nothing she could do or say to make her change her mind. She was very concerned though. To Lydia's surprise, Tayce agreed, but just as she did so Emperor Honitonia arrived, bringing with him two realm cream hooded robes.

"Chief Traun – an honour," said the Emperor with politeness.

"Emperor, it's been a long time," replied Lydia softly.

"We heard your proposal, Marc, and the Empire have offered these as your disguise – one for you and one for Phean," said Emperor Honitonia, handing both the robes to Marc.

"Thank you. At what stage will you take control of Aemiliyana?" asked Tayce.

"Use your mind to tell us when you have her and I will take over. This time there will be no escaping for her. The Realm, as we speak, are making sure there will never be an existence in any form for her again," expressed the Emperor.

Phean entered the DC looking questioningly at Tayce. She explained what was required of him for the present Quest. Marc handed him the cream full-length hooded robe and suggested he find a way to disguise himself further in some way, so he couldn't be recognised. Phean nodded, then turned to Tayce, telling her he wouldn't let her down. He knew just what Aemiliyana was capable of. He'd been looking into past Quest reports with Lance, doing his research on the present situation. Tayce glanced at her Wristlink time display. It was time to get changed into combat attire for the Quest. Marc, upon her saying as much, thought about it, then suggested that if he was going to hand her over to Aemiliyana, didn't she think it would look better if she dressed in off-duty casual dress? Tayce thought about it for a moment, wondering if he was taking this idea of her being handed to the Witch Queen just a little too far. Did it matter what she was dressed in? She glanced at her mother, who was thinking about what Marc had just said.

"Marc has a point. If you go dressed in Quest combat attire she's going to know you've not come as someone to be innocently handed over," said Lydia, seeing Marc's point.

"Maybe you're right. OK let's go. Marc, tell Nick to have Amal pick a team for the later part of this Quest and have them get ready. It's time," ordered Tayce.

"Right!"

Emperor Honitonia stayed talking with Lydia as she had asked for a private word regarding Tayce's training to date and her new abilities. She also wanted to discuss Aemiliyana and what was to become of her when she was caught.

Tayce, with Twedor in tow, walked off to her quarters to change into her normal off-duty attire. She wondered, as she went, if she could find something loose enough to wear to conceal the Power Arrow Launcher herself, so Aemiliyana couldn't see she was concealing the weapon to finish her off and Marc wouldn't have to discreetly hand it to her. She'd feel a lot happier carrying the weapon herself.

Kelly rose to her feet and left with Craig and Marc to go and get changed – Amal had announced that they were going on the risky Quest. On Marc's orders, Nick contacted Donaldo to tell him it was time to get the Medical Crisis Kit ready and for Treketa to get changed into her combat attire. She was needed. Marc, Kelly and Craig walked briskly along Level 1 towards the Level Steps in discussion about what might lie ahead.

***

Out in space Auran Amalthea Three was now surrounded by Quest 2 fighters from Enlopedia and the fleet of eighty or more fighters from PT-2 as backup. They were all moving towards the now impressive sight of the fortress, armed for battle, coming within a one-million radius. Fighters were surrounding not only Auran Amalthea Three, but Enlopedia as well. Aemiliyana's fighters were all around the fortress, ready to act on their Queen's orders to attack. It was going through everyone's minds, as they flew, just what kind of pilots were at the controls of Aemiliyana's fighters – human or machine. Knowing Varon Vargon and his merciless evil ways, he was likely to have pilots who had had their minds altered so they would only work on his orders: to destroy the Quest 2 fighters from Enlopedia and PT-2 and finally bombard Enlopedia with weapons fire, and if they could take out Auran Amalthea Three it would be a bonus.

***

A while later on Auran Amalthea Three, Marc had disguised himself so no evidence of who he truly was under the robe the Emperor had given him would be easily detectable. He checked his appearance in the quarters imager. Perfect, he thought – especially when he pulled the hood over his head to show just a slit for his eyes. He looked more like a rough space traveller peddling wares than the commander he was. He headed towards the quarters entrance and, as the doors parted on his approach, he found Phean in an equally good disguise. Marc suggested they check if Tayce was ready and what she'd decided to wear, considering she might want to conceal the Power Arrow Launcher. Tayce's quarters doors drew apart on approach and she walked out in a cream heavy panelled wrap-over gown. Marc raised his eyes, wondering if it was a case of dressed to kill.

"You wear that off duty?" he asked in surprise and admiration.

"No, but I wore this when I did my first Telepathian test during the second voyage and it has deep discreet pockets which will easily conceal the Power Arrow Launcher."

"You look nice," said Phean under his mask and robe.

"Shall we go?" Marc suggested.

Twedor followed on behind, ready for his Quest duty ahead. He wanted a chance to shoot Aemiliyana, considering the last time he was on her fortress, she'd placed him in a purple liquid and suspended him from the ceiling in a rather undignified way. It was something he wasn't likely to forget for a long time to come. Craig and Kelly fell into line, checking their Pollomoss handguns as they went. Aldonica also handed the Power Arrow Launcher loaded with the new more powerful arrows to Marc, who declined, gesturing to Tayce, who went about concealing it in the gown she was wearing, hoping that it wouldn't be seen. The padding of her gown disguised it as just another curve in the design. This everyone was pleased about as it wouldn't look suspicious. The team looked a true crime-busting team, ready for action. But Tayce, Phean and Marc were hoping Aemiliyana was fooled enough to think that Tayce was being handed over as an innocent victim. They would travel to the fortress first, followed, after a delay, by the rest of the Quest team.

Jan Barnford stepped aboard. His concerned thoughts as he stood waiting at the Docking-Bay doors were on what Marc had had for an idea. Lydia Traun had called him about it earlier. He knew the idea had to run very smoothly – one wrong move and it would all come crashing around his and his officers' ears and Tayce and everything would be no more. Tayce came towards him, walking briskly up the corridor followed by the others and Twedor. Jan, upon seeing how Tayce was dressed, wondered if she was going to a celebration, rather than going into a combat situation and confronting Aemiliyana. Tayce could see he was in thought as he studied her, looking her up and down.

"I don't mean to be rude here, but are you sure what you're wearing is the best kind of attire for what lies ahead?" He gestured to her gown, finding it somewhat unusual.

"You're not and it's perfect for what Marc and Phean are going to be doing," replied Tayce, to the point.

"Very well – it's your choice. Shall we go?" asked Jan.

"You're coming in with the backup team after we arrive. Understand?" said Tayce to Jan.

Jan thought for a moment, then he remembered what Admiral Traun had explained and nodded in agreement. Everyone walked out through the Docking-Bay doors, back aboard the Patrol Cruiser. Once on board, as it departed from Auran Amalthea Three, Tayce explained what the idea was once they docked with the space fortress, if they did. She glanced out through the nearest sight port, noticing the Enlopedian fighters were now engrossed in a full-on attack with the fighters belonging to the fortress. Explosions were full on, on both sides. Jan watched and noticed the slim-looking fighters from Aemiliyana's and Vargon's forces. They were shaped like a hammer head at the front and were trying to lead

Jan's men and their fighters away from protecting Auran Amalthea Three and Enlopedia, but he was glad to see that they were being unsuccessful in the attempt. The Enlopedian fighters were blowing many of Vargon's and Aemiliyana's fighters to bits, evading them with their expert combat fancy manoeuvres. It made Jan smile to think that Aemiliyana and Vargon had thought they had it made, but they hadn't anticipated his men and their flying ability. It was decided that Tayce, Marc and Phean would be put aboard as soon as they docked at the fortress, then himself, Craig, Aldonica, Kelly and Twedor with his men would follow on after a delay, with backup. Tayce stood watching the battle unfold silently for the rest of the crossing to dock at the fortress. Her thoughts were on Dairan and what state she would find him in when they reached Aemiliyana. She was hearing Marc's words in her mind about Dairan not knowing Marc when he'd let Marc be tortured during Aemiliyana's vicious attack on him, almost killing him. Marc put a friendly reassuring hand on her shoulder. It was as if he could somehow miraculously read what she was thinking at that moment.

"He'll be all right – you'll see. We may have to stun him for not cooperating, but when we get him back to Auran he'll be back to normal after help – you'll see," he said softly.

"I dread to think what that bitch has been doing with him, using him as her slave under her powerful hold," began Tayce, feeling both angry and disgusted at the same time as various thoughts went through her mind.

"If you say he has no idea what he's doing, perhaps when he comes back to normal he won't remember what happened," said Phean, sounding optimistic.

"Yes, you could be right," replied Tayce, deep in thought.

"Quite!" said Marc.

"Marc, ready to make the first drop?" said Jan.

Tayce, Marc and Phean readied themselves. Marc pulled up the hood of his robe and it draped over his face, allowing only his eyes to be seen through the slits in the mask he wore as a disguise. Phean did the same. Soon the three Amaltheans were being sent from the Patrol Cruiser to the docking area aboard the fortress. It was fast, to avoid being shot at and attacked, but it was a success.

***

Tayce, Marc and Phean were soon aboard the space fortress, where action was very much the scene. Marc grabbed Tayce by the upper arm and discreetly suggested she should play along. They had arrived below the main Operations Deck. All three had to steady themselves as weapon fire bounced off the fortress's protection shields. They began walking in the direction of Marc's last meeting with Aemiliyana with Tayce as a convincing unwilling victim, to be handed over to the Witch. Men ran here and there in urgent duty action, to protect the fortress and take up positions that had become vacant when other members of the crew had been killed. Marc watched, knowing that what was proposed was not going to be easy. He figured so far they'd been undetected as intruders as there was so much going on. But as they ran up the steps to the next level they were caught. Right in front of them stood two armed guards and in the middle was Count Vargon, and he looked as if he wouldn't hesitate to give the order to kill. Luckily for Marc and Phean they were heavily enough disguised to fool Vargon. It was time to play out the proposed scenario.

"Who are you? How come you have this young woman? What's your business here?" demanded Vargon.

"We come to deliver her to your Queen. We believe she's the woman you seek," said Marc, putting on an accent under the mask, and for some strange reason it was working as the mask muffled his voice.

"Where did you hear of this – the fact that Witch Queen Aemiliyana is wanting this young woman brought before her?" demanded Varon, testing Marc.

"We just heard. We figured there would be some kind of reward. We boarded Auran Amalthea Three and abducted her. Not even her team know she's missing," replied Marc in muffled sound.

"Aemiliyana will be pleased to finally give this woman her just deserts. Bring her – you'll certainly be rewarded," said Vargon, pleased to think that Tayce was going to finally meet the perfect end.

Tayce thought to herself, 'Not half as much as Aemiliyana will be when I get my chance to finally finish her for good.'

Marc said no more and looked at Phean. He wanted to thank him for using his powers to disguise his voice. It had certainly worked. Marc shoved Tayce forward and marched her along with Phean behind Vargon along the fortress corridor, towards the main Operations Deck. Tayce began to focus herself within, preparing to come face-to-face with Aemiliyana again, hopefully for the final time. She hoped this plan of Marc's worked.

They entered through the arched doorway into the vastness of the main Operations Deck. Aemiliyana slowly rose to her feet, unperturbed by the fact that her surroundings were under full-blown attack. She walked towards Tayce, studying her coldly as she came, full of calculating thoughts about what she was going to do, considering she was sent to the equivalent of Tartarus in their last encounter. She looked at Marc, in disguise. He had hold of Tayce by the upper arm, but she was unsure who he was. Tayce looked at the seat where Aemiliyana had been seated and saw an emotionless-looking Dairan. It shocked her for a moment. He seemed to be vacant, unaware of the fact that she was present. God, what had that Witch done to him? wondered Tayce. A slight evil smile crossed Aemiliyana's features as she saw Tayce looking towards Dairan. She figured she now had everything she wanted: Tayce Amanda at her mercy and Dairan helpless to do anything and not even knowing who Tayce was.

"What the hell have you done to him, Aemiliyana? Just do what you have to, but let him go. You have me now – what more do you want?" retorted Tayce, playing along with the act to fool the Witch Queen before her. She was itching to pull out the Power Arrow Launcher and put the evil bitch where she could never come back from again.

“He's my perfect companion. Why should I let him go? Sorry he broke your heart, Tayce Amanda, but that's men for you,” said Aemiliyana, much to Marc's surprise and Tayce's fury.

“Keep him! I wouldn't want to deprive you of your final hourons of happiness,” replied Tayce spitefully, not letting Aemiliyana'a words affect her because she knew what would soon unfold.

The fortress jolted and shook from the continuous onslaught of weapon fire bouncing off the protection shield. The operatives, in their circular working area, smoothly but excitedly made sure their surroundings stayed whole whilst returning fire on the Quests and Auran Amalthea Three.

Vargon sauntered over to Tayce, asking Aemiliyana to permit him to show Tayce what he had in store for Enlopedias Admiral Traun, her father. Tayce scowled spitefully at Vargon. What she wouldn't give to finish this bastard once and for all. She was finding her anger hard to suppress. Her hand reached discreetly into her pocket, where the Power Arrow Launcher was, and Marc loosened his grip on her arm. She felt the smoothness of the launcher within her grasp. The screen on the far wall of the main Operations Deck flashed into life, showing Vargon's identical twin, alike in every detail, at the controls of a fighter, heading across space towards Enlopedia.

“Saron is on his way with instructions to eliminate the one being that stands in the way of me taking command of my first base of many. Say goodbye to your father, Tayce Amanda,” said Vargon coldly, pleased he was making her angry beyond words.

“You bastard, my father will never fall for this. He'll never hand over Enlopedia to your clone. You're an idiot if you think he will,” retorted Tayce, finding it extremely difficult to resist drawing the launcher and shooting him.

“Once he's gone, you, your mother (wherever she may be)and your Amalthean Quests team will be either destroyed or under my ruling – a pleasing thought,” said Vargon, revelling in the idea.

“You keep that dream in mind because that's all it's going to be,” replied Tayce, enraged.

“Ruling this part of the Universe will be a new system. It will change everything dramatically,” he continued, ignoring Tayce's words, walking over, coming to a pause in front of her and looking down at her intimidatingly.

“You certainly are sure of yourself, I'll give you that, but what you don't see is you're sitting right in the middle of the biggest target practice this sector of space has seen for a long time, and you're the main target. Soon this fortress will be wide open and, eventually, no more in existence,” said Tayce plainly.

"You two, come here and escort these two back to their vessel. Give them what they want as a reward," ordered Vargon, beckoning to two of Aemiliyana's guards, still unaware of the fact that the men with Tayce were Marc and Phean.

Aemiliyana turned to walk back to her command seat, in continued pleasurable thought regarding what pain she was going to put Tayce through now that she was in her long-awaited presence. Suddenly she paused in mid step, reminding Vargon he was not going to think that taking over Enlopedia was a sole command; she was going to command also, at his side. Phean was silent, using his powers, standing beside Tayce, still not having moved since Vargon's instructions to the guards to take him and Marc back to a vessel that didn't exist. He was silently making Eltarin lose his stability and his hold on reality. As he stood the other side of Aemiliyana's throne Phean drove him into a unconscious powerless stupor. Suddenly Eltarin put his hands to his head, crying out in agony for the pain to stop. Aemiliyana turned sharply towards him, her eyes wide with alert horror, wondering what might be happening to her powerful friend.

"What's the matter with you, you numskull? Get yourself together," she commanded sharply.

"Looks like he's losing it. He's probably taken enough of your orders and your demands on him," replied Tayce, looking at Eltarin going crazy, trying not to laugh.

"You – you're doing this, Tayce Amanda. Cease this or I'll..." said Aemiliyana, coming back towards Tayce.

"Or you'll what?" asked Tayce, reaching for the Power Arrow Launcher and withdrawing it from her gown pocket quickly, ready to fire.

She aimed it right at Aemiliyana with intent and without a further thought of what she was doing. She'd taken enough. Aemiliyana, having felt the power of the launcher the last time, glared at Tayce and the weapon in her hand. Both Marc and Phean heard Vargon order the guards to kill Tayce. They pushed back the disguise of their attire and aimed their Pollomoss handguns directly at the advancing guards. Vargon was angry beyond words to think he'd been fooled in such a way.

"Foolish move, Commander Dayatso! There are armed men of mine on duty all over this fortress."

"I thought I'd killed you the last time we met. How did you return?" asked Aemiliyana, astonished to see Marc very much alive.

"Maybe your powers aren't as good as you think they are, Your Wrathfulness," said Marc sarcastically.

"Would you like a further demonstration? As I recall, you made a feeble opponent," retorted Aemiliyana.

"I wouldn't try it. I sent you back where you belong the last time, and if you don't give up this act to take Enlopedia I'll do it again sooner than you anticipate.

And this time you won't surface ever again – you can count on that," said Tayce, stepping in front of Marc.

"Dairan, kill Tayce Amanda," ordered Aemiliyana, thinking it would unnerve Tayce.

As Dairan, void of all reality and unaware of his present surroundings, walked like a dummy towards Tayce. His brown eyes showing no warmth and no soul. Marc slipped the Pollomoss setting to 'stun' and quickly took out Dairan as he approached. Dairan dropped to the floor in mid walk. As Aemiliyana glanced at Dairan, and became enraged by what Marc had done, Tayce activated the weapon in her hand and a power arrow sailed across towards Aemiliyana and impacted right in the middle of her chest. The higher level of power dispersed on impact, spreading rapidly throughout Aemiliyana's body like a spectacular electric display. Tayce fired another. This backed up the first, impacting in the same area, sending Aemiliyana reeling backwards in agony, much to Count Vargon's surprise. She then used her own Witch Queen abilities and unleashed a ball of red energy at Tayce. Tayce stood ready to block it using one of her new abilities. Suddenly she was bathed in a white shield, which surrounded her protectively.

"Nice try – try harder," said Tayce.

The battle was on between Tayce and Aemiliyana. Powerful bursts of energy from Aemiliyana came at Tayce, bouncing off the powerful aura that surrounded her. From out in the corridor came Jan Barnford, his men and Aldonica, Kelly, Craig and Twedor, shooting at the many guards and operatives as they entered the main Operations Deck. The onslaught of attack had now materialised in the centre of the deck. Vargon knew it was a no-win situation and left the scene swiftly, firing into the onslaught as he ran out. Twedor hurried to Marc's side, his Slazer finger activated. He was joining in the shooting. He had scanned the operatives and found they were of human origin but with their minds programmed to serve, so he figured he was releasing them from their locked-in torture. Tayce found herself suddenly thinking of her father and Saron, Vargon's clone, and the fact that he was on his way to kill him. If his protection wasn't what it should be, she knew she could lose him. Looking at Aemiliyana and her fight to stay on her feet under the effects of the new more powerful power arrows, she figured it was time to call the Emperor. It was time for him to take over and send the Witch Queen out of reality forever.

"You're a foolish girl, Tayce Amanda. I will return. You'll never win – never!" announced Aemiliyana, losing the ability to fight the effects of the power arrows, battling on without much success.

"I think I just have. This time you're going where you belong for all eternity, with no escape," retorted Tayce as she fired another power arrow at Aemiliyana, putting her all the way down on to the floor.

Aemiliyana was losing her fight to stay in control and alive. She glowed brilliant red, changing from being in full form to becoming almost transparent.

Emperor Honitonia materialised in the chamber. He announced in a loud commanding Emperor's tone, looking at Aemiliyana, that the Empire was waiting for her. She glared at him.

"I will not go back. I will not," she shouted, continuing to uselessly fail at holding on to reality.

With this, Emperor Honitonia pointed the first finger of his right hand at her and emitted a yellow laser right into her heart, telling her she would cooperate – she had done enough harm. Within cencrons she screamed and vanished from the deck, protesting in a fading way until she was gone into nothing. All weapon fire ceased. Tayce looked around, hoping to find the dead form of Count Vargon, realising that in all the weapon fire he'd as usual vanished to fight another dayon. Jan met Tayce's disappointed and angry look, which said it all. He raised his Wristcall, standing beside a dead operative, and contacted his deputy, the head of the battling fleet of Quests outside, and ordered that any escaped fighters from the fortress were to be destroyed immediately. His deputy quickly came back, much to his surprise, announcing that there was a small vessel leaving the fortress as he spoke.

"Destroy it now!" commanded Jan in urgency.

"Sorry, sir – too late. It just vanished."

"Damn!" said Jan under his breath, lowering his Wristcall.

He was far from pleased as he deactivated his Wristcall. His men that had been taking out Aemiliyana's staff were now ferrying back into the deck, their weapons poised ready for further action. Tayce crossed to Phean.

"Phean, I have to get to Enlopedia. Father's in danger from Vargon's clone."

"Allow me, then I must return to make sure Aemiliyana never returns to this life ever again to cause any more trouble," cut in the Emperor.

"I want to take Twedor," said Tayce seriously.

"Go and hold him tightly. I will put you there," said Honitonia, readying to do so.

Tayce crossed and took hold of Twedor by the shoulders. He raised his metlon arms and applied just the right amount of pressure to hold her. Together they disappeared from the main Operations Deck through space, leaving behind the turmoil of the now badly damaged fortress. It had been coming apart at the seams since Aemiliyana's demise as the protection shield had failed the moment she was sent where she would never return from again – to the furthest depths of the Honitonian Empire.

***

The clone of Vargon, Saron, was in a near-deserted E City Square. He had been hiding from sight until two security patrol officers had gone for their short relief break. He walked out into the open, entered the Vacuum Lift and ascended to the required level, so that he could do what he had to do. Once out on the Level for Admiral's Chambers, he entered the outer Anteroom. Before Adam had a chance to alert Darius, who was present, Saron shot Adam. He fell forward over his desk, silent, out cold. It wasn't known if he was dead or stunned. Saron continued on, proceeding in the same slow, calm way as his original master would have gone, in search of Darius Traun. On in through the entrance doors to Admiral's Chambers he went with intent to kill.

***

Tayce materialised with Twedor in the near-emptiness of E City Square. She checked the Power Arrow Launcher in her grasp and Twedor activated his Slazer finger. She had a couple more power arrows. She called Twedor, then began moving urgently towards the Vacuum Lift, breaking into a light sprint. Twedor followed as fast as his little metlon legs would allow him to go. Tayce entered into the Vacuum Lift, which had returned to ground level. Soon she and Twedor were heading up to her father's chambers, hoping that she wasn't going to be to late.

Up on the required level, Tayce cautiously but alertly and quietly crept into the outer Anteroom leading to her father's chambers, followed by Twedor. She refrained from gasping when she saw Adam sprawled over the desk, injured. Was she too late? she wondered. Then she heard male voices from within her father's chambers. One was her father and the other sounded like Vargon. Tayce gestured to Twedor not to make a sound. She walked forth through the doors, the Power Arrow Launcher primed in her hands, ready to shoot. Twedor held his hand out in a way that made it look like he was holding a gun. Tayce stood just inside the entrance. Saron detected her and spun round to face her, opening fire. Tayce fired back, but missed. She dropped to the floor from the pain, sheltering behind the nearest cabinet, but not before she saw the weapon he was using. It was the Catronic weapon. She felt something wet on her uniform. He'd struck her in the thigh and it was smarting like mad. She fought to keep her concentration going long enough to shoot back again at him. She opened fire with the Power Arrow Launcher and ordered Twedor to shoot too. Saron dropped to the chamber's carpetron floor. Tayce stumbled to the nearest chair, but missed and fell to her knees. Darius ran forth in urgency.

"Father, we have limited time. You've got to get me medical attention quickly. It's the Catronic weapon," said Tayce, near to tears as she knew she had very little time to get medical help.

"My God? Twedor, over here quickly! Keep monitoring Tayce's vital signs," said Darius, hurrying to his desk to summon the emergency medical team.

Darius watched on as he demanded that an emergency team should come to his chambers at once and told the person on the other end it was a Catronic injury. Tayce lost all awareness of where she was. She was trying to fight off the onslaught of the weapon's effects using her own power abilities, but they weren't working. She could hardly keep her eyes open and soon lost all consciousness. The last she knew was her father telling her not to worry, help was coming. Darius took her in his arms and held her reassuringly, trying not to think he was going to lose her, after she had so bravely entered into a situation that could have caused them both to lose their lives. Their immediate surroundings were not a pretty sight: a dead Saron; Darius himself kneeling holding an unconscious Tayce in his arms; Twedor standing by, keeping a constant check on his mistress's vital signs; and, out in the Anteroom, Adam Carford out cold, hit by the same weapon, slumped over his desk. Darius realised he'd come within inches of losing his own life; he would of died if it hadn't been for Tayce.

The emergency medical teams soon arrived, rushing first to Adam and then in to Tayce. Dr Carthean and Dr Sellecson both had Medical Crisis Kits in hand. Dr Carthean also carried a loaded Comprai Inject Pen. She immediately put down her kit and proceeded to administered the drug into Tayce's upper arm to counteract the effects of the Catronic weapon. She glanced at her Wristcall time display. They had less than ten minons before Tayce became the dead leader of the Amalthean Quests team. She crouched beside Tayce, pushing her blonde hair back behind her right ear, and continued to monitor Tayce's vital signs with the Examscan.

***

On Auran Amalthea Three Donaldo steadied an injured Dairan on to the waiting Hover Trolley. Marc contacted Lance up in Organisation, telling him to get Auran Amalthea Three out of their present orbit as the fortress was going to blow in a matter of cencrons. As the cruiser began moving away from the fortress, Marc watched through the sight port. The Quest 2 fighters were leaving the area, also heading back to Enlopedia before they got caught in the aftershock of destruction. Marc's thoughts drifted to Varon Vargon. How he wished he'd shot the bastard when he'd had the chance, back in the Operations Deck. Where had he gone? He sighed and turned, alone in the now empty Transpot Centre. The others had gone, either back to duty or to the MLC. He walked from the centre, wondering how Tayce had faired. He raised his Wristlink, ordering Amal to take Auran Amalthea Three to Enlopedia.

***

Lydia Traun was pacing agitatedly in Organisation. She was waiting for news of Darius and Tayce as she wasn't sure yet if both were still alive. All she'd heard from Jan Barnford via Nick Berenger was that Tayce, with the help of Emperor Honitonia, had gone to stop Vargon's clone from killing her long-time legal intimate partner. Nick suddenly turned at communications.

"Chief, there's an incoming transmission from Enlopedia."

"Put it through to the DC," said Lydia, hurrying in to take the call.

The Sight Screen activated and a very much alive but worried-looking Darius appeared. Twedor was down at his side. Lydia held her breath for bad news. Darius soon explained that he was fine thanks to their daughter, but she unfortunately wasn't. She'd been injured by the Catronic weapon Saron, Vargon's sent assassin, was using. He further explained that Adam had been wounded by the same weapon also, but nowhere near as seriously. It had just been a nick. Dr Carthean had luckily managed to give counteracting injections to both their daughter and Adam. He glanced behind him at the first personnel returning to normal duty and the every-dayon life once more returning to normal in E City – something that might not have happened if it wasn't for the brave men who refused to let the fighters and fortress force their way through the Quest protection squadron. He looked back at Lydia.

"You're safe to come home now," he assured her.

"I'll be there just as soon as Auran docks," replied Lydia casually.

As communications ceased, Lydia realised she'd come really close to losing the two people she loved the most. Marc entered the DC, still unchanged from the Quest. He wanted to find out if there was any news of Tayce. Lydia immediately explained that Tayce had been injured, but was going to be fine. He hugged her as she suddenly broke down, relieved it was all over. Marc had always been like the son she'd never had, and he'd always given her the kind of loving respect a son feels for a mother.

***

This Quest had been somewhat hard at times for all of them. But they'd won through in the end. Aemiliyana was in the hands of the Empire, never ever to return to the present time again. They would no doubt punish her in their own powerful way for her escape from eternity. As for Count Vargon's Saron, he was no more. But Count Vargon, himself had simply vanished in his usual way, being once again elusive. No one knew when he would next appear. But, wherever it would be, Tayce would be ready for him and so would the forces of Enlopedia and PT-2.

15. One Task to End

Enlopedia Headquarters Base was returning to near normality, except for the damage that had been done in various sections when enemy fighters had managed to land a few direct hits against the protection shield. Darius Traun was playing a vital role in making sure Enlopedia was open for business. He'd asked Marc Dayatso to stand in for Adam Carford until he'd been declared fit to return to duty as his assistant once more, like in the old dayons. Marc accepted, as he had no orders from Tayce to take Auran Amalthea Three back into space urgently because of her current condition. Maintenance Chief, Jamie Balthansar, wanted to complete the maintenance check and replace the much needed components on the cruiser while they were docked. His reason: he had to start work soon on another important project, and this would have delayed the check if it had been left until it would normally have been done. Marc decided to declare off-duty time for the whole team as there was little they could do aboard during the check. This meant the team could do what they wished until the maintenance was through. Darius wouldn't need Marc until Tayce was hopefully back on board, back to her normal self.

Dairan Loring had fully recovered from his experience with Aemiliyana, thanks to Professor Adrien Maylen. He'd given Dairan a full examination of his mind in a sedated state and found that Aemiliyana hadn't done any permanent damage with her mind tricks. She'd merely brainwashed him and shut down his regular thoughts and the emotional region of his brain, which Adrien had successfully unblocked with a simple yet highly skilled procedure, which had to be carried out over five dayons.

***

She lay in the medical bunk, sleeping peacefully. The medical overseer over her bunk monitored her vital signs. Phean Leavy sat by her side with Twedor. It was Phean's turn to sit with Tayce. He was trying to reach her with his mind and trying to bring her gently back to the present. But it was like reading through fog. Tayce had been in a deep unreachable sleep state for well over two weekons, since she'd been shot by Saron's Catronic weapon in her father's chambers. The drug Dr Carthean had administered had reacted badly. Fair enough, it had stopped Tayce from dying in an hourons time from the injury. But it had sent her spiralling into a deep seemingly irretrievable unconscious state, where she'd remained. Emperor Honitonia had visited her to try and help bring her back to reality, but even his great powers couldn't revive her, which, considering his higher state of power ability, left him totally baffled and concerned. Dr Carthean took a blood sample from Tayce and met with the head of the team that had made the original antidote, to find an alternative to counteract what had happened to a certain degree, to bring Tayce out of her sedated state. A new drug had been found using Tayce's sample and this had been administered eleven hourons previously. All anyone could do now was wait and hope.

Tayce's present state was a great source of stress for everyone around her, including Dairan, Marc, the other team members, and her mother and father, owing to the fact that they all cared for her. Dr Carthean was almost at her medical wits' end to think of what to try next for the best. Twedor stood watching the still and sleeping Tayce, going through past memories of happier times. He hoped they would have many more.

Without warning the overseer above Tayce's head began to sound the alarm. Phean jumped to his feet from sitting near her, alerted by the sound. He was about to head off and get Dr Carthean when she entered the room with Dairan not far behind. They'd both heard the alarm whilst talking outside.

"What's going on, Doc? What's this mean? Is she coming back to us?" asked Dairan in urgency.

"Yes, that's just what it means – and not before time," replied Elspeth, looking at the overseer and keying commands into the keypad she'd picked up, making sure there wasn't a malfunction in the equipment and it was reading true.

Phean moved out of the way so Dairan could come near to Tayce's side. He sat down on the nearby bunk stool and took hold of Tayce's delicate hand, stroking the back gently. He looked at her silently almost pleading for her to come back to him.

To everyone's relief, Tayce's eyelids began to open and she began blinking to focus on the sterile surroundings. Dr Carthean looked down at Tayce with caring eyes and a gentle smile of relief, pleased that it looked like everything was going to be fine.

"You're going to be fine," she assured Tayce.

"How long have I been here?" asked Tayce groggily.

"Since your injury over two weekons ago. You've been unconscious this long. We've all been worried – can't say we haven't," replied Elspeth.

"Good to have you back," said Dairan softly at her side.

"Dairan! You're all right, thank goodness!" said Tayce, much relieved.

"I'm fine, thanks to Professor Maylen and Donaldo," he assured her, looking at her lovingly.

"According to my readings, you're back to normal. The antidote worked. I'm going to suggest that Dr Tysonne have some stored on Auran Amalthea Three incase this should happen again," announced Elspeth Carthean.

"Good idea," said Dairan, realising so.

"I'll check in on you at first light. If you're still fine, which I have no doubt you will be, I may discharge you," replied Elspeth, heading back to the entrance to leave.

"I will leave you two. Good to have you back. See you tomorron?" said Phean, following on behind the Doctor.

"Sure. Thanks for sitting with Tayce, Phean," said Dairan in appreciative tone.

"You're welcome. See you at first light," replied Phean, continuing on out through the entrance.

Phean walked from the Medical Stay Room, following Dr Elspeth Carthean along the corridor, talking with her as they went. When the door closed Tayce sat up. Dairan stood wondering what she was going to do. She pushed back the coverlet and slid to her feet, proceeding to get out of the bunk. He stood ready to catch her if she dropped, as the drug was no doubt still leaving her system. She stood and began walking to the sight pane that looked out over E City. Dairan walked cautiously behind, waiting to catch her should she fall. Twedor watched her saunter over in her long grey silkene chemise. She was doing great so far, he thought, considering she'd been in the bunk for over two weekons solid. She rested on the sill. Dairan paused by her side. She looked at him, admiring his handsome warm features, glad to be seeing them. She thought Aemiliyana had stolen him forever. He fully turned and gently took hold of her, bringing her into a gentle reassuring hold against his warm chest.

"Do you remember anything about being on Aemiliyana's fortress?" asked Tayce softly.

"Only up to when she ordered her men to take me away to some sort of Obligation Chamber. After that nothing, though Marc and Phean have told me some of what happened since. You were brave going after Vargon's clone like you did," said Dairan in soft reply.

"Bravery wasn't in it. I had help from Twedor, and my father was in extreme danger. I had to get to him and help stop what was going to happen. Oh, have you heard how Adam is doing? He was injured at the same time as me," said Tayce, slightly pulling away, looking up at his brown eyes.

"Fully recovered. Your father said he'll be back on duty in a matter of dayons."

"That's good. Father would feel useless without him."

Dairan tried not to yawn – it had been a busy dayon. Tayce suggested he head back to the cruiser. They could talk first light. He agreed as he could hardly keep his eyes open. He'd been helping her father with Marc in the absence of Adam.

It had been decided Marc would return to Auran Amalthea Three and he could be available to visit her after assisting her father in Marc's place. He gave her a warm hug and then, as she looked up, he kissed her gently full on the lips for a moment, then let her go. He guided her back to her bunk. He then announced that he'd leave Twedor with her until the mornet. With this, he walked from the room.

The door opened and closed, then opened again in quick succession, and to her surprise it was her father. He was glad to see she was getting back to normal.

"Nice to have you back with us. You gave us quite a scare, you know – but thank you," he said, sitting on her bunk, giving her a warm fatherly hug.

"How's Mother? Is she all right? I thought she would come with you?" said Tayce, glancing over to the door.

"She's fine. She's finishing up an urgent meeting about stopping the use of the Catronic weapon and forming a task team to track it down at its source and destroy it. She'll see you at first light," he promised.

"Do you think Vargon's gone for good this time?" asked Tayce, looking at her father questioningly.

"With him it's hard to tell. I would like to think so, but I really don't know," replied Darius in wondering thought.

"So you think he's back at large again, then. God, why can't he give up this pathetic game?"

"I think it's time we drop this. We have all the necessary power to handle him if there's another strike."

"Unless he uses another Saron, Father. If he's alive, he has to be stopped now, before he gets another clone lookalike or whatever to come after you and this base. The next time I might not be able to get back here in time to assist and stop you or Mother from being killed. I don't want him to win and you both to be wiped out," she said, moving to hug him.

"You've no worries on that one. I'll see you tomorron. Now, I know you've been sleeping a long time, but I'd make the most of this time as you'll be back out cruising in no time and you'll wish you took this time to rest," said Darius softly.

"All right," replied Tayce, relaxing back on the bunk.

Darius ordered Twedor to look after Tayce, then walked over to the entrance and off out of the room, letting the door close behind him. Tayce sat in thought for a moment, now resting back against the pillets. She wanted to know if Varon Vargon really had escaped.

"Twedor, I'll be OK now. I want you to head back to Auran and fetch me my Porto Compute. If any of the team see you, just say you're getting a clean uniform for me, for first light. Don't trust any strangers en route – we don't want you disappearing. Understand?"

"I don't like crossing the square at this time of night, with the many after-hourons travellers, etc., worse for wear," he said, not moving.

"You'll be fine. Just stay on alert and make a run for it when it's clear," suggested Tayce, looking down at him.

"Very well. I don't know how long this is going to take," he said, not really wanting to go.

"While you're at it, find my replacement Wristlink. You can put it in my Port Compute case," replied Tayce.

"What if Dairan sees me?" asked Twedor.

"You'll think of something. Now go!" ordered Tayce. She knew he would do what she asked.

Twedor turned and reluctantly walked across the room to the entrance, turning over in his little plasmatronic thoughts what he would do in order to get what he wanted for his mistress. He walked out through the automatically opening door into the corridor. Tayce watched him go and wished she could have done the job herself, but she still had the medical alert disk attached, still taking her system readings, which were returning to normal. If she left the room the alarm would sound and all hell would break loose. She had to admit she too didn't like him crossing E City Square either, especially after hourons, but there was no choice. Now all she could do was wait and hope he would be all right.

***

Twedor walked down the corridor past the night medical staff heading on out into the main arrival area. Some staff that knew he was Auran Amalthea Three's Romid just glanced, then went back to what they were doing at that moment. He walked out through the main entrance and hurried through E City to the Docking Port Area, where Auran Amalthea Three was docked. He took a look ahead and, when it was clear, broke into a sprint, sidestepping quite a few awkward situations and avoiding beings who suddenly appeared from places where loud celebrations were in progress. He ran until he'd made it to the walkway up to the cruiser. But someone was watching him – not in the desire to possess him, but concerned he would be OK. This watchful eye was that of Chief Jan Barnford. He was stood checking the smooth emergence of patrons from one of the bars that had proven rowdy in the last hourons. He had had reports that the nightlife was slowly becoming out of control. He figured he'd hang around for a while just in case Twedor returned, as he knew how important he was to Tayce.

***

On Auran Amalthea Amal had let Twedor on board and closed the Docking-Bay doors behind him. The little Romid headed along Level 2 to the Level Steps. He was trying to work out how he was going to get the three things Tayce wanted without being caught: her replacement Wristlink, her Porto Compute and a clean uniform from her quarters. Without anyone seeing him, he walked down the Level Steps on to Level 3 and passed the doors to the team's quarters. To his relief, there wasn't anyone coming or going. He wondered if Dairan would be in the quarters or in Organisation. It would be great, he thought, if he could get what he wanted undisturbed. As he approached Tayce's doors, they drew open, picking up his presence. He activated his night vision and looked around as he quietly stepped inside into the darkness. First he checked to see if Dairan was present and in deep sleep, which he was – and he generally slept like a brick, so he wouldn't be disturbed unless a considerable noise was made.

Twedor continued on, firstly to get the Porto Compute case. He found it, keeping one eye on a sleeping Dairan, trying not to make a noise. He took it from the third storage shelf and crossed, setting it down on the soffette. Luckily for him, Tayce's Porto Compute was on the central small table. Twedor slowly and quietly opened the lid. It unfortunately made a click sound. He paused, waiting, looking in the direction of Dairan, hoping he wouldn't wake and make a sudden appearance. Nothing. He was safe. He continued on, pushing back the lid, then lifted the Porto Compute and placed it down inside. He was pleased that the first item his mistress wanted was ready to go. He proceeded to fetch the clean uniform, which he knew would require him to open a cupboard door, which opened with a push of the panel. All the time he was undertaking the task he had one eye on Dairan, but nothing happened. The only one that was silently watching him was Amal. He returned to the case and set inside the replacement Wristlink and folded clean uniform, which he'd found in the same place. He closed the case, making sure all the contents were safely inside. He picked it up, applying just the right amount of pressure so it quietly rose from the soffette and didn't drop to the floor with a bang, and so he could carry it by the handle like a normal person. Once he was ready, he glanced back in the direction of the Repose Centre, thinking, 'Mission accomplished.'

It was time to head back. He headed for the quarters' entrance doors. They drew apart in front of him. He walked through, off down the corridor under the continuing watchful eye of Amal. Soon he was back outside and heading across E City Square. As he paused to check the area ahead was clear, so he heard footsteps approaching from behind. He'd picked up that they belonged to a security officer of some rank. he couldn't tell who, but he knew he was being followed.

"Oh damn! I've been rumbled – now I'm going to hear it," said Twedor under his breath.

"Twedor, what are you doing out here in the middle of the night?" asked the familiar voice of Jan Barnford.

Twedor stayed silent. He wasn't going to incriminate himself. He was disappointed to think he hadn't managed to get to Auran Amalthea Three and back to Tayce without being spotted. He turned and looked up, noticing the questioning look on Jan's features. He figured he had to come clean – that way he would at least be escorted safely the rest of the way back to Tayce.

"Tayce asked me to get some things from the cruiser. Is there a problem?" asked Twedor, wondering if he'd done something wrong.

"No – no problem. It's just not safe for you out here at this time of night. I'll walk you back. Tayce should have known better than to let you out here at 03:00 in the mornet. Even though security is still tight, you never know if some traveller and untoward person is hanging around to take you and sell you on. Let's go," said Jan.

Jan placed his hand on Twedor's small shoulder and took the case from him. Together the Romid and the security chief walked the rest of the way on across the square, in the direction of the Medical Dome.

***

Tayce sat thinking, turning over different thoughts in her mind. One in particular seemed to be nagging at her even though her father had suggested she let it drop: was Vargon alive somewhere, planning his next attempt? The door to the room opened. Twedor walked in empty-handed, Tayce looked at him, somewhat surprised, wondering why he hadn't got what she'd sent him for. Then Jan Barnford walked in behind him carrying what Twedor had been sent for, much to her relief. Tayce glanced out through the sight pane, thinking that of all the people Twedor had to run into, it had to be him. Now she was in for a lecture.

"Tayce! Firstly, welcome back to reality; secondly, do you think it was wise sending Twedor after whatever is in this case at this time of the night? It's not like he's going down a Level corridor on Auran. You know what some after-houron travellers through this base are like – he would have been the booty of the century if he was taken," said Jan, displeased with her irresponsibility.

"Finished? I can see your point, but I need what's in that case as I'm looking into something that needs immediate attention."

"Couldn't it have waited until first light? You should be resting, considering what you went through. That was one tough mission," he said, sauntering over to the sight port and turning upon reaching it.

"I've been lying in this medical bunk for over two weekons. I'm far from needing any more sleep or rest," replied Tayce plainly.

"So what's so important Twedor had to risk being stolen for it?" asked Jan.

"My Wristlink, Porto Compute and a clean uniform."

"Looking into something interesting? Want to share?" he asked, interested.

"Not at the moment. It's something I hope to draw to a finish soon, when I've done my research," replied Tayce, opening up the case he'd placed down on the bunk beside her.

"I'll leave you to it as I'm heading off duty. I've already been on after-hourons duty longer than I should have been – three hourons, to be exact," he confided, glancing at his Wristcall time display.

"OK, see you at first light if I turn up anything interesting," replied Tayce, already beginning to key instructions into her Porto Compute, concentrating on what she was hoping to find.

"Goodnight, Jan," said Jan in mockery, seeing her watching the screen in front of her with interest.

"Goodnight, Jan," replied Tayce, not taking her eyes from the screen.

He laughed and walked from the room, shaking his head as the door opened and closed behind him, amused.

Tayce waited until he'd gone, then took out her Wristlink and placed it on her wrist. Twedor took away the case and set it on the far chair. Tayce depressed the Comceive on her Wristlink and began talking to Amal back aboard Auran Amalthea Three.

"Amal, this is Tayce. Download the Quest file involving Aemiliyana and Vargon, via Twedor. Play the scene of Vargon's possible escape from the fortress," commanded Tayce.

"Awaiting your command to commence, Tayce," replied Amal.

"Twedor, time to use that new computer link to Porto Compute," said Tayce.

Twedor moved to Tayce's side and held his thumb to the infrared port of the Porto Compute for immediate transfer pickup. Tayce gave the word to Amal. A pencil-thin beam of red light emitted from Twedor's thumb containing the information that would transfer into film to be played back at Tayce's request. She waited as the download occurred. When complete, Amal contacted Tayce on Wristlink, informing her that the information was successfully downloaded. Tayce ceased communication and began working on the Porto Compute. The scene unfolded of the unauthorised departure from the fortress. Tayce slowed the scene down with a few key commands until it was almost at a standstill. The film moved slowly, but became crystal-clear. Next, Tayce brought the small craft up to full magnification. As she studied it Twedor watched her and the scene on screen by her side. In the hourons that followed, going from darkness into artificial daylight, Tayce worked on the scene to discover if Varon Vargon had made it out alive.

***

Daylight filled the room and Tayce opened her eyes. She had drifted off with the Port Compute and her stored findings on her bunk a little before first light. The doors to her room opened and Dr Elspeth Carthean entered. She looked at Tayce, far from pleased that her patient had been working during the night hourons when she should have been sleeping, but she said nothing. Tayce was to be released as everything had returned to normality.

"Well, it would appear you're still feeling fine, which I'm glad to see. I just want to run the Examscan over you one last time. Working on anything interesting?" enquired Elspeth.

"Just a private project I wanted to complete," replied Tayce, waking up, not giving anything away.

"You're fine. According to this, your health level is back to normal and I can release you from my care," announced Elspeth, pleased.

"Good! Sorry – that wasn't meant how it sounded. I'm grateful for what you've done, it's just…"

"You take care. I know what it's like when you want to get back in command, and it's understandable. Stay away from Catronic weapons if you can," replied Elspeth with a smile.

She turned, walking in an elegant doctor's manner over to the entrance. Before leaving, she advised Tayce to ease back into duty. With this, she continued on out of the room, off to another patient. Tayce closed the Porto Compute and slid from the bunk. She retrieved the clean uniform and headed into the side Cleanse Unit, leaving Twedor to look after things until she returned ready to leave.

The first person into the Medical Stay Room was Lydia, as Tayce's father had promised the night before. She waited patiently for Tayce.

After she'd cleansed and put on her clean uniform, Tayce walked back into the room, putting her hair up in a clasp. Lydia turned to see her looking back to normal. Tayce began gathering up her Porto Compute and placing it in the case. Lydia looked at, her studying her. There was something on her mind – she could see it. She figured she wouldn't push it. Tayce would tell her when she was ready.

"I spoke to Dairan yesteron. Well, he came to see your father and me," began Lydia, waiting for Tayce's attention.

"Oh, why?" asked Tayce, looking up on closing the silver case.

"Well, to tell us the good news, that you and he are going to be joined together in an intimate joining ceremony," replied Lydia, happy at the thought.

"Oh, charming. He might have let me tell you first. did Father say anything?" asked Tayce, wishing Dairan had run it by her first.

"No, your father and I have noticed there's something growing between you two for a long time. Aren't you pleased to be joined again?" asked Lydia, a little concerned.

"Of course I am, but right now there are other matters that need my urgent attention and Dairan's proposal isn't one of them. I've wasted two weekons lying in deep sleep in that bunk and it's now time to sort those urgent matters out. They can't wait," replied Tayce, facing her mother.

"What matter is so urgent you can't put it aside for just a weekon more in preparation for your joining ceremony? Also you could have a little R & R with Dairan. It would do you good."

"I've been doing enough rest and relaxation in that bunk. No, Mother, there's too much to do in getting on with the Amalthean Quests voyage. You'll have to discuss intimate-joining ideas whilst I'm out in space. Come on, Twedor," said Tayce, picking up her silver case and heading towards the entrance.

"Tayce… can't Marc take care of this important matter and attend to duties on Auran just for a short while?" persisted Lydia, hoping Tayce would change her mind.

"Not what I have to do – no!" replied Tayce, not giving away what she wanted to take care of.

"Just hold on, young lady. What are you up to? You're hiding something," said Lydia, grabbing Tayce back by the upper arm, bringing her round to face her.

Tayce said nothing. She just looked at her mother's grip, then met her mother's questioning look. She had no intention of revealing what was on her mind: what she was going to do that was so urgent it couldn't wait. She pulled her arm free, saying that if there was nothing else, she wanted to go. Lydia knew better now Tayce was older to push her daughter for an answer if she didn't want to give one. Yearons ago back on Traun she could have demanded she tell her, but things had moved on a lot since then. All she could do was wait.

"There is just one more thing before you leave: I want you to attend a small gathering that the team are holding in the inner chambers in honour of you coming back to us. It's at 1850 hourons."

"All right – that's nice. I'll be there," replied Tayce, her mind still on the important matter ahead.

Both stepped out into the corridor. Twedor followed. Lydia was still wondering about Tayce's important matter she wasn't prepared to divulge. They all walked down the corridor to the Medical Dome entrance, where Tayce raised her Wristlink and contacted Marc, letting her mother go on to where she had to be next that dayon. As soon as Marc answered she requested he meet her in E City Square, by the fountain. He could be heard agreeing on the other end. Twedor looked up at her. He'd never known her to be quite so determined than she was now, over her conviction that Vargon had somehow eluded being blown to eternity. But he knew one thing: she had never been wrong in the past regarding the possible whereabouts of the evil man. He figured she was going to go it alone to find him.

Marc soon came into view. He walked towards her, dodging past people crossing before him en route. He looked at her, glad to see she was still very much his long-time friend and leader and a main part of the team's life.

"Welcome back. You're certainly looking better. It's good to see Vargon didn't win when his clone shot you, though we all had our moments of doubt about whether you'd pull through," said Marc, pleased.

"It's good to be back. I want to know everything that's been happening in the last two weekons. I also need you to take over command for a while," said Tayce to a surprised Marc.

"Sure, but where are you going to be that's stopping you from resuming command?" asked Marc, curious.

"Oh, I have something I need to take care of, so tell me what's been going on in my absence?"

"Anything I can help with? You know I always would try and help if I could," he said, a bit concerned.

"No, it's something I have to handle alone, but thanks anyway," replied Tayce casually.

"OK. Jamie has brought Auran's annual service forward, and it was completed yesteron. She's back to running at full capacity and ready to depart. The team, besides visiting you, have enjoyed a small break. Dairan has been assisting your father along with me in Adam's absence. That's it," he said casually.

"How is Adam?" asked Tayce, wondering.

"Doing fine. I hear he did ask after you when your father checked in on him yesteron."

"That's good. Look, I really want to get going. Would you take the Porto Compute back to Auran for me?" said Tayce, sounding as if she was really anxious to get going where she was proposing to go.

"I'll leave it in the DC for you."

Marc was curious, but didn't say anything about why she seemed to be agitated to get going to where this something she needed to take care of was.

"I'll see you later. Come on, Twedor, let's get this started," said Tayce, walking away.

Marc watched, a little worried about just what Tayce was attempting alone and why she wasn't telling him. But he knew Twedor would soon alert him if she got into any trouble doing what she didn't want him to find out. He took the silver-toned attaché case and headed back across E City Square to Auran Amalthea Three. Twedor, as he walked down at his mistress's side, couldn't understand why Tayce hadn't confided in Marc regarding her planned actions. What was she up to? She surely wasn't going to take care of the task ahead she wanted to finish once and for all, all on her own. It was dangerous, he thought. He knew he'd have to be on alert and stick by her, ready to come to her aid if it became apparent she was heading into danger during what she wanted to achieve. If it became too dangerous, even for him, he would contact Marc via Amal and get help.

Empress Tricara walked from the building where she taught gifted students and saw Tayce. She wanted to catch her urgently as Emperor Honitonia wanted to meet with her and speak urgently with her. Something made Tricara feel a feeling of powerful dread and it had something to do with what Tayce was thinking. She mind-transferred to Tayce. Suddenly Tayce paused whilst walking to where she was heading and turned, looking about. Then she caught sight of Tricara beckoning to her to go to her. Twedor looked up at her, wondering what she was going to do. Tayce figured she had better see what Tricara wanted, so as not to raise suspicion. Twedor followed. Upon reaching Tricara, Tayce picked up, using her abilities, that Emperor Honitonia was nearby.

"It's good to see you back with us. Dairan and your mother were really concerned," expressed Tricara.

"You wanted me? Is there a problem?" asked Tayce, ignoring what her long-time friend had said.

"Not here, but there's someone who has important information on something you're thinking of taking on and he wants to see you. You need to follow me. It's important that he sees you and so is the information he has to give you," said Tricara seriously.

"All right, let's go," agreed Tayce, thinking the sooner this was over the quicker she could continue with what she wanted to do.

"In here – this way," replied Tricara, heading back into the Schooling Centre.

Tayce ushered Twedor in first, then followed on behind, looking about as she entered the building. Soon they entered into the classroom and he walked into view from the shadows, glad to see she had returned to the Realm of life. She paused, waiting with interest and curiousness to hear what Emperor Honitonia had to say. He sauntered towards her, explaining that there had been proof found that Count Varon Vargon had escaped during the confrontation with Aemiliyana and was still at large. Since Vargon's escape from the fortress resources in the Realm of Honitonia had been tracking his escape route and he had gone up what was termed a Time-Shift Tunnel to a place called Alhenratt, a small deserted colony which was man-made and half completed. It had been deserted for a few yearons for reasons unknown.

"I knew he had escaped. If you knew all this why didn't you come and tell me last night, when I spent time doing research on my Porto Compute that could have been avoided? Another thing: why didn't the Empire step in an apprehend him?" asked Tayce seriously.

"You know in this matter we cannot interfere. He is human and not of the Realm, unlike Aemiliyana," said the Emperor calmly.

"So your people have gathered all this information for me, solely, to act on – is that right?" asked Tayce.

"Yes, Tayce Amanda. Put an end to this being Vargon once and for all. He cannot be allowed to cause any further danger in anyone's life ever again. The task ahead is yours. Use your abilities wisely – we will be watching," said the Emperor with a slight reassuring look.

"Thank you for this and thank your people too," replied Tayce, eager to get going on the information he'd given her.

"Be careful," said Emperor Honitonia.

"See you soon, both of you," replied Tayce, hurrying back to the classroom entrance, back out of the building, to go and continue where she was heading with Twedor in tow.

Both Empress Tricara and Emperor Honitonia exchanged concerned glances, hoping Tayce was going to survive what she had to do. It was extremely dangerous.

Tricara sighed. She hoped Tayce would come back. Tayce hadn't said anything about taking the team, and Tricara picked up on this whilst reading her young friend's mind: the idea of taking the team wasn't even in her thoughts.

Emperor Honitonia vanished in his usual way back to the Realm of Honitonia, leaving Tricara standing watching through the sight pane in thought as Tayce and Twedor hurried on across the square.

***

Tayce ran unavoidably straight into Marc and Dairan – something she didn't want. Marc caught hold of her, steadying her. She looked somewhat awkwardly at them. This was not a good moment, she thought to herself. She didn't want them involved in the plan she had. If they knew, they would try and stop her. Marc studied her as she began speaking.

"What a coincidence meeting you both here like this! I'll catch you later – I'm right in the middle of that matter we discussed earlier. I'll be back shortly," said Tayce without a further word, hoping it sounded convincing.

Twedor wanted to say something, but he knew Tayce would reprimand him if he did, so he kept quiet and figured he'd see what was going to unfold before he did summon help. Marc let Tayce go where she was heading, watching her walk away. There was something going on, but he couldn't put his finger on it. Dairan found her also a bit off in that she didn't ask either himself or Marc to help with what she was doing. Marc turned discreetly to Dairan and suggested that from that moment to departure, and maybe afterwards, they should keep on alert. If something arose, then he'd take charge of the situation quickly and he could take over the team if need be. Dairan nodded in agreement, wondering what might unfold with Tayce.

"Just be ready to take command when I say," said Marc, to the point, in a whisper.

"OK, you've got it. You're suspicious, aren't you?" asked Dairan, seeing as much.

"I can't explain what it is at the moment, but I've got a hunch regarding her secrecy over what she's up to. She isn't letting us fit in and I don't like it," replied Marc, uneasy.

"I share your concern about the way she's shutting us out and acting."

"I think she knows that if we knew what it was she was attempting she'd tell us where to go. This is what I'd term a solo Quest, whether we like or not. All we can do, like I said, is be ready. Look, I'm going to try and follow her. I don't like what I'm feeling right now. Can you take command until this is sorted?" asked Marc, watching the square and Tayce heading away in the distance.

"Yeah. Be careful – you're a good mate," replied Dairan.

"I'll call you on Wristlink," assured Marc, beginning to walk away with the notion of keeping a discreet distance from Tayce, so Twedor wouldn't pick up that they we're being followed by him.

Marc could see Tayce was heading back, surprisingly to the cruiser and it puzzled him, but he followed just the same. He thought she would have gone and hired a small craft, if she was heading off the base for whatever she had in mind. Maybe he was wrong. Maybe she intended to go on Auran Amalthea Three. What was so important that she wanted to do herself? Dairan in the meantime stood watching the whole scene unfold of Marc following Tayce, wondering about her strange actions and why she was being so secretive, considering they were to be legally joined soon. Something just wasn't right, he thought.

***

Tayce walked on board the cruiser and immediately ordered Twedor to do a cruiser-wide sweep to see if any of the team were on board yet. He immediately did as requested, and a few minons later he came back announcing, "All clear." No one had returned from what they were doing on base. With this Tayce continued, under the watchful Vid Cam view of Amal, on up the Level 2 corridor towards the Level Steps. As she hadn't closed the Docking-Bay doors, Amal took care of it and closed them.

Not long afterwards they opened again and Marc boarded. Raising his Wristlink, he ordered Amal that under no circumstance was she to divulge to Tayce that he was back aboard, but he wanted to be informed of any departure by Tayce. He'd be in his quarters.

"Yes, Commander," replied Amal.

"Good girl, Amal. This is an operation that is only for me. I need to know what Tayce is up to. Understood?" asked Marc discreetly.

"Discretion mode, Commander?" asked Amal.

"You've got it," replied Marc, hearing Twedor near the top of the Level Steps.

Marc was still unsure of what Tayce was attempting, but it looked like she was doing a good job in covering her tracks. Amal had informed him earlier that she'd checked on whether anyone was on board, like Tayce didn't want to run into anyone for a reason and she wanted sole control.

***

The time was 18:45. A small gathering of the Amalthean Quests team minus Tayce and Dairan were awaiting her arrival in the inner room of Lydia and Darius Traun's chambers. Drinks were being served and food was spread in a buffet fashion on the table by the wall for the team to help themselves. Lydia glanced at her Wristcall time display, growing concerned. Tayce was certainly cutting it fine for her recovery party. Lydia had made her aware earlier what time she had to be present. She sighed and glanced around the chambers and realised that there was no Dairan or Marc either. Why were they late? she wondered. Suddenly a bad feeling washed over her in a shudder. Lydia was far from pleased at her daughter's poor timekeeping, considering the party was something the team had wanted to do for her as a good gesture to welcome her back to full health.

"Well, I don't know where Tayce is. All I can do is apologise for her lateness," expressed Lydia to the team present.

On this, the doors opened to the chambers. Dairan sauntered in, not knowing how to break the news he had to say. Marc had contacted him in a purchase centre via Wristlink and informed him that what they were uneasy about regarding Tayce was under way and the cruiser was in departure mode. He was now in command of the team at short notice and the voyage break was now extended. The doors to the chambers opened again behind Dairan, and Darius almost walked into the back of him. Dairan turned, meeting his furious look.

"You're all still here. Would someone explain why I've just seen Auran leaving this base twenty minons ago? I thought I'd missed this," said Darius, glancing around at the puzzled faces of the team present.

"Actually, sir, I can explain. Can we talk somewhere private?" asked Dairan as the team looked on.

"My chamber's across here," said Darius, leading the way.

Treketa crossed to be with Lydia as she could see she was showing signs of great concern. Everyone on the team present were speechless as to what was happening. It didn't make any sense. Phean was the only one that knew what was unfolding with Tayce. She had informed him of her plan and had asked him to keep quiet until the situation became unavoidable. The chamber's doors closed behind Darius and Dairan as they entered.

Lydia shook her head, thinking, 'Now what had Tayce decided to take on single-handedly? One dayon her luck for doing something daring at short notice was going to run out.'

The team were at a loss of what to say or do.

***

Inside the chamber that Dairan and Darius had entered earlier, Darius walked over to the sight pane in a way that showed he was far from calm. After a few minons he turned.

"All right – not that I'm surprised – where has she gone?" said Darius, giving his full attention to Dairan.

"Marc called me on Wristlink a while ago. He's on board Auran and he said Tayce has taken the cruiser for important business that she wants to take care of herself. That's all I know," replied Dairan.

Darius sighed, thinking back to the conversation he and Tayce had had in the Medical Stay Room about Varon Vargon. He could only put two and two together and assume the nature of the so-called business was Tayce putting an end to the barbarous being once and for all, which he considered downright stupid. She didn't know what Vargon would have lying in wait for her when she arrived. He was glad in a way that Marc was aboard to make sure she didn't get herself killed.

"Marc has put forward that, as the end of the voyage isn't far off, the team could take an extended break until the next voyage or at least until this is sorted," said Dairan casually.

"Good idea. I guess all we can do is wait to hear from Marc," said Darius, far from pleased at his daughter's decision to put herself deliberately in danger without the team's assistance.

Both men headed across the chamber and back out into the awaiting gathered team. Darius would explain what was to happen whilst Auran Amalthea Three was away.

***

Auran Amalthea Three was en route to what Tayce considered the last important Quest of the yearon's voyage before she began the preparations to marry again – this time to Dairan Loring – and went for the voyage break. She sat in the navigation seat in Organisation, generally occupied by Kelly Travern. In less than an houron she would rendezvous with the Time-Shift Tunnel, which would take her to the supposed whereabouts of Varon Vargon for the last time. Twedor stood casually watching everything unfold as the journey progressed across the vastness of space. Tayce was already studying the Quest information, including the overall plan of Alhenratt, pronounced Al-hen-ratt. She was studying it to find the quickest route.

"Captain, Prince Tieman of the Charan Empire has granted you permission to travel through the Time-Shift Tunnel and wishes you good luck in your attempted personal goal," said Amal.

In through Organisation he walked. Tayce spun in her chair, her eyes wide in alert. Twedor was glad to see him – this meant he was going to assist his mistress, whether she liked it or not.

"You know this would have been better with the team, and right now I should imagine they are feeling sore at you for leaving them behind," said Marc, standing at ease.

"How did you get on board? Twedor, you said there was no one else here. You're wasting your time if you think you're going to stop me. If you do, I may not be held responsible for my actions," said Tayce, displeased, rising to her feet now that Marc was present.

"About to enter the Time-Shift Tunnel in ten, nine, eight, seven, six, five, four, three, two, one," announced Amal.

"What's this all about? Why are you trying to go it alone?" demanded Marc.

"If I tell you I have the solution to a long-term evil problem you have to swear that you won't interfere with what I have planned? Or, to achieve my aim, I will have you rendered useless," she replied plainly.

"All right – go on," he said, listening, but far from pleased.

"When I woke in the Medical Dome I had a strong feeling Vargon had escaped and was holding out somewhere licking his wounds. I had Twedor fetch me my Porto Compute and played the last moments on the fortress to find out if what I was strongly feeling was true. I found a small craft of great propulsion had left the fortress, as one of Jan's men confirmed. Something told me I had to pursue this, to put an end to Vargon before he has time to get another attack wave together," explained Tayce.

"Your father is going to think you've gone crazy, and I have to agree with him. So how did you find out where he is?" asked Marc, to the point.

"I'm getting to that. I was heading across E City Square when Tricara summoned me via mind transference. I turned and she beckoned. I walked over, thinking something was wrong. She told me Emperor Honitonia was in the school for gifted students and he had important information. To cut a long story short, he informed me that people in the Realm of Honitonia had information for me to act on: that Vargon was up the Time-Shift Tunnel on a man-made colony called Alhenratt. Hence it is up to me to go and stop him once and for all, so here I am," explained Tayce.

"But why not take the team? Why leave them out of this?" asked Marc.

"Because of the weapon Vargon has in his possession. It's bad enough me being shot by it; I don't want to put any of the team in a position of near and probable death just because I am doing what I'm doing. Actually I would have been a lot happier if you'd remained behind, like the others, on Enlopedia, instead of listening to your ego and deciding to put yourself in the line of danger. No offence."

"None taken. I'm still staying in case he has escaped. Remember, I have memories of what that bastard did to my life, that fateful night on our home world. Nothing would give me greater pleasure than to see the end of him," expressed Marc in thought.

"I understand," suggested Tayce, trying to sound fair.

Marc turned and walked to come and look in silent thought at the multicoloured journey up the Time-Shift Tunnel. He paused just a bit, angered still that Tayce couldn't see the danger she was putting herself in. He could see her point about not taking the team because they'd probably be killed. It was fair enough. He figured it wasn't going to be any different for himself and Tayce. They were deliberately going into danger, and he knew if they weren't careful they could both wind up dead. He glanced over his shoulder at her, busily seated back at the navigations console. He knew though that he couldn't let her down. He couldn't let her take this Quest on alone, no matter what the cost. He thought too much of her for that. He sighed, then headed away to get some refreshment as he figured she hadn't eaten since leaving Enlopedia. Tayce and Twedor watched him go from Organisation. Tayce wished he could see what she was attempting from her point of view.

"Time-Shift Tunnel has been achieved," announced Amal.

"Thank you, Amal. Keep us safe during transit," said Tayce, going back to the screen she was studying.

They were now heading 5,000 yearons into the future at hyper-thrust turbo speed. Alhenratt was ahead, and hopefully the end for Varon Vargon once and for all. Tayce turned to find Twedor down at her side.

"You were a bit tough on him, weren't you? He only wants to look out for you. He's here to make sure he returns to Enlopedia with you – you of all people know how your father would react if he didn't protect you and returned without you," said Twedor like he was telling her off in his own little way.

"I know I want him to be part of this, but he won't give me a sign that he agrees with what I'm doing. I'm not just doing this for me; I'm doing it for him and the people that lost their lives that fateful night. I know what I'm doing – that's why I'm doing all this studying before we get to Alhenratt," pointed out Tayce.

"Just thought I'd say what I was seeing, that's all," replied Twedor, realising he'd been told off too.

"Point taken," replied Tayce, calming her voice, continuing on with her studies.

"Let him help a bit. I want to see both of you and this cruiser return to Enlopedia," replied Twedor.

"I need to call up the blueprint on Alhenratt," replied Tayce, getting back to the studying.

"Tayce, Prince Tieman has urgent information for you," announced Amal. "Do you wish me open the link?"

"Yes, Amal. Activate main Sight Screen," ordered Tayce.

Tayce turned her attention to the main Sight Screen just as Marc walked back in with liquid refreshment and a small dish of purple snacks. They were boost snacks, which perk up the energy levels of those who eat them.

The Sight Screen flashed into life and Prince Tieman appeared. He hadn't aged a dayon in appearance since Tayce and the team had encountered him in the second voyage. It was miraculous how his whole body chemistry worked – young on the outside, despite his age, and continually replaced on the inside. Marc, having placed the tray on the nearby console top, glanced at the Prince, shaking his head in disbelief at the unchanged appearance of brown hair, the darkest of brown eyes and young looks.

"Captain, I have information on Alhenratt. The colony, as you are aware, is man-made. It's half completed. All main functions are operable, should they be needed, but extreme caution should be taken. The power system is unstable," explained the Prince.

"That's all we need. Sorry, Your Highness," said Marc in an outburst, sighing and looking away.

"Apology not needed, Commander. Like I've said, take extreme caution and good luck, both of you, in whatever you're attempting to undertake," said Prince Tieman, ceasing communications.

The screen message finished. Marc looked at Tayce, far from amused, considering the latest information on the destination of this personal Quest was somewhat concerning. The Sight Screen went blank.

"Alhenratt is now in orbital view ahead," announced Amal.

"Amal, put it on main Sight Screen. Let's see it," ordered Tayce.

Marc looked at the half-constructed triangular-shaped space colony hanging suspended in the new clearness of the time period 5,000 yearons from the original home space. He stood shaking his head. This was not going to be easy. Tayce glanced at him. She was beginning to see the same thing too, but there was a job to do and that's what she was there to do, with or without him. She flipped.

"Enough of this attitude! We came here to do a job – or I did anyway. If you're not happy about this whole Quest, even though I would like to include you, you can remain on board," snapped Tayce, feeling fed up.

"Oh, you're damn right I'm not happy! Why are you thinking of attempting this Quest to get rid of Vargon on a half-completed colony? God knows what dangers are over there besides that evil bastard. This is totally stupid, Tayce, and you know it," replied Marc, alarmed and worried.

"I came here to do this one thing, though in your eyes it might be stupid. I knew it wasn't going to be easy – that's why I've been researching, because of the possibility that Alhenratt wasn't the ideal environment – so if you don't want to drop this act of trying to protect me when I know what I'm facing, I hereby order you to your quarters until you can see my point of view in what has to be done. If you do come to your senses you know where to find me," said Tayce, much to Twedor's surprise.

"Fine! Get yourself killed, but let me tell you this: I'm not telling your father it was an accident. I'm going to tell him you ignored all the warning signs to forget the whole thing and did your usual irresponsible act. I'll tell him that's what got you killed," he almost shouted at her.

"Fine! Do what you have to," blurted out Tayce.

She felt so angry. What was suddenly wrong with him? Why wasn't he seeing sense – that ridding the Universe of the man who'd caused death and destruction to their people was necessary and it was in his best interest to help her? she wondered. Or was he just worried he was going to lose her?

Twedor felt he wanted to shout, "Time out!" He looked at Tayce. He'd seen this act between her and Marc many times before. There was Tayce, wanting the

Quest to succeed; then there was Marc, with yearons' experience, seeing only that the whole situation to finish Count Varon Vargon off once and for all on a half-completed colony was downright risky. She could die. Silence filled the air for a few minons. Tayce looked at the refreshment tray on the console top. Marc walked out without a further word, not looking back. He felt he had to cool down or he'd explode and say something regrettable.

"Marc brought it in for you!" exclaimed Twedor, breaking the awkward silence that was filling the air.

"Why can't he see what I'm doing? What's he suddenly scared of? He knows what happened on Traun that night and that it had repercussions for him too," said Tayce.

"He does, but he's worried you'll get killed and he'll have to tell your father. He doesn't want to stop you; he just wishes there was a lot safer way to do want you intend," replied Twedor, seeing Marc's point of view.

"Well, there isn't. Amal, put us under Invis Shield and take us in to dock with Alhenratt," commanded Tayce.

"Preparing to dock, Tayce," replied Amal.

Tayce ate the snacks and drank down some of the refreshing drink. She then placed Amal in command and walked from Organisation to head off and get changed into combat attire for the environment she was about to face. Twedor walked down at her side, wondering if Marc, once he'd calmed down, would join her before she left the cruiser for the corridors of Alhenratt, in search of Vargon.

***

On board the half-constructed triangular-shaped Alhenratt colony Varon Vargon, once the great leader of the Count Varon Vargon Warrior Army and most renowned lawbreaker of all time, sat in a lazy lull in a chair he'd found. He was injured and trying to treat himself with provisions from the portable medical kit off the craft that had brought him to his present surroundings from the fortress. He grimaced every time he administered a painkilling liquid into his system using a Comprai Inject Pen. It was the third time in a matter of hourons that he'd given himself the strongest dose. He was bleeding uncontrollably, and blood was now plainly visible at the top right-hand side of his uniform top. His face was ashen-looking, as if he was near to death. His surroundings were sparse, half fitted and deserted. Lighting and air support were in operation, but the air quality was very thin, which didn't help his situation. There seemed to be only half the ceiling fitted. Construction tools were just left where they had been discarded by the construction crew in a sudden hurry. Slowly the pain-suspending drug began easing his immense pain and he could feel more normal for a few hourons more. Strangely, and out of character, he began thinking about all he had done in his life. Had he achieved what he wanted? Not quite. The one obstacle in his way had been present since his first crusading dayons without Carra, his legal intimate joining partner and Sallen's mother: the Trauns, especially Tayce Amanda.

"Damn and curse you, girl," he said, making a great effort to speak.

The air was silent, cold and deathly – almost perfect for death. He checked the Catronic weapon in his grasp at his side. It would be so easy just to take his own life. He was bleeding badly. Had time simply run out for him? He'd noticed how his breathing was getting more and more hard to achieve. Death certainly was calling his name. When he came to think about it, he knew he had nothing left, nothing to lose. His army were no more. Carra was no more. Sallen, his once promising daughter, no longer recognised him. He would be quite happy to just go, he thought.

***

Roughly an houron later on board the cruiser, Tayce came from her quarters dressed in combat attire. She didn't pause. She walked off down the Level 3 corridor with Twedor by her side to the Level Steps. Her main aim was to begin the Quest with or without the help of Marc, and rid the Universe of Count Vargon after all the yearons he and Carra had carried out the endless evilness they had. In a way she realised this had been her aim right from the beginning of the Amalthean Quests voyages: to make the Vargons pay for what they had done to the people of her home world and Marc's wife, Pamera. This was why she couldn't understand why Marc seemed so reluctant to help in making Varon Vargon meet his final end. She walked up the Level Steps, heading on to Level 2, Twedor, just behind her, following on in silent thought. Amal, overhead, announced that safe docking and orbital distance under Invis Shield had been achieved. Tayce, on this, walked along Level 2 towards the Docking-Bay doors.

He came into view unexpectedly, standing at ease in combat attire, checking his Pollomoss handgun, much to Tayce's delight. He looked up on her approach and they exchanged looks for a few minons. He held out the silver-toned Power Arrow Launcher, handing it to her, loaded.

"I wondered if this would be more useful," he announced casually.

"You've decided to come with me, then?" she enquired calmly.

"Yes. Look I was wrong earlier. You're right – we have to do this," replied Marc.

"I did some research to find out whether Vargon is actually on board, and he's there all right, but injured. I would have been surprised if you hadn't changed your mind, considering what his men put Pamera through on our departure night."

"Please, Tayce, don't talk about it. It still smarts, even after all these yearons. Believe me, it took me quite a while to come to terms with the fact that she was gone when I went back for her and I wouldn't see her again. Many times I've had to restrain myself from taking the chance to put an end to his galactic backside, I can tell you."

"I know," said Tayce, understanding.

Both hugged for a moment, each forgiving the other for the outburst earlier. After a few minons they both released each other. Tayce announced that she had a weapon that was better suited for the likes of Vargon. She, as Marc wondered what she was doing, reached into the nearby wall cabinet, to where she'd had Amal Transpot it from the gun certification unit on Enlopedia. Marc raised his eyes in surprise at the sight of the very weapon that had injured her, the Catronic weapon, wondering just what would happen if the unit found it missing.

"This is the ideal weapon to destroy Count Vargon once and for all. It would be like giving him a taste of his own medicine. He'll die an agonising death, just like Pamera and my friends did," expressed Tayce, not knowing that Vargon was already close to death.

She walked towards the Docking-Bay doors. Twedor activated his Slazer finger and Marc checked his Pollomoss handgun. Once ready, Amal opened the Docking-Bay doors on Tayce's request to do so, via Wristlink. The doors drew open and all three Amalthean Quests team members walked forth into the near darkness of the half-completed colony.

***

One thing that was operational on Alhenratt was the computer. Vargon, despite his pain, upon arrival rigged a module to provide a continuous scan to give him warning if anyone arrived in his current surroundings. Suddenly, for a split cencron, the computer alerted him to the fact that there was a vessel in Docking Port 3, then it went back to normal scan.

Varon staggered to his feet. With every ounce of strength he could muster, he sauntered over to one of the hexagonal sight ports running round the vast area of his immediate vicinity. Like everything else, it needed completing. At present there was a force field protecting him from being sucked into space. He paused, looking out into the near darkness of the vastness of space. Nothing but stars as far as the eye could see. Was it a computer glitch? he wondered. Had he over anticipated, thinking he would be safe in his present surroundings after the unstable journey up the Time-Shift Tunnel to his present orbit? Was there someone on board and a vessel he couldn't see in the vicinity?

***

Marc and Tayce walked up a half-completed corridor with white walls and blue flooring. Cables and wiring were hanging in half-completed installation. It made Tayce wonder why the colony was never finished. It looked like everyone had left in a hurry. She and Marc exchanged glances, noticing the very fact. They both looked down the corridor, wondering what lay ahead in the semi-darkness. Twedor stood with them.

"Twedor, run a directional scan. Find one life form – you know who we're here to find," ordered Tayce.

"Scanning now, Tayce," replied Twedor, beginning the scan.

Twedor was silent for a few minons. A life-sign reading came back. He turned and pointed in the direction they should go. The power and lighting fluctuated around them suddenly, rising and falling over and over again. They followed on behind Twedor in the forward direction, which seemed to take them deeper into the central part of the colony. They walked on, alert, for quite a while, weaponry poised ready to shoot. Marc caught sight of Vargon as he rounded a corner near Twedor's destination scan point. He quickly pulled Twedor back against him, then gestured to Tayce to alert her to what he was seeing.

"In there – Vargon. Careful. Take a look," he, whispering, suggested.

Tayce looked out, round and into a vast unfinished centre, which looked like it was to be the main central operations point when the colony was completed. In the middle of the centre sat Varon Vargon in the one and only available blue leatherex seat. He looked far from the normal active planning and scheming Vargon they had come to know and hate. He looked near to death thought Tayce. It did though make her wonder if it was an elaborate trap. Had he anticipated her arrival somehow? It was now or never.

"You're my backup. It's time to end this once and for all," announced Tayce with meaning.

Before Marc had a chance to stop her, Tayce walked out and straight in through the open entrance of the centre, her gun pointed directly at Vargon. In a way Tayce was pleased it was just him at her mercy once and for all. He looked up, hardly finding the energy to give her the old Count Vargon threat.

"What! How did you get here? Why are you here? Have you come to finish me off" asked Varon.

"How the mighty have fallen! Where's your army now, Varon?" asked Tayce, showing no mercy.

"You must do what you feel is right, Tayce Amanda. I can fight you no more."

"You expect me to take a plea of surrender when you didn't give my people the chance to."

"You're here for one reason only and we both know what it is," he replied weakly.

"How come you're in the state you're in? Did someone attack you? They made a good job by the look of it," said Tayce, delaying, watching him suffer. She knew she shouldn't, but was enjoying watching him do so.

"If you must know, I was injured during escape from the fortress. Use your weapon and kill me. I can do no more – it's over," he said, then dropped into a strained huddle.

Tayce took aim. She was going to let him die slowly, relishing his suffering for the remaining cencrons of life he had. She didn't see the weapon Varon was concealing down at his side. But Marc and Twedor did. Just as they rushed forth, Varon raised the weapon.

At the same time, Tayce was saying, "This is for the people of Traun. Justice has at last been served. You're going to die, just like they did at your evil hands." As she spoke Tayce was aiming for a part of his body that would only heighten his suffering before death.

"No, Tayce, don't! He's got a gun," shouted Marc, pushing Tayce to the floor and firing his Pollomoss directly at Varon also.

At this cencron the unstable power of the lighting dropped to darkness instantly, plunging everything into total darkness. There was the sudden illumination of weapon fire, followed by deathly silence. Who had been killed? Had Varon Vargon finally gone from the Trauns' lives forever? Or had Marc been the one to be shot in protecting Tayce? Had Tayce ignored Marc's words once again and made a fatal move in her eagerness to finally destroy the one being who'd haunted her every move in the Universe and murdered her people? Was it the end for all present?

The First Amalthean Quest

Lightning Source UK Ltd.
Milton Keynes UK
UKHW041946130922
408822UK00001B/68

9 780722 352304